Flimsy World

Susan Shaker

I dedicate this book to the young generation—especially those who, because of their gender, age, race, or background, have been made to believe they cannot go further in their lives. This is for the dreamers, the thinkers, and those who dare to challenge the limits placed upon them.

To young girls and boys, in particular, I hope this serves as a reminder that science, knowledge, and discovery are for everyone. Your potential is limitless, and the world needs your ideas, your curiosity, and your brilliance. Never let anyone convince you otherwise. You are capable of more than you know.

ACKNOWLEDGMENT

I would also like to extend my deepest gratitude to my employer, Larry, who was one of the best employers I've ever had, and especially to my wonderful manager, Caroline, who graciously allowed me to stay in the office to work on my novel. I am profoundly grateful for all the support I have received from everyone in the office, including Jennifer, Trisha, Kayla, Natalie, Pauline, and Bernie, whose kind smiles and encouragement have meant so much to me.

My story concept has a captivating and imaginative appeal, combining my love for superheroes with a thoughtful exploration of power and potential in the most unexpected of people.

Ever wondered about the true extent of a superhero's powers? Superman, with his effortless feats—crushing concrete like it's nothing, lifting trains, even bringing down airplanes safely—leaves us in awe. But is it really possible to defy Earth's gravity and perform such miracles?

Growing up, I dreamed of having powers like his—an impossible fantasy, or so it seemed. But what if I told you it's not so far-fetched? What if even the tiniest, slimmest teenager, or even a child, could unlock unimaginable strength? It may seem illogical, but sometimes, the impossible can be within reach. This is the story of Artemis, a girl who becomes a hero against all odds. Explore her journey, challenge the boundaries of what we believe is possible, and share your thoughts on how a small girl found the power to become something extraordinary.

PREAMBLE

In a world where gods and heroes seem like distant myths, I am thinking, what if power found its way to someone unexpected?

Artemis, an ordinary teenage girl, was never supposed to be a hero. She was just a student, balancing schoolwork and friendships. But when fate forces her into a mysterious, otherworldly journey, she discovers a truth that defies everything she's ever known. With the fabric of reality itself unraveling, Artemis realizes she must rise to the challenge—not only to save herself and her father but to protect an entire world on the brink of collapse.

She never asked for powers. She never wanted to be a legend. But sometimes, heroes are born from the unlikeliest places.

Now, caught between dangerous political schemes, old family secrets, and a ruthless villain bent on control, Artemis must harness strength beyond her wildest dreams—strength that might just turn the tide in a war she never saw coming.

Join Artemis as she steps into a destiny filled with extraordinary challenges, incredible powers, and choices that could determine the future of two worlds. What does it take to become a hero? Artemis is about to find out.

Table of Contents

A NEW STUDENT

It was January 30, 2007, just five months before the anticipated school closures. The cold was biting, and snow blanketed everything in sight. The Avicenna[1] High School was renowned for its gifted students, earning a strong reputation among the public and the scientific community alike. Students were busy moving to their next class, and the hallway was packed with bustling activities. The office hummed with a lively energy while the principal's door remained firmly shut. Through the small glass window, Principal Kelly, a man in his forties with salt-and-pepper hair, could be seen. He was very tall, with a bushy mustache and beard that matched perfectly with his round tummy. He appeared visibly impatient, yet he made an effort to keep his tone steady as he spoke on the phone with a parent.

Suddenly, the door swung wide open. Principal Kelly glanced up from the letter he had been reading to the parent over the phone. His gaze met the eyes of a gentleman standing by the hallway entrance, a sleek black suitcase in hand. This man exuded an air of obsessive refinement, the hallmark of the fabulously wealthy—as befitting the CEO of one of the world's most prestigious companies. His impeccably tailored suit spoke volumes of his status.

The gentleman cast a cursory glance at the secretary, Mary Ann, a tall and slender figure known to all as Mary, and without uttering a word, strode purposefully towards Mr. Kelly's office. Mary attempted to intervene, her voice rising as she admonished him about the necessity of scheduling an appointment with Mr. Kelly. She dashed toward Mr. Kelly's office door, blocking it with her slim frame, and she kept reiterating, "Sir, I've already informed you that you must schedule an appointment to see Mr. Kelly, especially this week with midterms starting—he's extremely busy," she exclaimed, turning toward the principal. She then gestured to her desk, inviting him to sit, before addressing the stranger.

"The appointment book is right there. Could you please sign in and schedule an appointment with the principal?" she continued, offering a polite yet firm tone.

"Let me get you a pen," she added, moving toward her desk to find one. However, the moment the door became accessible, the stranger seized the opportunity, quickly opening it and stepping into the office. She ran to the principal's office, turned towards the principal and tiredly said, "I apologize, Mr. Kelly. I attempted to inform him of your busy schedule, but he simply disregarded my words."

The stranger reached the principal's desk, extended his hand, and firmly shook Principal Kelly's hand before handing him an envelope. Without a preamble, he launched into his purpose for being there.

"Hello and good morning, Mr. Kelly; I had to come as soon as possible," he began earnestly.

"You see, my son and I have been searching for the right school for quite some time now. We've conducted extensive research, and your school has captured our hearts."

Mr. Kelly fixed his tie and focused on him again.

"I understand that it's the middle of the school year, but I'm compelled to enroll my son here. It means a great deal to both of us."

Principal Kelly listened with a sense of pride swelling within him. However, as he began to open the envelope, a wave of confusion washed over him. His gaze shifted from the stranger to the envelope a couple of times, his brows furrowing in bewilderment. He closed it abruptly, leaving it on the desk, his curiosity piqued by the sizable stack of $100 bills contained within.

His voice tinged with skepticism, Mr. Kelly turned back to the stranger. "What is this? I'm at a loss. Who are you?"

The stranger, visibly moved by the encounter, endeavored to maintain his composure as he responded, struggling to contain his excitement as he addressed Principal Kelly with a polite apology, "My apologies for the oversight. I'm Robert Gonzales," he introduced himself, his tone measured but brimming with enthusiasm.

"I reside in Ottawa, but my son recently discovered the sterling reputation of your school's education, which is renowned for its exceptional faculty. He's immensely impressed, you see. As the only family he has left, ensuring his happiness is my utmost priority. I'll go to any lengths for him. After an exhaustive search, he has chosen your school, and he's eager to join as soon as possible. The name of this school perfectly matches its reputation. Avicenna, a brilliant Persian scientist, left a legacy of knowledge that continues to be taught in universities across America."

Mr. Gonzales took a deep breath and continued, "I'll make sure he has a place to stay and transportation to Toronto, and I'll guarantee his punctuality throughout the school year. He's earned a stellar reputation as one of the top students in his current school and I believe he'll be a valuable addition to yours. As you can see in his reports." He handed over a file of his son's record to Mr. Kelly.

Mr. Kelly took the file and scanned through the pages with a keen eye. The achievements listed were indeed impressive top grades in all subjects, numerous awards in science and math competitions, and glowing comments from teachers about his work ethic and leadership skills.

"This is quite impressive," Mr. Kelly said, looking up from the file. "We'd be delighted to have a student of his caliber join our school."

With a confident flourish, Mr. Gonzales handed Principal Kelly a folder containing detailed information about his son's academic achievements, emphasizing his exceptional grades.

"This folder contains all the pertinent information about his schooling and his outstanding academic record," he explained. Pausing briefly to allow the information to sink in, he gestured toward the envelope resting on the desk. "That envelope is yours upon his admission. Shall we proceed with his registration?" Mr. Gonzales inquired, his voice steady and resolute. "Furthermore, there is seventy-five thousand dollars enclosed. I urge you to count it."

He sat back confidently while he watched every move Principal Kelly made, observing him. Principal Kelly quickly looked at him distrustful and suspicious. He pushed the envelope on his desk in front of Mr. Gonzales. He was unclear about his request and was uncertain about the truth. There was something about the stranger that Mr. Kelly couldn't spot, and he didn't feel right about him. Simply put, he couldn't trust him.

Confidently reclining in his chair, Mr. Gonzales observed Principal Kelly's every movement with keen interest, his gaze unwavering. However, Principal Kelly's response was swift; his demeanor was tinged with distrust and suspicion as he regarded the envelope on his desk. Uncertain about Mr. Gonzales' intentions and uncomfortable with the situation, Principal Kelly hesitated to act.

Turning his attention back to Mr. Gonzales, Principal Kelly reached for a pencil, his expression guarded as he posed a pointed question. "Why the sudden urgency to enroll your son here? Moreover, students are required to pass a special test to gain admission to this school." Is this an attempt at bribery?" he inquired, his tone conveying a mix of caution and firmness.

Noticing the expression on Mr. Gonzales' face, he continued, "Regardless, I'm afraid I cannot accept this money. It goes against the policies of the board, and I must adhere to those standards."

Mr. Gonzales nodded resignedly, glancing at Mr. Kelly as if he had anticipated the response then rose from his seat, pushing the envelope further toward Principal Kelly. Leaning forward, he pressed his hands onto the desk, his gaze intent on the principal. "I anticipated as much," he acknowledged. "Very well. Would more be to your liking? I can easily double the amount to one hundred and fifty thousand. You know I have the means to make it happen. There are others who would gladly seize this opportunity if you do not.

Consider this—twice your annual income, tax-free and in cash. I'm aware of your aspirations, including your desire for a cottage. As I mentioned, I've studied everything about this school. This could be your chance a secret between us. Help me, and we need never speak of it again."

Mr. Gonzales watched Principal Kelly meticulously, noting the subtle change in his complexion and the slight tremor in his hands. The offer had struck a chord. After a moment's hesitation, Principal Kelly cautiously reached for the envelope, setting it aside before pulling out a sheet of paper. With deliberate movements, he began to write, then handed the paper to Mr. Gonzales, his resolve evident in his demeanor.

"You'll need to provide an address in Toronto within close proximity to the school. Simply fill in the blank areas marked with 'X' and leave the rest to me. Your son can begin attending tomorrow," Mr. Kelly instructed, his smile masking a sense of satisfaction as he settled back into his seat.

After swiftly filling out the necessary information, Mr. Gonzales handed the completed forms to Principal Kelly.

"Thank you once again. Tomorrow, my son will visit your office first thing, and you can discuss the school regulations with him. He'll bring the remaining paperwork with him, along with the rest of my promise. However, he does have one final request—he wishes to be placed in specific classrooms. I trust you'll be able to assist him with that," Mr. Gonzales added with a knowing look.

As Mr. Gonzales made his exit, Principal Kelly watched the door close behind him before carefully opening the envelope to inspect its contents. Counting the money methodically to ensure its accuracy, he then stowed it away in his briefcase. Glancing around the office, he quickly reached for the phone and dialed a number.

"Hi honey, guess what! We can finally get your dream cottage," he exclaimed enthusiastically.

"Call David and let him know we'll take it. We need to make an appointment to sign the papers. I'll fill you in on the details when I get home." With a sense of anticipation, Principal Kelly hung up the phone, a newfound exhilaration coursing through him.

With a sense of urgency, Principal Kelly swiftly gathered his belongings. "I have to leave early today. Something has come up," he informed Mary, his secretary, who nodded understandingly.

"See you tomorrow," she replied as he made his way out.

As the school bell chimed, signaling the end of the day, the crowded hallway bustled with students. Mr. Gonzales navigated through the throng, struggling to make his way toward one of the classrooms to verify the accuracy of the information he had before heading toward the exit. His eyes flicked to the classroom numbers as he passed as if double-checking to ensure he had the correct information. Suddenly, he spotted the classroom number, and the door swung open narrowly missing him as a student, engrossed in conversation with her friend, halted abruptly upon hearing her name.

"Artemis[2], Watch out!" the friend exclaimed, prompting her, one of the school's top students, and her friend Matt, who was also renowned for his intellect, to rush into the hallway.

Her name was Artemisia but they used to call her Artemis because it was easier to pronounce it.

Holding the door open, Mr. Gonzales addressed Artemis with a smile, "Be mindful when opening doors, young lady. They can be hazardous. You must be Artemis."

Artemis, feeling contrite, responded, "I'm sorry, sir. I didn't mean to cause any harm. But how do you know my name?"

He remarked, indicating a nearby wall adorned with an article featuring her picture, declaring her as the school's top student.

"Your name and picture are right there, and your friend just called you," he explained, his smile unwavering. "It seems you've made quite a name for yourself."

Artemis exchanged a quick glance with Matt, her smirk indicating her usual confidence and pride.

He added with a warm smile, "I remember you from when you were just a little girl. You still have that same beautiful, youthful face."

"Who are you? How do you know me?" Artemis asked, her voice filled with confusion.

Mr. Gonzales, with a satisfied look on his face, replied, "I used to be your father's friend before the incident."

Artemis looked at him doubtfully, unsure of what to say. She simply replied, "Okay, he's gone, and I don't know any of his friends; good day, sir." She then turned to Matt and they began talking and walked away together.

TWELVE MONTHS LATER

Time flew by swiftly, and nearly a year had passed since Principal Kelly had admitted the new student to the school. It was February 27, 2008, and the bustling school corridors were teeming with students eager to head home. Artemis and Matt were among them, both feeling the urgency of the day's events. Tomorrow marked Artemis's birthday, and she was determined to tie up loose ends before the celebrations commenced. With a promise to her mother to return home on time, Artemis planned to make a quick stop at the library to pick up some study materials. However, Matt had to leave abruptly. Ricky joined them, his excitement palpable as he realized that Artemis had invited him to her birthday. They all began walking together toward the entrance of the school.

Matt was a genius, exceptionally bright for his age, but often overlooked because of his youthful appearance. He was tall for his age, yet his face had a boyish look, with dirty blond, silky hair and striking dark silver eyes. He always carried a big backpack slung over his shoulder.

"I'm sorry, Artemis, but I have to go right now," he said. "I'll catch up with you later," Matt explained hurriedly, leaving Artemis to make her way to the library. Ricky, brimming with excitement, glanced at Artemis and politely asked to be excused, promising to see her at her party the next afternoon.

Although his sudden departure took her aback, Artemis understood the importance of their commitments and assured them it was fine.

"It's okay, guys. I have to go to the library as well, and I'm in a rush, too. I'll see you tomorrow," Artemis replied with a smile, hiding any hint of disappointment she may have felt.

Despite the rainy weather and freezing temperatures of minus 31 degrees Celsius, Toronto retained its enchanting beauty, cloaked in a pristine blanket of snow and ice. Even amidst the rain, the city exuded a magical charm, captivating all who beheld its wintry splendor.

Artemis, a 16-year-old beautiful girl with a passion for biology and computers, possessed an insatiable curiosity about the world around her. Her love for animals led her to create websites dedicated to their biographies, detailing their lifestyles and habits. A skilled researcher with extensive knowledge of both animals and computers, she was familiar with nearly every species known on Earth despite her age.

In spite of her slim frame, Artemis possessed captivating eyes that hinted at her intelligence and determination. Her lifestyle revolved around her commitment to her mother and sister, and she approached everything with caution. Fearful of the darkness, Artemis always made sure to be home before nightfall, harboring a deep-seated unease about being out after dark.

Today, Artemis found herself at the library, returning books and searching for new ones. She hoped to discover something extraordinary, a book that would enthrall her with its contents. Lost in her quest for the perfect read, Artemis lost track of time, only realizing the lateness of the hour when the librarian announced the library's impending closure.

As Artemis hurried out of the library, dusk had descended, casting a faint glow across the sky. Though relieved to see the clouds dispersing, she remained wary of the encroaching darkness, her unease growing with each passing minute. With a quickened pace, she made her way home, her thoughts consumed by her mother's constant worry and the ever-present fear of the unknown.

Her mother, Dorsa, had been deeply affected by her husband's mysterious disappearance years earlier when Artemis was only four years of age; her frustration was palpable in her daily demeanor. For

Artemis, witnessing her mother's distress was more frightening than any darkness she encountered. With each step homeward, she quickened her pace, casting nervous glances over her shoulder in a futile attempt to quell her growing unease.

Artemis felt a wave of relief wash over her as she reached home just before complete darkness enveloped the neighborhood. However, her relief quickly turned to concern as she noticed the unusual dimness of the house. Normally, her mother ensured that the living room and kitchen lights were left on to comfort Artemis's fear of darkness, and she would be waiting for her on the sofa, but tonight was different. Only one light, facing the street, illuminated the living room, casting eerie shadows on the walls.

Fumbling with her keys, Artemis finally managed to unlock the door and stepped inside, greeted by the faint sound of the wind rustling through the trees outside. The unsettling noise made her hasten to close the door behind her, feeling a sense of triumph as she succeeded.

"I've conquered the darkness once again," Artemis thought, a wry smirk playing on her lips.

Despite its unassuming exterior, the house held a special charm within. Professionally designed by her mother years ago, it bore the mark of Dorsa's creativity and love. Vibrant colors adorned the walls, complementing Dorsa's paintings and creating an atmosphere of warmth and comfort. As Artemis stepped further into the house, she felt a sense of familiarity and security wash over her, grateful to be back in the sanctuary of her home.

She turned on the hallway light, its glow reflecting off the carefully selected furniture and enhancing the vibrant colors adorning the walls, creating a harmonious and inviting atmosphere. A sunken area of sectional sofas faced a large plasma screen TV, inviting relaxation and comfort. Regardless of its outdated appearance, the house was a masterpiece of art and beauty, a testament to Dorsa's talent as a connoisseur of aesthetics.

Friends and family often referred to her as the 'moralist of art,' recognizing her keen eye for design and creativity.

While the house may have needed some updates, Dorsa was adamant about preserving its original charm and character, refusing to make any changes since her husband's disappearance. Each room held memories of happier times spent with Arsham[3], father to Artemis and Atossa, and Dorsa was determined to keep those memories alive.

Even with the challenges she faced, Dorsa persevered for the sake of her children, finding a job at an art store near OCAD, the University of Art in Toronto. Though the job wasn't particularly demanding, it allowed her to support her family while surrounded by her passion for art.

Offers to purchase the house came and went, but Dorsa remained steadfast in her decision not to sell. For her, the house held too much sentimental value to part with, serving as a tangible connection to the happiness she shared with her husband. In her heart, she knew that letting go of the house would mean letting go of a part of herself and the memories they had created together.

Artemis closed the door behind her, feeling a sense of safety as she flicked on the second light switch and shed her jacket. Hanging it up and leaving her shoes on the rack to dry, she made her way into the dimly lit hallway. The transition from the darkness of the hallway to the brighter living room was almost soothing, the colors gradually shifting to lighter tones as she approached.

However, her moment of comfort was shattered by a sudden wheezing sound, its origin was unclear amidst the noise of the wind outside. Artemis paused, her senses on high alert as she cautiously scanned the living room from the hallway. With trepidation, she made her way into the kitchen, hoping to distract herself by focusing on the routine of her mother leaving dinner on the counter.

But her attention was drawn back to the living room by another noise, something moving in the darkness. Panic seized her as she listened intently, the slow, rhythmic breathing sending shivers down her spine. Fear clenched her heart as she thought of her mother, who should have been home by now. Worried for her safety, Artemis couldn't bear the thought of losing her too. Scanning the room and staircase for any sign of her mother, Artemis called out her name, her voice trembling with fear. With each unanswered call, her anxiety grew, until finally, in a desperate plea, she called out once more, her voice filled with uncertainty and dread.

"Mom...! Mom...!" Artemis's voice wavered, her fear palpable in the empty silence of the house.

Her heart raced as she sensed the presence of more than one person in the living room, intensifying her fear. A clang echoed from the corner, prompting her to cautiously approach the fireplace, grasping a log defensively. With trembling hands, she braced herself, ready to either defend herself with the log, hurl it at whoever was lurking in the shadows, or, if panic took over, sprint upstairs to her room and lock the door. Her mother's name escaping her lips in a desperate plea.

"MOM...!"

Her mind raced with thoughts, but before she could fully comprehend the situation, the room was flooded with light as someone flicked on the switch. In an instant, screams filled the air, followed by a chorus of voices singing repeatedly, "Happy Birthday, Artemis... Happy Birthday, Artemis… Happy Birthday, Artemis."

Startled and disoriented, Artemis staggered back, her pale face drained of color as she struggled to catch her breath. As the initial shock subsided, Artemis surveyed the familiar faces before her. Her eyes searched for her mother's reassuring presence. When she finally spotted her amidst the crowd, a mixture of relief and gratitude washed over her, and a faint smile graced her lips. Her sister Atossa embraced her tightly, then, with a hint of surprise, Artemis asked, "Weren't you supposed to be at Aunt Azar's house?"

Atossa smiled and said, "No! That was just a setup to keep you from suspecting your surprise birthday party."

However, Artemis couldn't help but express her feelings of fear and frustration. "You all scared me half to death, and whether you think it's cool or not is irrelevant," she stated firmly, her voice tinged with a hint of reproach.

Dorsa's expression softened as she realized the extent of Artemis's distress. "Oh, my dear Artemis, I only wanted to surprise you. I had no idea it would frighten you so much," she admitted, compunction evident in her voice.

Artemis, touched by her mother's sincerity, mustered a soft and affectionate tone as she replied, "Thank you for the thrilling birthday surprise, Mom. But we agreed no party this year, only my friends and besides, my birthday isn't until tomorrow." Regardless of her initial fright, Artemis's love for her mother shone through, her words conveying both understanding and appreciation.

Dorsa hugged her and explained, "That's why you didn't expect it to be tonight—it was a surprise. And since your Aunt Azar[4] is leaving early tomorrow morning, she didn't want to miss your birthday."

Artemis nodded happily, her surprised expression turning to joy as she embraced each of her friends. Laughter filled the room as they shared hugs and playful banter. When she spotted Matt among the crowd, she couldn't resist teasing him about his earlier excuse.

"You little rascal… You told me you were in a rush, but you're a good liar because I completely believed you," she began, her words trailing off into laughter as Matt joined in, the tension of the earlier scare melting away in their shared amusement.

As the festivities continued, Artemis's attention was drawn to the dining room, where her aunt Azar had illuminated the space with a warm glow. The room was adorned with balloons, ribbons, and flowers, each detail meticulously arranged to celebrate her special day.

Gift boxes piled in the corner, promising surprises to come, while a banner above the window frame proudly proclaimed:

"Happy Sixteenth Birthday, Artemis."

Meanwhile, Dorsa entered the room with a basket of fresh fruit, the sweet aroma filling the air and adding to the festive atmosphere. Artemis couldn't help but feel a surge of pride and gratitude as she looked around at her loved ones, grateful for their thoughtfulness and affection. Her gaze lingered on her mother, who had undoubtedly spent hours preparing for the celebration. Dorsa's smile said it all, her love for Artemis evident in every gesture and expression. Artemis returned her mother's smile with a grateful one of her own, her heart overflowing with love and appreciation for the woman who had always been her rock.

Artemis listened as her mother explained the reason for the impromptu celebration, her heart swelling with gratitude and love. Dorsa's words touched her deeply, reminding her of her father's absence and the strength and pride her mother had always shown in her children. As Dorsa[5] expressed her pride and love for Artemis, kissing her on the forehead and whispering words of affection, Artemis felt a warmth spread through her, grateful for the unwavering support of her family.

But her sister, Atossa[6], couldn't resist teasingly interjecting, prompting laughter and playful banter among the family. Dorsa, ever the loving mother, reassured Atossa of her own worth and importance, expressing her pride in both her daughters. With laughter and smiles, they continued to celebrate, the joy of the moment filling the room with a sense of warmth and camaraderie.

Surrounded by her friends, Artemis felt a surge of happiness, grateful for their presence and the love they showed her. Megan, Ricky, Helen, Allen, and especially Matt stood by her side, singing "Happy Birthday" and cheering her on with infectious enthusiasm. As she looked at each of them in turn, Artemis felt a profound sense of gratitude for the bonds of friendship that surrounded her, knowing she was truly blessed to have such wonderful companions in her life.

As Artemis basked in the joy of her birthday celebration, her eyes caught Matt's quiet presence among the group of friends. With his black leather laptop case slung over one shoulder, he smiled brightly at her, his babyish features accentuated by his smooth, round face, silky dirty blond hair and light pink lips. His striking, dark, silvery eyes, a unique feature, added to his charm.

Despite his youthful appearance, Matt's intellect was far beyond his years, earning him the title of number one student at school. Yet, his academic prowess often isolated him from his peers, as his conversations veered towards scientific topics that few could understand or appreciate. Despite this, Matt remained unapologetically himself, steadfast in his beliefs and never hesitating to express his love for Artemis. Yet, she always saw him as just a good friend.

His dedication to science was evident in his daily habits, always carrying books with him and occasionally delving into their pages even amidst the festivities of Artemis's birthday party. Though he may not be the most social of individuals, his bravery and determination were unwavering–a testament to his character and integrity.

In spite of his affection for Artemis and his hopes for a future together, she gently reminded him of their similar ages, expressing her wish for a partner older than herself. Though disappointed, Matt respected her decision, holding onto the hope that she might change her mind in the future. His love for her remained resolute as they navigated the complexities of adolescence and young adulthood.

As Artemis observed the dynamics of her friends' interactions, she couldn't help but smile at their diverse personalities and talents. Ricky, with his knack for mimicry and impersonations, brought laughter to the room as he seamlessly transitioned between cartoon characters and celebrity voices, his curly dark hair and expressive brown eyes adding to his charm.

Helen and Allen, their hands intertwined in a silent display of affection, exuded an undeniable chemistry. Helen's captivating blue eyes and model-like stature hinted at her aspirations beyond high school and she was one of the great artists at school, while Allen, with his quiet confidence and steady presence, complemented her perfectly.

Meanwhile, Ricky and Megan, the dynamic duo on the dance floor, moved with grace and precision, their synchronized movements a testament to their shared talent and camaraderie. Ricky's unique heritage and magnetic personality made him effortlessly likable, his ability to connect with others transcending barriers of race and culture.

Artemis marveled at the diversity within their group of friends, each individual bringing their own strengths and quirks to the table. Despite their differences, they shared a bond that transcended superficialities, united by their shared experiences and mutual affection for one another. As she watched them interact and enjoy each other's company, Artemis couldn't help but feel grateful for the unique blend of personalities that made up her circle of friends.

As Artemis observed her friends enjoying the party, her thoughts drifted to Matt once more. She admired him greatly, appreciating his heroic nature and the unique way he approached life. His laughter at the end of the sofa brought a smile to her face, reminding her of the special bond they shared.

Regardless of her admiration for Matt, Artemis found herself grappling with her feelings for him. She valued their friendship immensely but couldn't quite decipher if her affection for him extended beyond that. There were moments when she imagined being with him romantically, envisioning themselves as two lovers embarking on adventures together. Yet, she remained uncertain about the depth of her feelings, hesitant to label it as 'love.'

Matt's resemblance to Superman only added to his allure in Artemis's eyes. She had always been captivated by the iconic superheroes, drawn to his strength, courage, and unwavering sense of justice. In her daydreams, she envisioned herself being rescued by Superman, with Matt watching proudly from afar.

She couldn't deny the undeniable attraction she felt towards Matt. His handsome appearance, combined with his unique personality and deep, manly voice, made him stand out in her mind as one of the most exceptional boys she had ever known. Yet, Artemis remained hesitant to fully embrace her feelings, uncertain of the kind of love she truly felt for him, often confused by the contrast between his mature demeanor, commanding voice, and youthful, almost boyish face.

As she continued to watch Matt from across the room, Artemis couldn't help but feel a sense of gratitude for his presence in her life. Whether their relationship blossomed into something more or remained rooted in friendship, she knew that Matt held a special place in her heart, his uniqueness and perfection leaving an indelible mark on her soul.

As the door swung open, Artemis was greeted by the warm embrace of her extended family. Aunts Padideh[7] and Parto[8], along with their spouses and children, flooded into the room, adding to the joyous atmosphere of the party. Their resemblance was uncanny, almost like twins, with their dark, shiny hair and smooth skin tone reminiscent of their grandfather.

Aunt Azar and her family joined the celebration, too, having spent the afternoon assisting Dorsa with decorations and baking. With everyone gathered around, Dorsa entered the room carrying the birthday cake. The sight of the cake prompted a burst of excitement, and the room erupted into a chorus of the birthday song, sung even louder than before.

Atossa quickly dimmed the lights, casting a soft glow over the room as the candles on the cake flickered to life. The 3D image of three white doves flying over the buildings in the sky captivated everyone's attention. Dorsa's intricate design, with the three connected pieces representing the dove's flight, was a testament to her creativity and thoughtfulness.

Artemis gazed in awe at the cake before her, the two numbered candles atop it signifying her age. The intricacy of the design, coupled with the vibrant colors and delicate details, left her speechless. She looked up at her mother, her eyes shining with gratitude and appreciation for the effort she put into making her birthday special. With a nod of approval, she signaled her acknowledgment of the cake's beauty, ready to make a wish and blow out the candles surrounded by her loved ones.

Ricky inquired about the three doves, wondering if they held any special meaning.

Artemis smiled and said, "Tomorrow, there will be three birthdays in our family—my grandma Tara[9], my father, and me."

"Wow, three birthdays in one day! That's quite extraordinary," exclaimed Ricky, breaking the silence with his observation.

Then he continued, "It must be a special day indeed. Artemis, may all your wishes come true as you blow out the candles."

Artemis smiled gratefully at her friend's words and took a moment to make her wish; her heart was full of gratitude for her loving family and friends surrounding her. With a deep breath, she leaned forward and blew out the candles, the room erupting into applause and cheers as the flickering flames were extinguished.

As the candles were blown out, Artemis closed her eyes, holding onto her wish with the hope that it would manifest into reality. With the warmth of her family's love enveloping her, she knew that no matter what the future held, she was blessed to have such wonderful people by her side. Her heart skipped a beat as she realized that she had spoken her wish aloud, her cheeks flushing with embarrassment. She hadn't intended for anyone to hear her innermost thoughts, especially not her heartfelt wish for her father's return. Then she realized it was just her imagination, and she felt a quiet joy in keeping her wish a secret between herself and the Lord.

Feeling a mix of vulnerability and uncertainty, Artemis took a deep breath and nodded slowly. "Yes, I made my wish," she replied softly, her voice barely above a whisper. "Thank you, everyone."

There was a moment of solemn silence as the weight of Artemis's wish settled over the room. Her friends and family exchanged meaningful glances, understanding the depth of her longing and the significance of her birthday wish.

Uncle Cenzio[10] broke the silence once again, his voice gentle and reassuring. "Artemis, may your wish bring you the peace and happiness you deserve," he said kindly, his words carrying a sense of warmth and hope.

Artemis offered a small smile in response, grateful for her uncle's comforting words. Though she knew that her wish might be a long shot, she couldn't help but hold onto the hope that, somehow, someday, her family would be reunited. And on this special day, surrounded by her loved ones, she allowed herself to believe in the power of wishes and the possibility of miracles. At that moment, everyone cheerfully stood up and simultaneously asked if it was time for gifts.

As the gift-opening tradition continued, Artemis couldn't help but feel overwhelmed by the generosity of her friends and family. They had already prepared a jar filled with folded chits, each one bearing a name. Each present was a thoughtful reminder of the love and support she had in her life. From books on biology and computer programming to art supplies and handmade crafts, every gift held a special significance. Each item was thoughtfully chosen, reflecting the unique interests and talents of its receiver. These carefully curated presents were more than just objects; they were tokens of appreciation and love, celebrating the diverse passions that brought joy and meaning to her life.

As she reached into the jar to pull out a name, Artemis couldn't shake the feeling of anticipation that washed over her. She wondered whose gift she would open next and what surprises awaited her. With each name called, the excitement in the room grew. Friends eagerly presented their gifts; their faces lit up with anticipation as Artemis unwrapped each one. The atmosphere was filled with laughter and chatter as everyone enjoyed the festivities.

Artemis picked another name from the jar and opened the slip. It read, 'Mom.' She turned to her mother with excitement and asked, "What did you get me?"

Dorsa hurried to the gift table, retrieved a small box, and held it out to Artemis. "Open it," she urged.

Artemis opened the box, and there it was—a cell phone. She couldn't believe her eyes. Overwhelmed with joy, she looked at her mother in surprise. "Mom! This is amazing. I've always dreamed of having one. Thank you so much, Mom."

Dorsa, beaming with happiness, kissed her and said, "You're welcome, my sweetheart."

All her friends gathered around excitedly, asking Dorsa for her phone number. "Miss Vedetta, what's the number?"

Dorsa smiled, handing the phone to Artemis, who quickly shared it with her friends. "The number is 416-555-3369."

Meanwhile, Atossa discreetly watched Matt from across the room, her heart fluttering with nervousness. She had admired him from afar for so long, but she never seemed to find the right moment to approach him. Despite her efforts to engage him in conversation, she often found herself at a loss for words in his presence. She was unaware of his love for Artemis, and from what she had always heard from Artemis, they were just good friends.

As Artemis continued to open her gifts, Atossa couldn't help but hope that maybe, just maybe, tonight would be the night she finally found the courage to speak to Matt and express her feelings. But for now, she remained on the sidelines, content to watch her sister enjoy her special day surrounded by loved ones.

Matt cherished his friendship with Artemis more than anything else. She was the one person who truly understood him, accepted him for who he was, and shared his interests and passions. From their early days in kindergarten, they had formed a bond that was unbreakable. Artemis was always there to support him, to listen to his ideas, and to encourage him to pursue his dreams.

Despite facing ridicule and bullying from other kids, Matt found solace in Artemis's friendship. She helped him navigate through difficult times and provided him with the confidence to embrace his uniqueness. Her unwavering loyalty and understanding meant the world to him, and he knew that he could always count on her no matter what.

As they grew older, their friendship only deepened. Matt admired Artemis's intelligence, creativity, and kindness, and he was grateful to have her by his side. They shared countless conversations about science, literature, and everything in between, and Matt cherished every moment they spent together.

Although he may not have realized it, Artemis's presence in his life had a profound impact on him. She helped him to believe in himself and to see the value in his own abilities. With her support, Matt continued to pursue his passion for science, eager to unlock the countless mysteries of the world around him.

For Matt, Artemis was more than just a friend—she was his confidante, his inspiration, and his rock. And no matter what challenges lay ahead, he knew that as long as he had Artemis by his side, he could overcome anything. Matt had been hoping for a closer relationship, but Artemis always told him that if she were to enter a relationship, her partner would need to be at least a couple of years older than her. Each time she said those words, it broke his heart, but it didn't make him give up.

As Matt handed the gift to Artemis, his excitement was palpable. He couldn't wait for her to open it and see her reaction. Artemis took the box from him with a smile, intrigued by what could be inside. She carefully unwrapped the gift, her fingers moving eagerly over the paper. When she finally opened the box, she was greeted by a beautifully bound journal that was included with a special pen carefully placed on the journal. The cover was adorned with intricate designs, and the pages inside were blank, waiting to be filled with thoughts, ideas, and dreams. Artemis looked up at Matt, her eyes shining with gratefulness.

"Thank you, Matt," she said sincerely. "This is such a thoughtful gift. I've been wanting a new journal to write down my thoughts and ideas for a long time. It's perfect."

Matt smiled and gently pointed at the box. "Look again," he said.

Artemis glanced back inside the box and found a beautiful bracelet with a heart charm hanging from it, inscribed with the words *My Best Friend.* She broke into the most beautiful smile and immediately put on the bracelet. Matt pulled up his sleeve and showed Artemis his bracelet too, and it was exactly the same, with a charm hanging from it, but his charm was inscribed with the words *Artemis, my best friend forever.*

Matt beamed at her reaction, relieved that she liked his gifts. He had spent a long time searching for the right present, wanting to give Artemis something meaningful and special. Seeing her appreciation made it all worth it.

As Artemis flipped through the pages of the journal, she couldn't help but feel touched by Matt's gesture. It was a reminder of the deep bond they shared and the countless memories they had created together. She knew that no matter what the future held, their friendship would always be a source of strength and joy for both of them.

"Artemis, this is a magnetic levitation device that I've been working on for your birthday, too," Matt explained with enthusiasm.

"Using magnets and electromagnetism, I've created a system that allows these three metal balls to levitate and move in the air without any physical support. But you need to wear this glove on your hand and place it beneath the balls for them to work. It's like magic, but it's all based on science!"

Artemis was mesmerized by the sight of the floating balls, her eyes wide with wonder. She reached out to touch one of them, but it moved away from her finger as if by its own will.

"This is incredible, Matt!" she exclaimed, her excitement growing. "I've never seen anything like it. How did you come up with the idea? I don't know what to say. Three beautiful gifts?"

Matt grinned proudly, happy to share his passion for science with Artemis. "I've always been fascinated by magnetism and how it interacts with objects. I started experimenting with different configurations and magnetic fields until I finally came up with this design. It's still a work in progress, but I'm glad you like it."

As Artemis watched the floating balls dance in the air, she couldn't help but feel grateful for having a friend like Matt. His creativity and dedication never ceased to amaze her, and she knew that with his ingenuity, he would go on to achieve great things in the world of science.

Artemis pondered for a moment, considering the unique qualities of the levitating device in her hand. She looked at the floating balls, their movement graceful and mesmerizing. Everyone was amazed by the unique and thoughtful gift from Matt, admiring his creativity and the special meaning behind it.

"I think I'll call it the Levitron," Artemis declared, her eyes bright with inspiration. "It's a combination of 'levitate' and 'electron,' representing the magnetic levitation and the electromagnetic principles behind its operation."

Ricky nodded in agreement, a grin spreading across his face as he grabbed it from Artemis's hand and started playing with the Levitron. "Levitron, I like it! It's catchy and futuristic. Thanks, Artemis!"

Artemis smiled, pleased with her choice of name. She watched as her friends continued to marvel at the Levitron, their laughter filling the room with joy. In that moment, surrounded by her loved ones, Artemis felt a profound sense of happiness and gratitude. And as she looked at Matt, she silently thanked him for his incredible gifts and for being such a remarkable friend.

"You're remarkable, Matt," Allen blurted out, clearly impressed.

"You're going to be a scientist one day, Matt. You can do anything you set your mind to," Ricky said with admiration, his voice ringing with certainty.

Artemis, trying to give everyone her attention, smiled at Matt and said, "Explain this invention to me later, after the party." Matt noticed Artemis's distraction, and he quickly changed the subject, understanding that she wasn't fully engaged in the conversation. He smiled and replied, "Yeah, I'll tell you about it later. Let's enjoy the rest of your birthday party for now."

Artemis nodded gratefully, relieved that Matt didn't press the topic further. She turned her attention back to her friends and family, basking in the warmth of their presence and the love they had shown her on her special day. As the evening continued, she cherished every moment, grateful for the joy and happiness that surrounded her.

Matt approached her again, holding the book he'd borrowed from her along with a couple of stones. Pointing to the book, he said, "I need to talk to you about this book later."

Artemis looked at Matt, sensing his discomfort. She nodded and felt a pang of guilt for not giving Matt her full attention, but she knew he understood.

As the party continued, Artemis made a mental note to talk to Matt about the stones and the book at a more appropriate time. For now, she wanted to immerse herself in the celebration of her birthday, surrounded by the people she loved. Matt read it and smiled at her. Artemis observed Megan and Helen chatting about the dress, their excitement infectious; then she saw Allen, who still was playing with

Levitron like a child playing with a toy and enjoying it. She knew he valued the gift he had given her, 'The Levitron,' and she didn't want to disappoint him. After a moment of consideration, she turned to Allen and said, "I'm sorry, Allen, but this gift means a lot to me, especially coming from Matt. I hope you understand."

Allen nodded understandingly, but he was a bit disappointed. "Of course, Artemis. No problem," he replied, handing the Levitron back to her while Matt was watching them. His expression softened as he heard Artemis's response. He appreciated her loyalty and felt grateful for her consideration. Artemis smiled at him reassuringly, silently expressing her gratitude for his thoughtful gift. Artemis laughed at Ricky's imitation of an answering machine, feeling grateful for her friends' enthusiasm. She knew they were all excited to celebrate her birthday together. As they finished getting ready to leave, Artemis thanked each of her friends and family for coming and making her birthday so special. She hugged them one by one, feeling a sense of warmth and happiness wash over her.

Ricky turned to Artemis and said, "Artemis, we all decided to go skating tomorrow, and since it's your actual birthday, we thought we could have a sleepover. We can watch movies and play games all night if that's okay with you?"

Artemis's face lit up with happiness. She immediately replied, "Yes, of course it's alright! Actually, it would be a great idea." As they headed out, everyone reminded Artemis of the plan for the next day. "Don't forget, tomorrow morning we're meeting at Finch Subway Station, the usual place."

"How could I forget? It's my birthday and my favorite sport!" Artemis replied with a grin. They all stepped out, laughter and smiles filling the air.

After bidding farewell to her friends, Artemis helped her mother clean up the remaining mess from the party. Despite her exhaustion, she felt content knowing that she had celebrated her birthday surrounded by the people she cared about most. As Artemis prepared for bed that night, she reflected on the events of the day. It had been a memorable birthday filled with surprises, laughter, and love. With a smile on her face, she drifted off to sleep, looking forward to the adventures that awaited her on the next day's skating excursion with her friends.

Artemis hugged her mother tightly, feeling the weight of her words showing the cell phone and happily pushed it into her pocket. She knew how much her mother missed her father, and she felt the ache of his absence keenly, especially on days like her birthday, which was his birthday, too. She whispered softly, her voice filled with emotion, "I miss him too, Mom. But I know he's watching over us, wherever he is. And we have each other; that's what matters most."

Dorsa nodded, her eyes glistening with unshed tears. She kissed Artemis's forehead, then embraced both of her daughters tightly. "You're right, my dear," she whispered. "We have each other, and we'll always be there for one another. Good night, my sweethearts. Sweet dreams."

With a final embrace, Artemis, and Atossa parted ways, each retreating to their respective rooms. Artemis climbed into bed, her heart heavy yet also filled with love for her family. As she drifted off to sleep, she held onto the memories of her birthday celebration, cherishing the moments spent with her loved ones, feeling grateful for the love that surrounded her; she hoped for the day her father would rejoin them, just as she had wished on her birthday cake.

Artemis's words resonated deeply with Dorsa, filling her with a mixture of hope and sadness. She marveled at her daughter's unwavering belief in her father's return, finding solace in the possibility that he might indeed find his way back to them. Dorsa cherished the connection she shared with Artemis, knowing that they were both united in their longing for Arsham's presence.

As Artemis retreated to her room, Dorsa remained downstairs, reflecting on her daughter's dreams and the profound impact they had on her. She, too, had experienced similar visions, moments of fleeting hope that Arsham might one day reappear, bringing their family back together. Despite the passage of time, the ache of his absence remained a constant presence in their lives, a reminder of the void left behind by his disappearance.

In the quiet of the night, Dorsa whispered a silent prayer, sending her hopes and wishes out into the universe, yearning for the day when they would be reunited with Arsham once again. With a heavy heart yet a glimmer of hope, she finally retired to bed, enveloped in the warmth of her memories and the love that bound her family together.

Artemis lay in bed, her heart still pounding from the intensity of her dream. The recurring vision had left her shaken, its vividness lingering in her mind even as she returned to reality. She couldn't shake the feeling of unease that gripped her, the sense of being drawn into a world beyond her comprehension.

As she reflected on the dream, Artemis couldn't help but wonder about its significance. The glowing door, her mother and grandmother waiting on the other side with outstretched hands, calling her to join them, and the sudden appearance of her father in pain, needing her help—all seemed like pieces of a puzzle waiting to be solved. She had always been fascinated by dreams and their hidden meanings, but this one felt different, more urgent somehow and a little scary.

Pushing aside her apprehension, Artemis resolved to delve deeper into the mystery of her dreams. She knew that there was more to uncover, more layers of truth waiting to be revealed. With determination in her heart, she vowed to unravel the secrets of her subconscious and unlock the mysteries that lay hidden within her mind. But for now, she needed to focus on the present, on celebrating her birthday with her friends and cherishing the moments they shared together. The answers would come in time; she was certain of it.

UNFORGETTABLE GATHERING

Artemis woke up to the sound of her phone ringing, sunlight streaming into her room, signaling it was time to get up. She glanced at the clock on her nightstand—it was 8:50. She immediately picked up the cell phone and answered, "Hello,"

Megan was on the other end of the call, reminding her that she was supposed to be at Finch Station by 9 o'clock. Artemis quickly assured her, "I'm on my way."

She hurriedly got dressed and rushed out of the house. She felt a pang of guilt as she arrived late to meet her friends. She hurried toward them, apologizing profusely for her tardiness. Despite her exhaustion, she couldn't bear the thought of disappointing her friends on her birthday.

"Sorry, guys! I'm here, I'm here," she panted, trying to catch her breath as she approached the group. "I lost track of time. Let's not waste any more and head to the city hall for some skating!"

Ricky interrupted, saying, "Artemis! Your mom's gift saved you, right? We could actually call you!"

"Let's go to Wonderland today!" Ricky suggested excitedly.

Allen chimed in, "Ricky, remember last time we went to Wonderland? She threw up and then passed out because she was extremely afraid of heights. Plus, Wonderland isn't even open during the winter."

Everyone glanced at him sideways, then turned to greet Artemis with understanding smiles, assuring her that it was all right. With their support, Artemis felt a surge of energy, ready to make the most of her special day. Together, they headed towards the city hall, excited for a day filled with laughter, joy, and, of course, plenty of skating.

As Artemis recounted her recurring dream to Helen, she felt a sense of relief to finally share her feelings with someone who understood. Helen listened attentively, offering comforting words and support.

"It's so strange, Helen," Artemis continued, her voice softening. "I always see this glowing door, and Mom and Nana Tara are waiting for me on the other side of that door. But I can never reach them. And then, just last night, I saw my dad's face in my dream. It felt so real like he was really there. He told me to search my pocket and the key was there. I think around my birthdays, I am thinking about my father a lot. That's why I have a dream about him."

Helen placed a comforting hand on Artemis's shoulder. "I can't even imagine how difficult that must be for you, Artemis. But remember, dreams are just dreams. They can't hurt you. Maybe it's just your mind's way of processing everything that's happened."

Artemis nodded, grateful for Helen's understanding. "Yeah, you're probably right. It's just hard sometimes, you know? I miss my dad so much."

As they sat together, waiting for Matt to return from the restroom, Artemis felt a sense of warmth and reassurance, knowing that she had friends like Helen by her side. Despite the challenges she faced, she knew she wasn't alone.

Artemis couldn't help but smile at her friends' playful banter, grateful for their lightheartedness in the midst of her own worries. As they made their way to the ice rink, she felt a sense of excitement building within her. Skating had always been a source of joy for her, a chance to lose herself in the movement and the rhythm of the ice.

She laced up her skates quickly, her fingers deftly working the laces as she prepared to hit the ice. Despite Ricky's earlier comment about birthday wishes coming true, she couldn't shake the feeling of anticipation that filled her. With a final tug on her skates, Artemis stepped onto the ice, feeling the cool surface beneath her blades. The familiar sensation brought a rush of exhilaration, and she pushed off, gliding effortlessly across the rink.

As she skated alongside her friends, the worries of the outside world melted away, replaced by the simple joy of movement and friendship. For now, at least, she could forget about her dreams and her fears and simply enjoy the moment.

As Artemis finished her breathtaking performance on the ice, she couldn't help but feel a rush of adrenaline coursing through her veins. The cheers and applause from the onlookers only added to her sense of accomplishment. Skating had always been her passion, her escape from the worries of the world, and in that moment, she felt truly alive.

Her friends gathered around her, their faces filled with awe and admiration. Allen, Helen, Megan, and Ricky all congratulated her on her incredible skills, their smiles reflecting their genuine excitement. Even Matt, who had struggled with his own balance on the ice, couldn't help but be impressed by Artemis's prowess. He watched her with a mixture of admiration and envy, wishing he could glide across the ice with the same grace and ease to stay closer to her.

As they continued to skate together, Artemis felt a sense of camaraderie and joy that she hadn't experienced in a long time. Despite the challenges and uncertainties that lay ahead, she knew that as long as she had her friends by her side, she could overcome anything. As they laughed and skated together, she couldn't help but feel grateful for the simple moments of happiness they shared. Artemis observed the bustling activity on the ice rink; she couldn't help but feel a sense of contentment wash over her.

Despite the fatigue setting in, she cherished these moments of camaraderie with her friends, knowing that they shared a bond that went beyond mere words. Turning her attention back to Matt, she felt a pang of sympathy for him as she watched him sitting on the sidelines, observing the skaters with a wistful expression. She knew that skating wasn't his forte, but she admired his willingness to try new things and be a part of the group.

With a gentle smile, Artemis made her way over to Matt and extended her hand to him. "Hey, Matt," she said warmly. "Why don't you give it another try? We're all out here having fun together, and it wouldn't be the same without you."

Matt hesitated for a moment, his gaze shifting from Artemis to the crowded ice rink. But then, with a determined look in her eyes, he took her hand and stood up, ready to join his friends once more.

Together, they joined the other skaters on the ice, their laughter mingling with the sounds of scraping blades and echoing across the rink. And as they glided across the ice in perfect harmony, Artemis felt a deep sense of joy and camaraderie that she knew would linger in her heart long after the day had ended.

After hours of skating, they were all exhausted. Together, they decided to pack up their things and head to Artemis's home to continue celebrating her birthday… follow through with their plans for the day and carry on through the night until morning.

As Artemis and her friends made their way to her room, they could already feel the excitement building for their evening together. Once inside, they wasted no time in setting up for their game and movie night. Matt helped arrange the setting while Helen and Megan took charge of selecting the games and movies.

Artemis couldn't help but feel a warm glow as she watched her friends bustling around her room, their laughter filling the air. Despite the ups and downs of life, moments like these reminded her of the joy and comfort that true friendship brought. Once everything was set up, they settled in for a lively game session, their competitive spirits shining through as they battled it out in various board games and card games. Laughter and banter filled the room as they cheered each other on and celebrated their victories.

After a few rounds of games, they decided to take a break and enjoy some ice cream, just as Dorsa had suggested and call out for them. They gathered around the kitchen table, sharing stories and jokes as they indulged in the sweet treat. With their energy replenished, they returned to Artemis's room to continue their evening with a movie marathon. They debated over which movies to watch, finally settling on a mix of classics and comedies that they all enjoyed.

As the night wore on, Artemis couldn't help but feel grateful for the bond she shared with her friends. In their company, she felt a sense of belonging and happiness that she cherished deeply, and as they laughed and joked together late into the night, she knew that these were the moments that she would treasure forever.

Artemis paused momentarily; a wave of emotions washed over her at Ricky's question. She took a deep breath as Ricky asked curiously, "Artemis, may I ask… was today your dad's birthday too?"

Artemis turned to face Ricky, her expression soft yet tinged with sadness as she replied, "It's okay, Ricky. Ask any question, and yes, it was… and also my Grandma Tara."

Everyone exclaimed loudly, "Wow…"

Allen, baffled, added, "But how is that even possible? Three birthdays in one day from one family?"

Artemis smiled faintly and said, "Why is it impossible? It happened in my family, so it's clearly not impossible."

Ricky sat down, hugging his knees, and asked, "What happened to your dad? I've heard about him but never heard the real story. Is it okay if you talk about it?"

Helen interrupted, "Do you remember anything from that night when your father went missing? You mentioned once that you were four years old and were in the room with him. Did you see him going out or doing something? What happened?"

Matt suddenly stood up and blurted out, "Wait a minute, guys! You all know this subject is really painful for her. Could you please change the topic?"

Artemis looked at Matt with a friendly smile and said, "Thank you for asking."

She began, her voice quiet yet steady, "My dad disappeared when I was just a little girl. It was exactly on a night like tonight—right here in our home—when he vanished. We never found out how or why. We searched everywhere and had his name and pictures in magazines and newspapers, but there was no sign of him. It's been years now, and we still don't know what happened. Even his friends were present that day, and after he disappeared, they tried to help, but they had no answers either."

She paused for a moment, scanning her friends' faces before continuing, "And yes, according to my mother, I was in the room. I have a very faint memory, but nothing clear enough to explain what happened."

"If they were together, then they should have some clue about what happened that night," Helen said, surprised.

"The only thing they said was he left the room, and they didn't see him again," Artemis explained.

She paused for a few seconds before continuing, "They kept coming back on his birthday, telling my mother they wanted to hold a ceremony for my father on the anniversary of his disappearance. I remember that because I was older then, and they asked me to stay with them while they performed strange rituals. My mother allowed it the first time, but after that, she refused to let them do anything more."

Artemis's gaze drifted to the picture on the dresser, her father's smiling face staring back at her. "I miss him every day,"

She continued, her voice tinged with longing, "I wish he could be here with us to see how much we've grown and to share in our lives. But wherever he is, I hope he knows that we love him and that we'll never stop searching for him."

Ricky jumped in again, "Maybe if your mother had allowed them to continue their ceremony, you might have found some answers."

Artemis glanced at him sideways, her expression thoughtful.

Megan listened intently, her heart going out to her friend. She reached out and placed a comforting hand on Artemis's shoulder, offering her silent support. "Thank you for sharing, Artemis," she said softly, then continued, "your dad sounds like a wonderful man, and I'm sure he's watching over you, wherever he is."

Artemis sighed softly, her thoughts drifting back to that fateful night. "It's complicated," she began, her voice tinged with a mixture of frustration and sadness. "The investigators searched for clues, but they couldn't find anything concrete. It was like he vanished into thin air."

She paused, her gaze dropping to her hands as she tried to gather her thoughts. "There were theories, of course," she continued, her voice barely above a whisper. "Some people thought my mother was involved or that he just left us. But there was never any evidence to support those ideas."

Artemis glanced up at Megan, her eyes reflecting the turmoil of emotions swirling within her. "I've spent years trying to piece together what happened that night," she admitted. "But it's like trying to solve a puzzle with no pieces at all. No matter how hard I try, I can't find the answers I'm looking for."

Megan listened quietly. She could see the pain etched in Artemis's features, the weight of uncertainty bearing down on her. "I'm so sorry, Artemis," she said softly, reaching out to squeeze her hand gently. "I can't imagine how difficult this must be for you. But you're not alone. We're here for you, no matter what."

Megan listened intently, her brow furrowing in concern as Artemis recounted the events of that fateful night. "That sounds... bizarre," she remarked softly, struggling to find the right words to express her thoughts.

Artemis nodded, her expression solemn. "It was like something out of a movie," she admitted, her voice tinged with a hint of disbelief. "One moment, everything was normal, and the next... he was gone."

Megan frowned, her mind racing with questions. "Did anyone else witness what happened?" she asked, her curiosity piqued.

Artemis shook her head. "Yes, but those two friends disappeared into thin air too, as I told you before," she replied, her tone somber. "My mom tried to explain it to the police, but they didn't believe her. They thought she was in shock, imagining things, or covering something up."

Helen's heart went out to her friend, the weight of her words sinking in. "I can't even imagine how terrifying that must have been for your mom," she murmured, her voice laced with sympathy.

Artemis nodded, a sad smile playing on her lips. "Yeah," she agreed softly.

Megan listened with a heavy heart, her empathy for Artemis and her mother growing with each word. "That's... incredibly unfair," she murmured, struggling to comprehend the depth of the injustice Artemis's family had faced. "To be accused and abandoned like that... I can't even imagine."

Artemis nodded, her expression reflecting the weight of her mother's ordeal. "It's been hard," she admitted, her voice tinged with gloom. "But my mom is incredibly strong. She's faced so much adversity, and yet she still keeps going, still holds out hope for answers."

Megan reached out to place a comforting hand on Artemis's shoulder again. "Your mom sounds like an amazing woman," she said softly. "To endure all of that and still be there for you and your sister... she's truly remarkable."

Artemis smiled gratefully, touched by Megan's words of support. "She is," she agreed, her voice filled with pride. "And I'll do everything I can to help her find the answers she deserves."

As they sat in quiet solidarity, Megan couldn't help but admire Artemis's resilience in the face of such adversity. She knew that with friends like her by her side, Artemis and her mother would never have to face their challenges alone.

Megan could sense the turmoil within Artemis as she recounted the pain her family had endured since her father's disappearance. It was a heavy burden for anyone to bear, especially for someone as young as Artemis. "I'm so sorry, Artemis," Megan said softly, her heart going out to her friend. "It's not fair that your family has had to endure so much uncertainty and pain."

Everyone was listening.

Artemis nodded, her eyes glistening with unshed tears. "It's been really hard," she admitted, her voice barely above a whisper. "But we'll get through it. Together."

Ricky got closer to her and squeezed Artemis's hand in a gesture of solidarity. "You're not alone, Artemis," he reassured her. "We're here for you every step of the way."

Artemis managed a small smile, grateful for Ricky's support. "Thank you," she said, her voice filled with emotion. "It means a lot."

As they sat together in silent understanding, everyone knew that their friendship would be a source of strength for Artemis in the days to come. No matter what challenges they faced, they would face them together, united in their bond of friendship and support.

Artemis's face grew pale, her lips turning white as if her energy had been sucked out of her. Sometimes, Artemis wanted to believe that her dad had left them, and her mother was simply trying to ignore the painful truth. Despite the love she held for her mother, Artemis couldn't help but feel a pang of frustration. It wasn't fair for her mother to suffer like this; she was innocent, yet forced to carry the weight of guilt on her shoulders.

Dorsa cherished her husband deeply, never uttering a negative word about him. She knew his love for her was immense, making it inconceivable that he would willingly abandon his family. Artemis vividly remembered the countless times she'd seen her mother quietly shedding tears, longing for her husband's presence. It tore at Artemis's heart to witness her mother's pain.

"Whenever I'm alone, I listen to 'Last Dance with My Father' by Luther Vandross," Artemis shared. "I love that song because it feels like it was written just for me and my pain."

Artemis sometimes lashed out, saying hurtful things about her dad in an attempt to distract her mother from her grief. But each time, her mother's reaction was a mix of sadness and anger, clearly showing how deeply she was affected.

Megan offered a gentle response, understanding Artemis's turmoil. "I understand why you might say those things, Artemis," she began softly. "But it's important to remember that your mom's love for your dad runs deep. Even though it's painful for her, she holds on to those memories because they're a part of who she is."

Artemis nodded, her expression reflecting the weight of her emotions. "I know," she admitted quietly. "I just wish things were different."

Helen reached out, giving Artemis's hand a comforting squeeze. She reassured her, "Your mom is lucky to have you by her side, supporting her through everything."

Artemis managed a small smile, grateful for Helen's understanding. "Thanks, Helen," she said, her voice tinted with emotion. "I'm lucky to have friends like you."

Artemis remembered once she was angry, and she said such things about her father and her mother was so angry when she reacted against her and said, "Artemis, you have no right to speak ill of your father. We still don't know what transpired that night. Perhaps he left for a reason, choosing not to disturb me, and met with an unfortunate incident. He could be in a hospital right now, perhaps even in a coma. Or maybe he suffered amnesia after an accident, wandering away without knowing his way back. There are countless possibilities, and unless we have concrete evidence, we shouldn't pass judgment. Do you understand, Artemis? It pains me to hear you speak this way about him. Please refrain from it. Stop it... Stop it," she pleaded with tears streaming down her cheeks.

Artemis, engrossed in her thoughts, was suddenly interrupted by a knock at the door. Dorsa opened it, breaking Artemis's reverie.

"Artemis, I just wanted to ask you something before saying goodnight. I didn't sleep well last night, and I have to wake up early tomorrow morning. If any of your friends need a ride home, I can drive them; otherwise, you can just call a cab." Dorsa stood by the door, waiting for their response.

Artemis looked at her friends and relayed her mother's offer, asking, "You heard her. Does anybody need a ride?" They exchanged glances and shook their heads, declining the offer.

Helen stood up and approached Dorsa, expressing their gratitude on everyone's behalf, "Thank you, Mrs. Vedetta. It's only six-thirty, and tonight's a sleepover for us. But don't worry—if any of us decides to leave early, we'll call a cab or ask our parents for a ride."

Dorsa smiled kindly, as usual, and looked at each of their faces before speaking, "That's lovely. I know it's Artemis's birthday, and I'm very fond of her friends."

Artemis kissed her mother's cheek and bid her goodnight, saying, "Good night, Mom. I'll see you in the morning."

Dorsa then retreated to her bedroom.

As soon as Artemis re-entered the room, Allen was already rummaging through the CDs. Suddenly, he jumped up and exclaimed, "Let's watch a movie!" He held up the Superman DVD in his hands.

"I love it. I say yes," Megan responded immediately.

They all watched the movie intently, interjecting with comments and jokes about Superman and his adversaries. As soon as the movie ended, Allen promptly put on "The Matrix," prompting applause from everyone.

"Hey guys! What do you think would happen if Superman was in the Matrix? Would he still be as powerful, or could the agents access him whenever they pleased?" Allen posed the question, sparking a lively discussion among the group.

"He'd still be Superman," Megan responded with a sigh, indicating her unwavering faith in the superhero.

"Well, Neo is kind of like Superman, too," Matt added, drawing parallels between the two iconic characters. Agents can not access him at all.

"I think Superman could enter the Matrix and exit whenever he wanted," Artemis chimed in, observing Megan's reaction with interest.

The door cracked open again, and Dorsa was halfway inside the room. As soon as she spotted Artemis, she asked, "Artemis! I found this book on the bookshelf last night after the party, and since then, I knew I had seen this book somewhere before. But I couldn't remember exactly where. I kept thinking about it, unable to shake it from my mind. Finally, I remembered. Your father had this book for a while, and a few days before his disappearance, he was very into it," Dorsa sighed, taking a few deep breaths before continuing.

"Matt had this book for a while, and he brought it back to me last night," Artemis replied calmly, trying to diffuse the tension in the room.

But Dorsa's tone betrayed her agitation as she asked again, "Where did you find this book? Why do you even have it? And how come you're interested in it?"

"It was in the basement, and somehow it caught my attention. I brought it to my room with the intention of reading it. Matt noticed it and asked if he could borrow it," Artemis explained quickly, hoping to reassure her mother.

As Artemis stood in the hallway holding the book, she asked Dorsa, "What is it about this book that makes it so important to you?"

"This is the book your father was reading in the last days of his life here, and that's why it's important to me. I've read it so many times, and I thought I might have felt the same way he did when he was reading it, but it doesn't make sense to me. Those signs are meaningless. Regardless, I still want to keep it safe. It might be a key," Dorsa explained, her voice filled with emotion.

Artemis took the book and examined its cover. "What's the name of this book again?" she asked, turning it over to read the title.

"Exquisite Incomparable Worlds," Artemis read aloud, feeling an inexplicable pull toward its contents. Her curiosity deepened, drawing her in even more.

Dorsa got the book back, looked at her daughter in surprise, and asked, "Do you know anything about it?

Artemis glanced at the book, hesitated for a moment, then picked it up again, unable to shake the feeling that there was something special about it. She opened it and quickly turned the pages over, then turned to her mother and said, "Mom...! Let me have it for a few more days. I think Matt was reading it, and he wants to talk to me about this book. He is smart, and maybe he can find something. I promise to return it to you as soon as possible. Can I have it?"

Artemis looked at her mother, who seemed hesitant to give the book away; she was so attached to it. Dorsa held it in her arms like it was a religious artifact with the power to bring back her loved one, and the only thing she needed to do was find the right spell. Artemis hugged her mother and gazed into her eyes for a moment, hoping to gain her trust.

Then she asked again, "Look, Mom," Artemis began gently, trying to reassure her mother. "Matt is very bright and has studied the book. He only wants to share his knowledge with me. I believe he may have more information about it than anyone else right now. If you want to know more, you'll have to trust me. I'm just borrowing it for tonight, and I'll return it tomorrow. Can I have it?"

Dorsa felt the warmth of Artemis's words in her heart. She glanced at the book in her hand and then held the book out to her with a smile. But after a moment, her expression shifted, and she took the book back with a tremble in her hands. Tears welled up in her eyes as she spoke, "No... I don't want anything to happen to you or anyone else." She choked out, "Please, don't insist on having the book. I can't bear to lose you too. I don't know why, but I have a bad feeling about this."

"Mom! What could happen to me? It's only a book," Artemis said softly

Dorsa looked at her and asked, "Can you explain what happened to your dad?"

Artemis's tone softened as she reached out to hold her mother's hands. With sincerity in her eyes, she repeated her request, "Mother, I love you dearly, and I would do anything to make you happy. Please listen to me carefully. I apologize for the intrusion, but we need to talk about it. Trust me on this. Let me have the book for tonight, and I'll return it to you as soon as I'm done with it. I just want to hear Matt's thoughts about this book and what he has to share with me. Besides, you often worry about everything, and it's not the first time you've had such a feeling. Just try to relax, and I'll see you in the morning."

Dorsa nodded with a mixture of apprehension and resignation. "Okay. But don't forget about your promise. Please be careful. I know it's just a book, but... be careful."

Artemis hugged her mother tightly, feeling a sense of relief wash over her. "Mom... Do you trust me? I am borrowing your book, and that's it. I'll return it to you very soon. Is that okay now?"

"Of course... I can do that... I'll be more than happy to know more about it too, but just promise me this: you won't do anything stupid," Dorsa responded with a mix of concern and hope.

"Mom...! When I'm done with the book, I will give it back to you for sure," Artemis reassured her, repeating her promise to emphasize her sincerity. She took the book from her mother's hands, holding it gently as a symbol of the trust placed in her.

Dorsa had a smile on her lips and kissed Artemis back on her forehead as she said goodnight again. She then headed straight to her room, leaving Artemis to rejoin her friends. Artemis gazed at the mysterious book in her hand, turning it over and examining its cover. There was nothing particularly special or unique about its appearance; it simply looked like an old book with an ordinary cover. Yet, something was intriguing about it, an air of antiquity and perhaps even a hint of sorcery or witchcraft.

The word 'Flimsy' was printed beneath the title 'Exquisite Incomparable World,' which the title was displayed above a circle featuring a five-pointed star at its center, giving the impression that the letters were being pulled into the star, or perhaps already halfway consumed by it. The design seemed almost hypnotic, as if the star held a mysterious power over the fragile letters, pulling them into its depths.

Artemis read the title again: "Exquisite Incomparable World…" Artemis repeated the title softly, mulling over its significance. To her, it seemed to carry a clear meaning, but in the context of the book, it likely held a deeper and more mysterious connotation. She couldn't shake the feeling that there was something extraordinary about this book, something beyond the ordinary. As she held it in her hands, questions swirled in her mind.

"What is it about this book? And what is the relevance between this book and my dad's disappearance? Are they connected?" Artemis whispered to herself, her curiosity piqued, and her determination to uncover the truth strengthened.

Artemis stood by the door, observing her friends engrossed in their game. They had chosen a racing car game with a four-player option on the Wii. Helen, Allen, Megan, and Ricky were the first group to play, with the loser being replaced by the next person in the room. As they cheered and laughed, enjoying their game, there was a knock on the door again, and Artemis cracked it open slightly. Behind the door stood Atossa, her sister. Artemis knew exactly why she was there; Atossa had a fondness for Matt. Although Matt had made it clear to Artemis that he wasn't interested in Atossa, Artemis never told her sister, not wanting to hurt her feelings. She hoped

Atossa would come to realize it slowly on her own and, perhaps, even fall in love with someone who truly adored her.

Atossa wore an angelic smile as she asked, "Can I come in and join you guys? I can't sleep either, and it's your birthday. I would love to be a part of it. I promise to behave. Please..." Her hands were clasped together as if in prayer, adding to the sincerity of her request.

Artemis responded with a warm smile and wordlessly opened the door wider for her. Atossa entered, and her eyes immediately found Matt sitting at the computer desk. She made her way directly to him. Matt felt a blush creeping up his cheeks as he sensed her fondness for him, but he was unsure how to respond. He harbored feelings for Artemis and saw Atossa only as a friend, yet he was too timid to address the situation.

Matt and Atossa watched as the others played the game, but Matt's attention was suddenly drawn to the rocks displayed on a nearby shelf. Curiosity piqued, he walked over and picked them up, closely examining them. Atossa observed him with interest, her eyes tracking his movements.

In the light, the rocks seemed to take on a new brilliance, their colors becoming more vibrant. Matt tested their authenticity, tapping them lightly and inspecting their texture. Satisfied with the results, he looked at Artemis, who had now turned her gaze toward him. "Hey, Artemis… Where did you find these cool rocks? They're completely different from the one I had," he asked, surprise evident in his voice.

Artemis turned her head towards where Matt and Atossa stood and asked, "Which rocks?" She furrowed her brow and glanced at Matt's hands, noting the rocks he was examining. "Oh, you mean those rocks. I found them among my dad's belongings the other day. Why?" she inquired curiously. This was the perfect opportunity for Artemis to engage Matt in conversation, and she intended to seize it. "My mom has taken great care of them because they belonged to my dad and are very special to her," Artemis continued, intending to provide more context until Atossa's interruption.

Atossa flashed a smile at Matt, who briefly returned it while keeping his focus on the stones. "These are called the five elements," he said, studying them intently.

Artemis and Atossa exchanged a puzzled glance before turning their attention back to Matt. "These are the five elements?"

Artemis repeated, her curiosity piqued. "What do you mean by that?" She leaned in, eager to hear more about Matt's revelation.

Megan looked at the screen then she frowned. "What are these? I can't understand a bit of it."

"You need to know something about the stones in order to be able to read and understand these," Matt replied while he was typing like a maniac. Suddenly, he stopped and tapped the submit button. As Matt hit the submit button, the web page refreshed, revealing a plethora of information about the symbols and their meanings. Matt quickly scanned the page, absorbing the details and cross-referencing them with the symbols they had observed on the stones and in the book.

He turned to Artemis and asked, "Do you have a printer?"

Artemis pointed at the corner of her room close to the door. "There is it."

"These symbols are ancient," Matt explained, his eyes quickly scanning the text before he pressed the key to print everything. "They have deep spiritual and mystical significance, often associated with rituals, spells, and protective magic."

Allen turned to Matt and asked, "How can just a few words and a couple of pictures create something so... magical?" Matt, visibly impatient, replied, "Have you ever seen *The Matrix*?"

"Of course," Allen answered.

Without turning away from Artemis, Matt said, "Then if you know how to make changes on a computer... well, you can figure out the rest."

Artemis leaned in closer, eager to learn more, as the symbols on the screen seemed to pulse with energy, drawing her deeper into their mystery.

"Each symbol represents a different aspect of magic and the elements, with each one releasing a unique energy or perhaps even a distinct power," Matt explained more and his voice animated with excitement. "By understanding their meanings and how they interact, we can unlock their power and potentially uncover the truth about them—and how they work together in harmony."

The group huddled around the laptop, engrossed in their research. With each discovery, they felt closer to unraveling the secrets hidden within the stones and the book. But as they ventured further and deeper, they realized just how little they truly knew. Their journey was only just beginning, and the mysteries that lay ahead would test their courage, determination, and bonds of friendship in ways they never imagined.

"After finding out about the signs and replicating the procedures then we have a chance to find out if we can reverse it. I think we can simply represent by drawing a pentacle in the air above your working space or on the floor, in the dirt if working outside, or on a piece of paper and to be discarded later," explained Ricky, as everyone suddenly turned their eyes toward him in surprise.

Artemis nodded positively, absorbing Ricky's words. Then she looked at Matt and both were speechless. "That was amazing, Ricky. How did you come up with that?" she asked.

Ricky shrank his shoulders and had a funny smile while he turned his eyes, focused on the screen again, and said, while the thought still lingered in his expression, "It just keeps coming up in my mind as we go."

The prospect of uncovering the truth filled her with determination. "We have to try," Artemis said, her voice tinged with both hope and apprehension. "If there's a chance to bring my dad back, I have to take it with your help."

The others nodded in agreement, their faces reflecting a blend of determination and uncertainty. They knew the path ahead would be difficult, fraught with challenges and dangers they couldn't yet comprehend. But with their newfound knowledge and the power of the stones at their disposal, they felt ready to face whatever lay ahead. They were determined to push forward for as long as they could, convinced that nothing could stop them.

Together, they would unlock the secrets of the symbols, master the rituals, and delve into the mysteries of the unknown. In doing so, they would embark on a journey that would test their courage, challenge their beliefs, and ultimately lead them to the truth they sought. With a shared sense of purpose, they gathered around the laptop once more, ready to begin their quest. Whatever obstacles they encountered along the way, they knew they would face them together, bound by friendship, determination, and the hope of uncovering the truth.

As Matt shared his knowledge with the group, he felt a sense of purpose and clarity, unlike anything he had experienced before. Artemis's presence seemed to amplify his abilities, sharpening his focus and enabling him to recall information with remarkable clarity. With each passing moment, Matt found himself drawn deeper into the mysteries they were unraveling. He reveled in the opportunity to share his knowledge with Artemis and the others, eager to guide them on their journey and help them unlock the secrets they sought. He realized there must be a purpose for him in that room at that very moment. Together, they pored over the information on the laptop screen, dissecting the symbols and rituals with precision and determination. Matt explained each concept with a blend of enthusiasm and patience, ensuring everyone grasped their significance and potential applications for their quest. He stood tall, exuding the presence of a scientist—or perhaps, a leader.

As they delved deeper into the mysteries of the stones and the ancient symbols, Matt's excitement grew. He relished the opportunity to explore the unknown alongside Artemis and her friends, confident that together, they could overcome any obstacle and uncover the truth they sought. With Artemis by his side, Matt felt the power of love, making him feel unstoppable. He knew that as long as they remained united, there was nothing they couldn't achieve. With each step they took, he felt a renewed sense of purpose and determination, ready to face whatever challenges lay ahead.

Excitement rippled through the group as they prepared to embark on their adventure. With Matt confidently leading the way and Ricky's sudden suggestions, they felt a renewed sense of purpose and anticipation. They listened intently as Matt outlined the steps they needed to follow, his contagious enthusiasm spreading through the group. As they readied themselves for the journey ahead, their anticipation heightened, each moment bringing them closer to unraveling the mysteries that had long eluded Artemis and her family. United, they knew that together, they could accomplish anything. Artemis's practical approach resonated with the group, grounding their excitement in a realistic understanding of the task ahead. They were willing to put in the time and effort necessary to uncover the truth.

With their determination fueling their efforts, they delved into their research with renewed focus and dedication. Each new piece of information they uncovered brought them one step closer to unlocking the secrets of the ancient symbols and rituals. As the night wore on, they worked tirelessly, fueled by their shared desire to solve the mystery. And though they knew they still had much to learn, they were confident that with perseverance and teamwork, they would eventually find the answers they sought.

"Matt knows almost all the answers, and, best of all, we have access to Google too. We're getting closer to uncovering the truth." Ricky looked at Artemis and then Matt constantly.

Ricky's acknowledgment of Matt's expertise and the group's access to information through the internet reassured them that they had the tools they needed to tackle the challenge ahead. With Matt's knowledge guiding them and the vast resources of the internet at their disposal, they felt confident in their ability to unravel the mysteries they faced. Artemis nodded in agreement, grateful for the support of her friends and the expertise they brought to the table.

Matt's question was directed at Ricky, acknowledging his contribution and seeking to understand the thought process behind his suggestion. It also highlighted Matt's appreciation for Ricky's input and his desire to involve everyone in the group's efforts. Ricky smiled at Matt's question, pleased to have made a meaningful contribution.

He replied, "Well, I just remembered something I read once and thought it might be useful. Sometimes, you just have to think outside the box, you know?"

Matt nodded, impressed by Ricky's resourcefulness. "Definitely," he agreed. "We all bring something unique to the table, and that's what makes us a great team."

Artemis smiled at the camaraderie between her friends, grateful for their support and collaboration. With everyone's contributions, they felt more confident than ever in their ability to unravel the mysteries they faced.

Ricky smiled when he said, "Let's just say I have my sources." Then he winked at Matt.

Matt grinned back at Ricky, appreciating his cryptic response. It added an element of intrigue to their discussion and hinted at Ricky's resourcefulness. With a shared understanding, Matt nodded in acknowledgment, acknowledging Ricky's subtle hint while maintaining the lighthearted atmosphere of their conversation.

Matt clapped a few times and said, "Listen up, everyone! We need a spirit circle first, then we can draw it on the floor, and one of us should represent the pentacle by holding these stones in special places," Matt said out loud without looking at anyone."

Matt's authoritative tone captured everyone's attention, drawing them into the plan he was laying out. As he spoke, his words resonated with confidence, indicating his leadership in the group's endeavor. Without needing to look at anyone, he projected his instructions clearly, establishing a sense of organization and purpose among his friends. "Come on, Artemis. Maybe we will be able to see what happened to your dad."

"A scientist and his followers are working on the case," Ricky broke his silence again, comforted the group, and encouraged them to support this idea.

Ricky's words injected a sense of urgency and motivation into the group, reminding them of the gravity of the situation and the potential to uncover crucial information about Artemis's father's disappearance. By mentioning the involvement of scientists and their ongoing efforts, he instilled hope and determination in the group, urging them to seize the opportunity to contribute to the investigation.

Matt didn't pay attention to him and cleared his throat for another question to ask from Artemis, "Artemis! It's a really tough question, but may I ask you when exactly your dad disappeared? Do you remember anything, or did your mother ever tell you about that? I mean, mainly the exact time of the incident?" He was tapping his lower lip with his index finger, a habit he had whenever he was deep in thought, especially when trying to solve a problem.

Matt's inquiry was direct and focused, aiming to gather critical information to assist in their investigation. By asking Artemis about the precise timing of her father's disappearance, he hoped to establish a timeline and potentially uncover clues that could aid their efforts. His methodical approach demonstrated his commitment to unraveling the mystery and finding answers for Artemis and her family.

"Yes... My mother once told me that happened on my fourth birthday," she said, slurping on her drink as memories of her father resurfaced—how he used to play hide and seek with her.

Though those memories were fading, they still brought her a sense of joy and comfort. Her recollection added a poignant layer to the mystery surrounding her father's disappearance. The fact that it occurred on her fourth birthday suggested a profound significance to the event, deepening the emotional weight of the investigation for her. This detail could potentially provide valuable context for understanding the circumstances surrounding her father's vanishing and may offer clues as to why it happened when it did.

Matt paused for a second, then asked again, "Artemis, I meant the time of day or night."

Artemis shifted uncomfortably before answering, "I think it was very early in the morning, but she wasn't sure of the exact time."

"You said your father and your grandmother have exactly the same birthday as yours?" Ricky threw his question out of nowhere, catching everyone off guard and causing a momentary pause in the conversation.

Artemis suddenly found herself the center of attention as everyone turned to her and exclaimed, "What?"

Allen was visibly surprised. "I thought you and your father shared the same birthday, but what are the odds of this? Are you sure?"

Artemis nodded slowly in response, while Atossa glanced around at everyone and said with a hint of playful frustration, "I'm the only one left out."

"Yes, that's correct. It's always been a special coincidence in our family," she affirmed with a soft smile then turned to Atossa and said, "You're not left out. Mom's birthday is different, too."

"What's your mom's birthday?" Helen finally chimed in, joining the line of questioning.

"She is February 28th. Why?" Artemis answered.

"How about Atossa?" Megan asked

Atossa answered immediately, "March 1st."

Everyone looked speechless and looked at Artemis and Atossa.

Ricky stepped closer to Artemis and, with a tone of genuine surprise, said, "Wait—you mean all of you were born at the end of February or the beginning of March?"

"Hey! Maybe this is something to do with all of your birthdays after all because all of you have a birthday around leap year?" Ricky seemed so convincing, and everybody looked at one another for quite some time. He kept quiet because he waited for the new idea to settle down in their mind. But his suggestions were exactly what they needed to hear, and they were meaningful, so they became facts. There is always the right question from someone that you never expected. His suggestion sparked a wave of contemplation among the group. They exchanged glances, each lost in their own thoughts, considering the possibility that Artemis's birthday and her family might hold some significance in her father's disappearance. It was a fresh angle to explore, one that could potentially shed new light on the mystery they were trying to unravel. With renewed determination, They refocused their efforts on unraveling the connections between Artemis's birthday, her father's disappearance, and the mysterious elements within the book they had to uncover.

"Today is your birthday, your father's birthday, and your grandmother's birthday, while your mother's was yesterday, and Atossa's will be tomorrow. It's fascinating," Megan repeated, almost in disbelief.

"It's amazing, right?" Artemis responded with a strange, almost enigmatic smile on her face.

Helen looked at Artemis with a sense of disbelief and said, "So that's why there were three birds on your cake—representing you, your father, and your grandma?"

Allen laughed and said, "You just figured that out?"

"Yes!" she replied, still sounding surprised.

Artemis couldn't help but feel a mix of emotions at the coincidence surrounding their birthdays. It was indeed fascinating and a bit eerie to think about. The alignment of their birthdays on the same day added another layer of mystery to the already enigmatic situation surrounding her father's disappearance. As they delved deeper into their investigation, Artemis couldn't shake the feeling that there was something significant about this particular day, something waiting to be uncovered.

"Artemis! Maybe this is the special night and it is because so many things had happened on this special night. There are three birthdays and one disappearance. All happened on this particular date. So... Why don't we do something tonight and try to recreate a similar action? For example, we can try to find out what your father was trying to do that night. We have some clues like the book and stones which they found after your father's disappearance. Also, you told us that your mother said something happened before your father disappeared, and you said your mother felt a movement as well as she found some kind of drawing on the floor too? These are all good clues," Matt said eagerly while Ricky placed a friendly hand on his shoulder and smiled.

Matt's suggestion sparked a wave of anticipation among the group. They were all eager to uncover the mysteries surrounding Artemis's family, especially on a night as significant as their shared birthdays. The clues they had gathered so far—the book, the stones, and the strange drawing on the floor—hinted at something larger at play. It was as if they were pieces of a puzzle waiting to be assembled.

Artemis nodded in agreement, feeling a renewed sense of determination. "You're right, Matt. Tonight feels like the perfect time to delve into this mystery. We have the tools and the clues—we just need to put the pieces together and see what we can find."

Ricky cheerfully exclaimed, "And this is the best game I've ever played in my entire life!" He glanced at Allen, who had been eager to play a game and kept complaining, and added with a grin, "Are you happy now?"

Allen looked at him and, unsatisfied, answered, "That's not what I was looking for."

With everyone on board, they began to make preparations for their investigation, setting up the spirit circle and gathering the necessary materials. As they worked, excitement and anticipation filled the air, mingled with a hint of apprehension at what they might uncover. But one thing was certain—they were determined to uncover the truth behind Artemis's father's disappearance, no matter the cost.

"The first thing we should do is to find this connection," Ricky interrupted

Ricky's interruption brought the group's focus back to the task at hand. They knew that finding the connection between the book, the stones, and Artemis's father's disappearance was crucial to unraveling the mystery.

"You're right, Ricky," Artemis agreed, her eyes alight with determination. Then she continued, "We need to understand how all these pieces fit together. Once we find that connection, we'll be one step closer to uncovering the truth."

With renewed resolve, they continued their preparations, each member of the group contributing their expertise and knowledge to the investigation. They were ready to dive deeper into the mystery and uncover the secrets hidden within.

"What about the game? Does anybody want to play?" Allan was bored.

Allan's suggestion of playing a game was met with disapproval from the group, who were fully immersed in their investigation. His interruption was quickly dismissed as they refocused on their task at hand. With determination in their hearts, Megan took the initiative to suggest calling their parents and informing them of their plans to stay at Artemis's place to celebrate her birthday. She looked around at the group, waiting for their reactions.

Allen appeared disappointed, clearly not as excited about the investigation that had everyone else so energized. He looked at everyone and asked, "Do you mind if I head out early? I'm really not into this kind of problem-solving."

Artemis looked at Allen and gently said, "I already appreciate you being here, and if you're tired, we don't mind if you go. We'll see you later." With that, Allen said goodnight to everyone, received a few responses, and then left.

Matt emphasized the importance of staying until the morning star appears, indicating that their gathering should extend beyond midnight.

Matt suggested to Artemis that they should go into the basement while their friends were busy calling their parents in order to search for more clues related to her father.

But before they proceeded, Ricky grabbed Matt's sleeve and said, "We have the spirit circle picture. Wouldn't it be better if we drew it on the floor while you're gone?"

Matt glanced at his friends, his gaze lingering on Helen when he said, "Helen, while we're heading into the basement to look for more evidence, I need you to follow Ricky's suggestion; I think it's a good idea. You're an excellent artist—could you draw the spirit circle on the floor? It shouldn't be too big or too small, just the right size. Follow this picture." He handed a printed image from a website to Helen.

Ricky interrupted, saying, "It should be the size of a person comfortably lying down in the middle of the spirit circle."

Matt looked at him in surprise, then nodded in agreement. "Exactly, Ricky. That's the right size. You can supervise the drawing."

As Artemis and Matt descended the stairs into the basement, Artemis asked Matt if he wanted to call his parents, too. Matt responded that he had already informed his parents about staying over for the night, so there was no need to call them again. Artemis felt satisfied and nodded approvingly.

As they walked through the basement, Matt expressed his curiosity about the space, having never seen it before. Artemis explained that it wasn't just any basement but rather a wine cellar. She shared that her father had a passion for wine and used to make it from family recipes. Despite the passage of time, there were still bottles of wine from fifteen or eighteen years ago preserved in the cellar. Artemis revealed that her mother hadn't allowed anyone to touch them or even go into the basement, holding onto them as a symbol of her hope for her husband's return. Her voice carried a calm tone, tinged with a hint of sadness.

As Artemis led the way into the cellar, Matt followed closely behind, closing the door behind them. With the flick of a switch, the basement was bathed in light, revealing rows of carefully arranged wine bottles. Matt's eyes sparkled with fascination as he inspected the bottles, each one holding a piece of history. He reached for one and examined its label, revealing a date: *1940*. Excitedly, he showed it to Artemis, his curiosity piqued by the age and story behind the bottle.

Artemis nodded knowingly as she inspected the bottle, acknowledging its age. Carefully, she returned it to its place on the wine rack, surrounded by others of similar vintage. The cellar held not just wine but memories and stories passed down through generations, each bottle a testament to the family's history.

As Artemis rummaged through the box, Matt glanced around the room, taking in the antique furniture and the dimly lit corners. Dust motes danced in the air, illuminated by the harsh overhead lights. He felt a sense of anticipation, wondering what secrets might be hidden in this forgotten corner of the basement.

Artemis…! Where are your grandparents? I mean, your dad's parents? I meant your father's parents or sibling?" asked Matt, uncertain if she was willing to answer.

Artemis sighed softly, her gaze dropping to the contents of the box. "They... They had a falling out with my parents before my dad disappeared. They haven't been in touch since then." She hesitated, then added, "I don't think they ever approved of my mom."

"I know what you're going to ask next. You want to know why they weren't here on my birthday. Am I right?" Artemis threw it at Matt.

"Yes. So...! What is it with them?" Matt stopped and looked into her eyes.

"They are living in New York," Artemis responded with a sad voice.

Artemis paused for ten seconds, and now she has had the time to ponder the spiritual side of what they've been through; then she had a deep breath and continued, "Well... Since my father is gone, they still won't accept it, and actually, they think it was my mother's fault for whatever happened to him. After my father's disappearance, every one of my father's family abandoned her. They'd stop visiting us ever since. Maybe, this way is easier for all of us. But my dad's sisters and brother still come here and visit us once in a while." Artemis fixed a box and sat on it with care.

Matt listened attentively, his expression softening with empathy as Artemis shared her family's struggles. "I'm sorry to hear that, Artemis," he said gently, moving to sit beside her.

"It must be really tough for your mom, dealing with all of this on her own. And for you, too." He reached out a hand, placing it comfortingly on her shoulder.

Artemis and Matt both jumped when suddenly Dorsa called them from upstairs, "What are you guys planning to do tonight? Is everything all right?"

Artemis and Matt exchanged a quick glance before Artemis called back, "We're just exploring the basement, Mom. Everything's fine down here!" She then looked at Matt, silently asking if they should share their plans with her mother.

Matt looked blank for a moment before suggesting, "I don't think it's a good idea, especially with your father's incident. She might be scared and think something bad is going to happen."

Artemis nodded in agreement. "You're right, we need to be careful about how we approach this." Then she said loudly, "Sorry to wake you up again, Mom. We were looking for scary books. Don't worry about us. I make sure not to disturb you again." Artemis had to come up with a story and Matt nodded in agreement with Artemis's explanation, silently going along with the story.

"Ok. If you need anything just call me darling. Have a good time." Dorsa went back to her bedroom and shut the door closed.

Artemis and Matt exchanged relieved glances, grateful that Artemis's explanation had been accepted without further inquiry. "Okay, mom. Thanks."

Artemis was very loud and Matt was holding his ears plugged with his hands and went backward. He tripped over a box and fell on it and before he knew the box was opened halfway. He peeked inside and couldn't believe his eyes; his face brightened.

Artemis frowned at him and said, "Look! You broke the box that is my father's."

Matt's excitement dimmed as he realized the significance of the box. "I'm really sorry, Artemis. I didn't mean to break anything," he apologized sincerely, feeling guilty for his clumsiness.

Matt even didn't realize her anger and he held the box in front of Artemis's face and said, "Look Artemis. I found something. There are lots of different candles and papers. There must be something useful in these papers."

Artemis's anger softened as she saw the contents of the box. She leaned in closer to examine the candles and papers. "You're right, Matt. Let's take a look at these papers. Maybe there's something here that can help us understand what my father was working on," she said, as her curiosity piqued.

Matt looked at the papers and recognized some of the symbols. "These are alchemical symbols," he explained. "They're used in alchemy, which is an ancient practice that seeks to transform matter, both physically and spiritually. These symbols represent different elements, substances, and processes."

Artemis's eyes widened with interest. "Alchemy? Like turning lead into gold?" she asked.

Matt nodded. "Exactly. But alchemy is also about spiritual transformation and enlightenment. These symbols might hold clues about your father's work and what he was trying to achieve."

Artemis's anger dissipated as she became intrigued by the possibilities. "Let's study these symbols and see if they can lead us to any answers," she said, her tone now eager.

Matt looked at her and said, "I know! But that just proves my point; these are sophisticated knowledge and must be read with care." Matt whispered after a pause, "There is lots of information here and your father polygraphed them all."

Artemis's eyes widened with realization. "You mean he transcribed all this information himself?" she asked, amazed.

Matt nodded. "Seems like it. These symbols and writings are not something you find in regular books. Your father must have been deeply involved in some esoteric studies."

Artemis felt a mix of emotions, a combination of curiosity and sadness at the thought of her father delving into such mysterious realms without her knowledge. "We need to go through these carefully," she said determinedly. "There might be something here that could help us understand what happened to him."

Matt agreed, his curiosity piqued as well. "Let's start examining them one by one," he suggested. "We might uncover something significant."

Artemis observed Matt with growing fascination as he sifted through the papers with remarkable speed. It was as if he absorbed the information effortlessly, his eyes scanning the pages with precision, and in less than a minute, he finished five pages. She marveled at his ability to comprehend the complex symbols and writings that seemed like a foreign language to her.

As Matt continued to read, Artemis couldn't help but feel a sense of admiration for his intellect. She had always known he was intelligent, but witnessing his rapid grasp of the material in front of them was truly impressive. It was as if he had unlocked a hidden talent that she hadn't seen before.

"Wow, you're really something," Artemis murmured, unable to contain her admiration.

Matt looked up from the papers, a faint smile on his lips, and caught sight of Artemis, her eyes captivating him. Even though he knew her likely answer, he couldn't resist trying again, hoping for a different response. "Artemis, you look so beautiful under this dim light," he said softly. He paused, then continued with a mix of hope and vulnerability, "I wish we could have a future together and build a family."

Artemis smiled and replied, "We're going to have a future together as good friends."

Matt looked at her, a hint of frustration in his eyes. "You know that wasn't my question."

Artemis met his gaze and said softly, "I know, but I've told you so many times—I really want my future partner, or husband, to be at least a couple of years older than me."

Matt kept quiet for a moment, then attempted to shift the conversation. "Just trying to make sense of all this," he said modestly. "But anyway, I think we're onto something here." Then he pointed at the box

Artemis nodded eagerly, feeling a surge of excitement. With Matt's expertise and her determination, they might just uncover the answers they were searching for and they delved deeper into the mysterious writings, eager to unravel the secrets they held.

He stared into the distance, captivated by a beautiful light emanating from one of the boxes. Drawn in, he approached and opened it, revealing a glimmering gemstone that seemed to radiate an otherworldly glow in the dim basement light. He looked over at Artemis as she approached, her eyes widening in astonishment. She reached out, her fingers grazing the stone's smooth surface as if to confirm it was real.

"This must be it," he whispered, his voice filled with awe. "The spirit stone."

She held it gently, her gaze shifting to Matt as she murmured, "It's the most beautiful thing I've ever seen in my life."

She was captivated by its presence, yet a sudden worry seized her. Turning to Matt, she asked, "Matt, I know this might sound foolish, but… what if I disappear too? There's even a one percent chance, right? What will happen? What will become of me? And… what would you do?" As she voiced her fears, a hollow feeling settled within her, filling her with a bleak sense of emptiness. Yet she couldn't hold it back—she needed to say it, just in case. She sensed the idea growing more real, taking root, deepening her unease.

Artemis's question hung heavy in the air, casting a somber shadow over the room. Matt's expression softened as he considered her words, understanding the weight of her fears.

"Artemis, I can't promise you that nothing will happen," he began, his voice gentle yet reassuring. "But I can promise you that I'll do everything in my power to find you, to uncover the truth, and to bring you back and that's a promise." He reached out to gently squeeze her hand, offering her a small but comforting smile. "You're not alone in this. We're all here for you, and we'll face whatever comes together." He paused for a moment and asked Artemis, "But if you want, we can stop right now. We can go and play games instead."

Artemis shook her head, her resolve unwavering. "No, Matt. We've come this far, and I want to see this through. We need to find out what happened to my father, and these clues might hold the key. Let's keep going. I don't want to live the rest of my life wondering, 'What if?'" Her determination mirrored Matt's own, and they continued their search with renewed focus and determination.

"We have everything we need," she announced, her voice ringing with determination. "Let's get started."

Artemis's mind swirled with a whirlwind of emotions and thoughts, each one vying for her attention. The possibility of her father's return filled her with hope and longing, a beacon of light in the darkness of uncertainty. Yet, the fear of the unknown, of what might happen to her, lurked in the shadows, threatening to extinguish that hope.

But amidst it all, there was Matt, a steady presence by her side, offering reassurance and support. She found solace in his wisdom and his unwavering determination to help her, to guide her through whatever challenges lay ahead. In his presence, she felt a sense of strength and courage, knowing that no matter what the future held, they would face it together.

With a deep breath, Artemis resolved to focus on the task at hand, to delve into the mysteries surrounding her father's disappearance, and to trust in the bond she shared with Matt and her friends. Whatever obstacles they may encounter, they would confront them head-on, united in their pursuit of the truth and their quest to bring her father home.

She held Matt's shoulder, looked into his eyes, and said, "Matt! Would you please just listen to me carefully? If anything happened to me… anything at all… I want you to give this message to my mother. I want you to tell her that I love her so much and I will be with her all the time."

Matt met Artemis's gaze with unwavering attention, his expression serious and compassionate. He reached out and gently squeezed her hand in reassurance before responding.

"Artemis, I promise you, nothing will happen to you. These are just metaphors and theories, nothing more." He looked into her eyes again, sensing her unease, and continued softly, "But if, for some reason, it comes to that, and we actually accomplish something, then we'll have to be ready. I'll make sure to deliver your message to your mother. I'll tell her how much you love her and that you'll always be with her, no matter what. But let's not dwell on such thoughts. We're going to figure this out together, and we'll make sure your father comes back home. That would be our goal."

With a soft smile, Matt stood by Artemis's side, a pillar of strength and support as they faced the unknown together.

Matt nodded, his expression filled with determination and resolve. "I won't let you down, Artemis. We'll get through this together."

With a reassuring smile, he gently squeezed her hand again before turning his attention back to the task at hand. Their bond grew stronger with each step they took towards uncovering the truth. With a sense of urgency, Matt's words spurred them into action. They knew they had to act quickly if they were to unlock the secrets hidden within the ancient writings and perform the ritual before the morning star graced the sky. Artemis nodded in agreement, her heart racing with anticipation. She took the box from Matt's arms, holding it close as they made their way out of the basement and back into the Artemis's room where their friends awaited.

Seeing the intricate symbols and signs drawn on the floor, Matt was impressed by the attention to detail that Ricky and Helen had put into recreating the spirit circle. He looked over at Artemis, a mixture of surprise and admiration in his eyes. Artemis returned his gaze, her own eyes filled with determination and excitement for what was to come.

Matt approached Artemis and whispered, "You have some really talented friends, Artemis. They've done an amazing job with the drawings."

Artemis smiled gratefully, feeling a sense of pride in her friends' efforts. "Yes, they're truly amazing," she replied softly. "Now, let's see if we can bring this all together and unlock the secrets hidden within."

Impressed by the precision of Helen's work, Matt turned to her with a smile and a hint of curiosity in his voice. "This is great! How did you know exactly where they were supposed to be? You made some changes to my description of the signs."

Helen returned his smile, a glint of pride in her eyes. "Well, I've always had a knack for attention to detail and Ricky was the main source and I just kept drawing," she replied. "And with a little intuition." She added briefly, "I thought it might be best to adjust some of the placements to ensure everything flowed smoothly and Ricky agreed too."

Matt nodded appreciatively. "It was a smart move," he acknowledged. "The circle looks perfect now. Let's hope it serves its purpose." With that, he turned his attention back to the preparations, ready to see what the night would bring.

Helen looked at Ricky then to Matt and said, "I had an angel to help me. Ricky looked into the book and told me which way is the correct way to draw them."

Ricky just smiled and his smile widened as he nodded in agreement. "Yeah, I just gave a little guidance based on what I saw in the book. Helen did all the hard work," he admitted modestly.

Helen chuckled and playfully nudged Ricky's arm. "Well, I couldn't have done it without your help," she replied warmly.

Matt observed their interaction with a grin, pleased by the teamwork and camaraderie among them. "Great job, both of you," he said sincerely. "Now let's see what happens when we put it all together."

As everyone settled around the spirit circle, Matt took a deep breath and began to read from the papers they had found in the basement. His voice resonated in the room, filled with a mix of excitement and determination. Each word seemed to carry weight as he recited the ancient incantations, invoking the power of the elements.

The candles flickered, casting dancing shadows on the walls as if responding to the words being spoken. The air seemed to grow charged with energy, and a sense of anticipation hung heavy in the room. Artemis watched intently, her heart racing with a mixture of apprehension and hope. She couldn't shake the feeling that they were on the brink of something extraordinary, something that could change everything.

As Matt reached the final words of the incantation, a hush fell over the room. All eyes were fixed on the spirit circle, waiting to see what would happen next. Matt laid out his plan, and everyone nodded in agreement, ready to contribute their thoughts and opinions. They gathered around him, eager to delve into the wealth of information they had collected.

Megan spoke up first, suggesting they start with the information they found on Google since it was likely to be the most comprehensive and easily accessible. Helen chimed in, suggesting they organize the information by topic or theme to make it easier to analyze and cross-reference.

Ricky suggested they create a timeline of events based on the information they had gathered, starting from Artemis's father's disappearance and tracing any relevant occurrences before and after. Allan proposed they divide the tasks among themselves, with each person responsible for researching a specific aspect of the mystery.

Everyone jumped suddenly, realizing Allen was still there. They wondered when he'd come back.

"When did you come back?" Helen tossed the question at Allen.

Allen chuckled and replied, "Come on, guys. I was about to head home, but then I thought, these gatherings don't happen often—why not stay and enjoy some time with my friends?"

Ricky hushed the group, then turned to Matt and Artemis, saying, "Go on, you two."

Artemis listened intently to their suggestions, feeling a sense of gratitude for her friends' support and dedication. With determination in her heart, she nodded in agreement and said, "Let's get started."

With everyone on board and eager to contribute, they began their exploration of the gathered information. Matt took the lead, guiding them through the details they had unearthed, while each member of the group added their insights and perspectives. As they delved deeper into the mystery, Artemis felt a surge of hope and determination.

"Would you please just give us some information about the spirit circle and what it does? Also, why do we need it here?" asked Helen

"Of course," Matt replied, adjusting his position to face the group more directly. "The spirit circle is a fundamental component in many magical rituals. Its purpose is to create a sacred space, a boundary between the mundane world and the spiritual realm. Within this circle, practitioners can perform rituals, invoke spirits, and channel energies without interference from external influences."

He paused, making sure everyone was following along before continuing. "In our case, we're using the spirit circle to focus and amplify our intentions. By creating this sacred space, we can enhance our connection to the spiritual energies surrounding us, making it easier to perform the ritual we have in mind."

Matt glanced around at his friends, gauging their understanding before concluding, "In essence, the spirit circle acts as a container for our magical workings, helping to channel and direct our intentions in a controlled and protected environment."

He paused for a moment, letting the information sink in, then continued, "I hope I was clear and answered your question?"

Ricky added, "As I did my research I found out that the spirit circle is useful in many cultural histories. A person would walk around an object, person or place during a ceremony of birth, marriage or death, or to bring good luck or destroy evil."

"That's correct," Matt nodded in agreement. "The concept of the spirit circle, or similar rituals involving circumambulation, can indeed be found in various cultural and religious practices around the world. Walking around a central object or space symbolizes the cyclic nature of life, the journey of creation and destruction, and the connection between the physical and spiritual realms."

He glanced at the others, ensuring they were following along. "In our context, the spirit circle serves as a boundary between our world and the spiritual plane, allowing us to work safely with magical energies. It's a universal symbol of protection and containment, ensuring that our intentions remain focused and undisturbed by external influences."

Matt paused, allowing his words to sink in before adding, "By incorporating the spirit circle into our ritual, we're drawing on this ancient tradition to amplify the power of our magic and achieve our desired outcomes."

Allan still didn't take any of these seriously and jumped in the middle of his talking and said, "You mean we have to dance around the fire like Indians or Africans for this ceremony?"

Artemis jumped from her seat and asked Allen, "I thought you were gone! You even said goodbye. When did you come back?"

Allen shrugged his shoulders and smiled.

Helen turned to Artemis and said, "You know, we figured it out when you two weren't in the room."

Everybody burst out into laughter and Allan started dancing and jumping up and down and he made some kind of sound and whistle while he was dancing. He jumped two times on his right foot and two jumps on his left foot and it continued for a couple of minutes. Matt was laughing too because it was very funny but this dance irritated Helen and Ricky. They took action to pull Allan down and made him sit down. Helen was very into listening and she was very concerned to learn about these stones.

Matt chuckled at Allan's remark. "Not exactly, Allan. While dances and rituals involving fire are indeed part of some cultural traditions, our ceremony will be a bit different. We'll be using the spirit circle to create a sacred space where we can work with magical energies safely and effectively. It's more about the intention behind the ritual rather than specific actions like dancing around a fire."

Allan was sitting down, Ricky said, "That's enough. We have no time." Then he turned to Matt and said, "Matt…! Please continue."

"Right," Matt said, acknowledging Ricky's prompt. "Now, let's dive into the information we gathered from Google first." He opened his laptop and began to review the details they found online, explaining each piece of information as he went along.

"As we've learned, the pentacle, or pentagram, is a powerful symbol representing the five elements and the unity of spirit," Matt began. "It's often used in rituals and ceremonies for protection, manifestation, and spiritual connection. The five points of the star correspond to the elements of earth, air, fire, water, and spirit."

He paused briefly again to allow the others to absorb the information before continuing. "Now, the specific arrangement of the pentacle and the positioning of the stones within it can vary depending on the purpose of the ritual and the tradition being followed. Our goal tonight is to use the pentacle to tap into the elemental energies and perform a ritual that may help us uncover the truth about Artemis's father's disappearance."

Matt glanced around the group, ensuring they were following along. "Any questions so far?" he asked, inviting their input.

"A spirit circle serves a similar purpose to a pentacle but with some variations in practice," Helen added.

Matt affirmed, acknowledging Helen's contribution and accurate drawing with a nod. "It's a boundary that's drawn or visualized around a space to contain and amplify energy during rituals or ceremonies. In our case, we're using it to create a sacred space where we can work with the elemental energies represented by the stones."

He glanced around the room, ensuring everyone was following along. "The spirit circle acts as a protective barrier, keeping unwanted energies out while allowing us to focus and direct our intentions inward. It helps to create a conducive environment for ritual work and can enhance the effectiveness of our ceremony."

Matt paused, aware of the subject's complexity, giving the group a moment to absorb the information. "Now, let's move on to the information we found in the book," he suggested, eager to delve deeper into their research.

Every once in a while, he would glance around the room to ensure everyone was following along. "Our focus will be on the symbolic aspects of the ceremony, drawing on the power of the elements and our collective energy to achieve our goals. So while dancing might add to the ambiance, it's not a necessary part of what we're doing tonight."

He glanced at Allen, noticing he had finally settled down. Matt cleared his throat and continued, "Alright, let's refocus here. Now, about the stones. Each of these stones represents one of the four classical elements: earth, air, fire, and water. They're essential components in many magical practices, symbolizing different qualities and energies."

He paused for a moment to gather his thoughts before elaborating further. "By arranging these stones within the spirit circle, we'll be harnessing the elemental energies they represent to amplify our intentions and the effectiveness of our ritual. It's like tapping into the fundamental building blocks of the universe to work our magic."

Helen nodded, seeming satisfied with the explanation. "So, the stones serve as conduits for channeling the elemental energies. That makes sense."

Matt spoke with the confidence of a teacher. His knowledge of science was incredibly impressive, far beyond that of the average person. He was a good teacher, not just because of his expertise, but also because of his patience and ability to explain complex ideas clearly.

He looked at Helen and answered, "Exactly," affirming with a smile. He continued, "And with each of us contributing our own energy and intention to the ritual, we'll create a powerful synergy that enhances the effectiveness of what we're doing."

"These elements hold significant symbolism and are integral to many spiritual and magical practices," Matt continued, his tone becoming more focused as he delved into the topic. "Earth represents stability, grounding, and the material realm. Air symbolizes intellect, communication, and the realm of thought. Fire embodies passion, transformation, and the creative force. Water signifies emotions, intuition, and the subconscious mind."

He glanced at the book for reference before continuing. "The fifth element, spirit, transcends the physical elements and represents the divine essence or the interconnection of all things. It serves as the binding force that unifies the other elements and infuses them with spiritual significance."

Matt paused, allowing his words to sink in again before inviting further discussion or questions from the group.

His sudden shift in focus intrigued the group, and they leaned in attentively. He continued typing, occasionally glancing at the screen to ensure he was gathering the necessary information. After a few moments, he looked up and addressed his friends, "I just need to gather some information about this month." Matt explained, "It won't take long, but it might provide us with additional insights or connections to our current endeavors."

With that, he resumed typing, his fingers flying across the keyboard with incredible speed. It was impossible to follow the rapid movements as he navigated through various sources, collecting the required data. The group watched with anticipation, eager to see what revelations Matt's research might uncover, while Allen stood frozen in awe at Matt's typing skills.

"I can't believe how fast and furious he's typing! I've never seen such fast and accurate typing before," Allen exclaimed, his eyes glued to Matt's flying fingers. He continued watching in amazement before asking, "Where did you learn to type like this, Matt?"

Matt paused briefly, a modest smile forming on his face. "I've been practicing since I was a kid," he replied. "I used to spend hours on the computer, learning different coding languages and working on various projects. The speed just developed over time."

Ricky chimed in with a playful grin, "Well, all that practice is definitely paying off today. You're like a human supercomputer!"

Artemis laughed softly, her eyes shining with admiration. "We're lucky to have you on our team, Matt. I don't think we could get this far without your skills."

Matt's cheeks flushed slightly at the compliments. "Thanks, guys. But we're all contributing in our own ways. This is a team effort."

Helen smiled as she gazed at her drawing on the floor, adding, "Speaking of contributions, the spirit circle is ready whenever we need it."

Matt's eyes lit up as he looked over at Helen. "Perfect timing! Once I finish compiling this data, we can proceed with the ritual."

The group exchanged excited glances, feeling a renewed sense of unity and purpose as they prepared to take the next crucial step in their quest. In less than ten minutes, Matt finished his research and returned to the circle, his focus sharp. "OK, guys, enough chit-chat. We're on a tight schedule!" he said, his tone commanding. "We need to draw another symbol—a diamond pointing north with a square in the middle. The corners of the square must be precisely aligned with the middle of two of the diamond's angles."

He looked around the group, making sure everyone understood the instructions. "Let's get to work. We don't have much time."

As Matt instructed, the group quickly set to work, with Helen taking the lead in drawing the new diagram. Matt grabbed the chalk and Helen along with Ricky held Artemis's Hockey stick as a ruler, and Matt drew the lines more accurately. They meticulously sketched out the diamond shape with its apex pointing to the north, ensuring the square was positioned precisely as described. Each member contributed to the task, carefully aligning the corners of the square with the midpoint between two angles of the diamond. Matt wrote fire on top, then Megan wrote water at the bottom, Helen wrote earth on the right and finally, Ricky wrote air on the left side of the diamond as Matt was leading them. Matt stood up again and looked at the floor. He pointed at Ricky to write hot at the left top of the square and on the bottom wet then Artemis wrote dry on the right, top side of the square. Also, Atossa wrote cold at the bottom. Matt was the one who controlled the situation and finished the job very professionally.

He read all the important parts loudly and looked at the drawing on the floor then with a hushed sound said, "It is a Pisces…!"

Allen stood up on top of the drawing and with the motion moved his head up and down and said, "We did a perfect job, didn't we?" when Helen pulled him aside and said, "Ahhhhhh, Shut up!"

Once the drawing was completed, Matt inspected it closely, nodding in approval. "Perfect," he declared. "Now, let's move on to the next step."

With focused determination, they continued their preparations, eager to uncover the mysteries surrounding the stones.

He turned to Artemis and repeated again, "IT IS A PISCES."

The group looked at each other in astonishment, processing Matt's revelation. Artemis felt a chill run down her spine as she realized the significance of Matt's words. The connection between the drawing on the floor and her father's disappearance was becoming clearer, but there was still much they didn't understand especially the meaning of Pisces.

"Pisces... What does that mean?" Helen asked, her voice filled with curiosity and concern.

Matt took a deep breath, his mind racing with possibilities. "Pisces is a zodiac sign, but it's also associated with the element of water. It's known for its intuitive and sensitive nature."

Artemis's heart pounded in her chest as she absorbed this information. Could her father have been trying to harness the power of Pisces in his rituals? And if so, what had gone wrong? But she has never heard of Pisces. But the way Matt described it, it looked weird and dangerous.

"We need to delve deeper into this," Matt continued, his voice determined. "There's more to uncover, and I believe the answers lie within these symbols and rituals."

The group focused their efforts on deciphering the mysteries surrounding Artemis's father's disappearance, guided by Matt's expertise and leadership. They knew they were on the brink of uncovering something extraordinary.

Artemis just looked at him puzzled and shrugged her shoulder while she said, "Never heard of it but your voice says it is important."

Matt nodded, understanding Artemis's confusion. "It's not something that's commonly discussed outside of astrology and esoteric circles," he explained. "But it seems like your father may have been tapping into its energy for his rituals."

Artemis furrowed her brow, trying to piece together the significance of Pisces in relation to her father's activities. "So, what do we do now?" she asked, her voice tinged with uncertainty.

"We continue our research," Matt replied confidently. "We need to understand the full extent of Pisces's influence and how it relates to the other elements and symbols we've uncovered. There's still much to learn, but we're making progress."

Artemis nodded, a sense of determination settling over her. Everyone was taken back then a chuckle swept through the room. Allen looked puzzled and asked, "I don't know what just happened?"

Megan looked at Allen and said, "I'll let you puzzle it out. It's okay." She turned to Matt and asked, "Matt! Would you please let us know what's going on? What was that we missed?"

"I just remembered, in astrology, Pisces is ruled by planets Jupiter and Neptune. It is from Feb 20 to March 20," Matt explained with such excitement.

Matt's revelation sparked a renewed sense of curiosity among the group. Megan's eyes widened with interest as she processed the information. "So, Jupiter and Neptune rule Pisces," she mused aloud. "That could explain why your father was drawn to it for his rituals, Artemis."

Artemis nodded thoughtfully, absorbing the implications of Matt's explanation. "And if Pisces is associated with Jupiter and Neptune, then perhaps there's a connection to the spirit stones and their elemental properties," she speculated.

"Exactly!" Matt exclaimed, his enthusiasm contagious. "We need to delve deeper into the significance of Jupiter and Neptune in relation to the spirit stones and the elements. There could be hidden meanings and powers waiting to be unlocked."

"Still don't know what's going on," Artemis said and looked at Matt while everybody else was looking at both of them in surprise and puzzle.

"This is the picture that we found in your dad's stuff and I knew, I saw it somewhere but I didn't know where," Matt replied and continued without breathing. "I just realized the meaning of it. It is a sign of you, your dad, and your grandma's date of birth." Matt's face flushed as he resumed breathing.

Artemis's eyes widened in astonishment as Matt's words sank in. "You mean… this symbol represents our birthdays?" she asked, her voice laced with disbelief.

Matt nodded, his excitement palpable. "Exactly! The pentacle we drew earlier, combined with the additional symbols we just added, forms a complex astrological representation of your family's birthdays. It's like a cosmic signature, connecting you, your father, and your grandmother through the celestial energies of Pisces."

Artemis was stunned by the revelation. "I never would have imagined..." she trailed off, trying to process the significance of what Matt had uncovered.

"It's incredible, isn't it?" Matt said, his eyes shining with enthusiasm. "And it might hold the key to unlocking the mystery of your father's disappearance."

As the weight of Matt's revelation settled over the group, a heavy silence filled the room. Each member of the group was lost in their own thoughts, grappling with the implications of what they had just learned.

Matt, still catching his breath from his excitement, finally broke the silence. "We have to explore this further," he said, his voice firm with determination. "There's something significant about these symbols and their alignment with your family's birthdays. It could be the key to understanding what happened to your father, Artemis."

She nodded, her mind racing with possibilities. "I agree," she said softly. "We need to delve deeper into the significance of these symbols and their connection to the events surrounding my father's disappearance."

By now, Artemis felt lost, uncertain whether to be happy, excited, or sad and worried. She slowly looked at Matt and asked, "So… what now?"

Matt took a moment to collect his thoughts before responding. "Now, we need to interpret the significance of these symbols and their alignment with your family's birthdays," he said, his voice steady and determined. "We'll need to research further into astrology, symbolism, and any other relevant fields to understand the full meaning behind these signs."

Artemis nodded, her mind racing with possibilities. "Agreed," she said. "We should also consider reaching out to experts in these fields for their insights. Perhaps they can offer us guidance on how to proceed."

Matt nodded in agreement. "That's a good idea," he said. "We'll need all the help we can get to unravel this mystery but not this time."

"What is special about this time?" Artemis questioned

"Because there isn't enough time—or rather, we could ask again in four years, but tonight is your birthday, and we might get the answer at the exact moment you were born. After that, we'd have to wait another four years," Matt said, his tone persuasive as everyone listened in silence.

They knew that the path ahead would be challenging, but they were determined to uncover the truth, no matter where it might lead them.

"We have to finish all the signs then we have to figure that out what we should do after. I began to realize that your father didn't do it alone and a friend must've been with him during all the procedures for that reason. Maybe his friend was gone with him that night too and nobody had noticed," Matt exclaimed

Artemis's eyes widened with realization. "You're right," she said, her voice tinged with eagerness. "If my father had a partner in this endeavor, they might hold the key to understanding what happened that night and how to reverse it."

Matt nodded in agreement. "Exactly," he said. "We'll need to explore all avenues to uncover any clues about your father's companion and their involvement in this ritual."

"But no other family claimed to lose any member of them?" Artemis explained

Artemis's question hung in the air, highlighting a crucial aspect of their investigation. Matt pondered for a moment before responding.

"It's possible that whoever was involved in this with your father might not have been a direct family member," Matt suggested. "They could have been a friend, a colleague, or someone with knowledge of these rituals. Perhaps they have kept their involvement a secret, either out of fear or for their own reasons."

Megan joined the conversation, suggesting, "Maybe your father's friend had no close family, or perhaps they both tried to keep this under wraps in case they wanted to be the only ones to benefit from it."

Artemis nodded thoughtfully, considering Matt and Megan's words. "So, we'll need to broaden our search beyond just family members," she concluded. "We'll have to delve deeper into my father's social circles, his work, and any other connections he may have had."

"Or, I think his friend knew what was going to happen and he was prepared but your father wasn't. He was just a bait. He was the reason to open a doorway to another world and his friend used him," replied Matt.

Helen stepped closer to say, "That's why they didn't report it but your family did."

"Maybe it's better we keep this under wraps until we know the full reason," Ricky suggested cautiously. "We might be in danger too. You never know. Approaching this cautiously is safer."

Matt's words and Ricky's suggestion sent a shiver down Artemis's spine. The idea that her father might have been unwittingly used as a pawn in a larger scheme was deeply unsettling. She glanced around at the faces of her friends, seeing the same concern reflected in their eyes, and then her gaze settled on Atossa, whose face was wet with tears streaming down her cheeks. Artemis walked over, wrapped her arms around her, and softly said, "These are just some ideas."

She moved to Matt again and murmured, "That's a chilling thought." She continued, "But it could explain a lot. If my father's disappearance was part of a larger plan, then there might be others involved who have information we need as Ricky suggested."

Artemis looked at the innocent faces of her friends and hesitated before asking, "Do you want to stop the procedure? We don't have to go any further if you're not comfortable."

The group exchanged solemn looks, realizing the gravity of the situation they were facing. They knew they had to press on with their investigation, no matter how daunting the task ahead might seem.

Allen stepped closer to Artemis and loudly said, "Are you kidding me? I'm interested now. It starting to be interesting."

Determined to uncover the truth no matter where it might lead them. They all responded loudly, "No chance! It's just getting more interesting!"

Artemis waved her hands, signaling for everyone to be quieter. "Shhhhhhhh. Remember, my mother is sleeping, and we don't want to wake her up." She then continued, her voice filled with concern, "In this case, maybe my dad was only a victim, and the other person used him to reach his goal. Please tell me if I'm right, Matt?" Artemis glanced at Atossa, then turned her gaze to Matt, seeking confirmation.

"It's a possibility," Matt acknowledged, his expression serious. "Your father might have been unwittingly drawn into something beyond his understanding. But it's also possible that he had knowledge of what was happening, though he might not have fully comprehended the consequences."

He paused, considering his words carefully before continuing. "Either way, we need to gather as much information as possible to understand what happened that night. And if there was someone else involved, we need to uncover who they are and what role they played—but that can wait. Tonight, we must focus on discovering the connection between these symbols and your birthday."

Artemis nodded, her mind racing with the implications of Matt's words. She knew they were facing a daunting task, but she also felt a renewed determination to uncover the truth, no matter what obstacles lay in their path.

Matt looked anxiously toward Artemis and requested, "Just don't push it. I need to go step by step and I don't want to make any mistakes. But I think so far you are correct and we are on the right page so far."

Artemis nodded in agreement, understanding the importance of proceeding cautiously. "You're right, Matt. We need to approach this methodically and carefully. We'll take it one step at a time and make sure we gather all the necessary information before we make any decisions."

Atossa felt so upset and asked loudly, "How do you know my father was a bait? How do you know if he did not know the result?"

Matt took a deep breath, understanding the severity of the situation. "I don't know for sure, Atossa. These are just theories based on the information we have. We're trying to piece together the puzzle, but we need to consider all possibilities."

He looked at Atossa with empathy, realizing the sensitivity of the topic. "I'm sorry if my words upset you. We're all just trying to find answers and understand what happened to your father."

Matt who was reading again looked up at Artemis and said, "If your father had known what was going to happen, he would have told your mother—or at the very least, he'd have left something behind, a note, a message, something. But he didn't know. He vanished without a word, without a plan. One moment he was here, and the next… he was just gone."

Artemis nodded slowly, absorbing Matt's words. She knew deep down that Matt's assessment was likely accurate, but accepting it was another matter entirely. "I understand," she said quietly, her voice edged with a soft sorrow. "It's just hard to come to terms with all of this."

Matt slowly stuffed his face in the book again while he was searching on the web then he walked back and forth. Suddenly he paused in the middle of the room as the knock echoed through the room, everyone's heartbeats seemed to synchronize and everybody jumped up together but they tried to look natural and cool. Helen hopped on the bed and sat straight up. Megan dived under the pillow beside Helen. Ricky was sitting on the computer chair and didn't move at all and Allan just was watching everybody else. Artemis covered the floor and sat on the carpet and tried to look at a book. Atossa sat beside Artemis, while Matt, closest to the door, cautiously approached. He slowly opened it, revealing a figure standing outside.

Dorsa pushed the door open and very quietly she peeked inside the room searching for Artemis. When her eyes met hers, she put a smile on her lips and asked, "Artemis…! Would you please be a little quieter? I really have a hard time sleeping. For some reason, I feel anxious tonight." She looked at Atossa then at everyone else again with a faded smile and left the room.

Artemis nodded in response, trying to mask the tension in the room with a forced smile. As Dorsa left, the group collectively let out a sigh of relief. They exchanged nervous glances, silently acknowledging the close call.

Megan pressed her point finger on her lips and with her other hand she slowly waved it in the air and said, "Please be quieter. We certainly don't want to disturb Artemis's Mother. So everybody behave please."

The others nodded in agreement, understanding the need for caution. They exchanged brief glances, silently communicating their resolve to maintain their composure and continue their investigation quietly.

They all moved to their previous position and Matt overlooked the drawing on the floor when all of a sudden his face turned brighter along with a happy smile that appeared on his lips. Matt's sudden change in demeanor caught everyone's attention. They looked at him expectantly, waiting for an explanation for his sudden excitement.

He picked the chalk from the floor, offered it to Helen, and said, "We have to draw the pentagram in the middle of the Pisces. It must be exactly in the middle of the square. It is important."

Helen hesitated for a moment and said, "Why me?"

"Because you're an excellent artist and did all the drawings, I want this symbol to be just as accurate as the ones you did before. Okay?" Matt replied, his tone both appreciative and firm.

Helen nodded and took the chalk from Matt. She carefully began to draw the pentagram in the square's center, ensuring it was perfectly aligned. As she worked, the others watched in silence, knowing the importance of precision in this task.

Watching everything from a distance, Ricky cast a strange, puzzled look at Matt. Finally, he stood, walked over, and observed the symbol where Helen sat in the center, focused intently on her drawing. Resting his hand on Matt's shoulder, he threw his questions at him, "How do you know all these things? Why in the sign should be in the middle and not on the side or above the sign? How do you know it works, and what makes it work? Magic, science or alien codes or what?"

"These are all secrets, and nobody really knows how they work or what makes them function," Matt began, his voice serious. "But I think if you have the right combination—like these special stones, along with the symbols, candles and information in this mysterious book—and if you know, whether by study or instinct, how to put them together, then it might open a gate or something like a portal to another dimension."

Allen jumped up and down, yelling, "I knew it, I knew it, I knew it! A portal! I'm so glad I'm here tonight!"

Ricky, fed up, shoved him back into his seat. "You were about to leave earlier, complaining it was boring—and now you're saying you *knew* something amazing was going to happen?"

Matt glanced at both of them briefly and said, "We don't know for sure—it's just a theory I have. But, in my opinion, this is technology left on Earth by extraterrestrials. They brought these things here with them. Think about it—most stones don't have any power, so why do only some of them? Why? The stones that do have power must be from another planet or created by extraterrestrials on Earth to ease their transportation. That's why these stones are so important—because if you have them and know how to use them, then you can say 'Olalla.'"

Matt's explanation hung in the air, filled with a mix of wonder and caution in a state of astonishment.

The idea of extraterrestrial technology and the possibility of opening a portal to another dimension seemed both fantastical and terrifying. Ricky, Helen, and the others exchanged bewildered glances, trying to process the information.

"What are you waiting for? Let's start…" Allen urged, his excitement bubbling over, all traces of his earlier disinterest forgotten.

Artemis glanced at Atossa and then broke the silence, her voice barely above a whisper, "So, you're saying that these stones and symbols could actually open a portal to another world? That's… incredible."

Matt nodded solemnly. "It's a theory, but it's the best explanation I can come up with based on what we know."

Artemis nodded slowly, absorbing the weight of the revelation. The thought of unlocking such power was both thrilling and daunting.

Still processing the information, Ricky asked, "But if these symbols and stones are so powerful, why haven't we heard about them before? Why aren't they more widely known?"

Matt shrugged. "Maybe they were deliberately kept hidden or forgotten over time. Or perhaps only certain individuals were meant to discover them."

The room fell into a contemplative silence as they all pondered the implications of Matt's theory. The idea of unraveling such ancient mysteries filled them with a sense of awe and trepidation, but they were determined to press forward in their quest for answers.

Matt approached the drawn pentagram, inspecting it carefully. He leaned down, tracing his finger along the lines, scrutinizing each angle and curve.

After a moment of contemplation, he straightened up and turned to Helen with a confident smile. "It's perfect," he declared. "You've drawn it exactly as it should be. The placement, the proportions, everything is spot on."

Helen beamed with pride at the compliment, relieved that her efforts had met Matt's exacting standards. The rest of the group gathered around to admire her handiwork, impressed by the precision and beauty of the symbol.

"Now that we have the pentagram drawn," Matt continued, "we must prepare and arrange the stones around the circle. Each stone represents an element, and their placement is crucial for the ritual to work."

He gestured toward the stones they had gathered earlier, each shimmering with its unique energy. "Let's begin," he said, a sense of determination in his voice. "We have work to do."

Helen looked at Matt and said, "Done…! But how do you know if this is the right one?"

Matt paused for a moment, considering Helen's question. He then replied with a reassuring smile, "We don't know for certain if it's the right one until we try. But based on everything we've learned and the symbols we've uncovered, I strongly feel this is the correct configuration." He glanced around at the group, his expression earnest. "Remember, this is all about belief and intention. If we approach this with focus and positivity, we increase our chances of success."

Allen shoved Ricky back, saying, "All you have to do is believe."

Ricky ignored him.

With a nod of affirmation, Matt motioned for the group to gather the stones and begin arranging them around the circle. "Let's proceed step by step and see where it leads us," he added, his voice filled with determination.

Everybody was around the sign and looked at the beautiful drawing. One by one congratulated Matt and Helen.

Allen was a nuisance to everyone; he tapped Matt's shoulder, his gaze shifting between the symbol and Matt, before shrugging and tugging at Matt's sleeve. "What now...?" he murmured.

Matt glanced at him, and without a word, he chose to ignore his excitement. Then he refocused on the task at hand, his expression serious. He took a deep breath, feeling a sense of responsibility weighing on him as the group turned to him for guidance. He scanned the room, meeting each person's gaze before speaking. "Now that the spirit circle is drawn and the stones are set, we should light the candles and arrange them by color. We need to ready ourselves mentally and spiritually for the next part of the ritual."

He continued after a quick silence, his voice steady with confident. "This is where things will become more intense, and we'll need to focus our energy and intentions."

He gestured towards the spirit circle, emphasizing its significance. "The spirit circle acts as a boundary, a barrier between our world and the realm we seek to connect with. It's a symbol of protection and containment, ensuring that we can safely explore the energies beyond without any harm coming to us."

He then turned to Artemis, his expression serious but reassuring. "Artemis, you're at the center of this ritual, as it's connected to you and your family. You'll need to be fully present and open to whatever experiences may come. Remember, we're here to support you every step of the way."

He glanced around the room, making eye contact with each member of the group. "As we proceed, it's important to remain focused and attentive. We'll follow the steps outlined in the research we've gathered, but we also need to trust our instincts and intuition.

This is a journey into the unknown, and we must approach it with respect and humility."

With a final nod of determination, Matt indicated that they were ready to begin. "Let's gather our thoughts and intentions, and when we're all prepared, we'll initiate the next phase of the ritual."

Everyone looked serious, waiting and hoping for something beyond their imagination.

Matt wasn't feeling satisfied, and he wouldn't take his eyes off the floor. He was staring at the signs. "Now... We have to put it into effect after I have finalized all the rules."

With confidence, he suggested as he settled on the floor, almost beneath the picture. Allan sat beside him, meeting his gaze and asking once more, "Now what...? Have we achieved our goal?"

Matt's face reddened at Allan's persistent, nonsensical questioning. Clenching his teeth, he replied, "Not yet, but... we have to figure out for ourselves what to do next. There's no right answer to your question anyway." He took a deep breath, inhaling deeply before exhaling slowly to ease his tension.

His response was met with a solemn silence as the group absorbed his words. Allan shifted uncomfortably beside him, sensing the weight of the moment. His expression softened as he glanced around at his friends, his gaze lingering on Artemis, who looked back at him with a mixture of anticipation and apprehension.

"We've come this far together, and we're closer to uncovering the truth than ever before," Matt continued, his voice steady but earnest. "But our journey isn't over yet. We still have more to learn, more challenges to face, and more mysteries to unravel."

He reached out and placed a hand on Allan's shoulder, offering reassurance. "Allan, your question is valid, and it reminds us that we're on a path of discovery. We may not have all the answers right now, but we're making progress, step by step."

Then he turned to Artemis, his eyes reflecting determination. "Artemis, your father's disappearance has affected us all, and we're committed to finding out what happened and bringing closure to your family. We won't give up until we have the answers we seek."

He glanced around at the others, his gaze lingering on each face. "So let's stay focused, stay united, and keep moving forward together. We have each other's support, and with that, I believe we can overcome any obstacle in our way."

With a final nod of resolve, Matt stood up, ready to lead his friends into the next phase of their journey. The room was filled with a sense of purpose and determination.

He regained control of his emotions and then continued again. "I know something is missing, but I don't know exactly what it is," Matt whispered without paying attention to anyone. He was whispering to himself, and he was looking at his friends at the same time and said, "We have to resolve it now or we'll never resolve it.

"If any of you have any suggestions, please speak up," Matt said, looking around the group, inviting their input.

"Why only now?" asked Helen

"Because it's her birthday, or better if I say it is their birthday and it is leap year too. If we don't do anything right now we might have to wait another four more years. It must be exactly on this day at this specific time, which is twelve midnight or by the time the morning star is in the sky," he explained.

Allen jerked his head toward Matt and asked, "When did you come up with this leap-year crap idea?"

"Suddenly, it came into my mind, and it plays an important role in this action tonight," Matt replied

As Matt spoke, the weight of their task seemed to hang heavier in the air. His friends exchanged glances, realizing the significance of the moment. Artemis's birthday, the alignment of their birthdays, and the rare occurrence of a leap year all added a sense of urgency to their mission.

"We can't afford to wait," Artemis said firmly, her determination shining through. "We have to act now while the stars align in our favor."

Her words spurred the group into action, each member feeling a renewed sense of purpose. They gathered around Matt, ready to follow his lead as he formulated their next steps.

"We need to review everything we've learned so far," Matt said, his voice firm. "Every clue, every piece of information, no matter how small. We must piece together the puzzle and find the missing piece to unlock the truth."

With a shared nod of agreement, they began to go over the details of their investigation, searching for any overlooked clues or connections. Matt's focused determination set the tone for their efforts, driving them forward with a sense of urgency and purpose.

As they delved deeper into the mystery surrounding Artemis's father's disappearance, they knew that time was of the essence. With each passing moment, they drew closer to uncovering the truth and bringing closure to their friend's family.

"What else do we have to do?" Megan got into the discussion again.

"That's the thing. I don't know what else…! All of us should put our minds together and come up with a decision." Matt started biting his thumb and then his nail. He overlooked all the sketches on the floor and kept biting his nails harder and harder.

"We need the spirit circle in the center. How about one of us sits in the middle of the sign and holds it? I don't mind doing that!" Ricky tossed the idea to Matt, standing up as if already prepared.

"It's Artemis's birthday, and it's all about her, so… let her lie down on the floor—maybe she's the key tonight. I mean, she could lie down on the sketches or those signs," Allen joked, feigning excitement, but quickly regretted it as he caught the irritation on Ricky's face.

Matt turned to Allen and hugged him. He said "YES" loudly. Then he said yes and yes again and again. "That's interesting and a good idea. Yes…yes…yes…!"

Artemis looked at Matt with surprise and a hint of apprehension. "Wait, what do you mean, lay on the floor? Are you suggesting I become part of the ceremony somehow?"

Matt nodded eagerly. "Exactly! You are part of the ceremony. Think about it, Artemis. Your birthday, the alignment of the stars, the significance of the symbols... You might hold the key to unlocking the portal."

Artemis hesitated, unsure of what to make of the suggestion. "But what if it's dangerous? What if something goes wrong?"

Matt placed a reassuring hand on her shoulder. "We'll take every precaution to keep you safe, Artemis. And besides, if anyone can handle this, it's you. You've shown incredible strength and courage throughout all of this. Trust me, I believe in you."

Artemis looked around at her friends, seeing the determination in their eyes. She took a deep breath, steeling herself for what lay ahead. "Okay," she said finally. "Let's do it. If there's a chance this could help find my father, I'm willing to try."

With their decision made, the group set to work, preparing for the ceremony. The knowledge that they were about to embark on a journey into the unknown sent a chill through each of them.

Matt took a deep breath, trying to gather his thoughts. "Artemis, I believe that by aligning yourself with the symbols and the energy of this ceremony, we might be able to tap into something powerful. Your connection to your father, your birthday, and the significance of this night… all point to something far beyond what any of us can grasp. You're like a vessel—maybe through you, we can reach your dad. If you want to talk to someone far away, you need a telephone to do that. Right now, you're like that telephone."

Atossa moved closer to Artemis, gently holding her hand. "I don't want to lose you too. What if you disappear as well? Don't do that, please."

Artemis wrapped her arms around her sister, hugging her tightly. "If there's a chance to bring Dad back and you were the only way to do it, would you?"

Atossa hesitated, her voice soft. "If you put it that way, I'd say yes... but it's not proven. Please don't do it. I can't bear to lose you too. Please…"

Artemis looked into her sister's tearful eyes, kissed her on the forehead, and whispered, "I have to try."

Matt gestured to the drawings on the floor. "If you lay in the center of the sign, it could act as a focal point for the energy we're trying to harness. I don't know if it's risky, but I know and truly believe it's our best chance at finding answers about your father's disappearance."

"Maybe a gate will open, and your father will be able to come back again," Ricky said, his voice devoid of any emotion.

Artemis looked at Ricky, then at Matt, uncertainty etched on her face, but she also felt a glimmer of hope. "But what if it doesn't work? What if nothing happens?"

Matt looked at her with determination. "Then at least we'll know we tried everything. But I have a feeling that tonight, something extraordinary is going to happen. Are you willing to take that chance with me?"

Artemis nodded, trusting in Matt's guidance. She carefully adjusted her position until she was lying exactly as he had instructed, her head pointing towards the north and her limbs aligned with the star points of the pentagram. As she settled into position, she felt a sense of anticipation building within her, a mixture of excitement and apprehension.

Matt stood back and surveyed her position, ensuring that everything was in place. "Perfect," he said, a note of satisfaction in his voice. "Now, just relax and focus on your breathing. Clear your mind of any distractions and let yourself be open to whatever may come."

"Think of your father," Ricky shouted out.

Artemis closed her eyes and took a deep breath, allowing herself to sink into a state of deep relaxation. She focused on the rhythm of her breathing, letting go of any tension or worry that lingered in her mind.

Around her, she could feel the energy of her friends, their presence a comforting presence that surrounded her like a warm blanket and allowed her to be enveloped by their support, drawing strength from their shared connection.

As she lay there, she felt a sense of calm wash over her, a feeling of peace and serenity that filled her entire being. At that moment, she knew that she was exactly where she was meant to be, surrounded by the people she loved, ready to face whatever challenges she had to face, and as she surrendered herself to the moment, she felt a spark of something deep within her, a flicker of hope and determination that burned bright despite the darkness that surrounded her. With each breath, she felt herself growing stronger, more resilient, more prepared to face whatever trials lay ahead.

As she lay there, bathed in the soft glow of the symbols surrounding her, she knew that she was ready to embrace whatever the future held, to uncover the truth, and to bring her father home. As Artemis settled into position, Matt looked around at his friends, a mix of nervousness and excitement evident on his face.

"Okay, everyone," he said, his voice trembling with anticipation. "This is it. We're about to embark on something incredible. I hope."

He took a deep breath and closed his eyes, focusing his thoughts on the symbols drawn on the floor and the energy pulsing through the room. "Now, let's all join hands," he instructed, reaching out to grasp the hands of those closest to him. "We need to create a connection, a bond that will amplify our intentions and guide us through this ritual."

The others joined hands one by one, forming a circle around Artemis as she lay in the center. Matt could feel the energy in the room, building a palpable sense of anticipation filling the air.

"Artemis," he said, his voice filled with determination. "We're here for you. We're here to help you find the answers you seek, to bring your father back to you. Trust in us, trust in the power of this moment, and together, we will uncover the truth."

With that, Matt closed his eyes and began to chant softly, the words flowing from him effortlessly as if guided by some unseen force. The others joined in, their voices blending together in a harmonious melody that seemed to resonate through the very walls of the room.

Artemis rolled her eyes at Allan's antics but couldn't help but smile at his attempt to lighten the mood. Despite the seriousness of the situation, his humor brought a moment of levity to the room.

Helen, however, was less amused by Allan's antics and shot him a disapproving look. "Seriously, Allan? Can't you be serious for once?" she chided.

Allan just grinned in response, unfazed by Helen's scolding. "Hey, laughter is the best medicine, right?" he quipped, earning a few chuckles from the others in the room.

Artemis couldn't help but agree, feeling grateful for the brief moment of lightheartedness amidst the tension of the situation. Even if Allan's jokes were a bit silly, they served as a reminder that they were all in this together, facing whatever challenges come their way as a team.

Meanwhile Ricky looked at Matt and tried to make another funny suggestion again. "Hey Matt...! Why don't you leave the special stone on her chest and make it even more interesting? When it looks more complicated, it'll be more exciting. Who knows, maybe it'll make things work better."

Helen looked at Ricky and said, "You look unusually sharp tonight. What kind of smoke did you indulge in?"

At that moment, Matt jumped at Ricky and hugged him repeatedly. The suggestion was brilliant, making Matt even happier. He held Ricky's shoulders and said, "You are a genius... brilliant, bright, and elegant tonight. Actually, I like your funny suggestions, and they help me a lot. Please don't stop and give us more of your ideas. You are completing our mission, and it's all thanks to you. Thank you."

As Matt arranged the stones around Artemis, his focus was unwavering, his movements precise. Artemis watched him intently, feeling a mix of curiosity and apprehension about what would happen next. Despite her uncertainty, she trusted Matt's judgment and immediately followed his instructions.

Meanwhile, Ricky jumped on the computer and started typing on the keyboard, his expression unreadable. His feelings of hurt and frustration simmered beneath the surface as he tried to distract himself from Matt's praise and the sense of exclusion he felt from the group's excitement.

Allen looked at Ricky and asked, "Who are you e-mailing now?"

Ricky replied briefly, "I know someone as brilliant as Matt. I'm asking him if he knows more about the stones."

"So, let Matt talk to that person who's smarter and knows more than you," Allen suggested.

Ricky glanced at Matt, who was staring at him, and responded, "I tried to reach him, but he's not available right now."

Artemis turned to Ricky, suggesting he stay quiet for the rest of the evening, but Ricky wasn't listening. His eyes were glued to the screen, and as soon as he heard his name, he turned to Matt, exclaiming, "Oh yes! We should lay the spirit stone on her heart and see what happens!" He giggled at his humor, but the laughter faded in an instant.

With a sense of unity restored, the group turned their attention back to the task at hand. As they waited in anticipation, the air in the room crackled with a mixture of excitement and uncertainty, each member of the group bracing themselves for whatever might come next. Ricky noticed the visibly displeased expressions around him, realizing that while his suggestion had amused Matt, it had sparked anger in Artemis and the rest of the group.

Artemis sat down on her spot in the middle of the signs, and unable to contain her frustration any longer, Artemis let out a piercing scream directed at Matt, "Come on, Matt, get real!"

Artemis shouted, casting an exasperated glare at Matt, who stood above her with the spirit stone in hand. Feeling deeply upset, she turned her gaze to Ricky and added, "I'll get you someday for that."

Then turned to Matt and said, "Really, Matt? You listen to his stupid suggestions?"

Matt placed the stone on Artemis's hand and, pointed at her chest and said, "We've come this far, please place it on your chest."

Angrily, while she was sitting, she placed it on her chest, and almost immediately, Artemis felt a wave of dizziness wash over her. Matt staggered back slightly and asked, "Did you feel it, too?" Even Artemis, still feeling disoriented, replied, "Felt what?"

Matt glanced at Artemis, then shifted his gaze to the others, rifling through his papers and notes once more. The group watched in apprehension, still reeling from the strange sensation they had just experienced. Still grappling with dizziness, Artemis felt her surroundings blur as Megan's voice faded into the background.

As they chanted, the symbols on the floor began to glow with soft, ethereal light, casting shadows that danced and flickered across the walls. A surge of energy coursed through Artemis, filling her entire being with a tingling warmth and light. In an instant, everything shifted—the room warped around them as colors swirled and merged in a dazzling display of light and sound. Artemis felt herself lifted momentarily, then pulled down at the speed of light as if swept by a wave of pure energy transcending space and time. She glanced around to see if anyone noticed, but everyone was arguing—

except Ricky, who was watching her intently. He shoved Matt and Allen aside and ran toward her.

Struggling to focus, she glanced at the clock beside her bed—5:29 a.m. It was long past midnight. At exactly five thirty, her eyes were drawn to the window, where she witnessed the magical appearance of the morning star.

Artemis's voice croaked as she struggled to comprehend what was happening around her. She glanced down at the magical stone in her hands and watched as it began to glow, its light casting an eerie glow in the dim room. To her amazement, she noticed that all the stones were now emitting light, illuminating the space with otherworldly brilliance. Desperately, she tried to draw attention to this phenomenon, pointing at the stones and then to Matt, but she felt like she was mute and Matt was engaged in a heated argument with the others. She glanced at the time again—still 5:30, stubbornly unmoving, as if frozen forever. Suddenly, she saw Ricky again, rushing toward her with his hand outstretched. But before she could reach for him, she felt herself pulled downward as if being drawn into an unseen vortex. Panic surged through her as she fought against the force, but soon she was swallowed by darkness, the only sound echoing in her ears like a pebble dropping into water. A sense of dread washed over her as she slipped into unconsciousness, and all the stones suspended above the floor suddenly dimmed and dropped, scattering in lifeless silence.

Matt and Allan's voices rose in a heated argument, echoing through the room. Allan expressed his frustration, declaring, "I thought it would be fun, but it's not. We've had enough of these... these magical and fairy tale moments."

Amidst their argument, the sound of stones clattering to the floor was punctuated by Ricky's frantic scream, "No... NO!" Overcome with regret, he dropped to his knees beside the symbols etched into the floor, anguish twisting his face. He should have watched over her more closely—he couldn't shake the feeling that it should have been him who disappeared, not Artemis.

"It should be me, not her," he muttered, anguish twisting his features. "I should've paid more attention. I should've been beside her." His voice grew more frantic with each word, tears streaming down his face. "No, no, no… This can't be happening." Desperation clawed at his chest as he slammed his fist against the ground, the weight of guilt and regret pressing down on him, threatening to consume him whole.

At the exact moment the stones hit the floor with a resonant clatter, the ground seemed to shift for a couple of seconds, drawing everyone's attention downward. Ricky turned to Helen, Atossa, and Megan, seeking their agreement, but the floor shifted beneath them just then, causing everyone to startle. After the brief tremor, Allen noticed Atossa frozen in place, her gaze locked on the floor. With a sinking feeling, he followed her line of sight to where Artemis had been lying—only to find her gone. Panic swept through the room as Helen and Megan frantically searched for any trace of her.

Atossa looked at Ricky and asked, "Did you see it, too? I saw everything. She's gone…." Then she burst into tears.

Allan persistently called out to Matt three times until Matt, exasperated, finally turned to him with a sharp "WHAT?" He noticed the excitement in Allan's eyes, then glanced at Helen and Megan, only to find them sharing the same expression. Their attention was fixed on the symbol on the floor, where Ricky now lay instead of Artemis. Their faces were wrought with tears and fear. Matt's gaze shifted to the symbol, and he paled visibly. They all stood in a circle around the symbol, which seemed oddly frosted and emitted an intense cold that permeated the room.

A tense hush settled over the room as a knock echoed against the door. Slowly, the doorknob began to turn, each creak heightening their hope that it was Artemis. But as the door opened, it was Dorsa's apprehensive gaze that met them instead. Her eyes, tired yet filled with anxiety, darted around, seeking out Artemis.

Urgency laced her words as she spoke, "Did you all feel that too? Is Arsham back? He might be in the basement or downstairs!"

She proceeded to the hallway and descended the stairs, her voice echoing through the house as she called out, "Arsham... Arsham?" Dorsa meticulously searched every corner of the house, her hopes dwindling with each passing moment. Returning to Artemis's room, a sense of resignation colored her words as she expressed, "I thought Artemis's father came back because it was exactly the same noise that I heard from the night of his disappearance. I kind of hoped to see him back."

It didn't take long for her to discern that something was amiss, though she couldn't pinpoint the exact nature of the problem. With all eyes fixed on her, Dorsa's frustration mounted, her gaze sweeping the room until it landed on Atossa, who was shocked, staring at the floor. Her gaze settled on Matt, and in a hushed tone, she inquired, "Where is Artemis?"

Atossa got closer to her mother, and while she was crying, she said, "I saw her on the floor, and then she just magically, in a couple of seconds, she disappeared just before my eyes. That can't be possible..."

Megan looked at Atossa when she said, "You're imagining things. She was here, or maybe when we were all arguing, she got tired and left the room. Ah, never mind, she's probably in the washroom."

Dorsa was very sleepy and tired when she asked again, "Would you all please keep your game a bit quieter? Thanks." With that, she closed the door gently behind her and left. The room fell into a state of panic.

Allan held a finger to his lips and whispered, "Quiet... shh..."

He motioned for everyone to take a seat, and they complied. On the verge of tears, Megan spoke with a trembling voice and tear-streaked face, "What happened to Artemis? How do we bring her back, and how do we explain this to her mother? What should we do now?"

Matt was still reeling from the shock and hadn't found any answers for this bizarre situation. But he knew he had to come up with something, anything, to explain what had happened. As goosebumps prickled his skin, he looked at the faces of everyone in the room, feeling the weight of their fear. He took a deep breath, trying to calm himself in the face of this horrifying moment. His terror only deepened as the door creaked open again, revealing Artemis's mother peering inside. Dorsa returned, her eyes scanning the room and picking up on the tension. She looked to Matt, who was now as pale as a ghost, and asked, "Matt! Where is Artemis? She's not in the washroom, nor is she in this room. She wasn't in the basement either. Where is she?" Dorsa's voice quivered with fear, her heart pounding audibly in her chest.

All eyes turned to Matt, who had unwittingly become the spokesman for the group. The outcome of tonight's endeavor was far from what he had anticipated. He had willingly shared his knowledge with them, and they accepted it eagerly. Now, faced with this unforeseen situation, his mind drew a blank. How could he possibly explain Artemis's absence to her mother? With a deep breath, he began to formulate an explanation.

Every word that left Matt's mouth seemed to push the others a step further back. Ricky retreated until he reached the computer chair, sinking into it. Allan collapsed onto the bed and then quickly sat up. Megan cried silently, comforted by Helen, who patted her back while nervously chewing her thumb. Atossa sat on the sign in the middle of the room, tears streaming down her face as she looked sadly at her mother.

With a hiccup, she stammered, "Mom! They didn't do anything. I was here—I saw her disappear right before my eyes." Turning to Ricky, she asked, "Right? You saw it too… and I didn't know you loved her that much."

Matt meticulously recounted the events from beginning to end to Dorsa, her face retaining its composure without betraying any signs of stress. Matt's face flushed red with every detail laid bare, his muscles frozen in anticipation of Dorsa's reaction.

Dorsa's initial reaction was one of disbelief, but as she looked at the others and observed their reactions, she couldn't contain herself any longer. Laughter bubbled up from deep within her, starting as giggles and escalating into uproarious laughter. Soon, the whole room was filled with the sound of laughter as they shared the absurdity of the situation.

Allan rose to his feet, his expression wary despite the laughter filling the room. He leaned into Ricky and whispered, his tone tinged with concern, "I'm not sure what's happening, but this doesn't feel right."

Ricky quietly answered, "Let's enjoy the laughter while we can because we might need all the help we can get after this."

Then, Ricky nodded, gesturing for silence, and Allan fell quiet.

Matt, however, remained motionless, standing at attention in the center of the room, anticipating Dorsa's inevitable outburst of screams and tears. He braced himself for the emotional storm he knew was coming. Dorsa's laughter faded after a few moments, replaced by a sense of unease. She approached Matt, her expression serious, and asked in a determined tone, "Where is she?"

She stood still, her gaze locked onto Matt's eyes for a long while. After a minute, her eyes welled up with tears. She struggled to speak through her sobs. "No... No... It can't be happening again. Not again. Not to my Artemis. Please tell me this is a joke, and you're kidding about this story, aren't you?"

Matt felt terrible, wishing with all his might that Dorsa was right. But he shook his head slowly from side to side before bowing his head, his voice barely above a whisper. "No. I wish I could say that."

Dorsa's breath quickened, her heart pounding louder with each passing moment. Everyone could almost hear the pounding of her heart. The room fell silent as everyone remained frozen in place. Ricky attempted to move closer to Dorsa to hear her better, but her mouth moved without emitting any sound. Suddenly, she turned white and collapsed to the ground.

Atossa swiftly rushed to her mother's side, cradling her in her arms as she pleaded for help. "Call 911! Oh, Mom! I'm so sorry..."

In a panic, Helen hurried to Dorsa's side, addressing her as Mrs. Vedetta.

Megan screamed and joined them, echoing the sentiment, "We killed her mom too... Oh God, help us."

Allan, taking charge, declared, "I know first aid. Let me help her."

Matt quickly rallied everyone, urging, "Everybody help! Let's get her onto the bed."

Dorsa felt dizzy and slowly slipped into unconsciousness. Matt turned to his friends and suggested, "Maybe when we were fighting, Artemis went out of the room, and she is in the basement or kitchen or somewhere else in the house? Please, someone, go and search the house again."

Megan rushed to the phone, and within two minutes, the sound of sirens filled the neighborhood as ambulances and police cars arrived. The flashing lights illuminated the house and living room as they reflected off the walls.

A heavy silence enveloped the room as fear and dread gripped everyone present. Panic began to spread among them, each one struggling to make sense of the situation. Still fixated on the sign, Matt felt the weight of responsibility crushing down upon him. He couldn't bear the thought of Artemis's disappearance and the anguish it brought. With desperation in his voice, he turned to his friends and uttered, "What in the world just happened? Where did she go?"

Allan asked everyone in the room, "Did she leave the room, or did something awkward just happen? I wasn't looking or paying attention to her when this happened. Can someone tell me what is going on?"

Allan's voice broke through the tension in the room, his words echoing the confusion and bewilderment shared by everyone present. He sought clarity, desperate for an explanation amid the chaos.

His inquiry pierced the tense atmosphere, his words resonating with the collective confusion and alarm gripping each person present.

Seeking illumination amidst the bewildering events unfolding, he implored for clarity, his urgency palpable in the room's charged air.

Ricky's voice cut through the uncertainty, laced with frustration and concern. His words echoed the shared bewilderment, grappling with the inexplicable absence of Artemis. Recounting his brief encounter with her and the enigmatic illumination of the stones, he voiced his apprehension, hinting at a connection to her father's mysterious disappearance.

Under the weight of mounting stress, Ricky's voice went unheard amidst the chaos. His trembling frame mirrored the unease that gripped the room, a palpable tension that seemed to suffuse every corner. Megan's plea cut through the turmoil, directed at Matt with urgency, beseeching him to conjure a solution from the depths of his troubled mind.

Megan said, "Matt...Matt... Please think of something. Think...think. We are in this mess because of your ideas."

As Megan's words tumbled out, they only seemed to exacerbate the situation, adding to the cacophony of voices clamoring for attention. Amidst the chaos, Helen took hold of Megan's shoulders, shaking them gently in an attempt to calm her frenzied friend. Helen's tears flowed freely as she implored Megan to calm down.

"MEGAN! MEGAN! Calm down," she pleaded urgently. "It's not Matt's fault. It's our fault, and everybody is as guilty as Matt. Don't try to dump everything on one person. If you were in the room, it means you are as guilty, too. You are as guilty as the others, and this is not improving the situation. Come to your senses, and instead of making yourself look innocent, at least try to be helpful and help Matt think of something. He is the only hope we have, and

Artemis has. He can unravel this mystery if we all stay together and help each other. He has the brain to unravel this mystery."

Dorsa opened her eyes, feeling exhausted, and glanced around the room. Atossa, her youngest daughter, was sitting beside her on the bed, and Azar was sleeping in the armchair nearby. As soon as their eyes met, Atossa rushed to the bed and embraced her tightly. Azar was quickly alerted by Atossa and hurried to her sister's side. She was relieved that her flight had been delayed by twenty-four hours, allowing her to cancel it and stay with her sister.

Azar looked exhausted, her eyes swollen and teary. She held her sister's hand tightly and asked, "How do you feel?"

Dorsa questioned, "Why are you here? Shouldn't you be gone by now? You should be on the airplane."

"My flight was canceled last night until tomorrow night," Azar managed to explain, her voice heavy with fatigue. Dorsa's smile quickly faded into panic. Clutching Azar's hand tighter, she pleaded, "Tell me that was only a bad dream! Please, Azar, tell me. I need to hear that from you… I want to hear that and nothing else!"

For hours, Dorsa cried and screamed, her anguish echoing through the house. Meanwhile, everybody else gathered in the living room, their own tears mixing with hers. Some remained in shock, unable to comprehend what had transpired the previous night. The atmosphere was heavy with uncertainty and grief, and a somber silence settled over the group. Matt, burdened with guilt, felt responsible for Artemis's disappearance. He knew that he had to confront the situation head-on and choose his words carefully.

Meanwhile, police searched all around the house and neighborhood to see if there were other witnesses. They talked to everyone in the house. It took them hours, and they found nothing out of the ordinary. Finally, they went to Dorsa, and they questioned her too.

"We haven't found any solid evidence to support her disappearance. The only logical explanation is that she left the house, perhaps to reunite with her father. The kids' responses don't add up, and we have no way to substantiate them. Just wait—it's likely they'll be back. If you come across any additional information, please don't hesitate to call. Otherwise, have a good day." With that, they all left the house.

As Matt made his way towards the bedroom, Ricky grabbed his sleeve and whispered urgently in his ear, "What are you doing? She doesn't want to see you or any of us. She hates us for what happened, do you understand?"

Matt pulled his sleeve out of Ricky's grasp and said, "She has every right to hate us." He looked at Ricky and then Allen when he said that, but Ricky wasn't giving up. He confronted him again and said, "Do you understand the meaning of hating someone? She doesn't want to see or hear us. Do you dare to get close to her again?"

Matt felt miserable, yet his voice was filled with determination as he declared loudly, "Leave me alone! I have to talk to her."

Ricky stepped aside, recognizing Matt's resolve, and gestured for him to proceed. "I thought robots had no feelings, but I was wrong. Okay, go ahead. Good luck," he conceded.

Matt approached the doorway quietly, listening to Dorsa and her sister's conversation. He hesitated to interrupt, aware of Dorsa's distraught state, but as soon as she saw Matt in the doorway, her voice went even louder, and it was filled with anguish as she cried out, "How could she disappear from her own room and in front of five or six people? How can I possibly believe that? Where is she? What did you do to her?" And with that, she burst into tears even louder.

Matt approached Dorsa with a desperate plea in his eyes, his heart heavy with the weight of her anger. He needed to convince her to listen, to believe his theory. His steps were cautious as he spoke in a gentle tone, "I believe you and I understand, Mrs. Vedetta, that you're angry, and we are as surprised as you are." His voice trembled slightly. "But, we don't know what has happened yet, and this situation feels eerily similar to what happened with your husband.

Nobody believed you then, and now you're doing the same thing to me, to all of us. There's something about this house, or..."

He faltered, realizing that continuing might only inflame her anger further. "Please, just hear me out," he added, his tone imploring. "Please give me some time, and I'll figure that out. I promise you that."

Dorsa's eyes blazed with fury as she screamed even louder, her words cutting through the air like a knife. "It's all your fault and your friends' fault. I don't know what you did, but it is your fault…YOUR FAULT…... I'm going to point the finger of blame squarely at you, where it belongs, and you can count on that."

Matt persisted in making her listen, knowing that logic and theories meant little in her anguish. All Dorsa wanted was her daughter back, and nothing else mattered to her at that moment.

"I know it sounds crazy," he pleaded earnestly. "But you've got to hear me out. Please, just give me a chance to find a way. If there's a way to go, then surely there must be a way to come back.

Dorsa was completely out of control, unable to comprehend anything in her distraught state. She had long passed her breaking point. With tears streaming down her face, she began screaming, her voice raw with anguish.

"What can I believe when you took her away from me?" she cried out. "Get out of my house. JUST GET OUT... ALL OF YOU! GET OUT!"

"Mrs. Vedetta! If you can explain your husband's disappearance, then I can explain what happened tonight," Matt insisted desperately, though his words seemed to fall on deaf ears.

Azar gently placed her hand on Matt's shoulder and guided him and others towards the door when she said, "Please, just go for now and give her some time,"

She implored softly, "You know this is a very painful time for her. Take all the time you need for your research, but you need to leave. Thank you."

Matt's frustration was palpable as he struggled to convey his message to Azar. He looked into her eyes with a sense of urgency, pleading for understanding. "Please listen to me carefully," he began, his voice strained with emotion. "This is the same thing that happened to Artemis's father, and I can help reverse it. I am the only chance to help her right now. I need more time to calculate everything again. Please let her know that and ask her to give me a chance to explain. Tell her that since I was able to open the portal, I can reopen it again. I won't stop until Artemis returns. I won't give up. I promised her... I promised her..."

His voice trailed off, choked with emotion, as he struggled to catch his breath amidst the overwhelming pressure and stress. Azar's tone, firm and resolute, escorted Matt and others to the door, trying to convey the gravity of the situation. "That's enough," she insisted. "I don't think you understand the situation. Enough is enough. Please just go."

Matt's frustration boiled over as he grappled with their refusal to believe in his ability to reverse the situation and bring Artemis back home. His voice cracked with emotion as he spoke loudly, almost yelling so that Dorsa could hear him. "I will never give up," he declared through tears. "I will bring Artemis back home, whether you believe me or not. That's a promise I made to her. I'm not just mourning for them; I'm working tirelessly to find a way to bring them back. I listen to the options rather than discarding them."

Azar cast a final glance at Matt and the others before retreating inside, closing the door firmly behind her.

INTO THE UNKNOWN

Artemis awoke with a strange headache, initially unaware of her surroundings. The first thing that caught her attention was the sky overhead, dotted with stars. She felt utterly exhausted and slipped back into unconsciousness. She opened her eyes again, and it wasn't until she tried to move that she realized she was no longer in her room, a shiver of fear rippling through her. As her mind cleared, she struggled to comprehend what was happening and where she was. Her attempts to sit up were met with dizziness, forcing her to wait until it subsided before trying again. She was so absent-minded that she couldn't even remember who she was; her mind was a blank slate devoid of any memories.

Gradually, she managed to sit upright and surveyed her surroundings. She appeared to be in an open field, devoid of any signs of civilization. Puzzled, she noted that her clothes were damp and sticky despite the absence of any nearby water sources. Suddenly, a strong odor assaulted her senses, causing her to recoil in discomfort.

Oh! I'm so sticky and smelly. What is this? she thought, puzzled by the sensation. Feeling exhaustion creeping over her, she drifted back into unconsciousness again. It was sometime later when she finally regained consciousness. Confusion and disorientation clouded her thoughts as she sat up and surveyed her surroundings.

"Where am I?" she wondered aloud, rubbing her temples in a futile attempt to alleviate her headache.

"Did I fall and hurt my head? Maybe that's the reason I'm hallucinating. Where am I? God…!!! Where is this place? This isn't the place with stars above my head! How am I under this huge tree now?" Her voice echoed into the darkness, unanswered. She felt utterly exhausted, not wanting to move, and knew She needed more rest; somehow, every bit of energy had been drained from her body.

Still, her vision was kind of blurry, gradually clearing with each passing minute. Artemis glanced around cautiously, her eyes falling upon the intricate and familiar silver balls laid beside her. Recognizing them as Matt's handiwork, she recalled him calling it the "Levitron." She reached out to them warily, knowing they wouldn't go anywhere as long as she had the base in her pocket to keep them close. A sense of unease crept over her. As she attempted to stand, her limbs felt strangely constrained, causing her to collapse back down. Sitting there, she pondered for a moment, the balmy air swirling around her, carrying with it fragrances that filled her nostrils.

Artemis scanned her surroundings, her eyes darting from side to side, searching for anything that wasn't a plant or a rock. The sounds of the woods enveloped her, the clattering of naked tree branches in the wind echoing through the night. Realizing she was in the middle of nowhere, she felt exposed, sitting there vulnerably. Drawing in a deep breath of the endless night air, Artemis wondered if she was dreaming or descending into madness. She wiped the salty sweat from her eyes, blinking away the sting, her fists clenched with visible worry as her hands trembled uncontrollably. Who could be behind this scare tactic, and why target her? Despite her fear, curiosity drove Artemis to raise her head and cautiously survey her surroundings. Glancing at her watch, she questioned whether the time was accurate or if her watch was broken, resigning herself to wait for either sunrise or sunset for some semblance of clarity. Suddenly, she remembered the cellphone her mother had given her as a gift, recalling that she had tucked it into her pants pocket. Her hand shot into her pocket, but it was empty. She began searching her surroundings, hoping it had simply fallen out, but after a long and fruitless search, she finally gave up.

"Oh, if only I had my phone. I could call my mom to come pick me up. But... where am I, anyway?"

Thank goodness I have my watch with me. At least it still works, she thought to herself while watching the second hand of her watch tick steadily forward.

Glancing at the time, she saw it pointing to nine-thirty. However, despite the darkness around her, her watch indicated it was daytime.

"Oh God... how long was I asleep? It's still night, but how can it be 9:30 in the morning? It's pitch black!" she wondered aloud, confusion lacing her voice.

To confirm her suspicion, She gazed toward the horizon, where a beautiful red sun hung low, either setting or rising. If she could be sure of which, she would know the direction of East and West. Feeling a bit uneasy and chilled, she became worried. Deciding to lie down a little longer due to her lingering dizziness, she glanced at her watch once more, then back at the sun.

The time read 10:35. "Either this watch is broken, or I'm going crazy. It can't be 10:35 a.m. or p.m.—the sun should be high in the sky in the morning, and it shouldn't be this dark at night."

Feeling increasingly weak, she knew she needed to rest more. However, the urge to explore further gnawed at her. Nevertheless, she found herself gazing out at the prairie grass, swaying in the breeze as she lay on her back. Suppressing her growing irritation, she noted the only visible lights were the moon and the Sun. She looked at the semi-dark sky, and her heart stopped at what she was facing.

She whispered, "Moon, or it's better to say moons," her voice trembling.

She glanced up at the sky and spotted two additional moons, their pale light casting an eerie glow over the field. With each blink, the sky seemed to shift—or perhaps she was blacking out for long stretches, which would explain the startling differences each time she opened her eyes.

After a while, she glanced at her watch again, then looked up at the sky. "That big one—it's not a moon; it looks like a Sun. But... it's been over an hour since I woke up, and the sun is still setting? And two moons? How…? I think I'm sick. Either that or I'm heading toward madness," she muttered to herself, her voice filled with a mix of bewilderment and dread.

Artemis was initially afraid, but then her curiosity drove her to understand what was happening. The fear of being in an unfamiliar place made her anxious and terrified. She couldn't determine if the issue was with her watch, the surroundings, or if she was in some sort of coma experiencing an imaginary world. Restoring her confidence was essential for her to muster the courage to explore further. Despite hours passing according to her watch, the Sun remained fixed on the horizon, indicating that it wasn't just her watch malfunctioning but rather something peculiar about the area. As she walked, time seemed to pass normally, yet the sun remained unmoved, creating an eerie atmosphere.

Artemis encountered a large rock obstructing her path, prompting her to navigate around it, where she discovered a small passage leading to an open area filled with what appeared to be orange trees. Intrigued, she cautiously made her way through and reached the end of the field. The sight of the luscious fruits dangling from the trees enticed her, and she couldn't resist tasting one. With its delightful blend of orange and cherry flavors, the fruit provided a much-needed refreshment for Artemis, who was emotionally and physically drained. Hunger gnawed at her stomach, urging her to hastily pluck one of the oversized, juicy fruits, which she cradled in both hands due to its substantial size. Its heavenly aroma enveloped her, filling her lungs with its enticing scent as she savored the unparalleled taste of the exquisite fruit.

"These oranges look incredibly juicy and massive. Oh my god. I wish everyone was here to taste them," Artemis exclaimed with excitement.

She effortlessly split the fruit easily into two halves, revealing a surprising interior. Mostly juice, it was incredibly refreshing and delicious. Artemis quickly devoured it and decided to climb one of the trees for a larger one. Surprisingly agile, she easily leaped and grasped the branches, ascending higher and higher with each jump. She couldn't help but wonder if the fruit had some sort of intoxicating effect or perhaps contained some kind of enhancing substance, as her climbing abilities seemed beyond normal. Nonetheless, she reached for another fruit and carefully plucked it, avoiding a repeat of the previous squishy mishap. She indulged in several more until she was full, marveling at their unique aroma and flavor. Despite their oddity, she found herself addicted to the delightful taste, unable to resist another bite.

With her mouth still full, Artemis exclaimed, "Oh... I think I know what's going on! These fruits must have something that makes people feel high. That's why I'm experiencing such an incredible sensation. I feel like I'm an angel!"

With her pockets stuffed full of the delicious fruit, Artemis set off on her journey. Recalling the view from the top of the tree, she decided to head in the direction she believed to be north, guided by the sun that appeared to be setting. She remembered seeing some traces of a path that way and chose to follow it. With determination, she began her trek in that direction, eager to explore more of the mysterious land she found herself in. She easily leaped down from the tall tree, feeling like she was in a slow-motion movie. The experience was both effortless and exhilarating.

Artemis marveled at the surreal experience of jumping from the tree. Feeling unscathed and invigorated, she couldn't help but exclaim, "Woo..." Her gaze shifted from her watch to the sky, where the sun remained unmoved, refusing to set—or perhaps to rise. Puzzled by the phenomenon, she questioned aloud,

"What is happening here? Why is the sun not setting at all? I can't deny the feeling that I'm in a coma right now. That makes more sense to me than a sun that refuses to move. Or maybe the world has been frozen, and I'm the only one alive?" she wondered, a chill running down her spine.

Artemis examined the large orange in her hand and muttered, "Yap! I'm high."

She continued along the path, nibbling on the fruit in her hand. She suddenly stopped in realization. "Wait a minute! I'm in a coma. Yes! I'll go with that. But how can I wake myself up?"

She whispered the question to herself a couple of times before repeating it aloud as she sat on a large cliff, attempting to pinch herself awake. The pain was sharp, causing her to relent. "I'm going to wait until I'm fully awake. Yes, that's what I'm going to do."

Artemis scanned her surroundings once more, feeling a sense of unease and profound loneliness. The weather was idyllic, with a gentle breeze brushing against her skin as she savored the tranquility of her surroundings. The verdant field stretched out before her, bathed in the warm glow of the setting sun, presenting a picturesque scene that captivated her gaze. To her left, the rocky wall loomed large, while to her right, the vast expanse of open prairie sprawled out, dotted with the lush orange trees she had encountered earlier. Beyond them, she spotted a towering mountain, its height not comparable to the likes of Mount Everest but still imposing in its own right.

Artemis's mind raced with conflicting thoughts as she weighed the risks of staying exposed in her current location. While the open field offered a higher chance of being found, especially with nightfall approaching, it also posed significant dangers. The presence of wild animals, with their keen sense of smell, meant that she could easily become prey if she remained out in the open. She knew she needed to find a safer shelter soon, balancing the need to be discovered with the imperative of protecting herself from potential threats.

Her mind whirled as goosebumps swept over her skin, sending a shiver down her spine. Deciding she needed to prioritize safety, she changed her plan and opted to seek higher ground for the night. Claiming the mountain as her temporary refuge offered the promise of better sleep and enhanced security. From its vantage point, she could also survey the surrounding field more effectively come morning, potentially spotting signs of civilization nearby. With this newfound determination, she leaped off the rock and began her ascent, seizing a large piece of stick along the way for both protection against wild animals and assistance in navigating the terrain.

Artemis found herself grappling with conflicting evidence and her watch indicated it was after midnight, nearing one o'clock in the morning, yet the landscape before her resembled a scene more typical of sunrise than sunset, suggesting a time closer to six-thirty in the morning. This discrepancy left her thoroughly bewildered and disoriented. Despite her confusion, she persevered, reaching the summit of the mountain around two o'clock in the morning, as per her watch.

"Thank goodness it wasn't that difficult," she whispered to herself, her breath forming small clouds in the chilly air. Fatigue weighed heavily upon her, a consequence of sleep deprivation. Feeling the chill seep into her bones, she sought refuge in a secluded corner, hoping to shield herself from the biting wind. After a moment of searching, she found a suitable spot and settled in. Pulling her knees to her chest, she wrapped her arms around them, seeking both physical warmth and a semblance of comfort as she attempted to steal some rest amidst the unforgiving night.

"When will I finally awaken?" she pondered, leaning back and tilting her head towards the skylights to better observe the stars that still twinkled above. The vast expanse above her was adorned with countless stars, a sight she had never before witnessed. Despite scanning the heavens, she found no trace of the morning star or the Milky Way. Resigned to her current predicament, she settled into a state of waiting, yearning for the arrival of morning. Her exhaustion weighed heavily upon her, and she longed for uninterrupted rest, hoping that with the dawn would come clarity of mind.

"If the sunset was so prolonged... how much longer until sunrise?" she mused aloud, a tinge of desperation creeping into her voice.

"God, help me, please," she whispered softly, a plea born from the depths of exhaustion and uncertainty. With a heavy heart, she allowed her eyelids to droop shut, embracing the temporary respite of darkness as she awaited the promise of a new day.

It didn't take much for Artemis to succumb to sleep. In the bewitching hours of the night, time seemed to stretch endlessly until the semidarkness was eventually engulfed by complete dimness, descending into absolute pitch blackness. She slept, unaware of the passage of time until she was stirred awake for reasons unknown to her. With a sense of disorientation, she fumbled for her watch, relieved to find its tiny light providing a faint glow in the darkness. "God! I wish I had my cellphone with me."

Six o'clock blinked back at her from the watch face, signaling what should have been the onset of sunrise. Yet, as she peered into the impenetrable darkness surrounding her, there was no hint of dawn on the horizon.

"So... it was sunset," she murmured to herself, a note of resignation creeping into her voice.

"It's good to know. Now I know I have to wait for morning." With that acknowledgment, she settled back into her makeshift refuge, bracing herself for the long wait ahead.

Suddenly, two crimson orbs pierced through the darkness, locking onto hers with an intensity that sent a wave of terror crashing over her. Panic seized her, overriding any rational thought as she succumbed to instinct. Without hesitation, Artemis turned and fled, her footsteps echoing against the unforgiving terrain as she ran for her life. Artemis was overwhelmed by the horrifying presence of the figure looming closer with each passing moment. Its menacing approach sent shivers down her spine, and she trembled in fear as it sniffed around her, the sheer enormity of its size overwhelming her senses.

Then, in a sudden shift, relative silence descended, broken only by the chirping of crickets that dared to resume their nocturnal chorus. Artemis's panic surged, driving her to the brink of desperation. As she prepared to flee, the creature lunged, its monstrous form launching towards her with terrifying speed.

With a surge of adrenaline, Artemis fought against the creature's grasp, summoning all her strength to break free. Somehow, she managed to wriggle out of its clutches, but the sense of hopelessness and weakness engulfed her. She stumbled backward, her back colliding with a massive rock, offering scant protection against the looming threat.

In a moment of sheer terror, Artemis instinctively scrambled atop the rock, her hands raised as feeble shields against the looming danger. But it was too late. Panic seized her as she realized the futility of her efforts. With a frantic leap, she sought to escape the creature's grasp, her heart pounding in her chest with a ferocity unmatched by any fear she had ever known.

In the dim light of the night, her vision blurred, rendering her surroundings a chaotic blur of shadow and uncertainty. Yet, amidst the darkness, one thing remained clear, Artemis had never felt such terror in all her life. Slowly, she realized that when she focused, the clearer everything became, as if she could see through the darkness. Yet, everything around her seemed to be happening so fast. As she landed on the precarious edge of the rock, her footing faltered, betraying her in her moment of desperation. With a helpless cry, she plummeted into the abyss below, her descent marked by a deafening rush of wind and the distant echoes of her own fear.

She screamed, "Oh my God... oh my God..." The words tumbled from her lips, but strangely, she felt an unexpected sense of tranquility wash over her. It was as if she were floating on a satin bed sheet, enveloped in a cocoon of comfort. A fleeting thought crossed her mind—was this sensation real or merely a figment of her imagination?

As she hung suspended in the air, her thoughts swirled in a whirlwind of uncertainty. Was she truly falling, or had she transcended the bounds of reality altogether? There was no sense of plummeting speed, no rush of wind against her skin. It was a surreal experience, leaving her questioning the very nature of her existence. Despite the chaos in her mind, fatigue weighed heavily upon her, pulling at her consciousness like a siren's call. With a sense of surrender, she allowed herself to succumb to the blissful embrace of sleep, finding solace in the midst of uncertainty.

As sunlight flooded the surroundings, Artemis stirred from her slumber, blinking against the gentle morning glow. As she sat up, taking stock of her surroundings, it became apparent that it was early morning. The tranquil scene before her offered a brief respite from the trials of the night. However, her moment of peace was short-lived as she became aware of the uncomfortable sensation clinging to her skin. With a frown of disgust, Artemis reached down and touched her clothes, confirming her suspicion.

"I'm sticky again? It's so gross," she muttered under her breath, frustration evident in her voice. Despite the unpleasantness, she knew she had to press on, steeling herself for whatever challenges lay ahead.

After a moment of contemplation, Artemis found herself acknowledging an unexpected realization. Despite the discomfort of her sticky clothes and the weariness lingering in her bones, there was an undeniable sense of vitality coursing through her veins. It was a sensation she had never experienced before, one that left her feeling truly alive. As she reflected on the events of the night and the brief respite of sleep she had managed to steal, Artemis couldn't help but marvel at the depth of her newfound vitality. It was as if a dormant energy had been awakened within her, revitalizing her spirit in ways she had never thought possible. In that moment, she realized with a sense of wonder that she had never slept so deeply, so soundly, in her entire life. The restorative power of sleep had eluded her for so long, but now, amidst the uncertainty and danger of her surroundings, she had found a sense of peace and vitality that she had never known before. And for that, she was grateful.

For the first time in her life, she wasn't tired or afraid. She was impressed to have such a good feeling with lots of energy. She got up and looked around, trying to piece together what had happened the night before. Why was she so wet and sticky? And worst of all, why did she smell horrible again? She surveyed the mess around her, where two enormous, broken trees lay beside her, and scattered pieces of wood were strewn all around. It looked as though a massive fight had taken place, with countless signs of struggle all around. She stood up and scanned her surroundings. Her eyes locked onto a cave in front of her, where two bright red eyes gleamed from the darkness. As soon as Artemis looked at them, the eyes retreated as if belonging to a beast that had been growling, threatening to terrify her, but then suddenly fell silent for a moment. Artemis's heart raced with fear as she stared into the piercing red eyes of the creature before her. Its menacing growls seemed to reverberate through the very earth beneath her, causing the ground to tremble in response. She watched in terror as the beast's breathing quickened, its agitation palpable in the air.

Then, with a sudden shift, the creature rose to its full height, towering over her in intimidating silence. Artemis's mind raced as she struggled to piece together the events of the previous night. She remembered the attack, the desperate scramble for safety, but for some reason, there was a gap in her memory. A sense of unease settled over her as she realized that she couldn't recall the moment of impact, the landing from her fall. It was as if a crucial piece of the puzzle was missing, leaving her feeling disoriented and vulnerable in the face of the looming threat before her. With a shaky breath, Artemis braced herself for whatever revelations the coming moments might bring, her instincts screaming for caution in the presence of such primal danger.

Immediately, she cast her gaze downward, inspecting her hands and legs for any signs of injury. With a sense of relief, she found her skin unblemished, devoid of any bruises or scratches. There were no damages to be found, not even a single scratch marred the surface of her skin, which remained smooth and unmarred, a stark contrast to the chaos that had unfolded the night before. As she struggled to piece together the events of her fall, Artemis couldn't shake the nagging sense of disbelief. The mountain loomed above her, its towering presence a reminder of the dizzying height from which she had plummeted.

But how was it possible? How could she have fallen from such a height and emerged unscathed? The sheer magnitude of the mountain, stretching upward like a towering skyscraper, only served to deepen the mystery. It defied logic and challenged the very laws of nature. Perhaps a superhero had swooped in and saved her, protecting her from the beast. She smiled, finding herself amused by the idea of a superhero swooping in to save her.

Artemis found herself at a loss, unable to reconcile the reality of her unharmed state with the unfathomable height from which she had fallen. It was as if some unseen force had intervened, sparing her from harm in the face of certain peril. As she grappled with the inexplicable circumstances, a sense of unease settled over her, casting a shadow over the tranquility of the morning light.

"Maybe it was just a dream... just a dream..." Artemis whispered to herself, the words a feeble attempt to rationalize the inexplicable events of the night. With each repetition, she felt a sliver of doubt creep into her mind, questioning the reality of what she had experienced. Nevertheless, she pressed forward, her footsteps a rhythmic cadence against the earth beneath her. Walking became her refuge, a means of grounding herself in the present moment and warding off the encroaching sense of unease. With each step, Artemis willed herself to focus on the tangible world around her, allowing the familiar sights and sounds of the forest to anchor her in reality. It was the only way she knew to stave off the rising tide of fear and uncertainty threatening to overwhelm her. After a few measured steps, Artemis paused and turned her gaze back towards the towering mountain.

"Yep... I've never been up there," she muttered to herself, the words tinged with a mixture of disbelief and apprehension. The memory of her fall lingered at the edges of her consciousness, a stark reminder of the inexplicable events of the night before.

"And last night, I was sleeping right here," she continued, gesturing towards the scattered remnants of broken branches and fallen trees surrounding her. The familiarity of her surroundings offered a small measure of comfort amidst the uncertainty, grounding her in the present moment. With a determined set to her jaw, Artemis reaffirmed her resolve to confront whatever mysteries lay ahead. She may not have all the answers, but she refused to let fear dictate her actions. Stealing a final glance at the imposing silhouette of the mountain, she set off once more, determined to uncover the truth lurking within its shadowed depths.

She paused for a moment, the weight of her words hanging heavy in the air. "You see," she began again, her voice a mere whisper in the vast expanse of the forest, "So many weird things have happened lately that very few things indeed seem truly impossible. Only when people are in a coma, do they hallucinate, right? That must be the logical explanation for all these strange things happening to me—even though everything feels so real." The truth of her words resonated within her, stirring a sense of unease that refused to be ignored.

"How can I find out which is real and which is not?" she questioned aloud, the uncertainty of her situation pressing down upon her like a suffocating blanket.

"Nothing makes sense here at all." With a frustrated sigh, Artemis shook her head in disbelief. The events of the past night seemed to defy logic, leaving her grasping for answers in a world where none seemed to exist.

"I must've been in a coma… or maybe I'm experiencing a near-death experience? Am I dead?" she reasoned, desperation creeping into her voice as she sought to make sense of the inexplicable. Yet even as the words left her lips, she couldn't shake the nagging feeling that there was more to her situation than met the eye.

Artemis absorbed the profound truth of her situation in this enigmatic place; nothing made sense. Yet, paradoxically, it was precisely this sense of wonder that fueled her determination to press onward. The inexplicable mysteries of the world around her served as a constant reminder that there was more to discover, more to unravel. Even as she traversed the unfamiliar terrain, Artemis couldn't shake the persistent belief that she would awaken from this surreal dream at any moment. The thought of recounting her strange experiences to others filled her with a strange mix of anticipation and dread. She was almost certain that she had heard the ominous growling of some unseen creature, and the memory of her fall from the cliff edge remained vivid in her mind. Yet, Despite the undeniable reality of these experiences, the question of how she had survived remained a perplexing mystery that haunted her.

Lost in her own thoughts, Artemis found herself engaged in a silent dialogue, accepting and rejecting her own thoughts in equal measure. Confusion clouded her mind, leaving her feeling adrift in a sea of uncertainty. Yet, amidst the chaos of her thoughts, a flicker of determination burned bright within her, driving her ever-forward in search of answers.

She rose to her feet, brushing off the leaves that clung to her hair like stubborn remnants of the night. A sigh escaped her lips as she realized her hair was once again damp and sticky, the remnants of an unseen moisture that seemed to linger persistently.

"What is this?!" she exclaimed in frustration, her voice carrying a note of annoyance as she attempted to shake off the dampness. The sensation of wetness against her skin only served to heighten her discomfort, leaving her longing for the simple comfort of dryness. With a resigned shake of her head, Artemis set aside her frustration, steeling herself for the challenges that lay ahead. Though the mysteries of this strange world confounded her at every turn, she refused to be deterred. Determination burned bright within her, driving her ever onward in search of the truth that eluded her grasp.

Artemis's heart pounded with a mixture of fear and confusion as she recalled the slimy, sticky substance that coated her hair and body. The memory of the events from the previous night flashed before her eyes, sending shivers down her spine. Goosebumps prickled her skin as she contemplated the possibility of being hunted by wild beasts or encountering other unseen dangers lurking in the shadows. Yet, amidst the fear and uncertainty, another memory surfaced—a glimmer of hope amidst the darkness. She remembered the distant lights, like the twinkling of a cityscape, beckoning to her from the northern horizon. It was a vivid recollection, one that she couldn't dismiss as mere imagination.

With a sense of determination fueled by this newfound revelation, Artemis resolved to trust in her instincts and follow the path laid out before her. Though the mysteries of this strange world still confounded her, she refused to succumb to fear. With each step forward, she moved closer to uncovering the truth that lay hidden in the darkness, her resolve unwavering in the face of adversity.

"Yes, I saw the lights from up there," Artemis murmured to herself, pointing toward the top of the mountain. Her voice tinged with a mix of wonder and confusion.

"If I've never been up there, then how is it possible that I managed to see the city lights from up there? And how did I get down? I don't even remember climbing down! It's so strange," she muttered, bewildered. Lost in thought, she turned her gaze towards the sky, searching for the sun's familiar glow. As she located its position on the left side of her, a sense of clarity washed over her.

"So... if it's morning, that must be east—the place where the sun always rises," she reasoned aloud, piecing together the puzzle of her surroundings. A spark of realization ignited within her as she connected the dots.

"I found it. That must be the north," she declared, her certainty growing with each passing moment.

"But how do I know it was north? Ah, that's because I saw where the sun was setting yesterday. And it is sunrise right now."

With a sense of accomplishment, Artemis allowed herself a small smile, grateful for the moments of clarity amidst the confusion.

Armed with this newfound understanding of her surroundings, she forged ahead, eager to unravel the mysteries that lay ahead on her journey.

As Artemis trudged onward towards the north, her stomach growled in protest, a stark reminder of her pressing hunger and thirst. Casting occasional glances around her, she sought to keep track of her surroundings in the vast expanse of the jungle—or whatever it was she found herself in.

"How can I find food and clean water in the middle of this jungle, or some kind of jungle, or maybe it's better if I say in the middle of nowhere?"

She mused aloud, the question hanging heavy in the air. The enormity of her predicament weighed on her, a daunting challenge in the face of the unknown. Glancing down at her watch, Artemis noted the time. Seven thirty in the morning on March 1st, according to her watch. Its display, showing both morning and evening along with the date, served as a constant reminder of the passage of time in this unfamiliar landscape. With each passing moment, the urgency of her need for sustenance grew more acute. Yet, despite the daunting task ahead, Artemis refused to succumb to despair. Armed with determination and steadfast resolve, she pressed forward.

Artemis's brow furrowed in confusion as she scrutinized her watch, its display contradicting the position of the sun in the sky. "It can't be seven thirty in the morning," she muttered to herself, her voice tinged with frustration.

"And it's not afternoon either, considering it's already been twenty hours since last night. So, what time is it?" She kept looking at the sky when she noticed something even more disturbing.

"Why aren't the sun and moons moving in harmony, in the same direction? That moon was on the right, and the sun was on the left, but now they're close to each other? How is that even possible?" She sat on the ground, holding her head as a wave of dizziness washed over her, feeling as if she were falling.

With a sigh of resignation, she shook her head, acknowledging the futility of relying on her malfunctioning watch for answers. "It's one thing for my watch to stop working, but what's the explanation for the sun and moon and the way they're orbiting the Earth?" she wondered aloud, confusion and fear gripping her. She concluded, a sense of defeat settling over her. In the absence of any reliable means of telling time, Artemis resigned herself to the uncertainty of her situation, focusing instead on the immediate task at hand—finding food and water to sustain her in this unforgiving wilderness.

Artemis furrowed her brow in perplexity, her fingers tapping on her lower lip, mirroring the rhythm of her thoughts. "It can't be the battery—I just changed it three weeks ago," she muttered to herself, trying to make sense of the situation.

Her confusion deepened at the inexplicable malfunction of her watch. Her attention shifted from her watch to her surroundings once more, her eyes scanning the unfamiliar landscape. Lost in thought, she began to calculate the time in her head, attempting to make sense of the discrepancy between the position of the sun and the time displayed on her watch. She began calculating the time since her arrival, but nothing added up—it was as if time itself had become unrecognizable. Suddenly, a burst of laughter escaped her lips, startling her with its unexpectedness. She remembered a humorous quip from Ricky when he said, "Do you know why you don't do math in the jungle?" he had once joked. "Because if you add 4+4, you get eaten... you got that... ate." She laughed more at the sheer stupidity of the so-called joke than the joke itself.

The memory brought a brief moment of levity amidst the confusion and uncertainty of her current situation. Chuckling to herself, Artemis realized the absurdity of trying to make sense of time in this wild and unpredictable environment. With a shake of her head, she resolved to focus on the immediate challenges before her, trusting in her instincts to guide her through the trials that lay ahead. Her laughter echoed through the wilderness, a stark contrast to the seriousness of her situation. Yet, even as she reveled in the momentary release of tension, her laughter faltered, replaced by a sense of awe and disbelief.

As she turned her gaze once more towards the sun, her eyes widened in astonishment at what she saw. "What... the... hell... is... this... place?" she whispered, her voice trembling with a mixture of wonder and uncertainty.

For there, against the backdrop of the sunlit sky, Artemis beheld a sight that defied all rational explanation. It was a moment of truth, a revelation of the natural world that shattered the boundaries of her understanding. In that moment, all the science she had ever known seemed to collapse in the face of the incomprehensible beauty before her. Artemis blinked in disbelief, unable to tear her eyes away from the spectacle unfolding before her. It was a moment of profound realization, a glimpse into the vast and wondrous mysteries of the universe that lay beyond the confines of human comprehension. And in that moment, Artemis knew that she stood on the threshold of something truly extraordinary. Artemis's mind raced as she grappled with the mind-bending realization before her.

"The sun didn't set like it usually does, from east to west," she murmured to herself, her voice tinged with awe and apprehension. "Instead, it's moving from north to south, following the strange paths of the moons and the few stars still visible, like the bright morning star, and strangely, It's being followed by a smaller sun that just revealed itself. "Two suns in the sky?"

Drawing upon her knowledge of the natural world, Artemis observed the movement of the stars overhead, seeking to make sense of the inexplicable phenomenon unfolding before her. "Yes, that's the morning star," she noted, her eyes tracing its path across the sky. "It was there on the left just a couple of hours ago, but now it's moved to the right."

The implications of her discovery sent a shiver down Artemis's spine. "It means we are turning naturally," she concluded, her voice barely above a whisper. "But it is the sun which is moving from north to south."

The realization was both fascinating and terrifying in equal measure, challenging her understanding of the fundamental laws of nature. As Artemis grappled with the implications of her discovery, she couldn't help but feel a sense of unease creeping over her. Yet, amidst the uncertainty, a spark of curiosity ignited within her, driving her to delve deeper into the mysteries of this strange and wondrous world.

Her sense of direction faltered in the wake of her startling discovery. As she watched the movements of the sun and moon defy the conventional norms she had once relied upon, the realization hit her—she was no longer on Earth. A wave of panic surged through her, and she felt as if she were choking, struggling to breathe in the unfamiliar air. With north and south now lost to her, along with east and west, she found herself adrift in a sea of uncertainty.

Her eyes traced the separate paths of the sun and the moon, each moving in a direction that defied all logic and reason. In her mind's eye, she envisioned the celestial bodies on a collision course, their orbits intersecting in a cosmic dance of light and shadow. Yet, it was the presence of a second moon, moving in perfect opposition to the first, that sent a chill down her spine again. The sight was nothing short of freakish, a stark reminder of the boundless mysteries of the universe that lay beyond the grasp of human understanding.

As she watched the celestial bodies move across the sky, Artemis felt a sense of awe mingled with apprehension. In this strange and wondrous world, where the laws of nature seemed to bend and warp with each passing moment, she knew that she stood on the threshold of an unimaginable adventure, one that would challenge her perceptions and redefine her understanding of the world around her.

Her heart skipped a beat as she beheld the sight of the third moon, its eerie presence casting a pall over the already surreal landscape. Unlike the others, which moved in seemingly chaotic and contradictory paths, This third moon followed a trajectory that defied all comprehension, moving from north to south as it trailed the smaller sun.

The realization sent a shiver down her spine, the implications of these new discoveries plunging her deeper into a state of unease. It was as if the very fabric of reality was unraveling before her eyes, revealing a truth far stranger and more unsettling than she had ever imagined. As she watched the celestial bodies dance their cosmic ballet across the sky, Artemis felt a creeping sense of dread take hold. In the presence of such otherworldly phenomena, she couldn't help but wonder what other secrets this mysterious realm held and what dangers lurked in the shadows beyond her understanding. With each passing moment, the world around her seemed to grow more alien and foreboding, leaving her with a sense of trepidation about the journey that lay ahead. Artemis's mind reeled with the weight of her discoveries, each revelation serving to deepen her sense of disorientation and confusion. As she pondered the erratic movements of the sun and moons, a sense of frustration welled up within her.

"It's not only the sun. The moons are different, too," she muttered to herself, her voice tinged with incredulity.

"If the first moon goes this way, why is the sun cutting its orbit? Either the sun is going from north to south, or the moon is. In this case, which way is north and which way is south? "But judging by the way the stars are moving, it looks like this planet is also turning clockwise while the sun is moving from north to south. How is it possible that the third moon is going North to South? What kind of nonsense world is this? I can't think clearly. I'm going crazy..." She closed her eyes, trying to calm herself, and took slow, deep breaths. The steady rhythm helped her center her thoughts, pushing back the rising tension within. After a couple of minutes, she opened her eyes and stared at the sky again.

"The universe is moving that way, not up and down," she murmured to herself. "That means north is that way, and south is this way, based on the planet's movement. Probably, this way is east, and that way is west. That's how I see it."

Her thoughts spiraled into a whirlwind of uncertainty, leaving her feeling adrift in a sea of chaos. Then, trying to steady herself, she said aloud, "But at least I came up with some answers."

"How... how is that possible?" she whispered, her voice barely audible above the turmoil raging within her.

"How... how did I come here anyway?" She still couldn't remember. It was as if she were in some kind of oblivion or amnesia, the details of her journey lost to the void.

She was happy to have solved one question, but the next minute, she was consumed by anger over everything else. It was as if she couldn't control her emotions, and they kept shifting uncontrollably, leaving her feeling helpless.

The questions hung in the air, unanswered and unsettling. Artemis's mind raced as she struggled to make sense of the inexplicable circumstances surrounding her. In the face of such overwhelming confusion, she felt herself teetering on the brink of madness, her grip on reality slipping with each passing moment. Her sensation was as if she had been spinning endlessly, only to come to an abrupt, disorienting halt. Yet, even as uncertainty threatened to consume her, a flicker of determination burned bright within her, urging her onward in her quest for understanding. Artemis knew that no matter how daunting the challenges that lay ahead, she could not afford to succumb to despair. She had come too far to turn back now. Artemis's throat felt dry as dust, her lips cracked and parched from the relentless heat of the sun. With a heavy sigh, she sank down onto a large rock, seeking respite from the relentless onslaught of uncertainty. Wrapping her arms around her knees, she buried her face in her palms, seeking solace in the darkness that enveloped her.

The wind whispered through the tall grass, teasing her hair and stirring the air with its cool caress. Yet, even as she welcomed the gentle touch of the breeze, she couldn't shake the overwhelming sense of uncertainty that gnawed at her insides. The mystery of this place twisted her mind into knots, leaving her unable to make sense of the surreal landscape that stretched out before her. With each passing minute, she found herself confronting new and inexplicable phenomena, each discovery serving to deepen her sense of unease. Reality seemed to warp and shift with each breath, leaving Artemis feeling adrift in a sea of chaos. Yet, amidst the confusion and uncertainty, a spark of determination flickered within her. Though the challenges ahead were daunting, she refused to succumb to despair. With each passing moment, she resolved to press forward, driven by a relentless determination to unravel the mysteries that shrouded this strange and enigmatic world. For Artemis knew that no matter how daunting the journey, she would not rest until she had uncovered the truth that lay hidden within the depths of this mysterious realm.

The relentless mysteries of this strange and unsettling place consumed Artemis' thoughts. With each passing moment, she found herself grappling with the overwhelming uncertainty that shrouded her surroundings. The revelation that the sun rose from north to south had shaken her to the core, challenging the very foundations of her understanding of the world. As she sat upon the rock, her mind raced with a whirlwind of conflicting thoughts and emotions. The events of the past hours seemed to blur together in a surreal haze, leaving Artemis unsure of what was real and what was mere illusion. She could vividly recall the animal's menacing growl, the sound echoing in her mind like a haunting refrain. And yet, despite their aggression, the creatures seemed unwilling to approach her, as if held at bay by some unseen force. Artemis felt a rising sense of frustration and confusion, her thoughts swirling in a maelstrom of uncertainty. She longed for clarity, for some semblance of understanding in the face of the inexplicable events that had unfolded since her arrival. Yet, try as she might, she found herself no closer to unraveling the mysteries that surrounded her.

In the midst of her confusion, Artemis clung to a glimmer of hope, a determination to uncover the truth that lay hidden beneath the surface of this strange and enigmatic world. For though she may be lost in a maze of uncertainty, Artemis refuses to surrender to despair. With each passing moment, she resolved to forge ahead, Fueled by an unwavering resolve to unearth the secrets buried deep within the heart of this enigmatic realm.

Artemis's frustration simmered as she gazed up at the sky, her brow furrowed in confusion and disbelief. The sight before her only served to deepen her sense of bewilderment as the celestial bodies continued their erratic dance across the heavens. Her eyes widened in astonishment as she beheld the third moon, its path cutting a swath across the sky from what she had always believed to be the North Pole to the South Pole. The realization sent a chill down her spine, the implications of this newfound discovery sending her mind reeling as the third moon intersected the orbit of the second, a sense of awe washed over Artemis at the sight of the celestial spectacle unfolding before her. The trailing tail of the second moon shimmered like a shooting star, casting a mesmerizing glow against the dark canvas of the night sky. She knelt down and began to pray, her voice trembling with desperation. "Oh God, my Lord, please help me."

Yet, despite the beauty of the scene before her, Artemis's frustration only grew, her attempts to reconcile her knowledge with the evidence before her proving futile. With each passing moment, she felt the grip of uncertainty tighten around her, leaving her feeling adrift in a sea of confusion. Unable to pinpoint the true positions of north and south, east and west, Artemis found herself at a loss, her sense of direction shattered by the surreal landscape that surrounded her. As she struggled to make sense of the incomprehensible mysteries of this strange and enigmatic world, Artemis felt a surge of determination welling up within her. For though the challenges before her were great, she refused to be defeated. With each passing moment, she resolved to press onward, driven by an unyielding determination to uncover the truth.

Artemis resisted the temptation to indulge in hope, recognizing the improbability of the situation. It felt as though a new world had unfurled before her, a reality she couldn't quite reconcile with her own. Despite her disbelief, she couldn't deny the palpable sense of curiosity that coursed through her veins. Drawing upon her own wisdom, Artemis reminded herself of the importance of perseverance.

"Going back may not be possible," she reflected,

"but I must endeavor to find a way forward."

The notion filled her with a curious blend of determination and trepidation, a sense of purpose guiding her steps into the unknown. A tingling sensation coursed through Artemis's entire body, a tangible reminder of the adventure that lay before her. Despite the uncertainty of her circumstances, there was a strange allure to the journey that beckoned her forward.

With determination in her heart, Artemis resolved to press on, her mind focused on the task at hand. As she scanned the surrounding trees, bathed in the soft light of the setting sun, she grappled with the challenge of choosing her next destination. How could she navigate this unfamiliar terrain without any knowledge of her location? It was yet another puzzle in the labyrinth of mysteries that surrounded her. Drawing upon her instincts, Artemis decided to retrace her steps, heading in the same direction she had started earlier. Surprisingly, she found herself starting to enjoy the sensation of walking through the field. There was something different about her now, a newfound sense of security that buoyed her spirits. Despite the hours of walking over rocks and sand, Artemis felt strangely invigorated, her feet carrying her forward with an ease that defied explanation. It was as if she were gliding effortlessly through the landscape, each step bringing her closer to the answers she sought. As the sun dipped below the horizon, casting a warm glow over the land, Artemis continued her journey with a renewed sense of purpose.

"Oh, damn it... it's so good. I love this feeling," Artemis exclaimed, a rush of exhilaration coursing through her veins.

But then, a wild idea took hold of her. "Maybe I am on the moon. No, wait, on Mars! Oh, yes... I'd like to agree with that, but none of them have two suns and three moons, all of which are moving in chaotic directions."

She paused, then whispered to herself, "Maybe—just maybe—I'm still on Earth, but somehow I've stepped into a different realm?"

A smile tugged at the corners of her lips as she entertained the thought. "I have gone too far in my thoughts, but nothing's wrong with that. Especially here, where everything is different. So be it... why not?" she muttered to herself, embracing the strange reality she found herself in.

A sense of accomplishment washed over Artemis as she surveyed her surroundings, her gaze alighting on the beauty that surrounded her. Tears threatened to well up in her eyes as she took in the breathtaking scene before her. Here, in this mysterious realm, the seasons seemed to dance to a different tune. While Toronto lay ensconced in the grip of winter, this place basked in the glow of a perfect autumn dawn. The contrast was stark and surreal, adding to the disorientation she felt. Artemis breathed deeply, relishing the crisp, refreshing air that filled her lungs. The sound of leaves rustling in the wind echoed through the air, adding to the serene atmosphere that enveloped her. Turning her attention to her surroundings, Artemis took note of the landscape that stretched out before her. To one side, a path shaded by towering oaks wound its way alongside the jungle, inviting her to explore its mysterious depths. The air was perfumed with the spicy scent of hay. On the other side, trees heavy with fruit beckoned tantalizingly, promising a bounty of delicious treasures. Behind her, a wide expanse of green field stretched out as far as the eye could see, a testament to the untamed beauty of this place. And ahead, another tall mountain loomed in her path, its summit obscured by clouds. Though not as imposing as the one she had slept on last night, it still presented a formidable challenge. With a determined shrug of her shoulders, Artemis set her sights on the mountain before her. There was no turning back now. With each step forward, she drew closer to the answers she sought.

Artemis murmured to herself, a wry smile tugging at the corners of her lips. "What the heck! This would be another unwanted and most likely, adventure for me today. Anyhow, this is the only way I get to see the land from a high place. I can decide better where to go."

With a mixture of resignation and determination, she began her ascent up the rugged slopes of the mountain, each step bringing her closer to the unknown. Though she knew not what lay ahead, Artemis faced the challenge with a courage born of necessity, ready to confront whatever obstacles fate had in store.

Artemis embarked on her journey towards the mountain, each step filled with a sense of anticipation and wonder. Despite the long walk, she found herself moving with an almost effortless grace, effortlessly navigating the terrain and leaping from one large rock to another. A funny feeling tingled in the air around her, infusing her with a sense of euphoria and excitement.

"Maybe it's the plants around here that got me high… and they're so beautiful," she mused aloud, her voice carried by the breeze. "There are so many colors I've never seen before—hues so unfamiliar that I can't even name them. But one thing is certain; these colors don't belong to the three primary ones we know on Earth. I feel like I'm flying. Wow... It's amazing."

With each jolt and bounce atop the rocks, Artemis felt a surge of energy coursing through her veins, her senses alive with the thrill of exploration. She scooped up a handful of pebbles, jiggling them in her hand as she marveled at the sight of the second moon rising once more in the sky. Despite the strangeness of her surroundings, Artemis couldn't help but feel a sense of exhilaration at the prospect of unraveling the mysteries of this new world.

As Artemis watched the two moons draw closer to each other in the sky, a thought occurred to her. "If they cross each other, they might make a plus sign in the sky. That would be cool. I wish everybody were here to see it."

Her mind drifted back to her family and friends, memories of her mother's loving eyes and her sister's familiar face flooding her thoughts. They were the ones who had given her the strength to face each agonizing day, their presence a source of comfort and courage in times of uncertainty. But now, as Artemis sat amidst the vast expanse of nature, a pang of longing swept over her. The faces she thought she'd never see again seemed to hover just beyond her reach, a bittersweet reminder of all that she had lost. They appeared like phantoms in the dim light, haunting her with memories of a life that felt increasingly distant.

Yet, even in the midst of her sorrow, Artemis found solace in the beauty of her surroundings. The scenes unfolding before her, the sights and sounds of this strange and wondrous world, felt too vivid, too real to be merely a figment of her imagination.

With a sense of conviction, she whispered to herself, "All of the scenes that I can see and feel here cannot be a hoax."

At that moment, amidst the quiet tranquility of nature, Artemis found a glimmer of hope, a faint light in the uncertainty,

as if the chaos around her began to make sense, a belief that perhaps, just perhaps, there was still a chance to uncover the truth that lay hidden within the mysteries of this enigmatic realm.

Artemis's thoughts drifted into deep contemplation, and she couldn't help but voice her concerns aloud, "How can I contact home? I'm worried, especially for my mom. She must've been worried sick."

She checked her pockets again while she was whispering, "I'm sure I had my cell phone in my pocket."

The weight of uncertainty pressed upon her as she grappled with the realization of being separated from her loved ones. With each passing moment, the ache of longing for home grew stronger, fueling Artemis's determination to find a way back to her family, no matter the obstacles that lay ahead. One moment, she felt a sense of calm, and the next, she was gripped by panic.

Artemis tapped on her watch in frustration, a sigh escaping her lips. "Hello... I changed your battery just three weeks ago, and it's supposed to last at least a year! Why are you not working properly? I paid for nothing! Why am I even angry at my watch? Clearly, this place doesn't make sense at all."

With a resigned shake of her head, she muttered to herself, "I know. As soon as I get back home, I have to change the battery again. It doesn't have any energy, and it's too slow or maybe too fast. I'm so confused, Oh..."

Glancing at the time displayed on her watch, she noted that it read eight-thirty in the morning, although the bright sun overhead suggested otherwise. Time seemed to pass differently in this strange and unpredictable place, its flow distorted and disjointed. Despite only being here for half a day, Artemis felt as though she had been immersed in this world for much longer, each moment stretching out into an eternity of uncertainty and wonder. Artemis's mind raced with wild conjectures as she grappled with the inexplicable nature of her predicament. She looked at her watch again and this time, she was wondering for the date.

"Maybe somebody dragged me and left me here just for fun. Whoever he or she is, possibly laughing at me by now. Maybe all my friends had this planned all together?"A sense of paranoia crept over her as she entertained the notion that she was being watched, that her every move was being observed by unseen eyes.

"Oh, they are watching me now. But they are not that devilish. Even a genius can't be this smart." She realized she was grappling with the mysteries of the universe, time, weightlessness, strange fruits, and new colors.

"No, that's not possible," she muttered to herself. "Not even scientists can do these things." She paused for a moment then she continued, "This is a serious phenomenon happening in my life," she whispered to herself. The weight of the situation finally began to sink in.

Despite her attempts to dismiss the idea as a mere prank or elaborate scheme, Artemis couldn't shake the feeling of being harassed, of being trapped in a bizarre and unsettling game. And yet, the more she contemplated it, the more it became apparent that this wasn't a game at all. There was something far more profound and mysterious at play, something beyond her comprehension.

Artemis's stomach churned with a mixture of anxiety and confusion, leaving her feeling unbalanced and disoriented. She couldn't fathom why she was experiencing such intense emotions, nor could she shake the nagging suspicion that her friends were somehow behind her current predicament.

"God, what's happening to me?" she whispered to herself, her voice trembling with uncertainty. "Where is this place? Who can answer my questions?" She broke into loud, uncontrollable sobs.

As she grappled with the myriad of thoughts swirling in her mind, Artemis couldn't help but feel overwhelmed by the sheer magnitude of the unknown. "I have lots of questions... but who can answer them?" she mused aloud, her words falling into the empty silence around her.

Realization dawned on her with a jolt. "Here is different from my home. Who can place three moons in the sky? Who could possibly be able to create two suns orbiting so closely around a single planet? "What kind of force or intelligence could wield the power to bend the very rules of the universe like that? No one! But then… what is it?" she exclaimed, the fragments of the puzzle slowly aligning in her mind.

"No, no... no… no. It's not a game, and I'm not on Earth anymore. Somehow, I was teleported here." Her mind continued to toy with her emotions, yet she still couldn't recall how it had all happened.

With each revelation, Artemis's sense of disorientation deepened, her world forever altered by the strange and mysterious forces at play. Yet, amidst the uncertainty and fear, a flicker of determination ignited within her. She may not have all the answers, but she was determined to uncover the truth, no matter where her journey might lead.

Artemis took a deep breath, willing herself to push aside the overwhelming sense of dread that threatened to consume her. "Yes," she affirmed, her voice steady despite the turmoil within. "I can't just wander around and waste my time. I have to know what's going on."

With a newfound sense of determination, she set out to organize her thoughts and embark on her research. Yet, as she delved deeper into her memories, a wave of unease washed over her. Suddenly, her memory flashed back. She vividly recalled the events of her birthday night. The cryptic signs, mysterious books, and strange stones from their game flooded back into her mind, sending a chill down her spine. Artemis hesitated, her resolve faltering in the face of uncertainty. This unknown place, with its eerie atmosphere and inexplicable phenomena, seemed more dreadful and nightmarish than anything she had ever encountered. But she knew she had no other choice. She had to be brave, to steel herself against the fear and uncertainty, if she hoped to survive and find her way back to her family and friends.

Yet, even as she steeled herself for the challenges ahead, a haunting question lingered in the back of her mind, threatening to unravel her resolve. "What if nobody knows where I am?"

The thought sent a chill down her spine again; this thought filled her with a profound sense of isolation and dread, as if the memories from that night held secrets far deeper and more dangerous than she had ever imagined. But Artemis pushed aside her fear, clinging to the hope that somewhere, somehow, there was a way back to the ones she loved.

Artemis's heart raced as she scanned her surroundings, a sense of unease settling over her like a heavy cloak. Every rustle of the wind and faint whisper of movement stirred a tremor deep within her and her senses were on high alert for any sign of danger.

With cautious movements, she lowered herself to the ground, her eyes darting back and forth as she listened intently to the sounds of the forest. The wind swept through the trees, tossing her hair about her face and carrying with it the faint scent of pine and earth.

But amidst the fear and uncertainty, Artemis couldn't ignore the gnawing hunger in her stomach, a reminder of her basic needs in this unfamiliar place. She longed for nothing more than a hot shower, a change of clothes, and a moment of respite from the chaos that surrounded her. Fumbling in her pockets, Artemis's fingers closed around a small pencil and Matt's birthday gift, the "Levi-tron" he had given her. Though it offered little comfort in the face of danger, the small token served as a reminder of her connection to her friend, a lifeline in the midst of uncertainty. With a sigh, she tucked the items away and focused on the task at hand, steeling herself for whatever challenges lay ahead. Artemis's thoughts drifted to her cell phone, a pang of longing coursing through her as she imagined reaching out to her friends and family, reassuring them of her safety and sharing in the adventure of this strange new world.

"I wish I had my cell phone with me," she muttered, her voice tinged with frustration.

"I'd call my friends and let my mom know that I'm okay. We could've had lots of fun here."

The absence of her phone only served to amplify her sense of isolation, leaving her feeling even more irritated, annoyed, and worried than before. But despite her frustration, Artemis refused to succumb to despair. With a determined shake of her head, she rose to her feet once more and turned her attention to the giant rock beside her.

With a leap, she bounded onto the rock's surface, the sensation of gliding through the air filling her with a sense of exhilaration that momentarily swept away her worries. In that brief moment of weightlessness, Artemis found a fleeting sense of freedom, a reminder that even in the midst of uncertainty, there were moments of joy and wonder to be found.

Artemis marveled at the sensations coursing through her body, a sense of euphoria washing over her like a gentle wave.

"Wow," she whispered to herself, a smile tugging at the corners of her lips. "That was something. I like it."

She glanced around at the field surrounding her, a suspicion forming in her mind. "I think it must be this field that influences my body and makes me feel this way," she mused aloud. "Definitely some kind of plants acting like drugs."

Despite the uncertainty of her surroundings, Artemis couldn't help but embrace the exhilarating experience. She said loudly, "But whatever it is, I like it." Then she declared with a laugh. "It's very cool."

Feeling buoyant and carefree, She found herself filled with an irrepressible urge to move, to dance, to soar through the air like a bird. She exclaimed with delight, her voice brimming with excitement, "I feel like I can leap or glide over the rocks in slow motion! Ahhhhhh, it's as if I could soar like a bird, too!"

She exclaimed, her voice tinged with wonder and excitement, "Yep... I feel like singing a song or doing whatever I want. Isn't that amazing?"

Artemis settled onto the ground, taking in the crisp, refreshing air that surrounded her. The sunlight warmed her skin, filling her with a sense of contentment as she reveled in the tranquility of the moment.

Her gaze fell upon a frog perched atop a nearby rock, perfectly still as if frozen in time. With a playful smile, Artemis addressed the amphibian. "Hmmm, how long have you been standing there? Are you on the lookout for food? I'll bet you love flies."

A moment passed before Artemis chuckled to herself, realizing the absurdity of her own question. "I know, I know the answer!" she exclaimed, her laughter bubbling forth. "You're watching closely and don't want to be disturbed because you don't want to miss a fly, do you, little guy?"

She felt a sneeze coming on, and with barely a sound, she sneezed. The water rippled, sending the frog skimming nearly ten feet away. Artemis stared in amazement and said, "Wow, I had no idea my sneeze was that powerful." Turning her gaze back to the frog, she added softly, "I'm sorry if I frightened you."

The frog remained motionless, seemingly unperturbed by Artemis's antics. But for Artemis, the simple exchange brought a moment of levity amidst the uncertainty of her surroundings, a reminder that even in the most unfamiliar of places, there was room for laughter and connection.

Artemis's voice carried through the stillness of the landscape, her frustration and exasperation evident as she called out into the empty air. She called out loudly, mimicking a funny accent as she repeated his name, "Ricky! Ricky! Ricky!" she cried, her tone tinged with a mix of irritation and nostalgia. "I don't know why I suddenly remembered all of your nonsense jokes!"

Her words echoed off the rocks and trees, a stark reminder of the friend she had left behind and said, "Besides," she continued, her voice tinged with bitterness, "because of your nonsense comments, I'm stuck here. Damn you, Ricky!"

Artemis's outburst gave way to a moment of quiet contemplation, the weight of her situation pressing down on her shoulders. "If only I could see you once more," she murmured, a note of resignation in her voice, "I'd... I'd..." Her words trailed off, lost in the vast expanse of the unknown.

Artemis's eyes widened with excitement as she spotted something resembling berries in the distance. Without hesitation, she broke into a run, her heart pounding with anticipation as she neared the field. With each step, her senses heightened, her anticipation growing with every breath. To her surprise, she looked back and couldn't believe she had run this far. The landscape behind her seemed to stretch endlessly, a testament to her desperate flight.

Finally reaching the source of her curiosity, Artemis reached out and plucked one of the berries between her fingers. She squeezed it gently until the juice oozed out, releasing a tantalizing aroma that wafted up to her nose. With a curious expression, she brought the berry to her lips and took a tentative bite.

The burst of flavor that flooded her mouth took her by surprise. The berries resembled strawberries in appearance but longer and no seeds, but their taste was reminiscent of cherries, with a hint of sweetness that danced on her tongue. Their light yellowish hue only added to their allure, and Artemis couldn't resist popping another one into her mouth.

As she savored the juicy sweetness of the berries, a sense of refreshment washed over her, quenching her thirst and invigorating her spirit. In this strange and unfamiliar world, the simple pleasure of tasting these berries brought her a moment of joy and contentment, reminding her that even in the midst of uncertainty, there were small moments of beauty and wonder to be found.

Artemis savored the last few bites of the delicious berries, relishing their sweet flavor as they danced on her palate. "Yes, it must be strawberry, but a different color," she murmured to herself, marveling at the unique taste of the berries. With each bite, she felt a surge of energy coursing through her body, invigorating her senses and filling her with wild, untamed vitality.

As she finished eating, Artemis couldn't help but feel a sense of awe at the transformation she had undergone. The berries had fueled her body with newfound strength and agility, and she could feel the urge to run coursing through her veins. With a sense of exhilaration, she rose to her feet and turned back to survey the field behind her.

To her amazement, she realized that she had effortlessly reaped two hectares' worth of berries in less than a minute, a feat that seemed impossible in her previous state. Her speed and agility had been enhanced in this strange new world, but how could that be? The question lingered in her mind as she pondered the mysteries of her surroundings, a sense of wonder and excitement driving her forward into the unknown.

Artemis stood up, determined and ready to press on with her journey. "Okay! I am ready to go. I know which way now."

For hours, she walked through the unfamiliar terrain, her mind racing as she searched for a solution to her predicament. Despite her best efforts, she found herself struggling to focus, the weight of her situation pressing down on her with each passing moment. In her previous life, she had been a top-notch student, adept at solving even the most complex problems. But here, in this strange and bewildering world, it was as if her skills had abandoned her, leaving her feeling lost and helpless. As the realization of her predicament sank in, Artemis felt a wave of despair wash over her. Tears welled up in her eyes as she grappled with the enormity of the challenge before her. All she wanted was to find a way to escape from this unknown world, to return to the safety and familiarity of her old life.

In that moment of vulnerability, Artemis felt utterly alone, the weight of her fear and uncertainty threatening to overwhelm her. But deep down, she knew that she couldn't give up. She had to find a way to overcome this obstacle, reclaim her confidence and forge a path forward. With that thought in mind, she wiped away her tears and resolved to keep moving, no matter how daunting the journey ahead might seem.

She stepped into the open campus, her eyes scanning the landscape before her. She could see that she was on the outskirts of a city, with a quaint little town lying straight ahead. As she gazed out at the view before her, she couldn't help but notice the similarities to Toronto, with its lush greenery and towering buildings in the distance.

However, as she drew nearer, Artemis began to notice subtle differences in the architecture and layout of the buildings. It was clear to her that this place was nothing like Toronto but rather a city that bore some resemblance to it from a distance. The streets were lined with beautiful oak trees, their branches providing shade from the midday sun.

Hidden behind hills and hedges, more homes came into view, their presence adding to the charm of the cityscape. The air was filled with the spicy scent of hay, a familiar aroma that stirred memories within Artemis. It was as if she had stepped into a city that had once been prosperous but now bore the marks of time and change. Toronto is cold and icy right now, with snow blanketing the city, unlike here, where everything is green, and the air is crisp and fresh. It's snugly warm and comfortable, with no sign of snow or coldness in sight.

"It's a completely different weather from what I'm used to." Artemis mused aloud, her thoughts drifting back to her hometown.

As she took in a deep breath of the unfamiliar air, Artemis suddenly felt a tightness in her chest, as if she were struggling to breathe. Panic threatened to rise within her, but she forced herself to stay calm.

"Where am I?" she whispered to herself, her voice barely audible. "Okay, Artemis, you need to give yourself a chance to breathe."

With each slow and deliberate breath, Artemis focused on calming her racing heart and easing the tightness in her chest. She reminded herself to stay grounded and present in the moment, knowing that panicking would only make the situation worse. As she regained control of her breathing, Artemis resolved to stay calm and composed.

The uncertainty of finding herself in a new and unfamiliar place was a heavy burden on Artemis's mind. Fear clung to her thoughts as she contemplated what lay ahead. For someone with a deep-seated fear of the unknown and darkness like herself, the idea of venturing into the city filled her with dread.

Walking along the edge of the town, Artemis found herself caught in a whirlwind of internal dialogue, her thoughts consumed by anxiety. Should she approach the city's inhabitants and inquire about her whereabouts, or would such an action be seen as rude or intrusive? Without any understanding of their culture or customs, she felt paralyzed by indecision.

Her gaze drifted to one of the houses, where she spotted a figure standing in the doorway. It seemed to be a person, possibly a woman, but Artemis was struck by the peculiar contraption covering their face, resembling a muzzle. The intensity of the woman's gaze sent shivers down Artemis's spine, causing her feet to falter.

She whispered, "Am I in the Middle East?" Then quickly corrected herself, "No, it can't be—remember, moons and suns."

A surge of fear pulsed through her veins, momentarily freezing her in place. Every instinct urged her to retreat from the unsettling sight, but a small voice within urged her to push forward, to confront her fears and seek answers. With a deep breath, Artemis summoned her courage and took a tentative step forward, readying herself for whatever challenges lay ahead.

"Which city is this?" Artemis murmured aloud to herself, her voice trembling with uncertainty. "It's definitely not Toronto."

She felt a knot of anxiety tightening in her chest as she considered the implications. "What is this place? What in the world is going on here?" She still refused to accept reality, fearing the truth that she might be on another planet or possibly even in a different dimension.

The realization dawned on her with suffocating weight, causing her breath to catch in her throat. A sense of alarm surged through her body, a visceral reaction to the mounting evidence that she was far from home and in a place unlike anything she had ever known. She kept refusing it, fear gripping her tightly. With trembling hands, Artemis sank to her knees, burying her face in her palms as she grappled with the overwhelming uncertainty of her situation.

"Oh my God, what is happening to me?" Artemis exclaimed, her voice echoing in the empty air.

"Why am I here in the middle of nowhere?" Her frustration and confusion threatened to overwhelm her, but amidst the turmoil, a new idea began to take shape in her mind.

"I'm here because I have to uncover the truth, and I need to finish this journey, in case it's my only way back home, I guess," she reasoned aloud, the words bringing a sense of clarity to her thoughts.

"I have to see this adventure through to the end, just like in games. If I can win, maybe I'll be able to return home." She pondered the possibility that she was caught in some sort of elaborate game or mission akin to the plots of children's movies she had seen.

"Perhaps I have a mission here, and I have to solve it," she mused, her resolve strengthening with each passing moment. She began to believe there was a mission or puzzle she had to unravel or conquer. Despite the uncertainty and danger that lay ahead, Artemis felt a newfound sense of determination coursing through her veins. She was beginning to realize the reality of the situation and knew she should take it seriously.

Standing atop the hill, basking in the satisfaction of her newfound resolve, Artemis was momentarily lost in her thoughts until a voice shattered the silence, calling out to her as a stranger. Slowly, she turned her gaze towards the source of the voice, her heart pounding in her chest as she braced herself for what she might encounter.

THE VISITOR BEYOND

"Hello Stranger! Excuse me, miss, but may I inquire as to what brings someone as lovely as yourself to such an inhospitable locale?" The stranger's tone carried a subtle hint of concern, though his words bore an undeniable edge of caution.

Artemis felt a shiver run down her spine as she assessed the situation, taking a cautious step backward. Her gaze flickered nervously over the unfamiliar surroundings.

As Artemis turned to face the source of the voice, her eyes fell upon a skinny figure whose skin appeared strangely translucent, allowing a glimpse of the veins beneath the surface. He seemed frail, almost as if he had endured hardships or struggled with addiction. As he approached her, his words carried a mix of curiosity and concern.

"Hello, stranger," he greeted her once more, his voice tinged with a hint of uncertainty, though his eyes revealed the respect he held for her. He stood before her like a servant, His posture was humble and attentive, a silent display of respect as he stood before her.

"What are you doing here? Are you lost or something?"

As the young man drew closer, Artemis observed his worn-out appearance and tired demeanor. Despite his tough exterior, there was a vulnerability to him that belied his demeanor. His clothes, though cheap, still retained a certain charm, and his ocean-blue eyes held a weariness that spoke of hardships endured. Artemis couldn't shake the feeling of unease as he approached. His intentions seemed unclear, his demeanor alternating between tough and tired. She couldn't discern whether he was looking for trouble or offering assistance. As he drew nearer, Artemis's discomfort grew, unsure of how to interpret his presence.

"You're new here—I can tell by the way you're dressed. What are you doing in this area? Do you know anyone here? Are you visiting someone, or are you lost?" he blurted out then he continued again with a more specific question. Are you lost or looking for someone?

Artemis felt a sense of unease at the stranger's abrupt approach and his keen observation of her attire. She couldn't fathom how he could discern her newness to the area simply from her clothing. Despite her bewilderment, she knew she needed to tread carefully. Artemis was taken aback by the stranger's comment. She glanced down at her own attire, finding it similar to his in many ways. As Artemis studied the stranger more closely, she couldn't help but notice the stark contrast between their respective appearances. While her own attire appeared sturdy and substantial, his clothing seemed almost translucent, as if worn thin by time and hardship. The realization sent a shiver down her spine, raising further questions about the nature of this peculiar encounter.

The stranger's words cut through the air, laden with an unsettling mix of concern and foreboding. "What brings a charming young lady like yourself to this perilous place?" he inquired, his tone tinged with a hint of skepticism.

"I'm afraid you won't find your way out of here," he added ominously, each step bringing him closer to Artemis, his intent unclear.

His sudden grasp sent a shiver down Artemis's spine, her initial fear palpable as she found herself at a loss for words. The stranger's wiry frame belied his forceful grip, and despite her apprehension, she remained uncertain how to react. His confident description of the city stirred a sense of unease within her, planting seeds of doubt about her own perceptions. Despite her trepidation, Artemis chose to conceal her fear, refusing to show any vulnerability in the face of this enigmatic stranger. Artemis's smile masked her growing distrust as she regarded the stranger with a cautious gaze. Instinctively, she sensed that he had ulterior motives, and she harbored no illusions about his intentions. As she mentally assessed her limited possessions—nothing more than the clothes on her back and a pencil tucked away in her pocket, along with the peculiar Levi-tron—

Artemis realized that trouble was the last thing she needed. With a wary resolve, she sought to reason with him, hoping to avoid any potential confrontation.

"Hey! I'm not looking for trouble or anything. I'm just passing through,"

Artemis asserted, her voice steady despite the fear coiled within her chest. She was determined not to let her apprehension show, holding it tightly in check as she addressed the stranger. The guy blocked Artemis's path, standing before her with a scrutinizing gaze. His eyes swept from her head to her toes before he burst into laughter.

"A cute little girl like you wants to stay away from trouble? Are you freaking kidding me? What trouble could you possibly bring me or anyone else?" he scoffed.

Suddenly and with surprising speed, he seized Artemis's arm once more, attempting to push her back. But as he strained to exert force, his face began to redden, then froze in place. Despite his efforts, Artemis felt no pain or discomfort from his grip. It was as if he was unable to apply any real pressure.

"Oh my Lord...!" he exclaimed, startled by the unexpected turn of events.

Artemis initially thought the guy was mocking her, pretending to be unable to push her away. However, as seconds passed, the humor of the situation faded, replaced by a sense of unease. When the guy eventually released her arm and looked at her once more, his demeanor had undergone a complete transformation. His hands trembled with agitation, and his gaze held a newfound respect and dignity as he regarded Artemis.

"Hey, where did you say you came from?" he asked, taking a step back as he addressed Artemis. "And what's your name?"

Artemis scrutinized the guy closely, observing the beads of sweat forming on his forehead. As she took in his appearance from head to toe, she sensed a palpable fear emanating from him. His demeanor had undergone a dramatic transformation, his previously confident facade now replaced by hesitancy and trepidation. Artemis couldn't help but wonder what had triggered this sudden change in him.

Artemis contemplated the situation, considering that the guy might have mistaken her for someone else. However, she recognized the importance of maintaining the facade he perceived.

With this in mind, she met his gaze and replied, "I didn't share my name with you, but I'm curious about yours. What do they call you?"

The man appeared increasingly agitated and apprehensive, his demeanor betraying signs of nervousness as he avoided meeting Artemis's gaze. But for some reason, he looked cheerful with a tremulous voice, he responded, succumbing to a panic-stricken episode.

"My name is Gilbert," he stammered.

Artemis glanced at Gilbert once more, her mind drifting to thoughts of her friends. "I wish Megan, Ricky, Allen, Helen, and especially Matt were here to witness this," she mused inwardly. "I could certainly put a scare into this guy."

She smiled briefly before her concern returned, prompting her to ponder further. "But why is he afraid of me? I've never seen him before, and yet he seems suddenly frightened and apprehensive when he's around me. But if he's scared, why does he also seem oddly happy?"

Meanwhile, Artemis continued to observe Gilbert from the corner of her eye, noting his gradual pallor with each glance. It struck her as peculiar, as she had never encountered such a reaction before in her life. *A man afraid of a woman?* Artemis was typically cautious around others, especially men or teenage boys her age. She was accustomed to being wary of their presence, yet this situation felt different. Despite Gilbert's evident fear, Artemis felt no threat emanating from him. In fact, she found herself strangely comforted by his apprehension.

"Would you be so kind as to tell me your name?" Gilbert asked, his voice barely audible as he addressed Artemis.

Artemis met his gaze with a confident demeanor. "My name is Artemis, and I must admit, I am quite famished," she replied, emphasizing the latter part of her statement and emphasizing her hunger. "And yes, I am indeed very hungry."

Gilbert's discomfort was palpable as he glanced at Artemis once more before hastily pointing towards the city. Without another word, he hurried away, his steps quickening as He headed towards one of the alleys or buildings, almost as if he were running for dear life. He kept looking back, his face a mix of confusion and fear.

"Just go ahead two blocks, then turn right," Gilbert replied, his voice tinged with urgency.

"You'll find a restaurant on your left side. They'll be more than glad to help you and your kind."

Your kind? Isn't that rude? she thought, then turned to him and said, "Are you joking? I thought you were tough and fearless. Look at you, so easily losing your humanity!" Artemis exclaimed.

Gilbert stood up and stared at Artemis for a few seconds, exhaling deeply before speaking again. "I'm not human! I am Rouhar. You are in Flimsy world."

He bellowed out the words, then swiftly turned and ran in the opposite direction, disappearing into a four-story apartment building. Artemis stood there, stunned and bewildered by Gilbert's revelation.

"My kind? Not human? They are Rouhar?" she murmured to herself, her mind racing with questions.

"I've never heard of any Flimsy world, race, or country—especially Rouhar. Perhaps I need to delve deeper into history or geography." She paused again and said, "Not human? What does that mean?"

Artemis surveyed the road ahead, which stretched straight toward a bridge leading into the city. Alongside the bridge, graffiti adorned the walls, adding to the urban decay. She noticed a group of guys congregating near a barrel, some seated on the steps of dilapidated townhouses. The scene unsettled Artemis; the group exuded an air of menace, their eyes scanning passersby with a mix of curiosity and hostility.

Desperate to avoid any confrontation, Artemis tried to ignore them, quickening her pace. However, their attention was drawn to her, their eyes lingering on her with an unsettling intensity. Artemis, accustomed to drawing attention for her beauty, now found herself uncomfortably aware of the danger it posed in this situation. She pressed on, hoping to pass by unscathed.

She couldn't shake the feeling of responsibility for Gilbert's abrupt departure just moments ago, but now she faced a more immediate threat. The group of individuals before her meant business, and she could feel the tension thickening the air as she approached. Attempting to slip past unnoticed proved futile; their eyes locked onto her, their expressions turning predatory.

As the leader of the group pointed toward his companions, they rose in unison, their movements deliberate and intimidating. Artemis felt a surge of fear coursing through her veins as they flexed their muscles, a silent but unmistakable challenge. She knew she had to tread carefully, but the sense of impending danger left her paralyzed, her heart pounding in her chest.

She cautiously traversed the intimidating encounter with the group, oblivious to Gilbert's discreet surveillance behind her. As she navigated the precarious situation, Gilbert shadowed her every move as if he were hoping to witness some action. His presence cloaked from the probing gazes of the gang members. With a mixture of apprehension and concern, he monitored the unfolding events, fully cognizant of the potential peril confronting Artemis.

Despite his own apprehensions, Gilbert remained watchful, meticulously analyzing the gang's behavior and gauging the extent of the threat they posed. Amidst his conflicting emotions towards

Artemis, a desire to shield her from harm warred or see her reaction with an underlying unease in her presence. Yet, he chose to maintain a cautious distance, patiently awaiting the opportune moment to step in and offer assistance.

Artemis found herself compelled to halt her progress as one of the gang members stepped forward, effectively obstructing her path and preventing her from traversing through their territory. It became evident to her that the gang placed significant emphasis on their collective performance and teamwork, viewing it as essential for bolstering their group's reputation and solidifying their dominance over their territory, particularly in the eyes of outsiders like herself.

Artemis felt a wave of panic wash over her as she scanned the faces of the gang members. One of them, notably shorter than the rest and with translucent skin akin to Gilbert's, rose to his feet. His eyes lacked color, reminiscent of albinos, yet they held a sharpness that belied their appearance. It seemed as though his vision was impeccable, capable of spotting the smallest detail from a considerable distance. Each member of the gang glanced back at him periodically as if seeking his approval or guidance.

As Artemis continued walking, she made the decision to veer across the road, putting some distance between herself and the intimidating group. However, her movements did not go unnoticed. One of the gang members, exceptionally slender and towering above the others, suddenly rose to his feet and pointed directly at Artemis, his gaze fixed intently upon her.

"Hey, little birdie! Why are you crossing the road? That's not how things work around here. You can turn back to where you came from—if we allow it. But I can see that you're mine. Come to me. You're going the wrong way." Laughter erupted among the gang members, echoing through the air with a menacing undertone.

For a moment, Artemis searched for an alternate route to evade the gang, but it soon became apparent that she was out of options. Reluctantly, she continued walking, feeling ill-prepared for the impending confrontation. Unlike her encounter with Gilbert, these individuals seemed altogether more threatening. As they advanced towards her in unison, Artemis felt a surge of distress and alarm.

Uncertain of what lay ahead, she found herself blurting out a response without thinking. "Maybe the little bird wants to prove she's not as chicken as she looks!" Immediately, she regretted her words, realizing the folly of her impulsive retort.

Their previously stern expressions dissolved into fits of laughter, catching Artemis off guard. Some of them even doubled over in mirth, unable to contain their amusement. The abrupt shift from seriousness to levity left Artemis perplexed, unsure of how to interpret their behavior.

However, the moment of laughter was short-lived. In an instant, they all composed themselves and began advancing towards her with synchronized precision. It was as though they moved as one cohesive unit, their movements coordinated with military-like precision. Artemis couldn't help but marvel at their seamless teamwork, even amidst the tension of the situation.

She attempted to make peace with them only seemed to exacerbate the situation, as their intentions became increasingly clear. She felt the weight of the predicament she was in, her mind racing through potential solutions. The thought of Gilbert crossed her mind, igniting a surge of anger and frustration.

Instinctively, she considered fighting back or fleeing, but a sudden weakness in her hand gave her pause. What if they weren't as vulnerable as Gilbert? She ended up in a losing battle? Faced with this dilemma, she opted for the third option which was shielding herself with her hands, preparing for whatever onslaught may come. At that moment, fear gripped her like never before, and Artemis braced herself for the worst.

As the menacing group closed in on Artemis, she couldn't help but yearn for the safety and familiarity of her neighborhood. These were not just unruly teenagers but a gang of hardened criminals, their malicious intent palpable in the air.

Artemis braced herself for the worst as the first assailant brazenly reached out and grabbed her hand, attempting to pull her toward him. But it was like trying to move a mountain—she remained immovable. He looked surprised. Then, another attacker approached, his fingers tangling in her hair, while a third poised to strike. The impending threat of violence loomed over her, and she resigned herself to the possibility of a fatal blow. Attackers looked at each other in surprise and Just when she felt all hope slipping away, a familiar voice shattered the tension, cutting through the air like a beacon of salvation.

"I wouldn't do it if I were you," Gilbert's voice rang out, his tone laced with a firm warning as he stood unwavering in the center of the street, radiating an aura of confidence.

Artemis's relief at Gilbert's arrival was short-lived, as the gang members laughed at him. Despite his warning, they continued advancing towards her. With her hair gripped tightly by one assailant, Artemis braced herself as another delivered a punch to her chest. Overwhelmed by fear, Artemis could barely see what was happening as the gang members began to rain down blows upon her, striking her relentlessly from all sides.

As the gang members examined their hands, now smeared with blood, which trickled steadily from their fingers, they exchanged satisfied glances, assuming it was Artemis's blood. However, their confidence wavered when they saw Artemis unscathed and staring back at them with fear in her eyes. Suddenly, a sharp pain shot through their arms and fingers, and they realized they were the ones injured. Blood flowed from their broken and battered hands, leaving them bewildered and uncertain about what had just happened.

Artemis observed the gang members closely as they grew increasingly confused and angry. Innocently, she noted their actions, including the retrieval of guns and knives from their pockets. Fear coursed through her as she contemplated how to survive this encounter unscathed. In a moment of disbelief, she couldn't help but wonder how they managed to conceal such weapons in their seemingly small pockets.

Artemis tried to identify the weapons pointed at her, but some of them were unfamiliar, unlike any she had seen in the movies. With her hands protecting her face and chest, she braced herself for what she believed would be a more terrifying onslaught. One of them yelled at Artemis and said, "Do you know women here must be owned by a man and cannot walk freely unless she's looking for another owner? A free woman is seen as a slut with no respect. Where's your muzzle? woman?"

However, despite hearing the sound of a few weapons being fired, she felt no impact. Confusion gripped her as she waited for the anticipated pain and damage, but nothing happened. It dawned on her that these individuals weren't simply toying with her; something else was amiss. Their reluctance to act left Artemis puzzled and anxious, wondering why they refrained from unleashing harm upon her. She opened her eyes to look at them, and then she saw Gilbert in the distance, standing tall with confidence. His unexpected presence left her puzzled, adding to the confusion of the situation.

With a mixture of exhaustion and curiosity, Artemis made the decision to uncover her face and assess the situation. Slowly, she parted her fingers and peered at the gang members before her. To her astonishment, she saw a barrage of bullets hurtling towards her, each one seeming to make contact with her skin. Panic seized her as she braced for the worst, her heart pounding in her chest and her hands trembling uncontrollably.

Uncertain whether she was gravely injured or if the gang members were wielding toy guns, Artemis's frustration began to mount. Gingerly, she checked her body for any signs of damage, relieved to find herself unharmed. Glancing at the gang members' faces, she detected a hint of embarrassment or perhaps a distraction.

Though her fear persisted, Artemis found solace in the fact that none of them dared to approach her any closer.

Artemis muttered to herself, trying to reassure her frayed nerves. As she continued to observe the gang members with a mixture of disbelief and apprehension, her primary goal remained clear to extricate herself from their menacing presence unscathed. With each passing moment, she inched away from them, determined to put as much distance between herself and the potential danger they posed.

Artemis turned to face Gilbert's voice, relieved to hear his familiar tone amidst the chaos. With his presence lending her a semblance of confidence, she surveyed the gang members, searching for any signs of hostility. As she met their silent stares, she addressed them directly, acknowledging their territorial claim while asserting her intention to leave without further conflict. As Artemis crawled on her hands and knees, scrambling to her feet and breaking into a run, she couldn't shake the feeling of unease that lingered. Despite her escape, she couldn't help but glance back at the gang members, observing the stark contrast in their demeanor. Where once they had exuded confidence and fearlessness, they now appeared vulnerable and diminished. It was a stark reminder of the unpredictable nature of their behavior and the potential for sudden shifts in power dynamics. With a mixture of relief and caution, Artemis continued on her way, mindful of the dangers that lurked in this unfamiliar cityscape. Artemis hesitated, taking a step backward as she warily assessed the situation. She couldn't shake the nagging suspicion that this might be yet another ploy by the gang members to further taunt her. However, after a moment of deliberation, she resolved to press forward and pass through their midst, determined not to let their intimidation tactics deter her from her path.

Artemis stood her ground, her expression unwavering as she watched the gang leader's futile attempts to harm her. In that pivotal moment, her true power was revealed, a force beyond comprehension or explanation. The bullets meant to inflict harm, were rendered powerless in her presence, flattening upon contact as if deflected by an invisible shield. This display of strength left the gang members stunned and bewildered, their confidence shattered in the face of such inexplicable power. For Artemis, it was a testament to her resilience and inner strength, a reminder that she possessed abilities far beyond the ordinary. As the gang members retreated, their resolve shaken by this undeniable display of power, Artemis remained undaunted. She had faced the ultimate test and emerged unscathed, a beacon of hope in a city shrouded in darkness and uncertainty.

Gilbert, looking so happy, turned to their leader, then glanced at each of them and said, "I told you not to do that."

Gilbert's words sliced through the tension like a knife, carrying with them a weight of warning and reproach. His voice held a mixture of concern and frustration, a clear indication that he had foreseen the potential consequences of the gang's actions. As Artemis glanced at him, she detected a glint of urgency in his eyes, a silent plea for understanding and restraint. For Artemis, Gilbert's admonition served as a sobering reminder of the delicate balance between power and responsibility. It underscored the gravity of her newfound abilities and the need for caution in their use. With a nod of acknowledgment towards Gilbert, Artemis silently vowed to heed his advice and tread carefully in this unfamiliar realm of uncertainty and danger.

Artemis stood in stunned silence, her chest tingling with an eerie sensation as she watched the bullets bounce off her, falling harmlessly and pressed to the ground. Gilbert's words echoed in her mind, a stark reminder of his earlier warning. The surreal nature of the situation left her bewildered and uncertain, struggling to make sense of the inexplicable events unfolding before her. As she looked around at the gang members, their faces a mix of disbelief and fear, Artemis couldn't shake the feeling of unease that gripped her. What had she become? And what did it mean for her future in this strange and unpredictable city? With more questions than answers, Artemis braced herself for the unknown, her resolve tempered by the newfound awareness of her own extraordinary abilities.

The leader's incredulous words reverberated through the group, his confusion mirroring that of his companions. Murmurs of disbelief rippled through the crowd as they struggled to comprehend the inexplicable events unfolding before them. Amidst the chaos, a hushed utterance of "My Lord Allom" escaped from the lips of someone in the rear, a phrase laden with reverence and awe.

Others whispered, "She's a God, like the others." The whispers grew, overlapping as they murmured, "But a girl can't be a God. Being a God is only for men, isn't it?" They looked confused, uncertainty flickering in their eyes.

Sensing the mounting tension, another voice urged the group to seek cover, recognizing the need to retreat from the enigmatic force that now stood before them. With a mixture of fear and uncertainty clouding their expressions, the gang members scrambled to find refuge, their earlier bravado crumbling in the face of this unforeseen and inexplicable phenomenon. Gilbert approached Artemis, standing by her side as he made his observation.

"She's just like Superman in the human world, as we were told, but only younger and female, and she's proven we were wrong. They taught us wrong. The truth is, being a God doesn't belong to a gender," Gilbert remarked, his voice tinged with awe.

"A female human?" echoed the gang members, their voices filled with disbelief as they struggled to comprehend what they were witnessing.

Gilbert looked at Artemis again, his gaze filled with curiosity, and asked, "Are you a human... I mean, a girl human? Are you from Lord Allom?"

Artemis struggled to catch her breath, her heart pounding fiercely in her chest. Her ears were ringing, and her eyes welled with tears. She glanced at the gun, then at the flattened bullets lying on the ground. Turning to Gilbert, she asked in confusion, "What?"

Artemis turned to Gilbert once more, her voice trembling with uncertainty. "What are you talking about? What's going on here? Is this a real gun or just a toy? Because if it's a toy, you've got me, and I'm scared. "And what do you mean by asking if I'm a human? Or if I am from Lord Allom? Isn't that insulting?"

Whispers started, "She is a human, but she doesn't know about Lord Allom. She is not from Lord Allom. She is a new Lord."

As Artemis stood up, causing everyone else to take a step back, clearly wary of her. She felt a trickle running from her right nostril, and when she dabbed at it, her hand came back with blood. Still panting heavily, she turned around to take another look at the gang. Judging by their expressions, they seemed more scared of Artemis than she was of them. Despite her anger, she couldn't shake the feeling that if they had the chance, what they would do to her. But why hadn't they? Artemis stood there, pointing at them with anger etched on her face. She demanded answers.

"What is going on here? I want to know the truth right now. Tell me what just happened?" She repeated her question, her voice firm and unwavering.

"Are these toy guns?" Artemis questioned, her tone incredulous yet tinged with a hint of desperation.

"You wanted to kill me with a toy gun or are they real? What have I done to you to deserve to die?" Her words hung heavy in the air, demanding an explanation from the bewildered gang members.

Artemis's anger boiled over as she bent down to pick up one of the flattened bullets from the ground. Gripping it between her fingers, she examined it closely, feeling the softness of the metal. With a mixture of annoyance and fury, she clenched her fist, flattening the bullet further as if it were nothing more than pliable tin foil. The disrespectful act had ignited a fire within her, fueling her determination to uncover the truth behind this baffling situation.

Artemis cast a piercing gaze at Gilbert, who stood proudly beside her, before turning her attention to the crowd who had attempted to harm her. With a voice filled with righteous indignation, she addressed them sternly.

"If you didn't already know, I have a moral compass, and I am infuriated. I am utterly fed up with all of you. Your behavior is despicable, barbaric, and utterly bloodthirsty. Your cruel actions are not acceptable to me or anyone else. They are inhumane. I am sick and tired of your twisted attitudes." She stepped closer to one of the gang members, yanked the gun from his hand, and, fueled by anger, folded it before throwing it to the ground. The gang members took a step back, visibly startled.

Artemis turned to Gilbert, who was nodding in admiration as she addressed the gang, her voice suddenly filled with urgency as she asked, "You're not human? What does that mean?"

"It means you're not on Earth, and we are not human. As I told you, my Lord, we are Rouhar, but the Lord before you called us Flimsy because we are like paper, so fragile compared to humans," Gilbert answered quietly.

Artemis stared at Gilbert, then she turned to gangs and seized the leader's gun, wresting it from his hand without hesitation. Gripping it tightly, her anger boiled over, and with a forceful motion, she slammed it into the ground. The impact was thunderous, echoing through the air as the gun disappeared into the ground, leaving behind a deep hole shrouded in dust. All eyes turned to Artemis in astonishment, their gazes shifting between her and the gaping cavity in the ground. Artemis herself stared at the scene, incredulous at her own actions.

She laughed triumphantly, turning to Gilbert with a grin. "Did you see that? You never know how deep that toy gun went, right...?"

Crossing her arms, she spoke with a newfound confidence. "I'm starting to like it here."

Gilbert, who had remained somewhat wary of Artemis, cautiously closed the distance between them and asked, "I know you would, but you didn't answer my question. Are you really a human?"

Artemis was about to respond to Gilbert when she turned to face him. Bathed in the sunlight, he glowed like glass, his organs faintly visible. She stared at him, speechless and stunned. Slowly, almost mechanically, she managed to say, "Yes." Then she turned to the group standing in the sunlight, noticing they all looked like Gilbert. She glanced back at him and asked, "Do you see your organs or other people's organs too?"

Gilbert wasn't surprised, as though he had been asked the same question before. He looked at Artemis and respectfully answered, "No, my Lord. Only humans have that ability."

She couldn't believe what she was witnessing. As the reality of her situation sank in, she pivoted back to face the leader, her tone firm and unwavering. "You think you're funny, don't you? Well, let me enlighten you about your little stunt, buddy. It fell flat. Not a chuckle in sight. Do you see me laughing? Ha... ha!"

Quaking before the wrathful Artemis, they seemed like they could be plucked up one by one and flung far from the scene. With a voice seething with anger, Artemis demanded another question, "What's your name?"

Cowering on his knees, the leader shielded his head with trembling hands. He spoke with a start, pleading, "Please, don't hurt me! I'll tell you. My name is Ugh."

Artemis lightly tapped his shoulder with her index finger, playfully poking him, intending to speak, but couldn't believe her eyes as she surveyed the aftermath of that seemingly simple touch. She was stunned by the profound impact it had on Ugh's shoulder, leaving her momentarily speechless. He had been launched into the air, now lying sprawled across the sidewalk with blood pooling beneath him. The once defiant gang members, now terrified, scattered in fear, scrambling for refuge from Artemis's newfound and unexplained power. She held her hands up, examining them as if expecting to find some clue to her newfound abilities. The sight of Ugh's injuries shook her to the core. She hadn't intended to hurt him with just a touch, yet there he was—bleeding profusely, writhing in pain. The overwhelming realization of what she had done left her trembling, unsure of how to control this power that now seemed to reside within her.

Despite her initial disbelief, Artemis couldn't deny the reality of the situation. This wasn't some elaborate prank or game—they were dealing with real consequences. With each passing moment, the world seemed to spiral further into chaos, leaving Artemis feeling overwhelmed by the weight of it all. Artemis was engrossed in trying to unravel the mystery before her, but it was like navigating through a labyrinth. The gravity of the situation hit her hard - these people were not jesting or putting on a show; their intentions were alarmingly real. Just as she was grappling with the gravity of it all, Artemis was jolted by Gilbert's voice coming from behind.

"Are you... a... human or someone above human—Superman they were talking about? Cause you are more strong than others?" Gilbert's voice trembled with fear as he whispered the question.

Artemis turned to find him standing there, an air of gentlemanly concern about him. She regarded him with impatience; these inquiries seemed utterly irrelevant. Even as the truth stared her in the face, she struggled to accept it, perhaps trying to convince herself that it wasn't real. Despite the clear evidence, she remained in a state of denial, grappling with the reality of what she was witnessing. Finally, she answered. "Are you joking? Of course, I am. I already told you my answer?" she retorted, her tone reflecting both irritation and disbelief.

She glanced at each person in turn, her expression incredulous. "What? Why are you staring at me?"

They all met her gaze and responded in unison, shaking their heads slowly from side to side. "No... no," they murmured, their voices filled with uncertainty.

Feeling a sense of relief, Gilbert found it easier to approach Artemis despite her evident distress. Drawing closer, he began, "I mentioned before that I'm not human, but you are. Although I referred to myself as a 'flimsy' guy like everyone else here, I recognized your mannerisms from my past experiences. I've shaken hands with others before, just like I did with you and my hand was unresponsive for hours because of the pressure on my hand, and that's when I realized you're a human." He paused before continuing, "The only difference is that you're the first female human to arrive here, and you're more powerful than the others. We always believed the gods were only men. In fact, everyone thought gods were male. But on your planet, are females more powerful than men?"

Gilbert took a moment to compose himself, inhaling and exhaling deeply before continuing with renewed enthusiasm. "Humans are powerful, almighty, forceful, and intelligent," he remarked then he added, "but females are super. You're impervious to our most potent weapons. I've witnessed them standing in the face of missiles and emerging unscathed."

Gilbert paused for a moment, observing Artemis's reaction before continuing. "I witnessed something extraordinary today—I saw a superman—or rather, a superwoman. Everything that has unfolded has convinced me that we don't just have a hero among us. We have the best of all—a supergirl. Wow!"

Artemis gazed at Gilbert in disbelief, her voice taking on a robotic tone as she repeated, "Supergirl, superwoman! Yes, I like it. But how do you know I'm a girl if you've never seen a girl human?"

Gilbert offered a reassuring smile and replied, "Well! I've actually never seen one, but our women are like human women. They have breasts, with gorgeous faces and beautiful bodies."

Master Ugh managed to sit down sideways, still leaning on the wall for support, as he directed a surprised query to Gilbert, "But just now, you said you could recognize her because you've seen one before?"

Laughter erupted among the group as they eagerly awaited Gilbert's response. With a gleam of excitement in his eyes, Gilbert turned to Artemis and explained, "I'm sorry. My dad always told us stories about mighty men supermen, and how they saved the day. I always wished to see one of you guys and I did. That's the reason from the moment I saw you, I believed all the stories about humans. I could see the differences immediately. I knew you're not a flimsy and you are a human girl."

Artemis interrupted him in the midst of his explanation, her face radiant with excitement. "Wow… wow. You mean there are others like me?"

"Of course there are!" Gilbert replied. After a brief pause, he continued, "There were so many humans before you, even before my grandfather was born. But I've only seen two like you. One was taller and more muscular, while the other was slim yet powerful, and… well, unstoppable, forceful, but…"

Interrupting him, the group chimed in unison, "Oh… shut up."

Master Ugh rested his head against the wall and pointed at Gilbert once more. "I'm getting angry at this nonsense. He just said he saw two superheroes. Have you seen a superhero or not? I'm confused!"

At that moment, all eyes were on Artemis. Her gaze widened, her eyes tinged with a hint of red. A sudden hush fell over the crowd as they fixated on her. Artemis, typically a reserved girl despite her prowess on the skating rink and in academics, felt a wave of discomfort wash over her as she met the gaze of those around her. These looks were different from the usual attention she received; they carried a weight of expectation as if the onlookers were hopeful witnesses to a superhero in their midst. Artemis sensed their need for her help, and a flicker of hope illuminated their eyes.

She shifted her gaze back to Gilbert, hoping to divert attention away from herself as a superhero, a title she didn't feel worthy of. Instead, she was curious about the others like her. Thoughts of her father lingered in her mind as she posed the question, "Where are they right now?"

Artemis's mind raced with possibilities and concerns as she awaited Gilbert's response. If her father was indeed trapped in this unfamiliar place, it would explain the communication blackout from home. Despite the ominous implications, the thought of her father's presence also provided a glimmer of hope. With both of them here, they could collaborate and strategize on how to navigate this mysterious situation. Perhaps together, they could uncover a solution and find a way back to their loved ones. The prospect of reuniting with her family filled Artemis with a sense of determination and resolve, anchoring her amidst the uncertainty surrounding her current predicament.

Artemis felt the weight of everyone's expectations resting on her shoulders. She was now the focal point of their hopes, their aspirations for salvation. Despite the pressure, she remained steadfast, her resolve unwavering. Turning to face Master Ugh and then to Gilbert, she said firmly,

"We'll find them. With your help, together. Can I count on you guys? I mean, if you know anything about them, you'll tell me, right?"

The group exchanged glances before scattering in different directions, murmuring, "Yes... yes... yes."

Gilbert stepped closer to Artemis and softly said, "I'll help you if you let me."

With those words, Artemis pledged to embark on a journey not just for her own sake but for the countless others who found themselves trapped in this enigmatic realm. She understood the magnitude of the task ahead, but she was determined to rise to the challenge, fueled by the strength of her convictions and the collective resolve of those around her.

Oppressive heat and suffocating humidity weighed heavily upon her, sapping her energy and leaving her feeling drained. With furrowed brows and a troubled expression, she raised a hand to shield her eyes from the glare while the other instinctively rose to shield her face from the relentless onslaught of sunlight.

In that moment, the physical discomfort mirrored her inner turmoil and weariness. Despite her determination, the challenges ahead seemed daunting, and the uncertainty of their journey weighed heavily on her mind. Yet, even in the face of adversity, Artemis remained resolute, steeling herself for the trials that lay ahead.

Artemis turned to Gilbert, her eyes reflecting a mixture of hope and desperation as she posed her question, "Can you help me find them?"

Gilbert's expressions were marked by surprise and curiosity while his gaze shifted briefly to the others before returning to Artemis, a warm smile gracing his lips. It was a question he had longed to hear, a chance to embark on an adventure that held the promise of discovery and perhaps even redemption.

"I'll help you," he replied, his voice tinged with optimism. "We can try to find them, but I must warn you, it's not guaranteed."

Despite the uncertainty that lay ahead, Artemis felt a surge of gratitude towards Gilbert. In him, she found a companion willing to venture into the unknown alongside her, offering support and guidance as they navigated the treacherous path ahead. With a nod of determination, he accepted her offer, ready to embark on their quest together.

He paused for a moment, his expression thoughtful, before adding, "I will help you. It has been my dream to see a superhero with my own eyes, but I never imagined I would have the opportunity to walk side by side with one." Gilbert's eyes sparkled with a mixture of amusement and pleasure as he spoke.

Then he murmured, "My wish came true, but I could've wished for wealth. Ahhhhhh, no—this one is better."

This delightful moment meant the world to Gilbert, filling his heart with pure joy. The opportunity to investigate and conduct research alongside a superhero not only fueled his passion but also forged a deep and lasting friendship between them. However, for the rest of the gang, it was a complete disaster—a harsh blow to their pride. They were forced to smile, speak politely, and maintain a positive attitude with Artemis—an act that felt utterly demeaning to them.

Artemis, knowing that Gilbert would be loyal to her, put on a smile and tried to rest a hand on his shoulder to show their friendship. She knew this gesture would mean a lot to Gilbert. However, to her surprise, he ran to the other side. Realizing the unintended harm she might have caused, Artemis quickly became aware of the potential damage and apologized sincerely.

Artemis nodded a solemn expression on her face. "I'll be more cautious next time, I promise," she said to Gilbert.

She took a deep breath and said, "I need to know where they were spotted most often—maybe even where they lived. Can you tell me their last known location before they disappeared, or share any insider stories? There must be reports—articles in magazines, newspapers, or maybe even pictures. Any advice on how I can access that information would be incredibly helpful."

Artemis caught her breath, turned to Gilbert, and asked, "Can you help me get to know the town too?"

Feeling tired and hungry, she longed for a shower and some quality sleep. Her energy was low, and she needed a boost. Not wanting to waste any more time, she asked Gilbert about nearby restaurants. She admitted she had no money but needed to eat and find a place to rest. "How can I get those?" she asked.

Gilbert smiled, his usual innocent enthusiasm shining through as he responded, "Yes, I'll be more than glad to help you. My father once assisted one of your kind, and according to him, the superman was huge and incredibly strong. I'm grateful to be assigned by you, and I want to thank you for that. It's amazingly awesome."

Artemis looked at him doubtfully, noticing that his stories about meeting superheroes seemed different each time. However, she didn't want to make him uncomfortable for as long as he was helping her, so she let it slide.

"What was his name?" asked Artemis.

"His name was Lord Leo," Gilbert replied, his pride evident as he explained everything passionately.

Artemis paused for a moment, her mind grappling with Gilbert's response. Then, she came up with another question, "Is this his real name or is it a nickname?"

"I really don't know." Gilbert's eyes remained fixed on Artemis as he described Lord Leo, but Artemis's gaze seemed distant, lost in thought.

With a mysterious expression, Gilbert slowly turned his face away, his voice low as he replied, "I think they all knew each other, but they just didn't want to admit it."

"Why do you think that?" she asked, her curiosity piqued.

"I don't know for sure," Gilbert admitted, "but it felt that way—the way they act."

Gilbert turned his eyes toward Artemis, seeking her reaction, before continuing. "You know, my father was honored by the president, and he gained so much respect from our people because of them."

Artemis remained silent, attentively listening to Gilbert's words and eager to learn more about the information he possessed. Slowly, she turned her gaze to him, formulating her questions carefully.

"How did your father assist a superman?" she inquired. "Or rather, why would a superman require aid if he was supposedly indestructible? What happened to him physically? Did something occur that rendered him vulnerable and in need of assistance? It doesn't quite add up to me. Where is your father? What happened to him?"

Gilbert recounted the moment with pride, describing how his father had witnessed the unprecedented sight of Lord Leo bleeding. "My father offered him water, and he actually accepted it. And look at us now—I'm helping you get to know the city or do research to find other supers, taking you to a good restaurant, and so much more," he added with a hint of pride.

"Ah, now I understand what you mean," she said with a nod.

Gilbert continued, his gaze fixed on Artemis. Despite his pride, Gilbert seemed to be growing anxious, evident in his tightly clasped hands and tense posture. However, to his surprise, Artemis appeared engrossed in his narrative, her attention fully captivated by his words. Gilbert pressed on with his tale, elaborating, "Lord Leo required rest and medical attention for his wound. My father provided him with care until he had fully recovered."

"So... there's a possibility we could get hurt?" she asked, her voice heavy with a hint of depression.

"Only from other Lords. They have something that can hurt each other easily," Gilbert added.

"Nothing here can hurt us, then... could they have brought something from Earth?" she wondered aloud, lost in her thoughts.

Artemis's sweet voice carried her question to Gilbert's ears, but it seemed to strike a chord of sadness within him. His gaze shifted away, and a flicker of emotion passed over his features. For a moment, he remained silent, grappling with the weight of her inquiry. Then, with a heavy heart, he gestured toward the road ahead, wordlessly indicating their next steps. Artemis understood his unspoken response, recognizing the pain behind it, and refrained from pressing further.

Artemis stood her ground, surveying each member of the gang with a mixture of caution and resolve. Despite the urge to apologize for the chaos, she couldn't forget their earlier intent to harm her. With a steady gaze, she addressed Master Ugh directly.

"You should be ashamed of yourselves," Artemis began, her voice firm and unwavering.

"I'm deeply disappointed in all of you. If I catch wind of any further trouble-making, harassment, or nuisance directed at the citizens of this town, rest assured, I'll take action. Consider this your warning. Next time, I won't be so lenient."

Artemis felt a surge of satisfaction as she turned to Gilbert, casually resting her arm on his shoulder. But her moment of triumph was interrupted by Gilbert's sudden cry of pain.

"Ouch!" he exclaimed, his voice filled with agony as he fell to the sidewalk, his gaze fixed on Artemis.

Realizing her mistake once more, Artemis attempted to help Gilbert up again, but her strength inadvertently sent him flying to the other side of the street, eliciting laughter from the watching gang members. Their amusement quickly turned to silence when they noticed the anger in Artemis's eyes as she turned her gaze towards them.

As she rushed to Gilbert's side, Artemis saw the purple marks left on his arm from her grip, a stark reminder of her own overpowering strength. With Gilbert unconscious and covered in blood, Artemis felt a wave of panic wash over her. Unsure of what to do next, she sat down beside him, feeling utterly lost.

Artemis's attention shifted to Gilbert's body, and to her surprise, she could see all his bones and internal organs, none of which appeared to be broken. After a few tense moments, Gilbert slowly opened his eyes and began to regain his senses. Turning to Artemis, he managed a weak smile and said, "Watch out, my friend. I'm like paper to you."

She couldn't contain her excitement, blurting out as soon as Gilbert opened his eyes, "Hey! When I focused on your body, I could see all your organs and bones." However, Gilbert's response was unexpected as he went unconscious again, though only for a few seconds this time. Concerned, Artemis gently held Gilbert's hand and helped him sit down, but Gilbert began to whine and complain of pain even louder.

Artemis placed her hands on Gilbert's back very softly and, offering support, and apologized, saying, "I'm sorry. I'm sorry. I don't know how to hold you! But the good news is that nothing in your body is broken or damaged, I checked them all."

Artemis turned to one of the gang members and inquired, "What is your name?"

"My name is Ron, sir… my Lord," he answered back promptly, his voice breaking slightly.

Artemis pointed at Gilbert and instructed Ron, "Help him. He needs attention. Hurry up!"

She hesitated, fearing that her attempts to help Gilbert might worsen his condition. That's why she refrained from touching him any further.

Gilbert opened his eyes again and looked at Artemis proudly. "I'm okay," he assured her.

"Just give me a few minutes to put myself together." Artemis nodded in relief, and in no time, they were ready to head into the city.

As they embarked on their journey, Gilbert couldn't help but notice the surprised expressions of the onlookers.

With a hint of defiance in his gaze, he directed his eyes towards Artemis and then gestured subtly to the others, silently conveying, "She chose me! Just remember that. You can go back to your pathetic life now."

Gilbert strode past Master Ugh and his cohorts with purpose, deliberately avoiding any direct eye contact. As he was passing by, Master Ugh said, "Does she know about you? "And what had your father done?" Master Ugh said to Gilbert, his tone dripping with suspicion."

Gilbert glanced at Artemis, who was in the distance and ignored him, and once he felt they were at a safe distance, he turned to them and asserted firmly, "Couldn't you hear her? Now back off."

Artemis sensed Gilbert's emotional state. Instead, she followed his lead, recognizing that it was time to depart. Gilbert's smile and eager demeanor signaled his readiness to accompany her, and Artemis reciprocated with a reassuring smile of her own. Together, they made their way down the road, leaving behind the curious onlookers and the mysteries that lingered in their wake.

As they left the gang members and their territory behind, making their way down a steep hill, they walked along a road lined with wild berries in a color Artemis couldn't quite recognize. Gilbert kept describing the vegetation, the fruits, and the nature around them, eagerly pointing out everything they passed.

Artemis held a flower with a color she had never seen on Earth and asked, "What color is this?"

Without hesitation, Gilbert replied, "It's red."

Artemis, picking up another red flower, said, "No, no, no. This is red, not that one. We don't have that color on Earth. It's beautiful."

Confused, Gilbert examined both flowers and said, "But they're both red, no difference."

Surprised, Artemis looked at him and said, "I think there are a lot of colors here, but Flimsy's can't tell them apart."

Gilbert ignored the flowers and their color and continued, "Isn't this a beautiful sight!" he exclaimed. After a brief pause, he realized he might be talking too much, worried that she could be tired of hearing him. "I talk too much." He fell silent.

Artemis smiled, appreciating Gilbert's thoughtfulness, even though she wasn't actually tired of his talking. "Oh, you can talk as much as you like. I actually enjoy learning more about your world," she assured him warmly.

Her words put a smile on Gilbert's face and as they traversed the remaining miles to the renowned restaurant, the slender man continued to chat incessantly about the picturesque scenery. At one juncture, they passed through an archway adorned with fragrant jasmine blossoms, their sweet scent filling the air and adding to the charm of the journey.

Gilbert regaled Artemis with tales of their history in the flimsy world, detailing the city's laws, weather patterns, natural surroundings, and seasonal changes. Artemis listened attentively as they strolled along the bustling city streets, passing crowded coffee bars and cafes where it appeared as though no one had homes to return to. For Artemis, being among them again felt comforting and familiar.

Artemis inquired, "What part of Earth is your city located in?" Her tone carried a hint of suspicion as if she were trying to confirm it wasn't Earth or catch him in a lie.

Gilbert regarded her with a soft expression, not surprised by her question. He replied, "Nowhere, my Lord. Flimsy is not even close to your home or planet, as we've discussed."

"What do you mean... nowhere? How can you possibly know that your home is not even close to Earth? How can you be sure about that? What do you know about Earth?" Artemis asked, her voice tinged with desperation and fear. She didn't want to hear Gilbert's answer because she knew it would frighten her. She was struggling to accept the reality; after all, she knew there was only one moon around Earth, not three.

"I mean, clearly, this is not Earth!" Gilbert blurted out.

"If it's not Earth, then what is this place?" she asked, her voice filled with curiosity and a touch of unease.

Gilbert glanced at her and said, "This place and planet is called Zamin11."

Artemis knew Gilbert wasn't trying to deceive or fool her, But she also realized she had no clear memory of how she had arrived here. While she vividly remembered her friends and her birthday night, the details of how she ended up in this place were hazy, as if fragments of her journey were missing or shrouded in mystery. The question loomed, "If it's not Earth, what is this place?" How could she return to her family on Earth? And the bigger question, "How did she manage to travel here?" She fell silent for a couple of seconds, her mind racing in search of answers to the mystery surrounding her situation.

She tried to rephrase her question, "Do you happen to know how the others got here?"

Gilbert looked at her, his expression a mix of concern and confusion as he tried to remember anything that might be helpful for Artemis. But there was nothing. Artemis's desire to see her father was consuming her thoughts more than ever and fear gripped her heart. Alongside that fear, however, was a deep curiosity about her father's appearance at an older age. Despite being a little girl when she last saw him, she remembered him vividly, retaining every detail of his face and their time together.

"Oh... this world is nothing like Earth, not even replicas," Artemis mused aloud as they arrived at the restaurant of Gilbert's choice. It was neither good nor bad, but certainly interesting. The interior was adorned with stucco to create a consistent aesthetic. Artemis found herself intently studying the drawings on the walls. From the artwork, it was clear that the owner must either be an artist or an admirer of art. Among the many paintings, one in particular caught Artemis's attention. It depicted a man of astonishing power and striking handsomeness, effortlessly controlling a tornado as tall and big as Everest mountain. The image portrayed him as both caring and mighty, with a sense of calm authority. But as Artemis continued to gaze at the drawing, she began to see something more, her father's face seemed to emerge from the lines and strokes of the artwork.

Her heart began to race with apprehension as she whispered, "I don't know whether to hope that the man in the picture is truly my father or if it's merely a coincidence."

Gilbert was talking to a wait staff, then walked over to Artemis and said, "The table will be ready in a moment."

Artemis glanced at the picture on the wall and asked, "Who is that? Is he one of the supers? What's his name?"

Gilbert looked at the picture and replied, "He was one of the heroes. His name was *Baerion.* He was one of the best." Then added,

"He disappeared too, like the others. All of them are missing... except Lord Demah."

Customers and wait staff stared at Artemis, visibly upset by the sight of a woman in the restaurant. Women weren't allowed to be seen in public, and soon, complaints began to rise.

"How dare they bring a woman into this restaurant?" they muttered, their voices laced with indignation.

As they approached an empty table, Gilbert gestured towards it, interrupting Artemis's contemplation of the wall drawings. The enticing aroma of food intensified her hunger, and she eagerly stepped towards the table. However, her attention remained fixated on the captivating artwork adorning the walls. Though beautiful and creatively crafted, Artemis couldn't ignore the discomfort of her wobbly chair, fearing she might topple over at any moment. Glancing at Gilbert, she hoped he understood her silent plea for assistance.

Gilbert looked at Artemis, then at the waiter, who came instantly. Gilbert explained about the chair, "She is exceptional and needs a special chair, if you know what I mean. Hurry up because she is very hungry."

The waiter looked at Artemis and said, "She is human?" At that instant, he hurried into the kitchen to inform the owner and staff about the presence of a human. But, before leaving the table, he gestured to another waiter to take their order.

As the word "human" echoed through the restaurant, now, all eyes turned toward Artemis, intensifying her discomfort. With a gentle yet firm tone, she addressed the curious onlookers, "Please, go back to your dinner and don't mind me. Thanks."

Her words were met with hesitation, making the customers angry. One stood up and said, "It doesn't matter if she's from Flimsy or a human. She is a woman, and she is not allowed here or in public. She must leave instantly."

Gilbert glared at the customer and retorted, "If you don't want to see a woman here, why don't you ask her to leave yourself? Go ahead, tell a human girl to leave if you have the nerve."

Gilbert turned to Artemis and said, "They have no respect for women here. It's up to you to show them otherwise."

The customer stood beside Artemis and demanded she leave the restaurant. Artemis glanced at Gilbert and his suggestion, then straightened up, locking eyes with the customer. "Do you want me to puff you out of here?" she asked, her voice steady. "Go back to your table—I'm very hungry, and I just gave Mr. Ugh and his gang a good lesson."

As soon as he heard Mr. Ugh's name and she punished him, the man's expression changed. He quickly returned to his seat and quietly resumed eating without another word.

Other customers nodded as soon as they heard a human and witnessed Artemis answer to that customer. All the diners returned their attention to their meals, allowing Artemis a moment of respite from their curious stares. When Artemis looked at Gilbert, giving her two thumbs up, she felt a wave of relief and happiness wash over her.

Later on, customers recognized her as gracious and polite, their conversations subtly shifting away from her presence. However, even as they resumed their discussions, Artemis sensed lingering glances and whispers directed her way. Despite their attempts to be discreet, she could feel the weight of their scrutiny, leaving her feeling uneasy and distressed.

The second waiter initially smiled, but as soon as his eyes met Artemis's, the smile faded, replaced by a forced expression. His hands trembled as he took down Gilbert's order, and he quickly assured them, "Yes, sir. I'll bring you the special chair in a minute," before darting into the kitchen. The waiter left, walking backward and bowing slightly toward Artemis as he exited.

Artemis chuckled, then turned to Gilbert with a hint of incredulity in her voice. "That was a lot of food you ordered, don't you think?"

Gilbert responded with a confident smile. "Believe me when I say the quality of our food is like us to you. That's why you need even more."

Artemis looked at him in disbelief and retorted, "I know my limit and my stomach capacity."

Gilbert maintained his smile as he offered an explanation. "The food here is too light for you guys. You need to eat more to ensure you get enough energy for your body."

The waiter returned promptly, accompanied by two sturdy individuals carrying a heavy armchair. With the grace of athletes, they replaced Artemis's chair with a new one crafted from top-notch, handmade wood. The new chair boasted intricate details on its handles and legs. The fabric, a beautiful blend of green and gold, was custom-made to Artemis's taste, resembling a chair fit for royalty.

As the chair was replaced, a wave of excitement rippled through the restaurant. Customers marveled at Artemis's special chair, and the atmosphere shifted from one of wonder to one of respect and admiration.

The towering figure rose from his seat with a warm smile, straightening his attire before clearing his throat in preparation to speak.

"Hello, my name is Khorram, and I'm one of the owners," he began, addressing Artemis with genuine hospitality. "My wife and I are delighted to welcome you to our humble establishment."

At this point, he gestured towards the kitchen door, where a woman stood, her mouth obscured by what seemed to be a muzzle. Despite this, a warm smile reached the owner's eyes as he acknowledged Artemis. He motioned to his wife, signaling her to come and greet their guest. Without hesitation, the owner's wife approached their table with a warm smile., extending a gracious welcome to Artemis. Her demeanor exuded politeness and refinement, suggesting a well-educated background.

"Good evening. Thank you for choosing our restaurant," she began, her tone respectful and welcoming. "My name is Mary, and please feel free to order anything from the menu that appeals to you. It's all on the house, and we sincerely appreciate your patronage."

Artemis nodded in appreciation of Mary's kindness, feeling welcomed and valued as a guest.

At that moment, the same customer who had previously asked Artemis to leave and stood up to complain about the owner's wife.

"Why is she here? Now we have to deal with another woman, all because of a human girl?" he complained, his voice filled with frustration.

As the customer approached Artemis and Mary, his anger palpable, Artemis watched in shock as he launched into a tirade, demeaning Mary and asserting that she belonged behind walls, unfit to speak or act. His aggression escalated as he made a threatening move towards Mary.

Reacting swiftly, Artemis stepped in front of Mary, positioning herself as a shield between the aggressor and his target. Before she could fully comprehend the situation, the customer's fist collided with her chest. In the blink of an eye, he recoiled in agony, clutching his injured hand and accusing Artemis of breaking it. Despite the pain shooting through her, Artemis remained composed, her mind racing with the realization of her newfound strength and the responsibility it entailed. She glanced at Mary, ensuring her safety, before turning her attention back to the disgruntled customer, her resolve firm. Artemis's smile remained unfazed as she locked eyes with him, her expression calm but laced with anger.

She responded firmly, "Did I?"

Her words seemed to catch the customer off guard. His face flushed with embarrassment from his outburst. He met Artemis's gaze, his voice lowering as he attempted to justify his behavior, trying to reason with Artemis by saying, "I wasn't trying to cause trouble. It's just... the rules here, you know? We don't allow women in public like this. I was only following what we've always known. She is female, and she mustn't speak in public. She is not allowed."

Artemis held her gaze steadily, her tone unwavering as she countered, "I'm a female too, and I talk anytime I feel like it." Her assertion hung in the air, leaving everyone present taken aback by her confidence and defiance against societal norms.

"But you're human, not Rouhar or, as other humans say, Flimsy," the guy retorted, his frustration evident as he tried to defend his stance, attempting to rationalize his prejudice.

Artemis's anger flared at his disrespectful attitude towards Mary and women in general. Pointing towards the entrance door, she issued a stern ultimatum, then she stood tall, her voice firm as she addressed the complaining customer. "I remember a story my mother used to read to me when I was a little girl. Now! If you don't go back to your seat or don't leave this place immediately, I'll huff, and I'll puff, and I'll blow you out of this house! Leave the restaurant immediately, or face the consequences," she declared, feeling incredibly empowered, her gaze unwavering.

"You have no business here anymore. If you can't respect others, especially females, I suggest you leave before you see me angry. And you don't want to see me angry. Do you? "You don't want to test me."

As Artemis spoke, the man's demeanor shifted dramatically. He began to writhe in apparent agony, screaming and pleading for the burning sensation to stop. Confusion and concern etched across Artemis's face as she turned to Gilbert for answers, asking, "What's happening?"

She found out that every body got away from her. Gilbert's quick reaction surprised Artemis, but she followed his lead, taking a deep breath to calm herself before meeting his gaze. She listened intently as Mary explained the situation, mentioning something about

Artemis's eyes and body temperature having the ability to cause harm when she was angry. If she stayed angry, she had the power to burn anything around her, much like other individuals in their world.

Artemis felt a wave of disbelief wash over her as she processed Mary's words. She turned to Gilbert, seeking reassurance and clarification.

"What just happened? I didn't burn that guy's face! Did I?" she asked, her voice tinged with concern and confusion.

As the commotion settled and the crowd dispersed, leaving behind whispers of the superhero in their midst, Artemis turned to Gilbert with a furrowed brow. The customer bolted, running out of the restaurant without looking back.

Khorram looked proudly at Artemis and said, "You handled that well. It seems they're starting to understand who they're dealing with.

Then he continued, "We weren't prepared for this incredible incident tonight, but as always, we are most honored to have you here, and we are very familiar with your needs and food requests. I've immediately prepared your favorite dish. With your permission, I'll return to the kitchen, but please be careful when you pull your chair to sit on it." With that, He hurried back into the kitchen, with Mary following closely behind.

"Why are they treating me so kindly? I don't even have money to pay for the food, yet they offer it to me with such honor and happiness," Artemis pondered aloud, perplexed by the generosity she had encountered.

Gilbert's smile was gentle as he responded, "My dear, they love you. To them, you are everything. And to us as well. You don't realize how long we've prayed for the return of a God." His words carried a weight of reverence and gratitude, underscoring the depth of admiration and hope that Artemis's presence had brought to their lives.

Artemis's frustration boiled over as she vented her exasperation. "Listen! I woke up in the middle of nowhere with no food, no water and had to sleep on rocks. Then out of nowhere, I become a superhero? And now they're all so happy to offer me food and even gave me a special chair???? What's going on here? Are all these people crazy or what?" Her words echoed with frustration and confusion, expressing the overwhelming sense of bewilderment she felt at the sudden turn of events and the inexplicable adoration she now received.

Artemis's mood shifted as soon as she laid eyes on the food, her complaints fading into the background as hunger took precedence. Almost involuntarily, a big smile spread across her face as she eagerly approached the table. Standing up, she inquired about the location of the washrooms to clean and wash her hands. Gilbert, ever respectful, gestured in the direction and addressed her as "my Lord."

Artemis chuckled softly at his formality and, with a playful smile, whispered back, "My Lord." then gently requested, "Thanks, Gilbert, but would you call me Artemis?" Her request carried a sense of familiarity and camaraderie, signaling her desire to be treated as a peer rather than a deity.

Gilbert looked at her and very politely answered, "No, I can't, my Lord."

Artemis's brief moment of embarrassment quickly turned to amusement as she encountered an unexpected situation at the washroom door. With a startled exclamation, she chided the occupant for leaving the door open, only to realize too late that the handle had come off in her hand, crumpling like tin foil in her grasp.

Turning to Gilbert with a sheepish grin, Artemis explained the mishap, "The door wasn't locked."

Gilbert's smile remained, his eyes twinkling with amusement as he replied, "Of course it wasn't. Take the other restroom." His response was lighthearted, offering a solution to the awkward situation with ease.

Artemis's embarrassment deepened as she emerged from the washroom, soaked from head to toe and water still spouting from the broken tap. She found Khorram standing before her, holding a new tap in his hands as if always prepared for situations like this. His readiness for any incident was something she had come to expect, yet it still surprised her how effortlessly he handled things.

Gently, Artemis examined the damaged tap and realized what had happened. With a soft touch, she squeezed the top of the tap, effectively stopping the flow of water. Her cheeks flushed with embarrassment as she apologized, "I'm sorry! I forgot that they're so delicate compared to my strength. I think I broke it."

Her admission carried a sense of remorse, acknowledging the unintended consequences of her superhuman abilities.

Khorram smile remained unwavering as he reassured Artemis with calm confidence. "No problem, my Lord. I have enough experience to know what to do. I'll fix it in no time."

His words carried an air of reassurance and competence, putting Artemis at ease despite the mishap. With Khorram assurance, she felt a sense of relief, knowing that the situation would be swiftly resolved.

She gazed at the chair, taking in all its intricate details. Crafted from dark walnut wood with a rich cherry hue, it exuded an aura of elegance. The seating area was adorned with lush green satin fabric, adding to its beauty. Though the men who had carried the chair had mentioned its considerable weight, she felt compelled to readjust its position, desiring it to be closer to the table.

Feeling hesitant to ask for assistance in relocating it, she resolved to handle it herself. With cautious determination, she pulled the chair slightly closer to the table and shifted it a tad to the right. As she exerted effort to lift the seemingly heavy chair, a sense of trepidation washed over her, adding to her apprehension.

She seized the chair and began to pull it towards her, oblivious to Gilbert's frantic screams to halt. Before anyone could react, the chair lifted into the air as if weightless foam, crashing into the nearby table, fortunately vacant, and sending another table, along with one of its chairs, hurtling through the window.

Artemis acted swiftly to contain the situation, her heart racing with surprise and disbelief, mirroring the astonishment of everyone present except for Gilbert, Khorram, and his wife, who had observed the scene unfold from the start.

With quick reflexes, Artemis managed to regain control, swiftly setting the chair back on the ground and taking a seat. She glanced uncertainly at Gilbert, still grappling with confusion over the inexplicable event that had just transpired.

Wow!!!" exclaimed Gilbert, utterly amazed by the unexpected turn of events.

Artemis, still reeling from shock, turned to Gilbert and blurted out, "What the heck just happened? I thought it was only light, but surprisingly, it felt like air and had no weight at all."

She found herself unable to utter that word in front of her mother or anyone else back home, yet here, its occurrence seemed almost involuntary since her arrival. Was it fueled by her simmering anger? Perhaps it stemmed from a sense of indifference she perceived in those around her. Or maybe, just maybe, it was the newfound power she had discovered that emboldened her to speak without restraint.

She shook her head, feeling a rush of exhilaration. She had always admired the superheroes back on Earth, but none of them exuded this kind of confidence, nor had they ever seemed this brash. For a fleeting moment, she was overcome with a sense of shame for wielding her power in such a manner as if she were somehow above others.

But deep down, she knew better. Despite her extraordinary abilities, she genuinely cared about people and had never treated any citizen with disrespect. The realization grounded her, reminding her of the responsibility that came with her powers and the importance of using them for good.

She dreaded the thought of being remembered as a brash superhero, unlike the revered figures she had admired. Here, everyone adored the superheroes because they brought goodness into their lives. But possessing powers changed everything; it forced a dichotomy of good and bad, with no room for ambiguity. Living an ordinary life became an impossibility.

The weight of expectation pressed heavily upon her shoulders. People looked to her, relying on her abilities to make a difference. There was no middle ground; she had become a pillar upon which they leaned.

As she reflected on her recent behavior and the impact of her powers, Artemis couldn't shake the memory of a line from the Spider-Man story, one she had always despised. "With great power comes great responsibility," Uncle Ben had told Peter Parker. At the time, she had dismissed it, viewing it as cliché and overly simplistic.

But now, faced with the reality of her own abilities and the consequences of her actions, she understood the weight of those words. This wasn't just a lesson from a comic book; it was her own lived experience. With every power came a corresponding responsibility, a duty to use it wisely and for the greater good. Artemis realized that this was her journey now, and she was determined to embrace it with all the gravity it demanded. She wondered if this was her destiny to be here in this moment, because these people—especially the women—were in dire need of a profound change.

"I'm sorry, Gilbert, for being impolite," Artemis apologized, attempting to gloss over her recent behavior.

But Gilbert was unfazed by her slip of demeanor. To him, Artemis was his superhero, a formidable force to be reckoned with. He simply smiled at her as she gingerly settled into the new chair and remarked, "Well... At least it's a little better than the other one."

As Artemis sat on her chair, eagerly awaiting the dishes of food, her anticipation grew with each passing moment. Soon enough, the waiter arrived, presenting three or four courses of different delicacies. With each bite, Artemis noticed a subtle difference in taste compared to Earth cuisine, leaving her pondering whether it was the style of cooking or the ingredients themselves that lent the unique flavor.

Unable to resist the temptation, she eagerly sampled each dish, savoring the delightful flavors that danced across her palate. In between bites and sips, she peppered Gilbert with questions about the origin and ingredients of each dish. Without hesitation, Gilbert answered each query, providing insight into the culinary delights they were enjoying. Despite her voracious appetite, Artemis's curiosity remained insatiable, fueling her desire to learn more about the cuisine of this new world.

Artemis inquired about the dish before her, pointing to the roasted meat on her plate which was like a roasted chicken breast. "Is this a roasted chicken breast?"

Gilbert looked at Artemis with a smile. "My Lord Artemis! The other gods said the same thing, but it's not a chicken. So, what is a chicken anyway?"

Artemis furrowed her brow in confusion at Gilbert's response as he continued. "By the way, we call it Parandeh12," he replied.

Artemis glanced at Gilbert, puzzled by the unfamiliar term. "This is chicken, but somehow tastier. Chicken is a type of domesticated bird on Earth, and almost everybody loves it," she explained, attempting to bridge the gap between their worlds with a familiar comparison.

"What is a bird?" Gilbert asked, his curiosity evident.

Artemis, focused on her hunger, nodded in response to Gilbert's question. "A bird, Yes, the ones with wings," she confirmed, her attention fixed on the tantalizing food before her.

However, Gilbert's explanation caught her off guard. "No, it's something that grows in the middle of trees, kind of like a vegetable similar to what you have on Earth," he clarified before taking a big bite of the dish.

Artemis paused mid-chew, intrigued by Gilbert's explanation. "What do you mean by growing in the middle of the trees?" she asked, seeking further clarification.

Gilbert's response was gentle and understanding. "Dear my Lord, I understand it may seem strange to you to eat something that grows in the middle of trees, especially if it resembles vegetables to you,"

he began, his tone reassuring. "But look at the bright side. It's delicious, and it's one of the most expensive foods around here. Not everyone can afford it, but the owner went out of his way to prepare this delightful dish just for you. So, as long as you're enjoying it, forget about where it comes from and simply savor the moment, relish the taste."

He emphasized the importance of enjoying the food for what it was, regardless of its origin, and encouraged Artemis not to be too picky. "Even if you don't particularly like the food, remember that it's sustenance that helps you survive," he added, highlighting the practicality of appreciating the meal provided to her.

As Artemis gazed at the spread of food before her, she couldn't deny its appeal. The dishes looked beautiful, and the aroma was enticing, promising a delicious meal. With a determined nod, she made a conscious decision to follow Gilbert's advice and set aside her reservations about the food's origin.

In that moment, she recognized the importance of nourishing her body for the challenges ahead. Surviving in this unfamiliar world required her full strength and focus, not unnecessary distractions. Artemis understood that her priority was to gather her energy and wits, to embark on her quest to find other humans, perhaps even her father, and ultimately, to find a way back to her home planet.

With renewed purpose, Artemis dug into her meal once more, savoring each bite as she steeled herself for the journey ahead.

Artemis's exhaustion began to catch up with her after what felt like an endless cycle of eating, yet she couldn't shake the feeling of perpetual hunger gnawing at her stomach. Puzzled and somewhat embarrassed by her insatiable appetite.

"It's been hours, and I've been eating continuously, but why do I still not feel full?" she asked, her voice tinged with frustration and confusion. "What's wrong with me? I still want to eat more, but I feel embarrassed," she admitted, her discomfort evident.

Artemis's exhaustion began to catch up with her after what felt like an endless cycle of eating, yet she couldn't shake the feeling of perpetual hunger gnawing at her stomach. Puzzled and somewhat embarrassed by her insatiable appetite, she leaned back in her chair and turned to Gilbert for answers.

"My Lord Artemis, as I mentioned before, our food is very light for a human's stomach. You need to eat until you feel truly full. Don't be embarrassed; this is how all the gods are. Providing food for our Lord is an honor to us. So please, don't be ashamed and eat as much as you need. Remember, we have a long journey ahead of us."

Artemis smiled, finding Gilbert's explanation quite logical. Glancing once more at the table, she observed an array of new dishes brimming with delectable foods. Meanwhile, amid their conversation, the attentive hosts had seized the opportunity to replenish her feast. Artemis had never experienced such culinary delight before. She indulged herself, savoring each bite until she was fully satiated and content.

Gilbert turned his gaze toward Artemis and inquired, "Do you need some rest, even if only for a short while?"

Artemis's eyes traversed the array of dishes on the table, her response tinged with surprise. "Yes... How many orders did I consume?" Her eyes widened as she looked at Gilbert.

"Oh, precisely twenty-one orders," Gilbert responded. "To be honest with you, I was expecting more, but I suppose you are much younger and slimmer than the others."

As Artemis finished her dinner, she noticed a sizable crowd gathering outside the restaurant. Word of mouth, she realized, held a formidable sway, far beyond the reach of mere advertisements. Glancing around, she observed other customers smiling at her, a silent acknowledgment of her remarkable feat.

Some of the young girls outside were screaming and crying with excitement at the sight of Artemis. For them, she represented a revolutionary idea in their world, where they had been told that only guys could be heroes. Artemis, a super girl, shattered that misconception. She proved that a girl could be a hero, too, possessing powers that even men were hesitant to approach. Her presence instilled courage and hope in girls and women everywhere, allowing them to openly express their excitement and aspirations. They have found the courage to speak more openly and with broader minds.

Artemis glanced at Gilbert and then subtly gestured toward the girls outside the window with her eyes, silently questioning the muzzle covering their mouths.

"Women have to wear it at all times. It's part of our new religion," Gilbert explained.

Artemis expressed her disbelief, "It's not fair. What kind of religion is that?"

"Our religion is Etah, and it mandates that women wear muzzles at all times. They're also prohibited from speaking in public or at home unless their husbands permit it," Gilbert explained with a tinge of sadness in his voice.

"Who is the prophet of your religion? Is he still alive? I already hate him anyway," Artemis said remorsefully.

Gilbert glanced around and whispered to Artemis, "Please lower your voice because it's our new religion, and people are prejudiced when it comes to beliefs."

Artemis looked around at the customers, then glanced outside, where mostly men were visible. She gave Gilbert a pointed look and asked, "What people? You mean men? Are women considered people here? And do their feelings matter?" Artemis asked, her voice edged with concern and curiosity.

Gilbert seemed to struggle to maintain a smile, but he managed to reply, "Yes, they are, but it's their men who would express whatever their feelings are."

Artemis appeared upset as she turned to Gilbert once more, pressing on, "This is ridiculous. It means the answer to my question is no. They are nobody in your world. And by the way, who is the prophet anyway?"

"Our leader is Demah, and he remains alive. All Flimsies must adhere to his guidance, or they will face punishment by death. God desires our happiness, which is why this religion is the sole path to joy and freedom," Gilbert whispered.

"Gilbert! Do you truly believe in this nonsense? Do you hear yourself?" Artemis exclaimed, her voice tinged with disbelief and anger.

"We must be cautious; God may hear us and punish us if we engage in such discussions," Gilbert whispered once more.

"What sort of punishment is that? Can't you simply refuse to be an Etah? I don't recall agreeing to that name," she asked persistently.

"Etah...! No, we cannot renounce it. We are bound to remain Etah, with no alternative, "That's why, with one religion, everyone would be happy and under one law," he stated, as if it were the only solution to harmony. He continued, "Death awaits as our penalty," he replied solemnly.

"You mean your god is killing people if they disobey him because he wants you to be happy? Do you listen to yourself?" She looked into his eyes for a couple of seconds then she continued

"Gilbert! This goes against the freedom of individuals. What kind of God sanctions this? Religion seems more like a business or voluntary slavery," Artemis remarked, her tone sharp.

"It enslaves everyone without leaving room for complaint. Are you truly a devout person? And how can you know if the women are genuinely happy? Have you lived their lives to understand them?" Artemis felt uneasy as the attention of everyone in the room turned toward her.

Gilbert maintained his gaze on Artemis, offering no response. She sensed that Gilbert didn't wish to discuss it at the moment, but his eyes hinted that he might later. To ease the tension, she shifted the conversation to a different topic, aiming to comfort him for the time being.

Outside the restaurant, chaos erupted as more and more people gathered, eager to catch a glimpse of the new superhero. A loud siren blared, signaling the arrival of security personnel to maintain order and keep the growing crowd at bay, ensuring Artemis's safety and the smooth operation of the restaurant.

Artemis felt a twinge of apprehension, though she was determined not to let it show. She glanced at Gilbert and quipped, "Are they here to see me, or have I inadvertently made a spectacle of myself by indulging in such a colossal and magnificent feast?"

As the crowds swelled by the minute, Artemis found herself torn between two conflicting emotions. On one hand, she was beginning to embrace her newfound identity as a superhero, yet on the other, she felt an overwhelming desire to remain unnoticed for the time being. There was an urgency gnawing at her, a need to locate the others and unravel the mysteries that undoubtedly held significance to her.

But amidst her anticipation, a trace of apprehension lingered. What if her father truly was among the crowd? The prospect of their reunion filled her with a sense of warmth and longing, envisioning a future where they could be a family once more.

As Artemis pondered the potential reunion with her father, her thoughts naturally turned to her mother. She envisioned her mother's face, contemplating how she might react upon seeing her husband again after so many years apart. Repeating to herself, Artemis affirmed, "That is cool. I've always dreamed of having my dad back, even though my memories of him are fleeting. This is my chance to make that dream a reality."

With a growing sense of excitement, she eagerly scanned the crowd, hoping to catch a glimpse of her long-lost father amid the throng of people. The owners of the restaurant approached Artemis with beaming smiles adorning their faces. "Thank you, Lord Artemis," one of them said with genuine appreciation. "We trust that you found our offerings to your liking. It was an honor to serve you. We've long been accustomed to catering to mighty men, but today, it was our privilege to serve a lady of your stature, Lord Artemis."

Artemis was momentarily rendered speechless by their graciousness. Despite the immense feast she had just enjoyed, they still expressed gratitude towards her, and their invitation for her return struck her as both unexpected and heartwarming. As she observed Khorram and Mary's amused and happy expression, she couldn't help but feel touched by their sincerity.

Artemis's genuine warmth radiated as she expressed her gratitude, saying, "Thank you for your kindness. I truly enjoyed the food immensely. I would be delighted to return again. Your generosity has been truly appreciated, and I hope that I may be of assistance to you in the future." Her words were imbued with sincerity and gratitude.

"You were... when you entered our restaurant, and most importantly, when you stood up for female rights. That was truly amazing," Mary expressed warmly, accompanied by a smile from both her and Khorram. Their acknowledgment filled Artemis with a sense of pride and affirmation.

Artemis turned to Gilbert, noticing the disappointment etched on his face. Concerned, she inquired, "Why do you seem upset?"

Gilbert made an effort to rein in his rising anger before responding, "You should never, ever say that again. They might try to exploit you for their own gain. You don't owe them anything, now or ever. That's my suggestion, if I may." His words carried a note of caution and protectiveness, urging Artemis to be cautious of others' intentions.

Artemis shot a glance at Gilbert and responded with a hint of humor in her tone, "You've said it all... and I'm not afraid to help a friend, especially those who've come to my aid when I need it the most. Are you suggesting I ignore their kindness and merely seek their help without any thought of return? I'll take it as a suggestion." Her words carried a playful defiance, indicating her resolve to remain true to her principles while also acknowledging Gilbert's concerns.

As Artemis scanned the faces outside, her heart raced with the hope of spotting her father among the crowd. However, her thoughts were interrupted by a sudden burst of muffled cheers and scattered applause from the hundreds of people gathered to witness a female hero. Realizing she didn't want to navigate through the throng any longer, she turned to Gilbert with a determined expression.

"Do you have any ideas on how we can navigate through this crowd?" she asked. "I really want to explore the city without being part of this spectacle. I don't feel ready for that yet."

Her tone was resolute, conveying her desire to maintain a sense of anonymity while she acquainted herself with her surroundings. Artemis's face lit up with anticipation as Gilbert suggested a way to navigate through the crowd without drawing attention. "How?" she inquired eagerly.

Gilbert leaned in close, his voice barely above a whisper as he outlined his plan. "We can slip out through the back door and make our way through an alley. But we have to move quickly before anyone notices," he explained.

Artemis nodded, understanding the urgency of the situation. With a determined nod, she signaled her readiness to follow Gilbert's lead and make their escape unnoticed. Artemis's expression shifted to one of discomfort and misunderstanding as she interrupted Gilbert's plan.

"Whoa, whoa, my friend," she interjected, her voice wavering with unease. "Take it easy. I asked for your help, but I didn't mean in an alley—"

Gilbert's frustration flared, his anger evident as he cut her off abruptly, speaking louder to ensure she understood.

"BEFORE THEY REACH US, AND YOU CAN FLY OUT OF HERE AND GO WHEREVER YOU DESIRE," he emphasized firmly, his tone leaving no room for further misunderstanding.

As Gilbert finished speaking, he crossed his arms and stood resolutely in front of Artemis. Sensing the weight of her misunderstanding, Artemis felt a pang of guilt. After taking a moment to truly listen to Gilbert, she mustered a sheepish smile and gave a hesitant thumbs-up. Feeling the weight of her misguided assumption, Artemis's cheeks flushed with embarrassment. She felt insignificant and ashamed for misinterpreting Gilbert's intentions, especially considering all the help he had provided since her arrival. Determined to make amends, she sought to shift the focus back to him.

"I meant, what about you?" she began earnestly, her voice tinged with sincerity.

"I won't leave without you. You've been such a tremendous help to me, and I believe you can assist me in finding the others. Right?" Her words were a genuine acknowledgment of Gilbert's importance and a reassurance of her commitment to their partnership.

Gilbert observed Artemis's suggestion with suspicion, his tone tinged with humor as he replied, "R...I...G...H...T...!!!"

Artemis's response was curt, a hint of frustration evident in her voice. "But the problem is that I can't fly," she snapped.

"You're like a baby here and I have to teach you walking, not touching, being careful when you hold something and how to fly. You don't know yet how to fly, but it's all part of the package. If you're human, then you can fly here, in our world. It's a fact, period. End of sentence," Gilbert retorted, his frustration palpable. He shot Artemis a reproachful look, mostly because of her persistently negative attitude.

"I think you're so touchy now, Gilbert," said Artemis with some kind of accent. Artemis' comment was met with a pause from Gilbert, who then replied with a hint of amusement, "Touchy? Me? Never."

His tone carried a playful sarcasm, a subtle attempt to lighten the mood despite the underlying tension between them. Then he continued, "I'm touchy, or are you just a coward with meager, timid goals that offer no fulfillment?" His words were laced with frustration and a hint of resentment.

"You're merely seeking out other humans, but do you even understand your purpose here? I doubt you'll ever find one if you remain ignorant of the complexities of life and pain on this planet." Gilbert's tone grew more impassioned as he continued, his words carrying a weight of conviction.

"Have you ever considered that perhaps you were meant to come here for a reason? These people are eager to see you, to engage with you. They've harbored hopes of being part of something extraordinary, something as brilliant as you. They were looking for hope and you came and lit their hope. They're offering you their hearts, and all you do is say thanks and move on, just to keep searching for the others?" he asked, his voice tinged with frustration and disbelief. His disappointment was palpable, stemming from a deeper concern for Artemis's understanding of her role in this world.

As Artemis observed the sad faces around her, she felt a pang of empathy, recognizing the truth in Gilbert's words. Her eyes glistened with unshed tears, but she fought to keep them at bay, unwilling to show her vulnerability, especially to Gilbert. A lump formed in her throat, stifling her words as she grappled with a wave of emotions.

Despite her weariness and the overwhelming weight of her thoughts, Artemis knew she couldn't afford to falter. Her determination to find her father and reunite him with his family burned within her, driving her forward even as exhaustion threatened to consume her. She longed to be a superhero, to wield the power to bring her father back home where he belonged. With every fiber of her being, she clung to that hope, drawing strength from it as she pressed on, refusing to let fatigue or doubt deter her from her mission.

Artemis's words, though brief, carried a weight of sadness as she struggled to articulate her thoughts. "Wishing to be something or someone you're not... is the biggest recipe for me," she murmured, her tone heavy with emotion. The weight of her longing and the reality of her situation hung heavily in the air, casting a somber shadow over her words. Gilbert's words resonated deeply with Artemis, his conviction stirring something within her.

"Work on those plans if that's your goal," he urged, his voice filled with determination.

"But in the meantime, don't dwell on your sadness. We will find them, together. But you have to believe that this is not your planet. This is Rouhar, or as other supermen called it, Flimsy World. And in Flimsy World, a human can fly, as you've experienced before, even if you don't want to admit it."

Artemis felt a rush of emotions coursing through her veins, the intensity of Gilbert's words leaving her breathless. His unwavering belief in her potential sparked a glimmer of hope within her, dispelling the clouds of doubt that had lingered in her mind. She nodded slowly, her resolve strengthening as she embraced the possibility of a new reality, one where she could soar beyond her wildest dreams.

Artemis gently tapped her hand on Gilbert's shoulder, a silent gesture of belief and respect. As she turned to express her gratitude to Mary and Khorram once more, she noticed Mary's smile, her hand covering her mouth as she glanced toward Gilbert. Artemis's heart swelled with appreciation for their kindness.

Turning back to Gilbert, Artemis's expression shifted to one of concern, but her worry intensified when she realized he wasn't there. Panic surged through her as she saw him lying on the floor. Rushing to his side, she knelt down, her voice trembling as she called out his name, "Gilbert, are you alright?" Her hands hovered over him, uncertain of what had caused him to collapse. Then, she realized her mistake once again.

Artemis's apology was tinged with a sense of helplessness as she tried to come to terms with the situation. "I'm sorry, it wasn't my fault. I mean, it was my fault again, and I'm still trying to adjust," she explained, her voice tinged with frustration. "You have to bear with me, okay?"

Gilbert whispered softly, "I'm afraid that by the time you learn, I'll already be in my grave."

As Gilbert struggled to his hands and knees, pain evident in his movements, Artemis felt a pang of guilt. She knelt beside him, offering a supportive hand. "Is there any other choice for me?" he asked, his voice laced with resignation.

Artemis's heart ached at his words, realizing the gravity of their situation. "We'll figure this out together," she promised, determination shining in her eyes. "We'll find a way."

Artemis and Gilbert stood side by side against the door and the restaurant window, their gaze fixed on the throngs of people filling the street outside. Without turning to look at Gilbert, Artemis broached the subject that had been weighing on her mind.

"You were saying we should run to a valley and fly somewhere that nobody could find us?" she asked quietly.

Gilbert's response was equally subdued, his eyes still fixed on the scene outside. "Yes, I did," he confirmed, his voice tinged with determination. Artemis's voice trailed off as she voiced her concerns, her words reflecting the weight of the dilemma she faced. However, before she could finish, Gilbert interjected with a firm tone.

"Come on, my Lord Artemis! These are just excuses. Deep down, do you really believe that you can't fly?" he challenged.

Artemis's gaze faltered, uncertainty flickering in her eyes. Despite her desires and the extraordinary experiences she had encountered, a lingering doubt gnawed at her. She remained silent, grappling with her own doubts and fears. Artemis found herself at a loss for words, her mind consumed by fleeting memories of past encounters and moments of uncertainty. However, as she exchanged glances with

Gilbert, a sense of resolve washed over her, they both turned to the restaurant owner, their expressions marked by determination and a hint of anticipation.

Gilbert broke the silence, addressing Artemis with a question. "What do you think?" he asked, his tone earnest.

Artemis's smile grew, a reflection of her newfound determination. "Agreed," she affirmed, her voice steady with conviction. With a shared understanding, they made their decision. Mary swiftly moved to the window and closed the blinds, shielding Artemis and Gilbert from the view of the crowd outside. Meanwhile, Khorram stepped toward the entrance door and addressed the gathering with a loud, commanding voice.

"I'm sorry, my friends," he announced, his voice carrying over the murmurs of the crowd. "The lord is exhausted and in need of rest, having entered our world today. Please forgive us and return tomorrow. Thank you for understanding."

His words were met with a murmur of disappointment from the crowd, but they gradually began to disperse, respecting Khorram request. With the immediate pressure alleviated, Artemis and Gilbert exchanged a grateful glance, knowing they had a moment of respite before their next move. As Khorram closed the door, the disappointed murmurs of the crowd echoed through the restaurant, with some expressing regret at missing the chance to see the esteemed royalty of Flimsy World. A few of the girls even shed tears, their longing to catch a glimpse of the new Lord, particularly a female one, evident in their distraught expressions.

Once the windows were blocked from view, effectively concealing Artemis and Gilbert from the outside world, Khorram led the way as everyone moved to the kitchen. With a cautious glance outside, Khorram confirmed his suspicions – the back of the restaurant was deserted, providing the perfect opportunity for Artemis and Gilbert to make their escape unnoticed.

As Artemis looked at Gilbert, seeking guidance in their precarious situation, she was met with a glare. Gilbert's frustration was evident as he responded sharply.

"Now what?" asked Artemis.

"You don't know? Fly...?" Gilbert said in return.

Artemis felt a pang of guilt at Gilbert's reaction, realizing her question had only added to the tension between them. Taking a deep breath, she attempted to diffuse the situation.

"I mean, what's our next move?" she clarified, her voice calm but tinged with uncertainty.

Artemis's attempt to lighten the mood with her funny accent was met with a different response from Gilbert this time. His expression became more complex, tinged with a sense of discomfort.

"We can't just fly off without a plan," Gilbert replied, his tone reflecting a mixture of frustration and concern. "We need to think this through carefully, he suggested."

Despite his attempt to maintain composure, there was an underlying sense of unease in Gilbert's voice, a recognition of the challenges they faced and the gravity of their situation. Artemis's suggestion was met with a skeptical look from Gilbert, who appeared unconvinced by her proposed method of flight. He held a bucket and mimicked her instructions, pressing his feet against the ground and attempting to jump. His efforts resulted in only a small hop, an inch off the ground.

"Just like that! Is that hard?" he remarked sarcastically, his tone laced with frustration. Despite his attempt to replicate Artemis's suggestion, it was clear that flying was not as simple as he made it out to be.

As Artemis glanced around at the faces of those who had shown faith in her, a sense of gratitude and determination welled up within her. Their unwavering support had helped her to find belief in herself, and now, faced with the possibility of flight, she felt a newfound sense of wonder and excitement.

"I lived sixteen years on Earth without a single moment of excitement, not even one. But here, in less than a day, I'm surrounded by a river of new powers, excitement, and the possibility of becoming a superhero in my life," Artemis thought, looking up at the sky.

Embracing the possibility that she may indeed possess the ability to fly, Artemis allowed herself to bask in the wonderful feeling of anticipation. With each beat of her heart, she felt a surge of energy coursing through her veins, propelling her toward the realization of her newfound potential. Artemis's gaze lingered on Gilbert, a flicker of uncertainty crossing her features as she sought reassurance from him one last time.

"But are you sure that it could happen? Flying, I mean," she asked tentatively.

Gilbert's expression softened, a sense of determination mingling with a hint of vulnerability as he approached Artemis. "Above all else, be kind, gentle, and understanding toward yourself," he advised, his voice filled with sincerity.

"Now, stop asking and just do it! Anyway, be very careful with me." His last words came out with a hint of nervousness, and he quickly rephrased them, his voice taking on a slightly squeaky tone. "Be careful because I'm fragile," he reiterated, his vulnerability laid bare in his words.

Artemis smiled at everyone once more before turning towards the bucket, ready to follow Gilbert's example. However, before she could step onto it, Gilbert's urgent shout stopped her in her tracks. Startled, she looked at him innocently, unaware of her mistake.

"I'm following your steps," she replied, confusion evident in her voice.

Gilbert quickly whispered to her, his tone urgent, "That was just an example. You don't have to use the bucket. Do you understand?"

She attempted a bit of practice before taking Gilbert with her. Before she was fully prepared, she pushed off the ground and shot up in a flash. For a moment, she blacked out but quickly regained consciousness. Frantically trying to stop her ascent, she waved her arms like a fish to slow down. Knowing that a fall wouldn't kill her, she aimed to descend as if diving into the water. This technique worked, and as she neared the ground, she used her hands again to reduce her speed. Despite her efforts, she still hit the ground, but fortunately, it wasn't too hard.

Gilbert laughed heartily, clapping with joy. "You are a natural, My little Lord! Excellent, bravo!" he exclaimed loudly, his voice brimming with enthusiasm.

Artemis nodded in understanding, her expression determined. She grasped Gilbert lightly and lifted him as if he weighed no more than a feather. With a gaze fixed upward, she pressed her feet against the ground and launched herself into the sky, soaring like Superman.

For the employees of the restaurant, it was a moment they would never forget – witnessing the extraordinary sight of their Lord, a girl with the ability to defy gravity and take flight. And as Artemis and Gilbert disappeared into the horizon, they couldn't help but feel a sense of awe and inspiration at the remarkable scene they had just witnessed. As she ascended higher, her fear of heights seized her; her vision dimmed, and all sensation slipped away."

She glanced down at the ground before everything went dark again, her body succumbing to unconsciousness as she slipped into her dreams mid-flight. Yet, in an instant, she jolted back, only to find herself enveloped in an all-consuming darkness. Her senses heightened as she searched frantically for the source of the desperate cries for help. The darkness seemed to press in on her from all sides, disorienting and overwhelming.

Amidst the darkness, a familiar voice broke through the silence, calling out to her repeatedly, "Lord Artemis, Lord Artemis... ARTEMISSSSSSSSS!"

The urgency in the voice stirred something within Artemis. Gasping for breath, she found herself back in the dimly lit room, the remnants of her dream still lingering in her mind. The sound of her name echoing in her ears sent a shiver down her spine, leaving her heart racing as she struggled to make sense of it all. As Artemis opened her eyes, she felt an odd sensation of weightlessness, as if she were floating. Gazing up, she beheld the vast expanse of the night sky, dotted with countless stars twinkling like diamonds. Lost in the beauty of the night, Artemis was suddenly jolted back again into reality by the sound of a desperate cry for help again. Turning her head to the right, she was met with the sight of Gilbert, suspended in mid-air, holding onto her leg with a look of desperation on his face. The urgency of the situation snapped Artemis out of her reverie, and with determination, she focused on the task at hand, ready to come to Gilbert's aid.

Artemis's initial reaction was one of fear and confusion as she processed the situation. "Wow... What happened?" she exclaimed, her voice tinged with apprehension, but Gilbert's response was laced with frustration and urgency.

"What happened? What happened?" he repeated, his tone incredulous.

"You mean you don't remember? We were supposed to fly our way out of the restaurant and that crowd, but you instantly blacked out. Do you remember now?"

His words hit Artemis like a bolt of lightning, jolting her memory back to the moment when she had lost consciousness while attempting to fly. Realization washed over her, and she felt a surge of guilt for letting Gilbert down. With a determined nod, she acknowledged her mistake and resolved to make things right.

Gilbert's voice boomed with rage as he confronted Artemis. "You're still confused about how to take control of your flying, aren't you?" he screamed, his frustration and anger palpable.

Artemis felt a pang of guilt at Gilbert's outburst, knowing that her inability to master her newfound abilities had caused him distress. Despite her fear and uncertainty, she knew she had to find a way to regain control and prove herself to Gilbert and to herself. Taking a deep breath, she steadied herself, determined to overcome her doubts and fears. Artemis's mind raced as she searched for a solution to their predicament. Despite feeling blank and uncertain, she refused to dwell on her doubts any longer. Recalling the mountain and the sense of safety it had once offered, she understood now that this world held no true danger for her. A new belief took root in this place, nothing could harm her—here, she was a super girl.

As Gilbert continued to panic and scream, Artemis felt a sense of calm wash over her. With a newfound resolve, she chuckled softly, her laughter mingling with Gilbert's frantic cries. Locking eyes with him, she conveyed a silent message of reassurance and determination. It was time to take control of the situation and find a way to set things right.

This time, Gilbert gave up and screamed loudly, "I'm going to die, die, d...i...e... because you don't remember where I am or YOU'RE A JERK. I'm sure about that right now and that's it." Then he kept saying, "I'm going to die, I'm going to die... die... die."

As Gilbert's words of frustration and despair washed over her, Artemis felt a surge of determination to prove him wrong. She refused to let him down and resolved to take control of the situation before it escalated further. She immediately grabbed Gilbert and, without hesitation, devised a plan. Realizing that swimming motions might help her gain better control of her flight, she gently positioned Gilbert on her back and instructed him to hold on tightly. With his arms wrapped securely around her neck, Artemis began to move her legs and arms in a rhythmic motion, mimicking the actions of swimming.

When Gilbert felt secure, he glanced at Artemis, observing her unusual movements, and said, "You're weird. This isn't how others usually fly!"

Gradually, she felt a sense of control returning, and soon, they were gliding through the air with ease. It was a moment of triumph for Artemis, a realization of her newfound abilities and a testament to Gilbert's guidance. Feeling reassured by Artemis's newfound control, Gilbert let go of his earlier frustrations and felt a sense of pride in her accomplishment. He knew he had been unfair in his outburst and resolved to apologize once they were safely back on the ground. For now, he could only marvel at the beauty of the moment and the incredible journey they were embarking on together.

As Artemis soared through the air, relishing the freedom and exhilaration of flight, she couldn't help but steal glances at Gilbert, who remained quiet beside her. His eyes were half-opened, his expression unreadable. Artemis couldn't discern whether he was scared or quietly enjoying the ride, but the sight of him brought her a sense of reassurance.

She glanced sideways at Gilbert, a hint of a smile on her lips, and said, "You know, we really should have bike helmets and goggles to shield our eyes from the wind. It would make the flight so much more enjoyable, don't you think?"

Despite the uncertainties and challenges they had faced, one thing was certain that Gilbert was alive, and they were navigating this extraordinary experience together. Artemis felt a surge of gratitude for his presence, knowing that they had overcome their differences and were now bound by a shared adventure unlike any other. Gilbert's complex personality intrigued Artemis from the moment she first laid eyes on him. Despite his slim or seemingly frail appearance, she recognized in him a deep sense of independence, rebellion, and intelligence. His demeanor may have initially confused others, but Artemis possessed a keen mind that allowed her to see through his facade and understand him on a deeper level.

Gilbert's allure was undeniable—he could be fascinating, funny, and captivating to those who didn't know him well. Many were drawn to him by his wit and charm, eager to follow him wherever he led. However, Artemis knew that beneath his charismatic exterior lay a more enigmatic and multifaceted individual. At times, Gilbert could display moments of brutal violence, his actions unpredictable and jarring. Yet, amidst his eccentricities, he also possessed a strangely endearing sense of humor and unexpected acts of humanity. Artemis recognized the complexity of Gilbert's character, understanding that he was not easily categorized or understood. Despite his flaws, she couldn't help but be drawn to his intriguing and multifaceted nature.

Artemis regarded Gilbert with a mixture of amusement and curiosity and looked at him again, who looked bored and asked him, "Do you have any particular place that you want to go?"

Gilbert as he responded with his typical nonchalant demeanor. His bored expression belied the underlying sense of adventure and intrigue that seemed to follow him wherever he went.

"Surprise me," he said casually, his words laden with a hint of mischief and anticipation.

Artemis couldn't help but smile at his response, feeling a surge of excitement at the prospect of exploring new destinations with Gilbert by her side. She felt a growing affection for Gilbert but wasn't quite sure what it was. With a mischievous twinkle in her eyes, she resolved to find the perfect surprise that would ignite Gilbert's sense of curiosity and wonder, eager to embark on their next adventure together.

Artemis's playful tone hinted at her mischievous intentions as she pretended not to hear Gilbert's response. With a grin, she teased, "What did you say? I can't hear you at all. Would you talk louder?"

Her lighthearted demeanor added a sense of fun to the moment, inviting Gilbert to join her in the playful banter. As they continued on their journey, Artemis couldn't help but feel a sense of excitement and anticipation for the surprises that lay ahead, knowing that with Gilbert by her side, every moment was sure to be an adventure. They saw a huge light in the distance, which looked like a massive fire. As they approached it, the warmth from the flames gradually enveloped them, growing stronger with each minute closer.

Artemis watched the flames rise high, mesmerized by the way they danced gracefully down there, flickering light reflecting in her eyes, creating a moment of peaceful beauty amidst the uncertainty. Artemis's playful demeanor faltered as Gilbert's sudden change in mood caught her off guard. His grumpy muttering and the suggestion sent a shiver down her spine.

"You want fun? How about going through this beautiful fire," he said, his voice laced with a dark challenge as the flames flickered menacingly below.

She turned to look at the flames, her heart racing with apprehension. Despite Gilbert's sarcastic tone, the idea of approaching the fire filled her with unease.

"Are you serious?" she whispered back, her voice tinged with concern.

The prospect of venturing into the flames seemed reckless and dangerous, and Artemis couldn't shake the dread that washed over her at the thought. A chill ran down her spine at Gilbert's response, his nonchalant demeanor only intensifying her unease. Despite his casual tone, the idea of going through the fire filled her with growing fear, making her question whether she could truly face what lay ahead.

"Ha ha ha, you know that fire doesn't do anything to me, but it would turn you to dust," she said with a smirk.

Gilbert remarked with a hint of amusement. "Interesting, but it's okay to me too. Your request is my command."

Artemis couldn't help but feel a sense of apprehension at Gilbert's willingness to entertain her request. The thought of going through into the fire, even if it posed no threat to him, filled her with a sense of foreboding. Despite her mischievous intentions, she couldn't shake the feeling that this was a risk she wasn't willing to take. As Artemis changed direction towards the looming fire, Gilbert's grip around her neck tightened with fear. His apprehension only seemed to fuel Artemis's mischievous spirit, and with an evil laugh, she plunged into the flames without hesitation.

In the blink of an eye, Artemis emerged through the fire unscathed, her incredible speed extinguishing the flames in an instant. As they heard the cheers and jubilant cries of onlookers, Gilbert's fear turned to awe, marveling at Artemis's incredible feat.

Amidst the cheers and celebrations, Artemis couldn't help but feel a surge of pride and exhilaration. Despite the danger and uncertainty, she had faced the fire head-on and emerged victorious, proving once again that she was more than capable of overcoming any obstacle in her path. Artemis's laughter echoed through the air as she playfully addressed Gilbert, her voice filled with exhilaration and amusement.

She turned to Gilbert and said, "Now! It's your turn." Gilbert shot her an angry look before turning his face away in frustration, clearly unwilling to comply.

Artemis continued her playful teasing and said, "Hey, buddy, I didn't hear you. Are you still there, or have you turned to dust?" Her tone was light, teasing yet affectionate, as she tried to coax a response from him.

Despite the adrenaline still coursing through her veins, Artemis couldn't help but feel a sense of relief at Gilbert's continued presence beside her. His unwavering support and companionship had been a constant source of strength throughout their journey, and she was grateful to have him by her side, even in the face of danger. Artemis's laughter faded as Gilbert's stern words cut through the air, his tone filled with offense and anger.

"Take me down right now. I thought you were one of the Lords, but you are still a childish person who is playing with people's lives. Don't you know the danger? Do you know what have you done?" Gilbert replied, offended. He was so angry and didn't think she would do it.

"I know I shouldn't listen to you anymore. I followed your lead, and now you're the one complaining about the danger?"

"Please, just stop somewhere," Gilbert asked her gently.

Artemis interrupted in the middle of his talking. "I know what I'm doing, but the thing I don't know is how I can land. It might be painful for you. Do you have any suggestions?"

Despite the tension between them, Artemis's words carried a sense of responsibility and concern for Gilbert's well-being. She recognized the gravity of their situation and sought to find a solution that would ensure both their safety. As they hovered in the air, she awaited Gilbert's response, hoping to find a way to safely descend from their lofty heights.

Artemis raised her right ear closer to Gilbert and emitted a soft "Hum," indicating her readiness to listen to his suggestions or concerns.

"I don't know how, and you should know by instinct! But I know I'm the one who'll be hurt. Just use your experience and land somewhere that I won't be hurt. Artemis, please make sure I'll be okay," Gilbert blurted out, his words tinged with a mix of frustration and concern for his safety.

"I need some time to come up with something," Artemis said soothingly,

her voice calm and reassuring as she continued to fly, deep in thought. It was beautiful up there. Gliding like this had never crossed her mind before, but now she found herself loving it despite her acrophobia. The sensation was both relaxing and comforting, allowing her to think clearly amidst the vast expanse of the sky. She felt so good, so happy, so alive—it was a strange and unfamiliar sensation, one she had never experienced before.

The effects she experienced felt almost indistinguishable from the pull of gravity itself. Artemis mused that sometimes it takes a true vintage piece to capture the specific feeling she had right now. Suddenly, she remembered Gilbert and wondered how he was feeling. But the good news was that Artemis didn't care if he liked it or not; what mattered most was ensuring his safety and well-being.

"Hey, Gilbert, are you still there? I can't feel you. Are you okay?" Artemis asked, her voice ringing out loud in the air.

"Yup... Why? I thought you'd forgotten about me," Gilbert muttered, his tone laced with a hint of annoyance.

"I did, but I have a question, that's why I remembered you now." She chuckled then she continued, "Can I ask you something?" Artemis teased, a playful tone lacing her words. She didn't wait for his response and simply threw her question at him, "Do you know where the other humans are?" Even though they both had to speak up, and it was annoying for both, somehow, it was also pleasurable.

"I told you before that nobody knows where they are and why they quit as being the guardian of Flimsies?" Gilbert replied loudly again, his voice shaking along with his hands.

His gaze remained as stoic as ever, but Gilbert was growing weary from holding onto Artemis. His fingers grew cold and numb, sending sharp pangs of pain through his hands. Despite his efforts to remain composed, he couldn't ignore the biting coldness any longer. Artemis, too, began to feel the chill creeping into her bones. She glanced at Gilbert's hands, now red from the cold, and realized they needed to find a solution—and quickly.

"At least I've found something that is similar to Earth and my world, and that is the coldness. As you go higher up from the planet, it gets colder," she said, noting the similarity between their current environment and her own world.

"Would you please land on the ground? I'm cold, and I feel sick. I don't have the right clothes for this flight, so I think I'll be sick for days—maybe weeks. Also, I can't hold on any longer, and I'm starting to slip," Gilbert requested, his voice trembling with discomfort and exhaustion.

Artemis agreed, secretly amused as the friendship between the two of them flourished. She scanned the surroundings, searching for a good and safe place to land. Her gaze fell upon the edge of the city, where a big bridge stretched across the landscape. Deciding that landing on her feet would be the safest option for both of them, Artemis carefully adjusted her position. Her hands moved in different directions, she turned up right then guided her descent as she gracefully touched down on the ground. Using her hands for balance, she took a few running steps before gradually coming to a stop. The landing was amazingly perfect, and both Artemis and Gilbert were safe on solid ground once again.

Gilbert was stuck to Artemis's clothes, shivering uncontrollably from the cold. Artemis felt helpless, knowing that any attempt to remove his hands might result in accidental harm. So, she simply stood there, offering her support as best she could.

After what seemed like an eternity, Gilbert managed to stand on his own feet, but he quickly collapsed, unconscious. Concerned for his well-being, Artemis gently lifted him and placed him on a nearby bench. Gilbert continued to shake violently, and Artemis felt a wave of fear wash over her. She knew she had to do something to help him. Knowing her body temperature was high enough to warm him, she sat beside him and gently placed her arm over his head, trying to warm the air around him with her breath. Gradually, he began to improve, the color returning to his face. She felt relieved, knowing he was okay now. Then, acting quickly, Artemis dashed into the woods and gathered a pile of broken branches and logs. With focused determination, she used her heat vision to ignite the wood, creating a blazing fire. They sat close to the warmth of the flames, and slowly but surely, Gilbert began to feel better, the shaking subsiding as his body absorbed the heat.

Artemis's face bore a look of guilt as she finally spoke up. "I'm sorry I put you through this. I didn't mean to make you uncomfortable,"

she admitted, her voice tinged with remorse. "I know that you've helped me a lot since I got here. If there's anything I can do to make you feel better, please let me know."

Her sincerity was evident, and she hoped that Gilbert would understand her remorse and appreciate her offer to help in any way she could. Gilbert's smile widened as he looked into Artemis's eyes, his demeanor shifting as he felt the weight of her apology and acknowledgment of his help. Her words held significant meaning for him, and he appreciated her sincerity.

As he glanced around, his gaze settled back on Artemis, and a sense of calm washed over him. With a smile on his lips, he finally spoke up, his voice calm and collected. "Why didn't you take me to the hospital? It could be serious?" he asked, his concern evident in his tone.

Artemis felt a pang of guilt at Gilbert's question, realizing that she may have overlooked the severity of his condition in her haste to provide aid. She took a moment to collect her thoughts before responding, determined to address his concerns and ensure his well-being moving forward. Artemis's expression softened as she listened to Gilbert's question, understanding his concern and feeling a renewed sense of responsibility towards him.

"I'm sorry, Gilbert. I was so focused on making sure you were warm and comfortable that I didn't think to take you to the hospital," she admitted, her voice filled with remorse. "But you're right, your health is important, and I should have acted differently."

She paused, contemplating her next words carefully. "If you still feel unwell, I can take you to the hospital now. It's not too late to make sure everything's alright," she offered, her tone sincere. Artemis was determined to rectify her oversight and ensure Gilbert received the care he needed.

Gilbert nodded, understanding Artemis's predicament. "It's okay, Artemis. I know you were just trying to help," he reassured her, his voice gentle. He appreciated her honesty and her efforts to assist him despite the challenges they faced.

"We can figure it out together," Gilbert continued, a faint smile gracing his lips.

"Maybe we can ask someone nearby for directions to the nearest hospital. Or we could try to find our way back to the restaurant and seek help from Khorram and Mary," he suggested, hopeful that they could find a solution together.

Artemis nodded in agreement, grateful for Gilbert's understanding and determination to find a solution. Together, they would navigate through this challenge and ensure Gilbert received the care he needed. Gilbert's words warmed Artemis's heart, and she returned his smile with gratitude.

"You're welcome," she replied softly, her tone filled with sincerity. Despite the challenges they faced, their friendship had grown stronger through adversity, and Artemis was grateful for Gilbert's presence in her life.

As they sat by the crackling fire, the warmth enveloping them, Artemis felt a sense of peace wash over her when Gilbert whispered, "Artemis, shut up and listen." His mood lightened as he spoke, "You're the Lord of Flimsy world. Nothing could possibly harm you. You're safe a hundred percent. And yet, you're worried about me? A Flimsy? You can walk in the city for five minutes, and hundreds, thousands of people would offer you their friendship and help. It's everyone's dream to be with a caring Lord like you."

Artemis paused, struck by Gilbert's words. His perspective offered her a new understanding of her role in this world and the impact she had on those around her. She realized that despite her own uncertainties and insecurities, she held a position of significance that inspired hope and admiration in others. Gilbert's words resonated deeply with Artemis, and she felt a sense of responsibility settle upon her shoulders. As the Lord of Flimsy World, she understood that her actions carried weight and influence, and she was determined to wield that power for the greater good. With a renewed sense of purpose, Artemis turned to Gilbert with a determined expression. Still in a playful mood, she looked at Gilbert and said, "You're right. Why am I wasting my time here? Let me go and find a hundred friends!"

Gilbert looked at her, puzzled, as Artemis burst into uncontrollable laughter. Suddenly, she composed herself and said firmly, "I'm sorry, Gilbert. You're right."

"I may be the Lord of the Flimsy world, but that doesn't mean I'm incapable of compassion and care. Thank you for reminding me of what truly matters."

But still, Artemis felt a pang of guilt as she responded, "Yes, you're correct. And yet, neither of them is you. You became my friend before you even knew who I am." Her words carried sincerity and a hint of regret as she acknowledged the significance of Gilbert's friendship. Gilbert's confession took Artemis by surprise. She looked at him, her eyes widening in astonishment as his words sank in.

"I knew who you were from the moment I saw you," he continued, his voice tinged with emotion.

"I was waiting for you for almost all my life. It was my father's final request, shared with a solemn weight as he revealed the prophecy to me and I did it. I knew you would come one day—that's why I was there. However, the surprise was that I had been expecting a Lord, as we all believed only men could hold that title. I never imagined our next Lord would be a young and beautiful woman like you."

Artemis was speechless, her mind reeling from the weight of Gilbert's revelation. She felt a deep sense of gratitude and awe for his unwavering dedication and the profound bond that had formed between them. Artemis's mind raced as she processed Gilbert's words. The weight of his revelation settled upon her, and she felt a mix of emotions swirling within her. She looked at Gilbert, her eyes searching his face for any sign of deception, but all she found was sincerity and vulnerability.

As Gilbert waited for her response, Artemis felt a surge of warmth and gratitude wash over her. The realization that someone had been waiting for her, believing in her, filled her with a sense of purpose and belonging that she had never experienced before.

Finally, she found her voice, her words laced with emotion. "Thank you, Gilbert," she said softly. "I... I don't know what to say. I never knew... I never imagined..." Artemis's words carried a mixture of awe and gratitude as she expressed her feelings to Gilbert. She turned to face him fully, her eyes reflecting the sincerity of her emotions.

"It's even better than I expected," she began, her voice filled with wonder.

"Which brings us back to the same answer! Neither of them is like you, and they will never be like you. You were waiting for me here all your life. It's like waiting for a prophet, and that's amazing to me. I don't know what to say! I'm happy that I saw you first. I'm happy that you were there."

Artemis's heartfelt words resonated deeply with Gilbert, filling him with a profound sense of validation. He had waited so long for this moment, and now that it had finally arrived, the weight of his emotions overwhelmed him. As they stood together, basking in the glow of their newfound connection, Artemis and Gilbert knew that their bond was stronger than ever. And as they looked ahead to the future, they did so with hope and anticipation, knowing that they would face whatever challenges came their way together.

Gilbert's pride swelled as he reflected on the positive turn their conversation had taken, feeling honored by Artemis's response. Her words had not only brought him joy and pleasure but also a newfound sense of self-confidence. As Artemis settled beside him, inhaling the dusty air around them, Gilbert watched with amusement until she began coughing uncontrollably. Concerned, he reached out to pat her back, but his efforts only seemed to exacerbate the situation. Artemis's coughs sent clouds of dust swirling around them, pushing everything in the vicinity away.

Realizing the chaos their unintentional disturbance had caused, Gilbert couldn't help but chuckle, albeit sheepishly. "I guess we should watch where we're sitting next time," he remarked his tone light despite the situation.

Artemis's confusion deepened as she struggled to catch her breath amidst the swirling dust. Worried about Gilbert, she turned to check on him, only to see him clinging to her sleeve, flapping like a flag in the wind.

While holding onto Artemis's sleeve, he said, "Please be more careful next time. You might destroy a city with one of your coughs or sneezes."

Gilbert's words struck a chord with Artemis, reminding her of the potential consequences of their actions. Despite the seriousness of the situation, she couldn't help but chuckle nervously at his remark, and before they knew it, both burst into laughter, momentarily easing the tension between them. "I'll do my best to control my coughs," she replied, a hint of amusement in her voice.

Artemis and Gilbert were overcome with laughter, sharing in the absurdity of the moment. As her laughter subsided, Artemis noticed a strange bubble emerging from beneath Gilbert's ear, near the underside. Confusion turned to surprise as the bubble suddenly popped, only for another to form. She stared in disbelief as the peculiar bubbles appeared one by one. Concerned for his well-being, Artemis's curiosity peaked, and she couldn't resist asking if he was alright, unsure of what to make of the strange occurrence.

Between fits of laughter, Gilbert pointed at his ear and said, "You mean this?"

Artemis's curiosity pressed him further for an explanation. "Yes, that! What is it? Don't you breathe through your nose?" she asked, her voice tinged with a mixture of apprehension and intrigue.

Gilbert pointed to where the bubble emerged again and answered, "You mean this? The Flimsies have it, and it's how we breathe. We don't use our noses for breathing—just for sniffing."

Gilbert chuckled, looking at Artemis with a grin. "You make me laugh, and no one else can make me genuinely laugh like you," he admitted warmly. Then, he explained the strange bubbles emerging from his ears. "These are where we breathe from. You should see us when we're running or exercising. So we don't have to worry about choking on food. Our air and food go through different tunnels. And when we laugh a lot, it gets runny—just like your nose—so our breathing switches to here," he said, pointing to the area under his ear where the bubbles appeared.

Artemis took a moment to process Gilbert's explanation, feeling a mixture of surprise and fascination. It was another reminder of the alien nature of this world, where even basic bodily functions differed from what she was accustomed to on Earth. However, she reassured herself that despite these differences, she was safe here. After all, the beings in this world seemed delicate compared to humans, which meant there was little danger for her to worry about, at least for now.

Artemis's gaze remained fixed on Gilbert's hand, which was still positioned beside his face. Her curiosity piqued, she couldn't help but ask, "You always had that?" Her tone was filled with genuine interest and a hint of wonder as she awaited Gilbert's response.

Gilbert giggled and said, "Of course, for as long as I remember. This is another way we can recognize a human from Flimsy. You don't have it and I don't know how that's even possible. You humans breathe partially from the same place you eat and that's amazing. Isn't it?" Artemis nodded, fascinated by Gilbert's explanation.

"It's definitely unique," she replied, her tone reflecting her intrigue.

"Can you eat and breathe at the same time?" she asked, her tone full of surprise.

"Absolutely! It must be quite uncomfortable for you to have to stop breathing while you eat, right?" Gilbert remarked.

"I don't know. I've never thought about that. I guess that's one of the many differences between our worlds. It's incredible how even the smallest details can be so different." She paused for a moment, reflecting on the vastness of the universe and the diversity of its inhabitants.

Gilbert chuckled softly. "No worries, Artemis. We all have our quirks," he replied, offering her a reassuring smile.

"Besides, it's just another reminder of how unique each of us is, right?" He gestured towards the sky, where stars twinkled brightly against the dark canvas of the night. Then he turned to Artemis and asked, "How do food and air move through the human body?"

Artemis responded, "In humans, air enters through the nose or mouth and moves down the lungs, where oxygen is absorbed into the bloodstream. Food, on the other hand, passes through the stomach for digestion. The key is the epiglottis, a small flap that directs food and air into their proper pathways, preventing food from entering the trachea when we swallow and helping us from choking."

She glanced at Gilbert, her curiosity piqued. "As for your 'thingy,' it's fascinating. Do you mind if I take a closer look?"

Gilbert's smile widened as he withdrew his hand from the opening beneath his ear, inviting Artemis closer with a nod. "Yes, of course you can. Go ahead," he said warmly.

Artemis observed the thin line beneath Gilbert's ear, her curiosity piqued by this unique feature. With careful precision, she placed her hand on it, her gaze unwavering as she sought to understand its nature. This discovery ignited a sense of urgency within her, driving her to learn more about these new lives and the world around her. The realization of this newfound knowledge left her mind reeling with astonishment.

Artemis was intrigued by the similarity and asked, "What do you call them? It's like fish gills."

"Yes, that's why all superheroes call it, but we call it shoosh13," Gilbert replied.

Artemis delicately ran her fingers across Gilbert's skin, marveling at its silky softness. Despite her careful touch, she noticed Gilbert's skin turning red, perhaps from sensitivity. Her attention then shifted to Gilbert's head, where she observed his fascinating gills with curiosity.

"You know, when I focus more, I think I can see through your skin," Artemis remarked, her voice filled with wonder.

"I can see these Shoosh are connected to tubes that go to the back of your lungs. I can also see two tunnels coming from your nose that are connected to the front of your lungs. It's incredible and unbelievable. I can see your heart and inside your body, even from on top of your clothes."

Artemis froze when she heard Gilbert's scream. He was yelling, "Stop it... stop it! You're burning me."

"What happened? I didn't do anything," Artemis said as Gilbert backed up a little.

"When you focus on me, the energy coming through your eyes is harming me. Remember what happened in the restaurant? It's too strong for Flimsies' bodies. It's burning me. Please stop," Gilbert explained.

Artemis's expression turned somber as she processed Gilbert's words. "I think I feel that I'm not good for this world because no matter what I do, I hurt you and your people. I don't feel comfortable anymore," she admitted, sitting down and leaning back.

After a short time, Gilbert's curiosity piqued and asked, "How are you able to see us and if you want to see inside of our body?"

Artemis smiled and, without looking at him, explained, "You know how, when you're at home and you stand in front of a window, you see the beautiful greenery, the street, people passing by, the sky, and the rain? But when you focus on the window itself, all you see is the glass and dust or marks on it. You have the choice to look either at the window or through it. That's how it works for me—I can choose what to focus on."

Today had been a strange day for Artemis, and despite everything that had happened, she still didn't feel tired. Sitting beside Gilbert, she tried to distract herself from the overwhelming thoughts swirling in her mind. Sensing her distress, Gilbert felt a strong urge to cheer her up, wanting to lighten the weight of the emotions she was carrying.

As Artemis gazed at the view before her, a sudden tension gripped her. The uncertainty of her future weighed heavily on her mind. Stranded in this unfamiliar world, far from her loved ones, she grappled with the harsh reality that she might grow old and die alone—a thought that filled her with pain. Without turning to face Gilbert, Artemis posed a question that had been on her mind before.

"I know I asked this question before, but do you know where the other humans are?" Her tone held a hint of urgency, reflecting her growing determination to find answers.

Gilbert's response was tinged with uncertainty, mirroring Artemis's own sense of confusion and frustration. "I don't think anybody knows what happened and why they've left without any explanation," he replied, his gaze fixed on her as he spoke.

He added, "I believe they're all in hiding now, unwilling to reveal themselves. Don't ask me why—I truly don't know."

"What do you mean by that? You mean they quit?" Artemis asked

Gilbert's voice held a somber tone as he continued, "Not exactly, because they were everybody's heroes, and heroes never quit. They brought us happiness, knowledge, and security. One day, they were simply gone—vanished without a trace. It had to be something far more serious than we could imagine. Not long after, our Lord Demah introduced us to a new religion.

"They just vanished?" Artemis asked, her voice catching as she froze in place.

Gilbert nodded solemnly. "Yes, they just vanished without a trace. No one knows why or where they went. It's like they simply decided to leave, leaving the rest of us behind. After that, this religion came along and we were forced to accept the new religion. That's how it started when my father's grandfather was a baby." He paused, his expression troubled. "It's been a mystery that's haunted us for years."

Artemis nodded, contemplating the gravity of the situation. "It's strange. You're right. It must have been something significant for them to leave without a word. Perhaps there's more to their departure than meets the eye. But whatever the reason, their absence has left a void in the hearts of many," she sighed, a sense of sadness clouding her features. "I just wish we had some answers."

Gilbert took a deep breath, his voice heavy with sorrow. "They were everything to me, and they were my heroes, and still are."

There was a silence for a while before Gilbert continued, his tone somber. "While they were here in the city, I felt safe, and everybody had the same feeling. The rate of violence and crimes decreased by almost 90%. And suddenly, poof... they were gone. We looked everywhere for them. We had search teams for months and years, but they were nowhere to be found."

"Do you remember what happened the day before their disappearance?" Artemis questioned again.

"I heard somebody had some kind of weapon that could hurt them. People still don't know if Leo is still alive or not." Gilbert couldn't talk anymore; his eyes were full of tears. He looked away.

"What was the name of the other hero?" Artemis pressed again.

"Bare," replied Gilbert.

Artemis liked the name because she thought it meant "bear." She turned to Gilbert and said, "Oh, he must've been very powerful and adventurous, heroic and fearless. That's why you called him bear, right...?"

Artemis glanced at Gilbert to see if he was proud, too, but strangely, he was staring at her with his mouth open.

Artemis continued, "Yap..."

"No... I didn't say B...E...A...R!!! I said B...A...R...E," said Gilbert.

"He must've been very powerful as a bear," she said

Gilbert nodded without listening, then he continued, still looking at Artemis and corrected himself and said, "No... that's not the reason again! We called him Bare because he was bald, and his head was 'bare naked.' It was strange to us because, in our world, everybody has hair on their head. That's the way it is in our world. But for some strange reason, women liked him a lot."

"Do you remember any other ones?" she asked.

"Yes, and actually, that one was the best and he was the best friend of Lord Leo, too. His name was Baerion." Gilbert's mood shifted instantly, a wave of happiness and contentment washing over him as he revisited the cherished fragments of his memory.

Artemis reclined on her back, seeking a moment of calm, and affirmed with a subtle nod. "Yes, I know. On Earth, it's like that too. Bald men are more attractive for some reason to some women and not all the women. Anyway, where is he now?"

"I told you, I don't know. No one does," Gilbert replied calmly.

Artemis sat on the bench by the street, feeling a sense of unease about Gilbert's demeanor. As people passed by, she started whistling her favorite song by Jason Mraz.

"Well, you've done done me and you bet I felt it
I tried to be chill but you're so hot that I melted
I fell right through the cracks
Now I'm trying to get back
Before the cool done run out"

Gilbert interrupted the song midway, asking cheerfully, "What is this song? It's nice. I like it. Just don't mind me and go ahead, and I'm listening."

Artemis sang for some time until she grew tired. Gilbert had fallen into a deep sleep, and the surroundings were quiet. Peering into the jungle, she found it difficult to discern anything in the darkness, which seemed ominous. Opting instead to recline and admire the beautiful stars, she drifted off to sleep with a sense of contentment she had never experienced before.

When she awoke, it was still twilight. Gilbert had also risen, and upon opening his eyes, he immediately looked for Artemis. Settling down beside her, he made himself comfortable, ready for whatever the day might bring.

Artemis turned to him, her curiosity evident, and asked, "Tell me about your city, its seasons, and your culture. How many seasons do you have? How long do children attend school to graduate? And how do people get married here?"

Gilbert leaned back, clasping his hands behind his head, a thoughtful smile forming as he prepared to share the intricacies of his world. "Well, we have two seasons here," he began, "which we refer to as the summer day and the winter night."

Artemis curiously asked, "What do you mean by that?"

Gilbert looked at Artemis impatiently and said, "I was going to explain it to you before your interruption.

Apologies for the interruption," Artemis said, eager to hear more. Gilbert's explanation revealed the unique celestial dynamics of his world, where two suns govern the seasons. "We have two suns here. One moves faster than the smaller one. For one month every year, both suns are visible in the sky. During that time, the city shut down because the heat made it impossible to walk outside or work. There's no night for the entire month until the second sun leaves. Afterward, we return to our normal cycle, with warm, cozy days while during the night is like winter, the bitter cold could be deadly without proper shelter." He emphasized the perilous nature of the winter night, where exposure could lead to freezing to death.

Artemis interrupted once more, "What do you mean by 'frozen to death'?"

Gilbert shot her a bemused glance before replying, "Oh my, I'm imparting knowledge to an infant! Perhaps I should first teach you proper decorum when adults are conversing."

Artemis regarded him with curiosity. "If that's the case, why didn't we freeze last night? How did we make it through?"

Gilbert paused, contemplating her question, "It's because your body temperature is higher here," he explained. "Even when I was beside you, I depended on your body heat to make it through the night."

He waited to see if she had any further questions, but instead, he was met with her chuckling and giggling, which only served to heighten his irritation and disappointment.

Artemis eventually ceased her laughter and retorted, "Look who's talking about good behavior. Perhaps a lesson in manners is something you should consider, and the sooner, the better. But for now, please continue—I'm all ears."

Gilbert glanced at Artemis, shaking his head slightly. Despite his frustration, he understood the importance of imparting information to Artemis for her safety in their alien world. "Another crucial detail to note," he continued. "Here, we experience rain roughly every other week."

Artemis grinned mischievously, her curiosity piqued. "Wait a minute! Are you telling me rain is considered a season here? I thought we were discussing the main seasons."

Gilbert sat down, meeting her gaze directly. "Indeed," he replied, "rain is considered one of our primary seasons."

Artemis cleared her throat and spoke with curiosity. "So, let me get this straight. Your planet stays the same distance from the sun all year, which means you don't have seasons?"

She paused before continuing, "They don't call it a season? A season isn't half a day or a week. It happens because of the planet's distance from the sun and brings long-lasting changes. Like three months of rain, snow, wind, and cold or extremely hot weather for an extended period."

She looked at him and said, "On this planet, there's only one season and two temperatures—one for day and one for night. Does it make sense?"

Gilbert nodded, then he said, "Ok, I understand." Then he nodded again in affirmation, crossing his arms as he confirmed her understanding.

Artemis listened attentively and as he spoke, she was gaining a deeper understanding of the unique environment in which Gilbert lived. Absorbing the intricacies of Gilbert's world and gaining a deeper appreciation for its unique climate and conditions.

She was lost in her thoughts before asking, "How many months are in your year?"

"We have fifteen months in a year," Gilbert answered.

Artemis suddenly sat up, exclaiming, "Fifteen months?!"

"Yes, why?" he asked, concerned.

"Tell me now, how many days are in a month?" she asked, puzzled.

"Each month has 50 days," he replied, staring at Artemis intently.

"Isn't that unfair? Working for fifty days straight before getting paid?" Artemis couldn't help but feel outraged for the workers, thinking of how long they had to wait.

"Every ten days, we get paid," he said, much calmer now, as if he had been through these questions before.

"Who decided on these regulations about the months and days?" she asked.

"I don't know because they were our rules for as long as I remember. How is yours?" Gilbert asked impatiently

Artemis looked at Gilbert and explained, "Our system is based on the rotation of our planet and its orbit around the sun. One full rotation creates a day and night, and it takes twelve months for our planet to complete one orbit around the sun, which makes a year. Nobody chose it—it was discovered by scientists thousands of years ago."

Artemis drifted into deep thought, the silence stretching between them. After a moment, she broke it, her voice curious. "How many different animals have you discovered so far? And how do they survive in the jungle and beyond, especially during the cold nights?"

Gilbert replied calmly, "We've discovered around 2,500 different species. Surviving at night is simple—find a shelter, like a cave or thick cover of leaves. It helps retain body warmth. Just cover yourself with something and stay close to the ground, which we call Zamin. That's how they make it through the cold."

"What is Zamin?" Artemis asked

Gilbert's reverence for the mighty humans was evident in his tone as he mentioned their names. "You are standing on it. We call it Zamin, as I told you before, as the other entire mighty human said the same thing," he explained calmly. His affection for them was palpable, and even their names had a profound effect on him, causing his face to glow with admiration.

When Artemis mentioned the name Zamin, Gilbert was intrigued and listened intently, his gaze fixed on her without blinking. "That's interesting because in some countries and languages, the word 'Zamin' means delicate, airy, and light," she explained.

Gilbert's curiosity grew as he pondered the linguistic and cultural differences between their worlds, fascinated by how one word could carry such varied meanings across different realms. Gilbert's remark sparked a thoughtful expression on Artemis's face. "Perhaps," she mused, considering the intriguing possibility. "It's fascinating how the same word can carry such different connotations depending on the context and perspective."

Artemis felt that she had hurt Gilbert's feelings by describing his planet as airy and light. She attempted to rectify her words. "When I explained the meaning of your planet, you seemed upset and agitated, but that was never my intention. Do you understand? On my planet, in certain cultures and languages like Persians, Earth is called the same as it is here—they call it Zamin," Artemis clarified her intentions.

Gilbert was surprised by the depth of Artemis's explanation and appreciated her effort to clarify. He knew his race well and didn't take her words as an insult. "What made you think I felt bad or upset? We appreciate all the help you provide in fighting crime here, and we understand that we are weaker compared to you. It's not an insult, it's simply who we are," Gilbert responded, reassured by Artemis's understanding, feeling a sense of comfort in her ability to grasp the complexity of the situation.

Artemis listened intently as Gilbert began to explain the various types of crimes prevalent in their world. However, her attention was diverted when she glanced at the sun and felt a cold sweat forming on her forehead.

Observing the sun's position, Artemis noticed something unusual—it was sinking in the east instead of the west. At first, she thought she might be mistaken or unwell. Confusion filled her as this defied everything she knew about the natural order. After quickly calculating the time since her arrival, she realized that over 45 hours had passed since she woke up, and the sun was now setting for the second time. Each sunset in this world stretched on, lasting approximately 40 to 50 hours in Earth time.

Here, the days stretched incredibly long, yet Artemis never felt the fatigue she would expect from such extended hours. It intrigued her deeply, as if the natural rhythms of this world had an entirely different effect on her body. Despite the unusual length of the day, she remained energized, a mystery that added to the wonder of this place.

Artemis turned to Gilbert with a weary expression. "I'm feeling quite tired and could use a rest. Would it be alright if I sat down for a while?"

Gilbert nodded in understanding. "Of course, resting would be fine, but not here. We're close to the edge of the city."

"Come on! Don't tell me it's not safe here. I'm with you, and nothing can harm me. I'll protect you if necessary," she said confidently. Then, she closed her eyes and quickly fell asleep.

Artemis felt a soothing sensation as she drifted into sleep. In her dream, she soared through the sky, gazing down at the planet below. But her awe turned to fear as the world below appeared fragile, like a giant balloon ready to burst. The thought of the planet popping filled her with dread, stripping away the meaning of existence.

Suddenly, a hand touched her arm, yanking at her sleeve. Startled, Artemis tried to see who or what it was, only to hear Gilbert's voice crying out for help. With a jolt, she opened her eyes to darkness enveloping everything. Only a faint glimmer of light in the distance provided any illumination. Artemis turned to Gilbert, whose eyes mirrored her own fear and panic.

Gilbert's urgent cries pierced through the darkness, jolting Artemis from her slumber. She followed his gaze to where he was pointing, her heart racing with adrenaline.

"Wake up, Artemis! Look! We're under attack," Gilbert shouted, his voice filled with desperation. "Help, Artemis! Help..."

Artemis's mind raced as she tried to make sense of the situation, her instincts kicking into high gear.

Artemis slowly turned her face toward the direction Gilbert was pointing, her heart pounding in her chest. At first, she froze, her mind struggling to comprehend what she was seeing. But then, as her eyes adjusted to the dim light, recognition dawned on her. She could distinguish those eyes, and the sound reached her ears like a distant echo, growing louder with each passing moment.

Artemis turned to Gilbert, her voice trembling with a mix of fear and confusion. "I know this animal. It's the same one that attacked me in the mountains. But for some reason, it pulled back and just followed me. I don't understand why it's not attacking now."

"I know it's not going to attack you, but it's here for me now because I'm the easy target. Help me before I pass out!" Gilbert screamed. "Send him away! Please!" Gilbert yelled, his voice desperate, before suddenly falling silent.

Artemis remembered the creature's previous attack on her, but she was filled with doubt about her ability to fight back. Despite her experiences since arriving in this world, she still questioned her own strength. The biggest hurdle was her belief in herself. On Earth, she would have had every right to be scared, but here, she knew she needed to overcome that fear. Gilbert could see the fear in her eyes as she hesitated to move forward.

Artemis hesitated, pulling back slightly as she voiced her uncertainty. "How can I possibly push away this enormous animal? It's ten times larger than I am! I think I need help. What do you think, Gilbert?"

Gilbert, frustrated with Artemis's hesitation, resorted to reverse psychology in a last-ditch effort to spur her into action. With the last of his strength, he confronted her. "Are you a mighty girl or a mighty mouse? I can't believe what I'm seeing! Artemis, you can do it, I promise you that. You just have to push him back, and you'll see! I believe in you."

The creature drew closer, stopping just a few steps from Artemis. It began to sniff both Gilbert and Artemis, hesitating for a moment before approaching Artemis. As it opened its mouth, it suddenly grabbed her hand. Startled and panicked, Artemis screamed, "Leave me alone!"

She struggled, waving her hand in the air, desperate to free herself from the creature's grasp. To her surprise, the creature was suddenly lifted into the air and crashed loudly a few steps away from her and onto the ground. It quickly got back up, glanced at Artemis, then turned its attention to Gilbert. A surge of anger overwhelmed her— she felt responsible for him and couldn't bear the thought of anything happening to him. Though she hadn't fought for herself, she charged at the creature to defend Gilbert. With one punch, she sent it flying through the air. As it hit the ground, the creature scrambled to its feet and ran away.

Artemis glanced at Gilbert, who appeared pale and shocked. She sat down beside him on the ground, taking a deep breath to calm herself. Her heart was pounding visibly in her chest. After composing herself, she turned to Gilbert and asked in a distressed tone, "What was that?"

Gilbert, still shaken by the encounter, struggled to find his voice. He answered weakly, "We call it Sheebr. It's one of the most dangerous and powerful creatures on Zamin." He took a few more breaths before continuing, "I knew I would be safe with you." Artemis felt proud. Gilbert's eyes gleamed with excitement as Artemis showed interest in learning more about the Sheebr. "They're one of the largest animals on Zamin, and they're known to eat just about anything. They're omnivores," Gilbert explained, his gaze fixed on Artemis to gauge her reaction. Then he continued, "No one had ever been able to face them, let alone catch them."

Gilbert leaned back, feeling a sense of relief as he explained, "Yes, you could say that Sheebr is like a combination of a lion and a tiger, but even more formidable and imposing," he elaborated, his voice tinged with a hint of awe.

"How do you know about Lions and tigers if you've never been on my planet before?" Artemis asked surprisingly

Gilbert's response was matter-of-fact, delivered with conviction and he explained, emphasizing his point. "You never listened. I've mentioned before that there were a few other humans who lived here, and they all came from the same planet as you,"

Gilbert's expression softened as he considered Artemis's question and he continued, "Ah, well, you see, I've learned a lot from the stories and knowledge shared by the other humans who have lived here. Their tales have painted vivid pictures of creatures from your world, like lions, tigers, elephants, etc. It's fascinating to learn about the diversity of life on different planets."

Gilbert recounted the recent events with a sense of urgency, wanting to reassure Artemis while also expressing his concern. "You were exhausted, and when you sat down, you just... fell asleep. I was right beside you, and I dozed off, too. Suddenly, I heard growling, and when I looked, the Sheebr was there, ready to attack. I rushed to your side, and then you woke up. Well, you saw what happened next," he explained, his voice filled with relief.

Artemis observed her hands intently, searching for any signs of harm or injury. Finding none, she glanced at Gilbert, her expression a mix of confusion and relief. Artemis wore a puzzled expression as she questioned Gilbert, her curiosity evident in her tone.

"But you said they are one of the strongest animals here and they're not even tamed because they are not tamable?" She paused, allowing the thought to settle before continuing, "But there is a problem here? Why this dangerous untamed animal is giving up its prey so easily?" She trailed off with a thoughtful hum, awaiting Gilbert's response.

Artemis emphasized her question by gesturing with her arms, ensuring Gilbert understood her inquiry. "But why did this huge and strong animal give up on its prey so easily?" she reiterated, her tone tinged with curiosity and a hint of bewilderment.

Gilbert hesitated for a moment, his gaze locked with Artemis's beautiful and lovely eyes. He felt an overwhelming urge to embrace her, to hold her close in his arms. Yet, he hesitated, fearful of misinterpreting his actions. He didn't want Artemis to perceive his gesture as merely an attempt to gain favor or admiration because of her power and allure. No, his feelings ran much deeper than that. Gilbert was willing to sacrifice everything for her, to give his life if necessary. But conveying the depth of his love and devotion was a daunting task, one he wasn't sure he could accomplish.

Gilbert rose to his feet, his gaze steady on Artemis. "My dear Artemis, have you not yet realized? When I say nothing in this world can harm you, I mean everything—anything—even the most dangerous bomb that could reduce an entire city to dust," he said, his voice gentle but full of earnestness.

As Gilbert prepared to express his love for her, he noticed a shift in Artemis's expression. It seemed to morph into a mix of puzzlement and anger, perhaps indicating that she either knew the answer already but was unwilling to accept it. Taking a deep breath, Gilbert settled down beside Artemis.

He scanned the surroundings briefly before reclining against the bench, beginning to explain without meeting Artemis's gaze. "Artemis, if it weren't for you tonight, I'd likely be in Sheebr's belly by now."

"No, you'd be at home, asleep. You're here because of me," Artemis interjected.

Gilbert struggled to maintain his composure amidst the chaos and potential danger. Though his heart was filled with love for Artemis, he knew revealing too much at once might push her away. He understood that remaining rational was crucial, even if it left him feeling drained and uncertain. Yet, despite the internal conflict, Gilbert stayed prepared to defend her at a moment's notice, knowing that alarming her was a risk he was willing to take should another threat arise. His loyalty and dedication to Artemis remained unwavering.

Without reacting to her answer, Gilbert continued, "They attack us periodically, and no one has been able to stop them. Only you, I mean you superheroes, could stand up and fight. We never had this problem when one of you superheroes was here."

Gilbert continued after a moment of silence, his tone steady, "You are not penetrable here. You are untouchable, whether you believe it or not. I don't know your situation in your world, but here it's like that."

Artemis was still in denial of such extraordinary power, as it didn't make sense to her. Yet, despite her skepticism, she found herself on the verge of becoming a believer, torn between disbelief and an emerging acceptance of what seemed impossible. She thought these powers were imaginary or temporary or even had limitations, but they were true. She stood up straight and gazed at the sky, which was beautiful and clear tonight. It was adorned with millions of stars spread across the expanse. Turning around, she began to touch everything around her—the ground, the bench, and even the trees. It was as if she had just been born, experiencing the world for the first time. She leaned against a thick tree and hugged it, but its rough bark felt smooth under her touch. She realized she could effortlessly peel off the bark with her nails, the sensation oddly reminiscent of pressing into jello. Then, she instinctively punched the tree, prompting Gilbert to scream, "Be careful!"

Artemis noticed Gilbert sitting underneath the tree, unaware of the danger he was in. Panicking at first, she was beginning to understand her true abilities and realized her power. Without hesitation, she held the tree with one hand and shouted at Gilbert, "Should I send you an invitation to move?"

Then, with a swift motion, she threw the tree in a different direction, ensuring Gilbert's safety. With a mischievous giggle, she urged him, "Move over a little!" She sat beside him briefly, then stood up again, glancing around.

Gilbert, though initially frustrated and soaked in sweat, recognized the playful innocence in Artemis's behavior. He couldn't help but smile as he stood up and straightened his pants. Meanwhile, Artemis was overjoyed, jumping up and down in celebration of her newfound power. With renewed confidence, she looked at Gilbert, who stood in awe of her abilities. Artemis examined her hands with a sense of wonder, then turned to Gilbert with newfound confidence.

"Well, I am the mighty power on your planet. I am incredibly strong and can break a tree as easily as breaking a cookie in two pieces." Gilbert nodded, his eyes shining with tears of joy as he looked at the tree and then back at Artemis, a radiant smile gracing his face.

Gilbert's expression contorted into a mix of shock and awe as he struggled to find his words. "Yes! Now you've got that," he managed to say, his voice barely above a whisper.

Artemis, however, wasn't satisfied. She picked up a large pebble and held it between her fingers, crushing it effortlessly like a piece of soft marshmallow. The pebble shattered into pieces, scattering onto the ground. Fascinated by her newfound power, Artemis scanned her surroundings and spotted a large rock. She approached it cautiously, studying it from different angles before reaching out to touch it. With a swift motion, she broke it into smaller pieces, the sound echoing through the air. She continued to break it until it was reduced to rubble, her movements almost frantic. Finally, she looked up at Gilbert and then at the sky before sinking to her knees.

She glanced at Gilbert again and joked, "I'm just glad I'm not obsessed with Mickey Mouse, or I might have ended up looking like him." She laughed at her own joke but then quickly fell into silence, her thoughts returning to the weight of everything around her.

Gilbert didn't quite understand her joke, but he could sense that she was beginning to transition toward believing in the powers she'd once denied. Her playful remark and momentary laughter hinted at a shift in her mindset, as if she was slowly coming to terms with the extraordinary.

Artemis's voice trembled with uncertainty as she voiced her inner turmoil. "What's happening to me? Maybe Ricky was right, and it's my wish that's twisting me around. Maybe I should've been more careful about what I wished for. Perhaps when I made a wish before blowing out the candles, it wasn't my true desire. Maybe deep down, my real wish was something else—something I've always longed for in my heart." Her belief was getting stronger and more logical to her now.

Artemis's breaths were shallow and rapid, her chest rising and falling with visible agitation. She reached out to Gilbert, her hands trembling with emotion, but he recoiled, retreating with a cry.

"Please, don't touch me," he shouted, his voice strained with fear.

"You might crush me or squeeze me like a pumpkin, especially now." His face turned white, and he looked scared

Artemis recognized Gilbert's fear and immediately halted her approach. Gilbert, however, found refuge behind a sizable tree, resembling a mouse sheltering behind a broom in a kitchen. He cowered, akin to a house cat in hiding. Aware that fleeing was futile, he remained rooted to the spot, gripped by terror at Artemis's seemingly erratic behavior. He feared she had lost control.

"Artemis! My lady! Please, just sit down and relax. I implore you, don't harm me. I'm not worth it. I can assist you in exploring our world further or perhaps even in locating the other humans. Please, calm yourself."

Artemis sat down and scanned her surroundings, contemplating the immense power she now possessed. She had no idea if she should be happy or sad. It was the kind of power she had always dreamed of—a power that could command obedience from even the wildest and most formidable creatures. Here, she was akin to a superhero, or perhaps more accurately, a superwoman. As she stood up, the wind tousled her hair, giving her a disheveled yet alluring appearance. Gilbert, watching her from behind the tree, was captivated by her presence.

"She's gorgeous and terrifying—God, I love her," he murmured, surprised to hear himself say it out loud.

"But the real problem? I can't tell her that. She might get angry and flatten me like a pancake," he thought, half amused and half terrified.

"You know, Gilbert," Artemis began, reminiscing about her world, "in my world, I used to have a crush on Superman. I watched every series or movie of Superman on television or in theaters. You know, I think I'd still give up these powers just to return to my family as an ordinary person, not a superhero. I missed them so much." As she spoke, she remained standing, savoring the increasing wind.

Despite her earlier discomfort with the darkness, she now felt braver than ever. But as the weather abruptly shifted, a thick cloud of dust enveloped her, obscuring her from Gilbert's view. Moments later, as the dust settled, Artemis emerged, standing powerfully amidst the chaotic swirl of wind and debris. The storm whipped around her, but she remained unaffected, almost as if she was part of the storm itself.

Debris brushed against her skin, even reaching her delicate pupils, but she stood firm, her wide eyes keenly observing every movement in every direction. Dust, pebbles, and leaves spiraled around her, yet she felt only invigorated, fearless in the midst of the tempest.

Artemis followed the traces cautiously, her senses alert for any signs of danger. She remembered the earlier encounter with the Sheebr and the sudden attack. She moved with a steady pace, scanning the area for any movement or unusual sounds. As she ventured deeper into the jungle, the traces of the Sheebr's presence became more evident, leading her to wonder why the creature had attacked and then retreated.

Artemis ventured into the jungle, following the traces left by the Sheebr, her determination driving her forward. Gilbert hesitated for a moment, torn between his fear and his desire to stay by Artemis's side. When he finally made his decision to go after her, he found that she had already disappeared into the dense foliage. Despite his trepidation, Gilbert took a deep breath and plunged into the jungle, determined to catch up with Artemis and ensure her safety. He knew there were forbidden areas ahead, places even a superhero should avoid.

Lost in the dense vegetation, Gilbert called out for Artemis, his voice echoing through the jungle. The unfamiliar surroundings filled him with unease, and he couldn't shake the feeling of vulnerability that washed over him. Despite his fear, he continued to call out, hoping desperately for a response that would lead him back to Artemis's side.

The sounds of movement in the jungle heightened Gilbert's fear, and he felt a shiver run down his spine. Goosebumps prickled his skin as he strained to identify the source of the sounds. Despite his growing panic, he forced himself to move backward, step by cautious step. Then, a surge of terror overwhelmed him, and he felt an urgent need to flee. Turning toward the safety of the city, Gilbert's feet froze in place, fear paralyzing him. His voice trembled as he called out for Artemis, desperate for her presence.

Gilbert's voice quivered with fear as he pleaded for Artemis's help, his words echoing through the jungle. "Oh... my... god...! Please, Artemis, help me. Help me? My dear Artemis, I shouldn't be scared of you, and I made a mistake. I should be with you. I'm so sorry."

"H... E... L... P... M... E...!" he whispered softly to himself. "It's not help I need... I just need to see you."

As the colossal Sheebr drew nearer, Gilbert found himself frozen against the tree, his heart pounding in his chest. The creature's presence was overwhelming, its breath heavy and hot. This wasn't just any Sheebr—it was the legendary giant, the one spoken of in hushed tones by all who had heard tales of its immense size and fearsome appearance. Gilbert knew he was facing a perilous situation, one that few had ever survived. Yet, in the face of such danger, he resolved to remain calm and think rationally, searching for any possible solution that might save him from this formidable foe.

As Gilbert grappled with the looming threat of the Sheebr and the relentless barrage of negative thoughts, he felt a wave of despair wash over him. The darkness of his own doubts seemed to consume him, whispering that he was insignificant, that his absence would go unnoticed. Despite the weight of these thoughts, Gilbert knew he couldn't succumb to despair. He clung to a glimmer of hope, a flicker of determination to survive and prove his worth, even in the face of seemingly insurmountable odds.

With a heavy heart, Gilbert wrestled with the harsh reality of his solitude. The absence of family and friends weighed heavily on him, a reminder of the isolation he felt in this moment of peril. Yet, amidst the despair, he found a sliver of solace in the thought that his voice would not echo unheard into the void. In this desolate moment, there was a strange comfort in knowing that his words, his fears, and his struggles would not fall on deaf ears, even if they were his own.

With a newfound determination, Gilbert embraced the resolve to face his fate head-on. Despite the overwhelming odds stacked against him, he refused to succumb without a fight. In that pivotal moment, he reclaimed his agency, refusing to let his Cranky be a passive surrender. Instead, he embraced the spirit of defiance, ready to confront whatever challenges lay ahead with courage and determination.

In a moment of sheer adrenaline-fueled bravery, Gilbert mustered every ounce of his courage and resolve. With his heart pounding in his chest and his senses heightened to a razor-sharp edge, he faced the charging Sheebr head-on. Though fear threatened to overwhelm him, he refused to back down, standing tall in the face of impending danger. As the creature closed in, Gilbert closed his eyes, a single tear tracing its path down his cheek, a testament to the gravity of the situation. Yet, even in the midst of his fear, he summoned the strength to stand his ground, ready to confront whatever fate had in store for him.

As Gilbert braced himself for what he believed would be his final moments, he uttered his last words, a heartfelt goodbye to Artemis, the only solace in his terrifying predicament. "Goodbye, my Lady Artemis, my love, whose place in my heart no one can ever fill. Goodbye, my eternal love."

With trembling hands and a racing heart, he awaited the inevitable impact, steeling himself for the end. But as the seconds stretched into eternity, nothing happened. With trepidation, he dared to open his eyes, expecting to confront his Cranky enemy. Yet, what he saw left him dumbfounded and incredulous.

For the second time one day in his life, Gilbert found himself face to face with the legendary Sheebr, a creature shrouded in mystery and terror. The tales he had heard, the whispered accounts of its size, shape, and the mesmerizing 100 different colors of its mane illuminate—all seemed like distant echoes now, replaced by the stark reality of its presence before him. This was the moment of truth for Gilbert, a moment he had never imagined he would live to see. The Sheebr, a creature of myth and fear, stood before him, the legendary being coming to life right before his eyes. Its form was both imposing and awe-inspiring in its enormity, a figure from stories now terrifyingly real. All around him, the air seemed to crackle with tension, as if the very forest held its breath in anticipation of what would transpire next. And in that moment, Gilbert realized that he was not just facing a creature of legend, but the embodiment of his deepest fears and the ultimate test of his courage.

As he gazed upon the Sheebr, he was hypnotized by its magnificence, struck by the intricate details of its form. Every aspect of the creature seemed both terrifying and mesmerizing, drawing him deeper into its awe-inspiring presence. Its towering height, adorned with a mane of long, flowing hair cascading down its back, mesmerized Gilbert. With each movement, the mane shifted to different brilliant colors, captivating his attention, leaving him both awed and unsettled by the creature's majesty. The colors of its body shifted and changed with each movement, like a rainbow illuminated, glossy and radiant, dancing in the dappled light of the forest. Golden hues melded into rich browns and blacks, forming patterns that seemed almost too perfect to be natural.

The Sheebr's massive limbs, adorned with sharp, curved claws that split into two at the tips, gleamed ominously in the early sunlight. Gilbert couldn't help but notice the intricate markings adorning its body—thick circles and intricate designs that spoke of a deliberate, almost artistic hand behind their creation. Its ears protruded from the sides of its head, adding to its otherworldly appearance. The most captivating feature was its tail, resembling that of a horse, moving flawlessly and fluidly with a strange allure. It swayed up and down in the air, and with each movement, it produced a soft, twinkling sound—angelic and enchanting, as if the very air around it shimmered with magic.

But it was the Sheebr's eyes that held Gilbert's gaze the most. Unlike any other creature he had seen, The Sheebr's eyes sank inward when it blinked and emerged again when it opened them, giving it a unique and unsettling expression. His father had always told him stories about the Sheebr, warning him that no one should ever look into its eyes. The creature was said to hypnotize its victims with just a gaze, rendering them helpless before it consumed them. As he couldn't escape after seeing the eyes, and he lost control of his body and stood there defenceless. As Gilbert's eyes traced over the creature's massive tusks and fangs, he realized the danger he had narrowly escaped, but strangely, he was not afraid anymore and kept staring into his eyes.

In that moment, Gilbert felt a surge of gratitude toward Artemis, whose quick reflexes had saved him from certain doom. He couldn't help but marvel at the Sheebr power and majesty of the creature before him, even as he felt a shiver of fear run down his spine.

In that breathtaking moment, as Gilbert's eyes fluttered open and he was frozen in his spot, he beheld an incredible sight—the Sheebr suspended in mid-air, held fast by Artemis's unyielding grip on its formidable fangs. The Sheebr strength and agility displayed by Artemis left Gilbert utterly speechless, his heart pounding with a mix of awe and relief.

For the first time in his life, Gilbert felt a surge of gratitude toward someone who had risked their own safety to protect him. Artemis's swift and decisive action had spared him from a grisly fate, and as he watched her effortlessly subdue the fearsome creature, he couldn't help but feel a newfound sense of respect and admiration for her.

In that fleeting moment, Gilbert realized that he was not alone—that there was someone who cared enough to stand by his side in the face of danger. And as he looked upon Artemis's determined expression, he knew that he could trust her to keep him safe, no matter what challenges lay ahead.

As Artemis studied the majestic creature before her, the Sheebr attempted to strike her with its colossal, razor-sharp paws. However, despite their menacing appearance, the creature's powerful claws proved futile against Artemis's seemingly invulnerable form. To her, it felt like being tickled with a feather, and she couldn't help but burst into laughter at the absurdity of the situation.

The Sheebr's failed attempts to harm her only served to reinforce Artemis's sense of invincibility, and she gazed upon the creature with a mixture of amusement and wonder. It was a surreal moment, watching as the fearsome beast struggled in vain against her impervious defenses, and Artemis couldn't help but marvel at the Sheebr strength and resilience of her newfound powers.

Artemis's radiant presence filled Gilbert with a sense of relief and gratitude, prompting him to drop to his knees with a mixture of tears and relief. As he composed himself, he cast his gaze upon Artemis, who stood before him, illuminated by the soft glow of the city lights behind her.

"Thank you for coming back for me, Artemis," Gilbert said, his voice choked with emotion.

Artemis regarded him with a puzzled expression. "What do you mean? I never left you. Did you think I abandoned you?" she asked, her tone tinged with genuine concern.

Artemis's expression revealed a profound disappointment as she gazed into Sheebr's eyes. Despite holding it firmly by its fangs, she gradually loosened her grip, making her movements deliberate and controlled. Gilbert yelled at Artemis, "Be aware of his eyes!!" She looked at Gilbert, then at the Sheebr. With a determined air, she released Sheebr, but not without a stern warning.

"I don't want to ever see you here again," she declared firmly, her voice echoing with authority. "Consider this your final warning. I won't tolerate your actions towards your victims any longer."

After landing gracefully on his paws, Sheebr paused for a moment as if assessing the situation. Then, with a sudden burst of movement, he bolted into the woods, disappearing into the darkness without looking back.

Artemis turned to Gilbert, a gentle smile on her face. "Did you really think I'd leave you here without any protection? Thank you for trusting me." Artemis smiled reassuringly at Gilbert.

"I understand. But remember, I'm here to keep you safe. You can always count on me." She extended her hand toward him, offering support and solidarity.

Gilbert's expression softened, a mix of regret and shame crossing his features. "I'm sorry. I didn't mean to doubt you. I just thought maybe you had left to explore the world, and I felt forgotten. That's all."

Artemis glanced at Gilbert, a hint of disbelief in her eyes, but then a smile played on her lips. She turned her attention back to the woods and remarked, "I waited for Sheebr to attack. I wanted to understand how they operate, and it was quite remarkable."

Gilbert's frustration boiled over as he confronted Artemis. He moved closer to her and exclaimed, "So, I was just baited to you, nothing more? How could you use me like that? You, the little mighty girl! You're being mean, and I don't appreciate it."

Artemis looked at Gilbert and teased, "That's how you talk to your Lord?"

They both remained quiet for a moment before she smiled and added, "But I didn't leave you behind, and I was here to protect you," Artemis blurted out, her tone softening with warmth.

Gilbert glared at her with anger and accused, "But you just admitted that you were waiting for him to attack because you wanted to see how he would do it, and you like to study animals, right?"

Artemis's face flushed with guilt as she glanced at him and simply shrugged.

Gilbert perched himself on a broken tree trunk, his gaze fixed on Artemis in amazement. Placing his hand under his chin, he exclaimed, "That was incredible, watching how you handled him— even though my life was on the line. Now... do you believe it?"

Artemis responded with a shrug and a smile. "Of course I do. I've believed in my power for a long time, but it's still hard to fully grasp that it's actually happening to me. After everything that's happened, I don't think I'll ever doubt it again. But still, I'd like to doubt it— it's just in my nature. I still live by the science of my world and everything that's happened here would be rejected by our scientific understanding."

Artemis walked toward a large tree nearby and casually pushed it from side to side. With surprising ease, she then pushed it forward until, with a loud crack, it snapped and fell to the ground. Glancing up at the sky and then down at Gilbert, she instructed him, "You just stay here and don't go anywhere. I'll be back in five minutes, but before I go, I'll make sure there aren't any wild animals around here."

As Artemis dashed away like the wind, leaving behind only faint traces of her footsteps, Gilbert remained seated, his senses heightened. Aware of the lurking dangers, he tried to remain as quiet as possible, knowing that not only animals but also the more menacing Flimsies posed a threat in this place. He couldn't shake the feeling that he was in the wrong place at the wrong time.

As Gilbert strained to discern any potential threats, his attention was drawn to two approaching figures. They advanced steadily, prompting Gilbert to ponder whether they were wild animals or individuals. However, the presence of strangers in such remote surroundings aroused a sense of unease within him. As they drew nearer, their silhouettes gradually took shape, though their identities remained elusive. Gilbert resigned himself to await their arrival.

Ultimately, the two figures materialized into recognizable individuals. Gilbert's apprehension heightened, particularly upon identifying one of them, and he wished those two figures were wild animals and not those two. This person had a history of imposing tasks on Gilbert, often with stringent conditions attached. Failure to comply with their demands invariably resulted in severe consequences. Gilbert instinctively rose to his feet, surveying his surroundings for any sign of Artemis's return. Yet, the landscape remained devoid of her presence.

Gilbert greeted them with a courteous smile and inquired, "Hi, guys. What brought you here?" His gaze shifted from one to the other as he addressed them by name, adding, "Hi, Cranky and Corrupt."

Cranky exuded an unsettling aura, his demeanor devoid of any discernible emotion. He seemed almost mechanical, akin to The Walking Dead, but far more unnerving. A faint odor of decay lingered around him, adding to his eerie presence. Always toying with something in his hand, this time, it was a small knife concealed within his sleeve, tethered to his arm by a chain. Gilbert couldn't fathom how Cranky managed to deploy the knife without injuring himself, and he observed cautiously as Cranky deftly retracted the blade, seemingly controlled by a concealed mechanism. Clad in his usual ensemble of baggy clothes adorned with numerous pockets, each layer a different hue, it was a challenge to distinguish one from the other.

In contrast to Cranky's somber demeanor, Corrupt was his steadfast companion, eagerly carrying out any task to earn Cranky's favor. Despite their partnership, Corrupt's appearance and style differed markedly from Cranky's. His hairstyle was particularly distinctive, featuring two ponytails positioned atop his head. One, situated above his eyes, transitioned from a deep red at the base to a vibrant yellow at the tip, while the second ponytail, positioned at the back, was entirely white. Corrupt's penchant for painting his teeth black and his tongue, coupled with the darkened skin around his eyes, lent him a menacing and unsettling air. He seemed to revel in the discomfort he inspired in others, a fact not lost on Gilbert, who couldn't help but feel unnerved in Corrupt's presence.

Cranky exuded an air of authority, his demeanor marked by an utter lack of concern for others. His visage remained impassive at all times, whether engaged in combat or amusement. His expression betrayed no hint of emotion. It was impossible to discern whether he was laughing, crying, or shouting. Despite the striking beauty of his eyes, Cranky possessed a distinctly rugged personality. His gaze held a mesmerizing quality, capable of immobilizing those who met his gaze. There was an inexplicable aura surrounding his eyes as if they possessed a hypnotic power over those who dared to look into them. Always at his side was a cane, a cherished possession that he guarded fiercely, never permitting another to handle it. The cane, with its peculiar spiky ball atop a regular stick, added to his enigmatic and unsettling presence. Cranky's stoicism was unmistakable, evident in every line of his face.

Gilbert remained rooted in place, refraining from advancing towards them. He harbored a reluctance to draw nearer, acutely aware of the unpredictable nature of Cranky and Corrupt, particularly the latter. Uncertain whether they intended to harm or had a new task in store for him, he chose to maintain a cautious distance.

"Hello, guys!" Gilbert repeated, his tone is cautious yet composed. He silently prayed for Artemis's swift return, hoping to avert any potential danger that might arise in their presence.

Corruptly approached Gilbert, his movement calculated and menacing. He placed a firm hand on Gilbert's chest, pinning him against the sturdy trunk of a nearby tree. The pressure was relentless, suffocating as if Corrupt had no intention of releasing his grip anytime soon. Gilbert's gaze remained fixed on the sky, his eyes swirling with fear and disorientation. Corrupt followed his gaze briefly before turning his attention to Cranky, a silent exchange passing between them.

"I've heard about your little hero," Cranky remarked, his voice tinged with a sinister edge.

"I'd love to have a go at breaking her myself. But don't worry my little friend," he said with a sinister grin. He continued, his gaze fixed on the sky as if lost in thought. "I know she's breakable, and I'm just the one to do it. If she's looking for an opportunity, she can come to me." He paused a second and said, "Hand this over to your little hero."

Cranky approached Gilbert, locking eyes with him in a way that sent a shiver down Gilbert's spine. His gaze, devoid of any hint of humor, seemed to penetrate straight into Gilbert's soul. As Cranky's hand made contact with Gilbert's neck, the coldness of Gilbert's own sweat against his skin sent a chill through him. With a swift motion, Cranky produced an envelope and tossed it onto Gilbert's chest before turning away, his attention drawn back to the city. Corrupt, always in tow, followed his lead, trailed behind as he turned back toward Gilbert and flashed him a mocking gesture with his finger.

Relieved to see them leaving, Gilbert sank down, feeling a sense of ease now that they were no longer looming over him. He quickly pocketed the envelope, his attention shifting as he caught sight of Artemis approaching. He managed a faint smile and chose to set the envelope aside, keeping it out of her reach.

Artemis returned with a jubilant exuberance, her voice ringing out loud and cheerful. It had been nearly twenty minutes since she had left, but to her, it felt like a lifetime of freedom she had never experienced before. She reveled in the sensation of liberation, relishing the absence of fear as she walked confidently through the jungle, even in the dead of night.

Gilbert remained seated beside the tree, his eyes closed in quiet contemplation, as Artemis returned and settled down beside him. Lying on her back, she found a comfortable position, gazing up at the expansive night sky. Above them, the heavens were adorned with thousands of shimmering stars, their brilliance accentuated against the deep, dark blue canvas of the firmament. A scattering of fluffy white clouds added a touch of texture to the celestial vista, making the scene all the more captivating. In this moment of serenity, free from worry or fear, Artemis gradually succumbed to the tranquility of the night, her eyelids gently closing as sleep overtook her.

THE WEIGHT OF TIME

Back on Earth, four years had slipped by since Artemis disappeared, leaving an unfillable void in Matt's heart. In the wake of her disappearance, he had searched tirelessly, scouring every corner of the world in hopes of finding a trace of her presence. But as the years stretched on, hope began to wane, replaced by a gnawing sense of loss and longing. Memories of their time together haunted him, a bittersweet reminder of the bond they had shared and the adventures they had embarked upon.

Despite the passage of time, Matt remained steadfast in his determination to find Artemis, clinging to the belief that somewhere out there, she was waiting for him. And as he gazed up at the stars, he couldn't help but wonder if she, too, was looking back, her spirit still intertwined with his in the vast expanse of the cosmos.

As Matt trudged through the knee-deep snow in Artemis's neighborhood, he found himself questioning how he had ended up in this area. But with each step, memories flooded his mind, reminding him of the deep bond he had shared with his best friend, making the journey both heavy and bittersweet. He wasn't sure why he found himself wandering through this neighborhood filled with memories of Artemis. Toronto's perpetual cold and snow seemed to mirror the icy ache in his heart, a constant reminder of the void her absence had left behind.

He couldn't shake the guilt that gnawed at him, blaming himself for the events of that fateful night. It was his insistence that had led Artemis down that path, and he couldn't forgive himself for the consequences. If only he could turn back time and undo the choices that had torn them apart.

But amidst the bitter cold and swirling snow, there remained a flicker of hope in Matt's heart. He refused to give up on Artemis, clinging to the belief that somewhere out there, she was waiting for him. And as he navigated the familiar streets, he vowed to do whatever it took to find her and make amends for his past mistakes.

As Matt trudged through the snow, his mind buzzed with conflicting thoughts and emotions. The weight of guilt pressed down on him, a heavy burden he carried with each step. He couldn't shake the feeling that there must be a way to undo the events of that night, to bring Artemis back from whatever realm she had disappeared into.

The once tight-knit group of friends had splintered in the wake of Artemis's disappearance, their bonds strained and frayed by the loss. Despite their attempts to move on, each of them harbored a secret longing for Artemis's return, a hope they dared not speak aloud.

Matt's attempts to reach out to Artemis's mother had been met with resistance, leaving him feeling even more powerless in the face of uncertainty. He knew the risks involved in attempting to bring Artemis back, uncertain if the procedure that had caused her disappearance could be reversed.

Yet, deep down, Matt couldn't shake the nagging sense of possibility. He had witnessed firsthand the inexplicable events of that night, and despite his doubts, he couldn't ignore the flicker of hope that burned within him. If there was even the slightest chance of bringing Artemis back, he was willing to risk everything to make it happen, ready to sacrifice even his own life if necessary.

Matt's mind churned with the analogy, finding solace in its simplicity yet grappling with its implications. How could Artemis's mother, knowing there might be a chance to return, choose to remain in pain? It was a question that gnawed at him, its answer elusive and enigmatic.

In his heart, Matt understood the depth of Artemis's mother's pain, the wounds that lingered unseen beneath her brave facade. He could empathize with her reluctance to embrace a solution that might bring her daughter back. Yet, with each step, he knew there was also a chance of reopening her old wounds, stirring emotions that had long been buried beneath the surface. It was a delicate balance, a tug-of-war between the desire for resolution and the fear of confronting the past.

As he trudged through the snow-covered streets, Matt found himself grappling with his own emotions, torn between the longing for Artemis's return and the uncertainty of what that might entail. Deep down, he knew that the journey ahead would be fraught with challenges and obstacles, But he was determined to face them head-on, fueled by the hope of reuniting with his dear friend—or, better yet, his love and soulmate—once more. He wasn't that shy boy anymore. He was a true scientist now, willing to do anything to find the answer, just like a brilliant mind or a dedicated and devoted researcher, giving up was never in his destiny. His resolve was unwavering, driven by a passion for discovery and the pursuit of truth.

As Matt grappled with his uncertainty and doubt, he found solace in memories of Artemis, her unwavering support and boundless encouragement. She had been his rock, the one who believed in him when no one else did, and he clung to those memories now more than ever. Yet, as he faced the daunting task of bringing Artemis back, Matt couldn't help but feel the weight of his own limitations. The fear of failure gnawed at him, the worry that he might not be able to bring her back in one piece haunting his every thought. It was a burden he bore alone, unable to reach out to his friends or Artemis's family for the support and encouragement he so desperately needed.

In his moments of doubt, Matt found himself questioning everything, from his own abilities to the feasibility of his plan. But deep down, he knew that he couldn't give up, not when Artemis's fate hung in the balance. He drew strength from her memory, her spirit a guiding light in the darkness of his uncertainty, urging him to press on, to keep fighting until he found a way to bring her home.

He was walking slowly along Finch and Yong Avenue, discreetly wiping tears from his eyes, making sure no one noticed.

Unexpectedly, he found himself standing in front of the coffee shop they used to frequent together. Pausing for a moment, he felt a heavy weight settle on his heart, making it difficult to breathe. Without overthinking, he headed inside, imagining for a moment that he might see Artemis smiling at him again. The aroma of freshly brewed coffee filled the air as he scanned the crowded shop, his eyes drawn to the display of cakes and muffins by the window. Most of the tables were occupied, and he decided to grab a soda and leave. As he made his way to the exit, a familiar face caught his eye.

Matt's heart raced as he caught sight of Megan seated in the corner, engrossed in her book. His mind raced with conflicting thoughts, unsure whether to approach her or flee the scene. Feeling overwhelmed, he opted to leave the shop, hoping to avoid any awkward encounters. As he hurried away, he heard his name being called from a distance, causing him to halt in his tracks.

He was startled to hear Megan's voice calling out to him from behind. Turning around, he saw her rushing towards him, a concerned look on her face. Despite his mixed emotions, he couldn't ignore her call, and he stopped to wait for her, his heart still racing from the unexpected encounter. Matt paused, then turned at once. He saw her, and he was amazed by how much she had changed. She had transformed into a fine and beautiful young woman. The last time he saw her, they were all sixteen, but now, at twenty, she exuded charm, elegance, and a captivating allure that left Matt at a loss for words to describe her beauty.

"Hi Matt... It's been a long time, and I wasn't even sure if it was really you. You've changed a lot," she said, blushing. After a quick pause, she added, "Oh my god, you're so handsome." She blushed again, but her tone was friendly.

"Hi there! I couldn't recognize you either. You've changed a lot since the last time I saw you. As long as I remember you, you had a baby face but look at you now. You've become a young woman. How are you now?" Matt replied.

"I'm doing well. Where were you going?" asked Megan.

"I was just going for a walk… I guess," Matt replied, unsure of what to say. He didn't know why he was there, and he wasn't sure if it was appropriate to bring up Artemis's name either.

"Oh, come on. We all made a plan to meet here—I mean, Helen and I did, but I'm not sure about the others. I left a message for them," she said, uncertainty creeping into her voice as she wondered if they'd show up and her voice trailing off. Suddenly, she held his arm and continued, "Just like before, if you remember? Come on. I'm sure Helen will be flattered to see you again. She always talks about you. Maybe we are meant to be here today, you never know." She looked straight into his eyes, a hint of sincerity evident in her gaze.

Matt felt a wave of warmth spread through him at the mention of Helen's name. While he cherished his friendship with Artemis, he also held a special place in his heart for Helen as a good friend; knowing that she had been thinking of him filled him with a newfound sense of happiness. Perhaps this encounter could mark the beginning of a renewed friendship, maybe it wasn't an accident to be here. Perhaps he meant to be here as if it was his destiny to meet them all. Matt thought to himself. It was comforting to know that despite the passage of time, the bonds they shared still held significance. Megan's words struck a chord with Matt, stirring up memories he had tried to bury. He could sense her melancholy as she spoke, and it reminded him of the pain they had all endured during those difficult times. Despite the weight of the past, there was a glimmer of hope in knowing that Helen still cared, even if it was tinged with guilt.

Matt nodded solemnly, feeling the weight of those four years pressing down on him. "Sure, that sounds like a plan," he agreed, offering her a reassuring smile.

"Time flies, doesn't it? It feels like just yesterday, yet it also feels like a lifetime ago." He sympathized with Megan's sadness, understanding all too well the pain of lost time and missed opportunities.

"It'll be nice to catch up with everyone." He hoped that the reunion would bring some warmth and comfort amid the cold and melancholic memories of the past.

Megan's sincerity touched Matt's heart, and he couldn't resist her genuine plea. With a sigh, he nodded. "Okay, you convinced me," he relented, offering her a small smile.

"Let's wait in the cafe for Helen and the others." Despite his lingering doubts and fears, he couldn't deny the allure of reconnecting with old friends and perhaps finding solace in their company.

As they walked back together inside the cafe where Megan had reserved seats for their meeting, Matt couldn't shake the uncertainty gnawing at him. Yet, he found a sense of comfort in Megan's presence. With each step, he wrestled with his conflicting emotions, torn between the longing for connection and the fear of revisiting painful memories. Despite his hesitations, he continued to follow Megan, silently hoping that this reunion would bring closure and perhaps even healing.

Matt felt a rush of mixed emotions as he stepped into the cafe again, greeted by the surprised faces of his old friends. He was met with a whirlwind of greetings and exclamations, enveloped in the warmth of their reunion. Despite the initial shock, the atmosphere quickly transformed into one of joy and camaraderie as laughter and conversation filled the air. For a brief moment, Matt allowed himself to be swept away by the familiarity and comfort of their company, grateful for this unexpected reunion.

Allan's request brought a hush over the group as they settled into their seats, eager to hear each other's tales of the past four years. One by one, they took turns sharing their experiences, from travels to new jobs and personal milestones to unexpected challenges. Each story was met with nods of understanding, laughter, and words of encouragement from the group. It was a moment of genuine connection and reflection, bridging the gap of time that had separated them.

Allan turned to Helen and asked, "What are you doing now? Are you working or studying?"

Helen smiled at Allan's question and replied, "I've actually been doing a bit of both. After finishing my degree, I started working at a local nonprofit organization that focuses on community development. It's been incredibly fulfilling, and I've learned so much in the process. But I've also been taking some online courses to further my education in urban planning, which has been a passion of mine for a while now." Helen's friends listened intently as she shared her journey.

"That's impressive, Helen," Allan remarked. "Combining work and study must be quite demanding, but it sounds like you're excelling in both areas."

When she finished, she asked the same question to Matt, "How about you Matt? We haven't heard from you almost in four years. What happened?" Helen couldn't take her eyes off of him

Matt paused, reflecting on the difficult time he had endured. "It was a challenging period," he admitted.

"I felt lost and uncertain about my future." He took a deep breath, gathering his thoughts before continuing, "It was hard for me and It took me six months to decide. I couldn't think clearly and I started to work as a boss boy in a restaurant. I didn't want to do anything. One day, Mr. Cuddle, our science teacher, came to the restaurant with his family and as soon as he saw me, he was very surprised and shocked. His presence was like a wake-up call for me. He reminded me of my potential and encouraged me to pursue my education."

Matt's voice softened as he recalled the impact of their conversation. "That meeting with him was a turning point. It gave me the clarity and determination to get back on track and continue my studies." Matt hesitated for a moment, feeling the weight of their expectant gazes.

He was interrupted by Ricky. "What are you studying right now?"

Matt's gaze shifted to Ricky as he posed the question. "I'm studying neurology," Matt replied, his eyes lighting up with enthusiasm. "It's a fascinating field that explores the complexities of the brain and nervous system. There's so much to learn, and I'm excited to delve deeper into it."

Then he turned to Allan and asked, "How about you?"

"I am studying journalism-broadcast. Ricky and I are in the same college. He is getting his bachelor's degree in civil engineering technology." He winked at Ricky

"Interesting choice, Allan. And it's great to hear that Ricky's pursuing civil engineering. It seems like you both have found your passions. How's the program treating you?"

Ricky smiled and teased Allen when he interrupted, "Yes, you heard him. I don't have to say anything while Allen is with me." Allan intercepted Ricky's wink with a playful gesture, crushing it metaphorically onto the floor. Laughter erupted from everyone around the table.

Megan glanced around the table, taking in the somber expressions of her friends, before drawing a deep breath. She looked at Matt again and asked, "What did you do after that fateful night? It was hard on all of us."

Matt paused for a moment, feeling a sense of relief that Megan had brought up the subject. It was something that had weighed on his mind, and he was glad it was finally out in the open, then said, "Well, after that night..." he began slowly, "I needed some time to myself to figure things out. I've been doing some research besides my education, trying to understand what happened to Artemis, trying to find a way to... bring her back." He paused, knowing he was about to reveal something they might find hard to believe. "I believe she's still out there, somewhere. My four years of research proved the truth about that night to me and how I can reverse the procedure."

Ricky kept looking at Matt then he asked, "Are you serious?"

Megan scanned the faces, feeling like she had finally found the right moment to say it, "I know we've all been wrestling with this every single day, but the truth is unavoidable. We need to confront it head-on. We have to visit Artemis's family, especially with next week marking the fourth year since her disappearance."

As Megan concluded her statement, her gaze lingered on Matt as if she were trying to convey something through her words or silently communicate a message.

"What can we do? Her mother never answered any of our phone calls!" Ricky whispered with a tone of frustration.

"Yes, I understand, but her sister always talks to me, and we can ask her, maybe insist on going," Megan suggested, looking around at everyone for agreement.

"With all respect to her mother, I don't think it is her decision anymore. You know, guys, February 29 is her birthday, and it's also a leap year! We have to do something. This is our chance, and even this meeting wasn't a coincidence—it was meant to happen," Matt said in a quiet voice. He paused for a moment, then his expression turned somber.

"Oh no... no..." Allen spoke those words aloud, then turned to Megan, his eyes a mixture of hope and anger. "Can't you forget about that? We still don't really know what happened that night. We can't go through that again?"

Ricky asked Matt, noticing his flustered demeanor as he scribbled on a piece of paper pulled from his pocket. His gaze shifted from Matt to Megan and Helen, then stopped on Allen, his expression earnest and shifted surprisingly. "What if it was you, stuck somewhere, needing our help to come back home?" He locked eyes with Matt before scanning the rest of the group.

"Do you all feel the same? What if the only ones who could help you were us?" Ricky persisted his tone a mix of urgency and determination, encouraging everyone to consider the gravity of the situation.

"Would you still expect us to forget about you and carry on with our lives? Would you?" Ricky's gaze bore into Matt, his words echoing the weight of their friendship and the importance of their collective responsibility.

Matt felt a tumult of emotions stirring within him, his chest tight with the weight of their words. He glanced at each of his old friends, finding solace in their familiar faces, but it was Megan's gentle smile that anchored him amidst the storm of uncertainty.

"When I think about it, I realize that she needs our help. If this happened and she disappeared right before our eyes, there's a chance we could bring her back home again. I say yes. Let's try it again," Megan said, her face brightening with newfound hope as she looked at the others, including Matt. Megan's words struck a chord with Matt, stirring a profound sense of responsibility within him. As her face lit up with newfound hope, Matt felt a surge of determination coursing through him. He met her gaze with a resolute nod, acknowledging the gravity of the situation and the collective responsibility they shared to bring Artemis back home.

"Listen, we managed it once before, and I made a promise to her that if anything ever happened, I'd never give up on her. I'd fight until the end to find a way. I'm bound by that promise. But I can't do it alone. I've been thinking about this a lot, and I have some ideas to bring her back, but I need all of you there. Help me help her," Matt's words carried the weight of his commitment, stirring emotions in everyone and plunging them into deep contemplation.

"You know I say yes, but what if we make it worse and put somebody else in danger?" suggested Ricky, his concern echoing the fears of the group.

"It's not possible. Only the person in that circle might be affected, but this time, nobody would be there, and we reverse the whole process. At least we can try. In ten years, when we look back, we can't regret it. It will always remain a question for all of us. And the question is, *What if we could return her home?*" Matt sounded convincing, his words resonating with determination and a sense of responsibility.

At that moment, everyone stood up and clasped each other's hands. Matt felt the weight of this moment settle in, knowing it would be etched into his memory forever, coloring his world with newfound hope. Gesturing toward the chairs, he invited everyone to sit down again and begin their planning. His breaths were shallow with anticipation, for this was the moment of truth He had endured over four agonizing years—or, more precisely, 1,460 excruciating days. As he looked at his friends, they appeared to him as a formidable team, the best allies he could hope for. They were more than just good friends now, they were his steadfast companions, his soulmates.

Matt's contemplation was cut short by Helen's gaze, prompting her to voice the question that hung heavy in the air. "How do we convince Dorsa to let us hold our ceremony in Artemis's bedroom again? Do you have a plan, and where should we begin?"

Megan clutched her purse tightly, leaning forward on the table as she spoke, "Perhaps we could just explain it to her."

Ricky smiled and glanced between Megan and Matt before suggesting, "Yes... maybe no plan is the best plan!"

Helen felt uncomfortable and reached for her cell phone. She dialed a number, pausing for a moment before pressing the call button. "Let me talk to Atossa first, and then we can all have a meeting with her. We have to convince her first before moving to the next level, which is seeing her mother. Am I right?"

With unanimous agreement, everyone nodded and chimed in cheerfully, "Yes, of course."

As Helen waited for Atossa to answer, a sense of anticipation filled the air. However, her hopes were dashed when Atossa's voicemail picked up instead. Disappointed but undeterred, Helen left a message, expressing her desire for a meeting to discuss an important matter concerning Artemis and a succinct yet heartfelt message for Atossa, hoping to convey the urgency and importance of their conversation. Helen's disappointment was palpable as she ended the call, but her determination remained steadfast. She knew that reaching Atossa was crucial for their plans to move forward. She glanced at her friends, who were waiting anxiously for any updates. With a reassuring smile, Helen assured them that she would keep trying until she got through to Atossa.

Matt's suggestion was met with understanding nods from his friends, acknowledging the delicate nature of the situation and the significance of Dorsa's role in resolving their predicament. With a shared sense of determination, they recognized that Dorsa held the key to unraveling the mystery of Artemis's disappearance and facilitating her return home. Their exchanged glances conveyed their readiness to confront the challenges ahead with unity and resolve. Matt turned to Helen, assigning her the crucial task of persuading Atossa when she returned her call.

"Helen, it's essential that when Atossa contacts you, you emphasize the urgency of our situation and the potential for bringing Artemis home. We need to convince her that seeing her mother is the next vital step in our plan."

Helen nodded determinedly. "I understand the importance of this task, and I'll do everything I can to convey our message effectively."

Matt nodded, then explained, "I have to go home and gather everything I have from that night and restudy them. Please notify as soon as you talk to Atossa." He nodded again at his friends and I left the cafe.

Matt stepped out into the slightly cold weather, his famous umbrella in hand. Despite its unassuming appearance, the umbrella held a fascinating secret. As the first drop of rain touched its surface, the spot would transform from dark blue to brilliant white, only to revert to its original color once the raindrop had passed. Each raindrop created a delicate symphony, sounding like breaking China as it hit the umbrella's surface. As the rain began to fall faster, the umbrella transformed into a stunning night sky adorned with countless stars, adding a touch of beauty to the otherwise dreary weather, accompanied by a sound like a symphony. Matt was proud of his magical creation.

He felt a surge of excitement coursing through him as he embraced his new mission. The prospect of bringing Artemis back filled him with a sense of purpose like never before. He meticulously gathered his belongings from that fateful night, carefully packing them away in a box. Every detail was important, and he made sure to document everything thoroughly, ensuring that nothing was forgotten. He felt the weight of the moment pressing down on him as he grappled with the challenge of convincing Dorsa to join him in their endeavor. He knew that winning her trust wouldn't be easy, but he was determined to find a way. Surrounded by boxes filled with memories and preparations for the upcoming night, he felt the urgency of the situation keenly. As his phone rang, cutting through the stillness of the room, he struggled to free himself from the tangle of boxes to answer the call.

His breaths came in quick, shallow bursts as he answered the call. "Hello?" he gasped, his voice strained with exertion.

Helen's voice on the other end sounded concerned. "Matt, are you okay?" she inquired, her worry evident in her tone.

His voice wavered with anticipation as he asked about Helen's conversation with Atossa. The weight of his hopes hung on her response, but Helen's hesitant tone hinted at uncertainty, casting a shadow over his expectations. Helen's words conveyed a mix of challenges and opportunities.

"Atossa's reluctance to discuss the past and her fear of disappointing her mother presented obstacles, but Helen's perseverance had secured an opportunity for them to be heard. With a wish for luck, Matt found himself with the opportunity to face this pivotal moment alongside Atossa.

Matt took a deep breath, steeling himself for the task ahead. While uncertainty loomed, he knew he had to seize this opportunity and turn the odds in their favor. With determination fueling his resolve, he prepared to confront the challenges head-on and navigate the complexities of Atossa's apprehensions. Matt's words resonated with a sense of urgency and determination.

"I understand and I'm ready, but I need your support, and I mean all of you must be there and back me up," he reiterated, emphasizing the importance of their collective effort in persuading Atossa and overcoming Dorsa's reservations.

Helen's response was resolute. "You've got it, Matt. If you say there's a chance, we believe you. That's why we're supporting you. We all want Artemis back," she affirmed, echoing the sentiments of determination and hope shared by the group.

"When is this gathering and where?" Matt inquired.

"It's tomorrow at 6:00 pm, back at the same cafe. Is that okay with you?" Helen replied, seeking confirmation.

"Yes, it must be, and I'll be there. Helen, please let the others know about tomorrow too, and I don't expect any excuses," Matt replied, his voice tense with determination. As he spoke, he wiped the sweat from his brow and hastily dried his cell phone with his shirt.

"Don't worry. I'll let everybody know and I'll see you tomorrow." Helen comforts him.

"Thanks, Helen. I'll see you tomorrow," Matt replied, feeling a mix of nerves and anticipation as he ended the call.

Matt's mind raced with a whirlwind of thoughts and emotions as he prepared for the crucial meeting tomorrow. Despite his determination, doubts and negative thoughts threatened to creep in.

He knew he couldn't afford to entertain them now; he had to stay focused on his goal of bringing Artemis back home. As he sorted through his preparations, he reminded himself that success was possible, especially with the support of his friends behind him.

Despite the internal conflict raging within him, Matt knew he couldn't afford to let uncertainty paralyze him. He reluctantly entertained both the negative and positive viewpoints, realizing that understanding them both was crucial for making informed decisions. It was like navigating a battlefield, with his conflicting ideologies waging war within his mind. Yet, amidst the chaos, he found solace in the guiding principles he had developed over the years. These principles served as his compass, guiding him through the uncertainty and helping him find clarity amidst the storm.

The next day finally arrived, though it felt like days or even weeks had passed for Matt. As he entered the cafe, he immediately noticed Ricky pacing anxiously back and forth.The rest of the group was already gathered, waiting for him. A pang of guilt struck Matt as he realized he was late because of an accident on the way to the cafe, causing him to be late for what was supposed to be a crucial meeting. Apologizing for his tardiness, Matt approached the table and stood before his friends.

"I'm sorry for being late. There was an accident, and I had to take a detour to get here. How's everyone doing?"

As Matt scanned the faces around the table, he noticed Atossa's absence. Turning to Helen, he inquired, "Helen, where is Atossa?"

Before Helen could respond, Atossa's voice came from behind Matt. "Hello, Matt! I'm right here."

Matt turned around to face Atossa, who appeared charming and magnificent. She looked so much like her sister, with long, silky hair shining over her shoulders. Her beautiful light golden-green eyes made her even more striking than he remembered. She was an admirable sight, and Matt was genuinely delighted to see her.

"Hi, Atossa...! Thank you for agreeing to see us again," he greeted warmly, gesturing for her to take a seat.

"How is your mother?" Helen throws it out

Helen's question hung in the air as Atossa's emotions spilled over. "She's sad, and since the incident, she's not herself anymore," Atossa admitted tearfully.

"She looks at me like she doesn't see me, but when I want to go to my room or outside, she goes crazy and begs me to stay with her. So... what can I say about my mother? Do you want me to say she's okay? But she's not. I don't blame any of you because I was there and I saw her having fun with you guys. I don't know what to think anymore." Her voice trembled with emotion as she struggled to find the words. She burst into tears

"She's right. How can she believe her daughter vanished from her room?" Allan said.

"The police keep coming to our house to update their information and let my mother know they are working on the case. But all of it is bullshit," Atossa continued, her voice tinged with frustration and sorrow. She kept her eyes fixed on the table, unable to look at anyone.

"Atossa… you were there when Artemis disappeared, right?" Helen asked gently.

"Yes, I was there too. That's why I believed you the first time. But what happened? Where did she go?" Atossa's voice broke as she started crying again, the weight of the mystery and her sister's absence overwhelming her.

"Atossa, listen to me carefully," Helen said, her tone serious.

"You have to help us see your mother. We believe she's crucial and could play a significant role in Artemis' returns. Will you help us talk to her?"

"What's the point? She wasn't there that night. How can she help?" Atossa's voice broke.

"I lost my father when I was a baby and never got to know him. Four years ago, I lost the only sister I had. Now, you want me to risk losing my mother, too? I can't lose her!" Tears streamed down her face as she cried even harder.

"What if this time we can bring back not just Artemis but your father too? Think about it. There's a chance—a big chance. Your mother told us your father disappeared the same way. Wherever Artemis is, your father is there too. We just need to reverse the process in the same place. You say your mother wasn't there that night? But she was in the next room. Think about it. Are you willing to help us, or do you want to live with sorrow and regret for the rest of your life, always wondering what if? Don't you want to know if this chance is real?" Matt stepped closer to Atossa, his voice earnest, and it was clear to everyone that he genuinely believed in what he was saying. He was ready to do whatever it took.

Everyone turned to Matt, their expressions shifting from skepticism to determination. His words resonated with them, and the sense of unity and purpose was palpable. They all nodded in agreement, their resolve solidifying. They all said together, "Yes, we're ready. Let's do it," they said in unison, their voices echoing with newfound conviction.

Matt felt a surge of hope and excitement. This was the moment they had all been waiting for, the chance to right the wrongs of the past and bring Artemis—and perhaps even her father—back. They all turned to Atossa, who looked at Matt with a mixture of amazement and hope.

Atossa felt a wave of relief wash over her and asked, "You mean that, right? Matt, you're the genius, and you can do it, right? I still remember that night—you were the one who promised my mother you'd find a solution and bring my sister back. I still remember."

Matt nodded, his expression serious yet hopeful. "Yes, Atossa. I mean it. I promised, and I intend to keep that promise. We can do this together."

Matt was shocked by everything he had just said. The words had flowed out of his mouth, driven by a deep-seated hope. He continued as Atossa was looking at him, "What if they both returned home?"

He looked at Atossa, his determination clear. "Yes, I remember, And I've never stopped thinking about Artemis."

"The problem is my mother," Atossa confessed, her voice tinged with frustration.

"She thinks all of you are guilty. She doesn't want me to see you guys either, and I'm in big trouble right now. I don't know how to convince her to see you or how to even start this conversation with her."

Matt took a deep breath, understanding the gravity of the situation. "We'll figure it out together, Atossa. We need to find a way to make her see that we're trying to help, that we care about Artemis as much as she does."

Helen nodded in agreement. "Maybe we can write her a letter explaining everything. Sometimes, it's easier to process things when they're written down."

Ricky chimed in, "And we can all sign it, showing our unity and sincerity. It's worth a shot."

Atossa looked around at the determined faces of her friends, feeling a glimmer of hope.

"Okay," she said slowly. "Let's try that. But we need to be very careful. My mother is fragile, and we can't afford to upset her more."

"We understand," Matt reassured her. "We'll take it one step at a time. And we'll be here for you, no matter what."

"We just want to open the gate," Ricky suddenly blurted out. Everyone turned to him, staring in confusion. Realizing his mistake, he quickly corrected himself, "To bring Artemis back... and maybe your father too. You never know."

Matt ignored Ricky and hesitated for a moment, his gaze fixed on Atossa's eyes as he carefully considered his response. After a few seconds, he spoke earnestly, his words carrying a weight of sincerity.

Matt looked at everyone, one by one, before turning to Atossa and saying, "Dear Atossa, I understand how difficult this situation is for you and your mother. But please know, there isn't just one path back to your family. We've all endured our own suffering and hardships, and now we're here, standing beside you, ready to support and help in any way we can. Writing a letter won't be as effective as talking to her face-to-face. We need to meet her in person, but it's your responsibility to convince her—at least to try to listen to us. However, that first step, reaching out to your mother, is something only you can do. It's up to you to take that brave first step."

He paused, his expression gentle yet resolute. "When you speak to your mother, try to keep in mind not just the present but also the future. Picture Artemis and your father, who need our help, and primarily your help, to come home. Let their faces guide your words, and let the love and longing in your heart speak volumes. We're all rooting for you, Atossa, every step of the way."

Matt stood there for a minute, contemplating his next words. Then he continued, his tone serious and urgent, "I have to warn you about the limited time we have left. If we don't succeed at the precise moment, we will fail, and we'll have to wait another four years for another chance. Trust me, talk to your mother as soon as possible. Each time it might get harder to bring them back, or there may not be a next time at all. Eventually, they would give up too."

With these final words, Matt offered a polite, personal farewell and left the cafe, leaving a sense of urgency hanging in the air. It was all up to Atossa now. Matt had done everything he could to reach Dorsa, hoping his words would inspire her to act or persuade her mother for one more chance. By the time he left, his speech had captivated everyone. It was convincing, like a sharp needle that pricks the skin—painful, yet awakening. His magical words had penetrated their minds, altering their perspectives and compelling them to get involved. Matt's unwavering confidence was infectious, encouraging others to participate willingly. They had all witnessed Artemis's disappearance, a terrifying yet magical event, which assured them that this was not mere fantasy. They knew it was real, and they wouldn't miss their chance to be part of it.

"If Matt did it the first time, then he can do it again," Ricky jumped in, his voice filled with urgency, pacing back and forth with restless energy. Then he continued, "But this time, when the portal opens, they'll be able to return."

Atossa was convinced enough to face the reality. She longed to see her sister again and possibly meet her father for the first time. People don't just disappear without a reason. Something extraordinary must have happened that night. She practiced how to start the conversation with her mother, fearing that she might upset her and cause another hospital visit. Unsure of how to broach the subject, she knew there was one person who could help and she whispered, "Aunt Azar."

Determined, Atossa didn't want to waste any time. She stood up, glanced at her friends, and said, "I know how to approach her." then she left immediately, heading straight to her aunt's home just a few blocks away. When Azar opened the door, her face instantly reflected her worry, fearing that something had happened to her sister. Sensing her aunt's alarm, Atossa quickly began to explain, hoping to prevent Azar from fainting.

She held Aunt Azar's shoulder and said, "Hi, Aunt Azar…! Everything is alright, but I have some questions for you. That's why I came here before going home—I really need to know the answers."

Atossa knew how to capture her aunt's love and ensure her support, so she chose her words carefully. She couldn't afford to lose this only chance. Aunt Azar was the key to making this happen. Azar's worried expression softened as she listened.

"Of course, sweetheart. Come in and tell me what's on your mind." She led Atossa inside, sensing the importance of the conversation.

Atossa took a deep breath. "It's about Artemis and Dad. I need your help to talk to Mom about it. There's something we need to do, and it can't wait."

Aunt Azar hugged her tightly and then guided Atossa to the living room. They settled on the couch, and Azar's eyes were fixed on her niece, full of concern and curiosity. "I'm listening."

"Aunt Azar, I know you love me just like your own children," Atossa began, her voice soft and earnest.

"And I know you would give anything to have Artemis back in Mom's arms." She paused, letting the emotional weight of her words sink in. She wanted to strengthen the bond and love in Azar's heart, ensuring she would be receptive to the difficult conversation ahead. Azar nodded, her eyes glistening with unshed tears.

"You know I would, Atossa. Just tell me what you need." Encouraged by her aunt's response, Atossa continued,

"I need your help to talk to Mom about something very important. It's about Artemis and Dad. We have a chance to bring them back, but it requires Mom's involvement, and I'm afraid of how she'll react. I need you to help me explain it to her, to make her understand without getting too upset."

Azar shifted her gaze, her expression suddenly turning serious, but she squeezed Atossa's hand reassuringly. "I'm here for you, sweetheart. Let's figure out the best way to talk to her together. "We'll do this carefully and with love."

Still, Azar regarded her with suspicion, sensing that Atossa was after something significant. Experience had taught her to tread cautiously whenever her niece approached with such fervent intensity.

"Alright, Atossa, tell me what this is truly about," Azar said, her tone laced with both curiosity and caution. "What exactly do you need from me?"

Atossa took a deep breath, knowing she needed to be completely honest to gain her aunt's trust.

"Aunt Azar, it's not just about talking to Mom. We have a chance to bring Artemis and Dad back, but we need to act quickly. I need your help to convince Mom to take this chance. I know it sounds unbelievable, but I promise it's real. I just need you to trust me and support me in talking to her."

Azar's suspicion softened a little, but she remained cautious. "Atossa, this sounds very serious. Are you sure this isn't just wishful thinking? I need to understand exactly what you're asking us to do." Atossa nodded earnestly.

"I know it sounds extraordinary and I understand your skepticism, and I know it sounds impossible, but I wouldn't come to you if I weren't absolutely certain. Please, Aunt Azar, just hear me out and help me explain everything to Mom. "We may never get another chance like this."

Azar squeezed her left eyelid, a gesture of both concern and determination. She looked directly at Atossa and asked, "Where is this speech going now? What do you want from me, Atossa? Just spit it out, and I won't get angry. You know I'll do anything for you and your mom! Please, be honest without twisting the words and tell me what is bothering you."

Atossa took a deep breath, feeling the weight of her aunt's sincerity. "Alright, Aunt Azar, I'll tell you everything. Matt told me that there's a chance to bring Artemis and Dad back, but we have to act quickly. We need to perform a specific task at a precise moment, and it involves Mom. I'm scared to bring it up to her alone because I don't want to upset her. I need you to help me talk to her to make her see how important this is without causing her too much stress. I know it sounds incredible, but I truly believe it can work. Will you help me?" Her eyes remained fixed on Azar, glimmering with an extraordinary brilliance brought on by unshed tears. Azar listened intently, her concern deepening. She could see the desperation and sincerity in Atossa's eyes.

"Atossa, it's not that I don't believe you. It's just... It's hard to accept something so extraordinary. But I can see how much this means to you. Show me what you and Matt have found. I understand your feelings. It's completely normal to waver between belief and doubt, especially when facing something as extraordinary or difficult as this. When we're confronted with the unknown or something that defies logic, our minds can struggle to reconcile what we want to believe with what seems possible.

"On one hand, you want to believe in the hope and the possibility that something incredible could happen. On the other hand, doubt creeps in because it challenges what you've always known to be true. It's a battle between your heart and your mind. In these situations, it's helpful to consider a few things:

1. **Evidence and Experience**: What evidence or experiences do you have that support one belief over the other? Reflecting on this can help you lean towards one side.

2. **Trust in Others**: Sometimes, our belief is strengthened by the trust we place in others. If someone you care about is deeply convinced of something, it can make it easier to lean towards believing, even if doubts remain.

3. **What's at Stake?**: Consider what it means if you do or don't believe. Sometimes, the cost of not believing can be higher than taking the risk of belief, even if it feels uncertain.

4. **Room for Both**: It's also okay to hold space for both belief and doubt. You don't have to fully commit to one side; you can acknowledge the doubts while still moving forward with hope.

"Ultimately, it's a deeply personal journey, and it's okay to feel conflicted. The important thing is to listen to your instincts, weigh the possibilities, and decide what you can live with—whether it's taking a leap of faith or holding onto caution. If there's even a small chance, I want to be there for you and your mom."

Atossa, still teary-eyed, nodded, feeling a glimmer of hope. "Thank you, Aunt Azar. I promise I'll show you everything. Just please, give us this chance."

"Okay! Go on, I'm listening. Enlighten me, convince me, because I need to believe it if I'm going to convince your mother. Go ahead, and I won't interrupt you," Azar said, bracing herself for what Atossa was about to reveal.

Atossa took a deep breath, her voice trembling slightly as she began, "It began four years ago. I was in the room when my sister vanished right before my eyes. I witnessed it that night. It was nobody's fault—somehow, it just happened. I'll do anything to get my sister back."

She paused, gathering her thoughts and trying to steady her emotions then she continued. "What if I told you that there's a chance they can return home? "According to Matt, there's a strong chance that Artemis went to the same place my dad did, and they both vanished without a trace. Are you with us, or are you willing to destroy our hope, maybe our only chance? Will you help us, or do you want to keep quiet and do nothing, only to regret it later? Time is passing by, the clock is ticking, and we're losing precious moments."

She took a deep breath and continued, "We're in a leap year, and it's the anniversary of that terrible night when my father vanished. Years later, at the same time, the same thing happened to Artemis— but this time, I was the witness. I saw how she disappeared. We need to act on this day because it's the only time we can reverse the process and bring them back. We have an amazing young scientist who cares and is willing to try. "We have Matt, who made it happen before. If we give him this chance, he could do it again—he can reverse the procedure. Maybe if someone like Matt had cared enough back then, my father might have had a chance to come back."

Atossa's voice broke, and she burst into tears. She whispered, "Are you with us, Aunt Azar?"

Azar's heart ached to see her niece in such distress. She pulled Atossa into a tight hug. "Is not that easy and how do you know if this will work?"

Atossa, who had been waiting for this question, took a deep breath and began, "It's not that easy, you're right, but it's doable. Matt was the key to the whole procedure. Artemis was so happy at the thought of bringing Dad back, and Matt promised her that if anything happened, he wouldn't stop until he made things right. He kept that promise. For the past four years, he's been researching. He's confident that if we reverse the procedure in Artemis's room, we will have a chance to open the portal and bring them back. The portal needs to be opened from this side and exactly at the same place, which is why Dad was never able to return."

Atossa's voice was steady, but the urgency was clear. "We either succeed or we don't. But even if it doesn't work, at least we'll know we did everything in our power. We won't have to live with the regret of wondering, 'What if?'"

Azar looked at her niece, her mind racing. The situation was overwhelming, and the risk was enormous, and it seemed too far-fetched and unrealistic, yet somehow, it made sense. But seeing the determination in Atossa's eyes, Azar knew this wasn't a decision made lightly. She took a deep breath and steadied herself.

"I'm with you, Atossa. We'll do this together. Let's figure out how to talk to your mother and make this happen. I promise I'm with you all the way."

Azar was shocked by the intensity of Atossa's belief. She watched as her niece laid out the plan, feeling unprepared for such a heavy, foreboding subject. The weight of the situation pushed her to the edge, but Atossa's clear belief in the possibility of Artemis's return made her pause. For a moment, Azar considered the potential devastation if it failed, but she also recognized the strength in Atossa's resolve.

Azar squeezed Atossa's hands reassuringly. "Atossa, this is a lot to take in," she said, her voice trembling slightly. "But I can see how serious you are about this. I trust you, and if there's even a chance we can bring Artemis and your father back, we have to try."

Atossa's face slowly brightened, and her lips opened wide with surprise. She hugged her aunt, kissed her all over her face, and said, "Thank you, Aunt Azar. Thank you so much for your help. I need you to come to our home and talk to my mom because we have to do it in the same place. You and Mom can be a big help, too."

"Okay, I will talk to your mom, even though I know it's one of the hardest things I've ever done," Azar said, her heart racing.

"But how do you know if it will work? How do you know this procedure won't risk someone else's life again?" Her curiosity piqued, she leaned in closer as Atossa continued with fervor.

"If you believe it might take someone else, then you have to believe there's a possibility for a reverse procedure. That's why we have to do it," Atossa insisted, her eyes gleaming with determination.

"I don't think it'll take anybody else because there's a specific area you shouldn't go to. As long as we avoid that, we should be safe."

Atossa suddenly became quiet, trying to catch her breath. She was relieved to have her aunt on her side. Slowly, she turned to her aunt and asked, "When are you coming to talk to Mom? According to Matt, we can't waste any time. Time is precious, and we only have a few days until leap day to prepare everything. We need to get the room ready."

Atossa could hardly contain her joy at convincing her aunt to help. She was bursting to share the good news with her friends and couldn't stand the thought of wasting any time. "Aunt Azar! Are you coming with me to talk to my mom right now?" she exclaimed, practically bouncing on her feet with excitement. She grabbed her aunt's hand, her eyes shining with a mix of urgency and hope.

"Atossa honey, I know you've told me we have little time, but let's not rush it," Azar said in a reassuring voice. "I need to organize my thoughts. This isn't the right time to approach your mother, and I don't want to risk losing your hope—because it's mine, too. If we rush this, there's a chance your mother might not only reject the idea but could also end up in the hospital again. So, how about I come tomorrow afternoon around five o'clock, and we take it from there?"

Atossa found Azar convincing and accepted her plan immediately, knowing her aunt was a reasonable person who had a knack for handling delicate subjects, especially with her sister. She kissed Azar on the cheek and hugged her tightly for ten seconds before heading home. The anticipation of what tomorrow would bring filled her mind, making it nearly impossible to fall asleep as she eagerly awaited the next day.

The next day, as promised, Aunt Azar arrived at five o'clock sharp, bringing her daughters with her. They all wanted to help. Dorsa was already complaining about the plumbing in the kitchen and how hard it was to find a good plumber. Atossa glanced at her aunt, then at her cousins Pietra and Anahita, feeling a mix of excitement and nervousness. The reality of what they were about to do was setting in, and she couldn't help but feel a little anxious. But seeing her cousins there, ready to support her, gave her a sense of reassurance.

Azar smiled reassuringly at Atossa before turning to her daughters. "Let's focus on the task at hand," she said gently.

"We're here for something important." Atossa felt a surge of gratitude.

With her aunt and cousins by her side, Atossa felt great. Aunt Azar approached her sister and gently said, "Dorsa, I've noticed that you tend to worry about everything. It's important to take some time for yourself and focus on positive thoughts. Try to relax and not let negative thinking overwhelm you."

Dorsa looked at her sister, slightly taken aback, but she could see the genuine concern in Azar's eyes. "I know you're right," Dorsa replied with a sigh. "It's just hard to keep calm with everything going on."

Azar placed a comforting hand on her sister's shoulder. "I understand, but we're here to help, and together we can handle anything. Let's take things one step at a time."

Dorsa looked at her sister with a defeated expression and said, "How can you expect me to be positive? I've lost the most precious people in my life. Positivity seems impossible right now."

Azar's heart ached at her sister's words, but Dorsa had steered the conversation exactly toward the topic Azar had been hoping for. She took a deep breath, trying to find the right words to comfort her. "I know you've been through unimaginable pain, Dorsa, and no one can take that away or make it easier for you. But holding onto even the smallest bit of hope, just a sliver of positivity, might help you find the strength to keep going. We're not asking you to forget or move on—we just want to help you see that there's still a chance, however small, to bring some light back into your life. And we're here to support you, no matter what."

It was difficult for Azar, but she had promised her niece and had to follow through. "Of course, you have to be positive. Look at your daughter and tell me if you're lucky or not. You have a daughter who looks up to you. Isn't she amazing?"

Dorsa felt a wave of happiness as she looked at Atossa. "I am happy and blessed to have her in my life, but I'm still sad about losing those two."

"My dear sister, there are so many people who dream of being in your shoes," Azar said, her voice steady and compassionate. "Thousands, even millions, have lost their loved ones and would give anything to see them just one more time."

Atossa watched her aunt carefully, appreciating the thoughtful choice of words. She could see the impact they had on her mother, who seemed to pause and consider them deeply. Azar continued, "I know it feels impossible right now, but think of this as an opportunity—a chance that so many others would never even get. We owe it to ourselves, to Artemis and your husband, to at least try. We're all here to help you through this every step of the way."

"What do you mean by that? I would pay or do anything to see them one more time, too, but how is that even possible?" Dorsa's voice trembled, a mix of hope and frustration making her blood boil.

Azar took a deep breath, understanding the intensity of her sister's emotions. "Dorsa, what if I told you that there might be a way? It's not guaranteed, and it might sound impossible, but Matt and Atossa believe there's a chance. A small window of opportunity to bring them back."

She paused, allowing the words to sink in. "I know it sounds unbelievable, and it's okay to be skeptical. But before you dismiss it, just hear us out. What if this is our one chance to see them again? Wouldn't it be worth trying, even if the odds are slim?"

"Do you remember telling me that Arsham disappeared from your home?" Azar began, her voice gentle but firm.

"You know he loved you like crazy, and you said he was at home and never left. You also mentioned there was a wave and a sound exactly when he disappeared," she continued, knowing she had touched on a memory that still haunted her sister.

Dorsa's eyes widened as the painful memory resurfaced, and she nodded slowly. Azar leaned in slightly, her tone filled with both urgency and compassion. "What if that wave, that sound, was more than just a strange occurrence? What if it was the key to understanding what happened to him—and to Artemis? We may not fully grasp how or why, but we believe there's a way to reverse it, to bring them back. I know this sounds unbelievable but think about it, Dorsa. We have to try. For them and for you."

"Yes, but what does that have to do with finding a plumber?" Dorsa asked, her concern growing.

"I'm not talking about the plumbing issue. I'm talking about your sadness. I know it seems unrelated but listen to me carefully.

"Yes, I told you that too. What are you getting at?" Dorsa asked, looking at Azar with a mix of curiosity and concern.

"How can two people disappear in exactly the same way, on the same day, but in different years? I mean, the day that appears only every four years? Yet they both were born on that special day, too." Azar asked, her voice calm but filled with urgency. "You've been blaming Artemis's friends, but listen to your own daughter, who was there and witnessed Artemis disappearing. There's a strong possibility that Artemis went to the same place her father did years ago. They might be there, alive, and they need our help to come back home. Are you with me?"

Azar spoke carefully, mindful of her sister's fragile emotions. She took a deep breath and continued, "Maybe this was supposed to happen. Maybe it was meant to be. We don't fully understand why, but what if this is our chance to bring both of them back? We can't ignore the possibility, Dorsa! We have to try."

"What is this? They are dead… DEAD. Nobody can bring them back, and I have to live with this pain for the rest of my life. What are you doing to me? Just leave me alone!" Dorsa 's voice cracked as she burst into tears, crying out loud, her grief pouring out uncontrollably.

Azar's heart broke seeing her sister in so much pain, but she knew she couldn't back down now. She gently reached out, trying to comfort Dorsa. "I know it's unbearable, and I'm so sorry for bringing this up. But please, just listen. What if there's even the slightest chance that they aren't gone, that they're somewhere else, waiting for us to bring them home? I'm not asking you to believe it right now, just to consider the possibility. We can't give up on them, not when there's still a glimmer of hope."

Azar knew she had reached a point where she could no longer back down. For Atossa's sake, she had to press on.

"Listen to me, Dorsa," she said, her voice firm but filled with compassion. "I know you're hurt and depressed, and I understand why you'd want to shut this out. But you have a choice, you can remain in this pain and cry for the rest of your life, or you can take the last chance you have to see them again and become a family once more. This opportunity is in front of you, and these kids are ready to help. If they could open that portal four years ago, they can reverse it now. Maybe it's destiny giving us a second chance."

Azar paused, letting her words sink in before continuing. "Are you truly ready to do anything to see them again, to hug them, and to have your family back? Or will you let this chance slip away, believe they're gone forever, and fill your life—and Atossa's life—with sorrow and regret forever? We have a window in just a few days, and if we miss it, then you may say we lost them forever. You have a chance, Dorsa. At least try, or you'll spend the rest of your life wondering, 'What if?' It's up to you. Don't blow it, and don't leave any regrets behind."

By this time, Dorsa had gone deep into her thoughts and was silent. She was ready to do anything for them. She looked at Azar again, who wasn't about to give up and continued explaining, "You have a second chance, and I know how much you love them. Don't lose it. Let's help these kids to help them and bring them back. This time, we'll be there to supervise and make sure everything is done right. I'll do anything for you, Dorsa, because you're my sister, and I love you so much. That's what sisters do for each other. That's why Atossa wants to talk to you—she wants to help her sister, just like I'm trying to help mine."

Azar took her sister's hands in hers, her voice pleading. "Dorsa, please don't miss this opportunity. If you don't take this chance, you'll regret it for the rest of your life, and the pain of missing them will only grow. Give your permission, and let's see if we can bring them back. For them, for you, and for all of us."

As soon as Azar finished, Dorsa turned to Atossa and said, "What do you mean? What meeting?"

"Mom...! There is no time left. This Friday is a leap day, and that's the only chance we have to try it out. You and Aunt Azar can watch us, but please don't stop us because this is the only chance, and I don't want to waste time explaining why I met with them or talked to them. They're our only chance, and Matt is the only one who can make it happen." Atossa's voice was shaking as she approached her mother, tears streaming down her face. She held her mother's hands, her desperation palpable.

Dorsa placed a hand on Atossa's hair, gently patting it. Watching her daughter cry, she felt her suffering and pain deeply. Tears welled up in her own eyes as she cried, too. At that moment, she resolved not to let her daughter down this time.

"I won't let you down, my darling. If you think it will help them, then I have no objection. When do you want to have the meeting?" Dorsa said softly.

Atossa, overwhelmed with relief and gratitude, hugged her mom tightly. "Thank you, thank you so much!" she repeated, tears of joy streaming down her face. She then turned to her aunt, ran to her, and hugged her just as tightly.

"Thank you, Mom, and thank you, Aunt Azar, for your help. I have to let them know as soon as possible because they need to prepare so many things. I'll keep you updated." Atossa ran to the kitchen to call her friends and share the good news.

The very next day, Atossa, her mother, Aunt Azar, and Azar's two daughters waited anxiously for Artemis's friends to arrive. Dorsa felt uncomfortable and kept glancing at Azar for reassurance. Tonight was the night everyone had been anticipating, each with their own reasons and emotions.

Dorsa couldn't bring herself to say no to her daughter, even though she was skeptical about the possibility of their return. Azar, on the other hand, wanted to see this through to finally put an end to Atossa's persistent requests. Atossa, full of hope, believed in Matt. She had witnessed what had happened that night and trusted that Matt could succeed. She was confident that if they followed his instructions precisely, they would bring Artemis and her father back.

Matt knew he could bring Artemis back again; it was pure logic to him. The others held onto hope, not wanting to be responsible for any failure. They all arrived at Artemis's home almost simultaneously, one by one, and sat in front of Dorsa.

Atossa had already prepared some drinks and served them one by one. Everyone settled in, facing Dorsa in silence, waiting for Matt to start. However, Dorsa spoke first, breaking the tension. Matt's explanation followed and was quite extensive. Initially, Dorsa struggled to look at them, especially at Matt, but gradually, her mind opened up to their new theory, which was compelling.

Dorsa looked at Matt with renewed hope, yet lingering doubts about his procedure remained. She had to ask her final question.

"Matt," Dorsa began, her voice tinged with skepticism, "I understand the theory, but what makes you so sure this will work? What if something goes wrong? How can you guarantee their safety and return? How do you know if it really works? Is there any evidence that it has worked before, or is this just another idea, giving me empty hope and wasting our time?" Her words were sharp, cutting straight to the heart of the matter.

"There is plenty of evidence to prove they are still alive," Matt began, his voice firm. "First, the way your husband disappeared, and second, Artemis vanishing in exactly the same way years later. Third, the witnesses in the room when it happened—everyone here is my proof. That's why they're all here, because they believe, just like I do, that this can work. We're not just clinging to empty hope. We have real reasons to believe they're still out there, and we can bring them back. Including you, Mrs. Vedetta!" His eyes met Dorsa's with unwavering conviction, hoping to break through her doubt.

By this time, everyone was silent, their eyes fixed on Dorsa. She didn't know what to say; Matt's certainty in his theory was so strong that even Dorsa wanted to believe him. He was here to help, and everyone else was there to support him.

At that moment, Azar moved closer to her sister, held her shoulders, and asked gently, "Dorsa, even if you still have doubts about this, I want to know—what is the worst thing that could happen? What do you think you will lose? At least you won't regret it later on. But if you disapprove, they won't continue and will leave this place immediately. Remember this moment because, for the rest of your life, you'll ask yourself, 'What if they were right?'"

Dorsa was deeply touched by her sister's plea and looked around at everyone again. She saw the dedication in their eyes, the way they stood united by a common goal. This was important—more than she had allowed herself to believe. They weren't here to waste time but because they believed in this, even if the chances were slim. She could feel their hope, see it in the way they stood together, ready to do whatever it took. It was their driving force, and in that moment, Dorsa realized that maybe, just maybe, she could let a little of that hope in, too.

She nodded, her resolve firming, and stood up to approach Matt. Resting her hand on his shoulder, she said, "Matt, Artemis always spoke highly of you and your intelligence. She trusted you, and tonight, I have to do the same. I have to trust you despite my doubts and the reasons behind them. But know this, I'm watching you, and if anything goes wrong—if anyone else disappears—you'll lose any respect I have left. I trust you because of my daughter, and I won't leave the room during the entire process. I'm watching you closely. I just wanted to make that clear."

Matt smiled at her, placing his hand over hers, looking genuinely happy and delighted. "Mrs. Vedetta, it would be an honor to have you with us during the procedure. In fact, I was going to ask you to stay because you are a crucial part of this. Your presence is necessary."

Dorsa looked surprised. She couldn't avoid the question and had to know why it was important for her to stay in the room. After taking a deep breath, she asked, "May I ask why my presence is important? If something happens to me, Atossa will be alone forever."

Matt still held her hand, acknowledging her fear. He said with his best reassuring smile, "Your mother and your daughter, Artemis, all share the same birthday. Artemis inherited it from you, just as you inherited it from your mother and passed it down to your daughter. All of you bear the power of that extraordinary day. Am I correct?"

Dorsa was taken aback and impressed by his unexpected question. "I guess the answer is yes. But what does that have to do with our problem?"

Matt felt more comfortable and decided to explain further. He turned to Azar, pointing at her, and continued, "With Artemis's absence, I wasn't sure if you were the key to opening the gate to the other world or if it was your mother. That's why I asked Azar to invite her here and explain the situation. This way, she won't be confused when she arrives."

Dorsa looked even more surprised. "What do you mean? How can our birthdays be related to this?"

Matt explained, "Leap years have a unique significance, especially for those born on leap day. A connection between your family members strengthens the bond between worlds. Having you all present, especially with your shared birthdays, creates a powerful link that can help us bring Arsham and Artemis back. It's not just a coincidence; it's a crucial part of the process. Your mother's presence will further amplify this connection, making it possible to open the gate and guide them home."

Matt looked at Dorsa and Azar and continued, "Actually, I found out that Artemis was strong enough to open the portal on her own, while your husband's friends believed he was the main power behind it. According to your report from that night, when he disappeared, he was with two of his friends. We already have a strong person on the other side—Artemis. On this side, we need as many people as possible who were born on that special day, or at least those connected to them. I also discovered that Artemis was a key part of the incident when her father disappeared. She didn't need to do anything, being just a little girl at the time—she only needed to be there. And they knew that. Your husband's friends knew, which is why they kept coming around with the excuse of honoring him by holding ceremonies at your home. They were trying to open the portal using Artemis's power."

At that moment, there was a knock on the door. As Matt finished speaking, Atossa entered the room with her grandmother. Dorsa looked at her mother and asked, "Mom! Do you know what is going on here?"

Her mother, more composed, slowly walked to the sofa and sat down. She smiled at her daughter as Azar brought her a glass of water. After taking a sip, she held Dorsa's hands and said, "I know what you're going through, but when Azar explained the situation to me last night, it made sense. You had an uncle, my brother, who disappeared when I was a little girl. We were all so afraid and confused about what happened that night. He had found some stones and a book; the stones were beautiful. Anyway, he tried to draw pictures on a big piece of paper and arranged the stones in a strange order, and we just laughed at him. That night, he asked me if I wanted to explore and discover the signs, and I said no. But I watched him through the keyhole and witnessed his disappearance. I told our parents and investigators what happened, but everyone thought I was making it up. Nobody believed me, and I was bullied at school almost every day because of that story. I had a very hard childhood."

Dorsa 's mother became quiet and took another sip of her drink, her mind racing. Dorsa looked upset and pulled her hands away from her mother. Then, she turned to her sister, disappointment etched on her face.

"You mean to tell me you knew what had happened to my husband and kept it from me? That you kept this secret—that I had an uncle who disappeared—and never told me? How could you do that to me? Why didn't you tell me that my uncle disappeared too?" her voice quivered with a mix of anger and hurt, the betrayal cutting deep.

Grandmother Tara smiled gently at her daughter and took her hands again. She called her name softly, "Dorsa, all my life, people made fun of me because I said my brother had disappeared in his room. My parents forbade me from speaking about it, and I learned to keep quiet. They never believed me, and in time, I started to doubt the story myself. When Arsham disappeared, I didn't know what to say. I was scared no one would believe me again. I didn't want you to endure the pain I had gone through. And even if I told you the truth, would you have believed me? This handsome young man and your own daughter are struggling to make you believe what happened that night, yet you keep blaming these innocent people."

Dorsa's anger began to fade as she saw the pain and regret in her mother's eyes. Tara continued, "I didn't want you to go through the same ridicule and disbelief I faced. I kept quiet because I thought it was the best way to protect you. But now, seeing what you're going through, I realize I should have told you the truth."

Grandmother Tara fell silent, waiting for Dorsa's answer. She pointed at Matt and extended her hand toward him. Matt immediately approached and held her hand in his. Grandmother Tara continued, "This young man is remarkable and an extraordinary scientist to me. His significant knowledge might help them come back to their lives and help us reunite with our loved ones. I didn't know what to think when I first heard about this. At my age, nobody wants to look foolish. But there was nothing I could do except cry every night. When Azar explained to me about this young man and how he wanted me to be part of this incredible procedure, I immediately said *yes*. There wasn't any doubt in my mind. I've been waiting for someone like him my whole life, and you are lucky to have him here."

Grandma Tara looked at Matt and asked, "I hope there's still a chance for my brother too. Even if he's old, I'm holding on to the hope of seeing him one more time."

Megan's attention shifted to Grandma Tara, and with curiosity, she asked, "Grandma Tara! What was his name?"

Grandma Tara had a smile on her lips and said, "His name was Timothy and we called him Tim."

Matt, deeply moved, squeezed her hand gently. "Dear Grandma Tara, I believe there is hope. If we can bring Artemis and Arsham back, perhaps we can find a way to bring your brother back, too. We will do everything we can."

Matt was more surprised than anyone else. He kissed Grandma Tara's hand like a gentleman, feeling grateful that she would be there with them tonight. Knowing there was someone who believed in him completely was a significant boost for him. Just then, the door opened, and Grandpa Avan entered, looking pleased as he explained his tardiness. "I couldn't find a parking spot close to your home, Dorsa. I had to park the car a block away. Thank goodness there was an empty space there; otherwise, I would've had to circle to the next street to find parking."

He saw the crowd in the room, and everyone was sitting formally. Without showing any surprise, he sat beside his wife, holding her hand. He looked into Dorsa's eyes and asked, "When are we going to start?" everyone burst into laughter.

Matt stood up and waited for everyone to quiet down, no longer the shy guy he was before. He felt more confident, knowing he had a believer and that he had the situation under control. He looked at everyone's faces, making sure he had their full attention. Clearing his throat, he began to speak, "As you know, four years ago, on Artemis's birthday, we came across an idea that wasn't just a theory but a rediscovery. Possibly, there are many others who were trapped there and are still stuck, needing our help to return. On the 29th, we will re-open that gate and bring them back. If we fail, it means they might lose their hope, too. So, we won't let them down."

He felt very calm by this time and continued, "Tonight is a big night for us and for everyone who cares about Artemis and her father, as well as Grandma Tara's brother Tim. We are all gathered here to be part of this incredible journey to get ready for that special day which is Feb 29th. I thank you in advance for believing in me—it means more than you know. We don't have a lot of time, so we must move quickly, but we also need to be careful and precise."

He took a sip of his drink to refresh his throat, then continued, "Today is Monday, February 27th, which gives us two days until the 29th, which is Wednesday. As you all know, because of the leap year, this date only appears every four years. I know Artemis, and I know she is a very intelligent person. She will try the same thing from the other side because she knows I will keep the promise I made to her, and that's why we have to do our part of this procedure exactly at the specific time. If we fail, she might think we don't care or give up on them. I believe Artemis will be exactly as I expect her to be. We have to prepare everything according to the list I've made, and we'll reconvene here on February 29th."

Azar looked around with her tired eyes, then at Matt, who seemed a little confused. She asked, "How do you know we have to do it here? Why can't they do the same thing and open the gate from their side?"

Grandma Tara immediately responded, providing a convincing explanation, "Because if they could do it from the other side, my brother would have come back a long time ago."

Matt nodded in agreement, finishing his theory. "My guess is that to get there, we can open the gate from this side. However, for them to return, both sides must be open and aligned. In this case, we'll need to open the gate here, and with Artemis on the other side, it should be easier to establish the connection."

Matt gave her a happy smile, clearly pleased with Grandma Tara's response. He stood up and pulled out a stack of papers, handing one to everyone. He wanted to ensure everyone understood the importance of their tasks.

"I've listed the items we need, and everyone has an assignment. Please make sure you do it right and exactly as it was mentioned here. For example, Atossa is tasked with finding the stones because she said she hid them four years ago, thinking they might be useful, and they really are now. Thanks, Atossa, you did a great job."

Dorsa looked at Atossa angrily, her eyes expressing her frustration. Atossa met her gaze and said, "I had to keep them because I knew someday they might be handy, like today. That's all!" She looked at Dorsa and continued, "Without these stones, we might never have a chance to see Artemis again."

Helen tapped Matt on the shoulder and read the paragraph aloud, "On a big piece of paper, draw the spirit circle, pentacle, and don't forget the pentagram and its five points. But this time, do it in the opposite order." She looked at Matt and asked, "Are you serious?"

"Yes, and as a matter of fact, I've never been this serious in my life. Please follow the exact procedure you used four years ago—no changes. The only difference this time should be the participants. I've already given you all the pictures."

Helen continued to look at Matt as she asked, "Aren't I supposed to do it on the room floor? Just like we did four years ago?"

Matt looked at her with the calm authority of a teacher and replied, "You're right, but this time, we'll post it on the wall to create a gate-like structure. That way, they just have to walk through to this side, and it ensures no one accidentally falls into it."

Helen, now convinced, looked at Matt again and said, "Why don't I draw it on the wall itself? It'll be safer that way."

Matt nodded in agreement and replied, "Once everyone is here, we need to erase all the signs immediately—just to be safe. We don't want it opening on its own, especially when Artemis, her father, and her mother are here all together. Just as a precaution."

Helen was speechless at his answer, impressed by the wisdom in his thinking. She nodded in agreement, quietly acknowledging his plan, and then she added, "May I draw one on the wall and one on the floor, just to be safe? If one doesn't open, hopefully the other will."

Matt looked at her and said, "It will appear on the wall. We designed it that way for safety, ensuring no one accidentally falls through it."

Helen stared at him and said, "Okay, No problem."

Then he looked at Grandma Tara and went over and sat down beside her on the sofa. Grandma Tara was excited, hoping to see Artemis, along with her father, and especially her brother, whom she lost when she was just a little girl. She smiled at Matt, anticipating his question. But Matt only wanted to share some of his ideas with her.

"Grandma Tara, I've studied your family over these four years to find a way to bring Artemis back. Your family has very interesting names that seem carefully chosen. For example, your name, Tara, means star. Your daughters' names—Dorsa, Parto, Padideh, and Azar—mean, in order, diamond, the ray of light, phenomenon, and fire. Other names in your family, like Zohreh, Storm, and Atossa, mean, respectively, the planet Venus, airy, and a stone. These names might hold deeper significance and could be connected to why this happened in the first place."

Grandma Tara looked at him curiously and asked, "My dear, what do these names mean to you?"

Matt smiled and replied, "They mean so many things. They are chosen names, and we need to find the connection between them."

He stood up and, very politely like a gentleman, kissed Grandma Tara's hand again when he said, "Grandma Tara, I have a lot of thinking to do, but we will bring them back for sure." He stood in the middle of the room and raised his voice to get everyone's attention.

"Everyone, please listen carefully! On Wednesday, the 29th, we all need to be here in the morning—no excuses. This is crucial. We have only one shot at this, and it's absolutely essential that everyone is on time. Those related to Artemis by blood are the key participants and must be present. We need to arrive early to prepare everything and be ready when the moment comes. If you encounter any problems, contact me immediately. Don't wait until the last minute, as that could cause us to fail, and nobody wants that. If you have a doctor's appointment, surgery, or any unthinkable event, please reschedule it—this is a matter of life and death. Remember, we can't reschedule this. We only have one shot."

"Helen, it would be best if you arrived even earlier to ensure you can draw the signs exactly as I explained on Artemis's bedroom wall. Thank you everyone. I'll see you all on Wednesday early morning, maybe 6 am sharp. And a special thanks to Grandma Tara and Mrs. Vedetta for trusting me and believing in me." His actions and the way he organized the event were those of a true leader. It was as if he was born for this role.

Helen turned to Dorsa and Atossa and asked, "Is that okay if I come tomorrow night with all my tools to start drawing and preparations?"

Dorsa looked at Atossa and immediately said, "Of course it's okay. I'm happy to see you tomorrow."

Matt had thousands of thoughts racing through his mind as he headed straight home, eager to dive deeper into his research about the unfolding events. He was both hyper and aggressive, driven by an intense determination to uncover more about the mystery at hand. The agitation within him was unsettling, and he knew he needed to find a way to calm himself down. Fortunately, he had kept his notes in a safe place. On the night of Artemis' disappearance, he had meticulously documented every detail from beginning to end. Now, he poured over those notes, reviewing everything again and again, hoping to find any clues he might have missed.

Matt reminded himself to stay focused and calm as he poured over his notes. This was their best chance to bring Artemis and her father back, and he needed to be at his best. The detailed observations and thoughts he had recorded four years ago could hold the key to their success. Each entry, no matter how small or seemingly insignificant, was scrutinized as he searched for connections and patterns. He knew that somewhere within these pages lay the answers they needed, and he was determined to find them. His mind raced as he pieced together the events of that night, looking for any detail that could guide them in the upcoming attempt. The pressure was immense, but Matt knew that with the support of everyone involved, they had a real chance to make this work.

Atossa felt a whirlwind of emotions—both scared and happy—as she struggled to control herself. After the guests had left, she ran downstairs into the basement. She knew exactly where she had left the box. The basement, filled with antique furniture, could easily pass for an antique store. Her mother never liked going down there because it felt spooky, which reassured Atossa about the safety of her hiding spot. In the dimly lit basement, Atossa made her way to a large chest that had been there for as long as she could remember. The chest was impressive, with numerous drawers and doors that made it fascinating. Taking a deep breath, she approached the chest, her heart pounding with anticipation and anxiety. She opened the chest carefully and began searching through its compartments, her mind racing with thoughts of the upcoming leap day and the crucial role the box would play.

Finally, she found the hidden box. With trembling hands, she opened it to ensure everything was still inside. The stones were there, just as she had left them four years ago. Relief washed over her as she realized the significance of what she held. This was their chance, and she was ready to do whatever it took to bring Artemis and their father back.

Years ago, when Atossa and Artemis were exploring the basement, they discovered a secret compartment in the chest that was nearly impossible to find at first. They had found the stones for the first time in this hidden compartment. The stones would glow at their touch, and they weren't just ordinary stones—they were extraordinary. The girls had never talked about them because their mom never wanted to touch anything that had belonged to her husband.

Now, Atossa took the stones out again and brought them upstairs. She sat beside her mother and slowly opened the lid of the box. Dorsa looked at them quietly, her eyes filled with curiosity and a hint of awe. She reached out and picked up one of the stones, which was like crystal but shone brilliantly like a diamond.

She held the stone up to the light, watching it shimmer. "These are incredible," she whispered, her voice tinged with wonder. "I can see why you kept them safe, Atossa."

Atossa nodded, feeling a mix of relief and excitement. "I knew they were special, Mom. I just had a feeling they would be important someday."

Dorsa continued to examine the stone, her skepticism slowly being replaced by a sense of possibility. "Maybe these really are the key to bringing them back," she said, her voice barely above a whisper.

Dorsa held the stone in her hand and said, "Look, Atossa! It is beautiful. Your father and I used to love these stones, and We placed them in every corner of the house for good luck, but we were wrong. They aren't meant to bring good luck—they hold a much greater, more significant purpose. They are truly extraordinary."

Atossa could clearly see the connection between the crystal and her mother. The stone shone more brightly, casting a soft, ethereal glow across Dorsa's face. The light intensified whenever Dorsa held the crystal as if responding to her touch, glowing even brighter in her hands.

Dorsa held the stone up to her eyes and said, "Oh… I told your dad these were not good charms and that we should get rid of them, but he insisted on keeping them. And just look at us now." Atossa watched as the stone seemed to rekindle a spark in her mother.

"Maybe Dad was right to keep them," Atossa said softly. "Maybe they're not just stones, but something more. We must trust them and ourselves to bring Dad and Artemis back."

WHEN HOPE MEETS HOMES

The day that Matt had been waiting for had finally arrived. Artemis's home was bustling with activity. Everyone had brought food for this special occasion, filling the dining table with a feast. The atmosphere was charged with anticipation as they prepared for the possibility of welcoming Artemis and her father back. As soon as Helen walked into the room, Matt was overwhelmed to see how amazingly she had done the job.

Helen drew the sign backward on the wall and on the opposite wall, she drew it exactly the opposite way from how she did it four years ago. Meanwhile, she did the same drawing on the floor, exactly the way she did four years ago, but completely opposite. She looked at Matt and said, "Just in case—let's see which one works better." Without any questions, Matt nodded.

Atossa, holding the glowing stones, showed them to her cousins Anahita and Parvin. Since seven o'clock that morning, they had all been working tirelessly except Helen, who was there the night before to ensure she had enough time to finish it. Even Dorsa was full of energy and feeling great today. Grandma Tara was laughing and joking with everyone, moving quickly as she set the table for lunch and made lemonade for everyone. She didn't want anyone to slow down, giving them hope and energy to work faster, better, and more accurately.

Dorsa went to Artemis's room to check on the rescue team and ensure everything was as it should be. They were working diligently to recreate the scene exactly as it had been four years ago, though disagreements arose over minor differences and their positions in the room. Now fully engaged in the process, Ricky took charge, directing the others on what to do and deciding which moves were correct. His sudden burst of energy made it clear how seriously he was taking the situation.

By eleven o'clock at night, they had finished their tasks and gathered in the living room. Exhausted and tired, they all took their places. The living room was full, and most of them were sitting on the floor, ready to listen. Matt stood up, looking around at the tired but determined faces.

"Thank you all for your hard work," he began. "We've done everything we can to prepare. Now, it's time for the final step. Remember, we need to stay focused and work together. This is our one shot to bring Artemis and her father and possibly Grandma Tara's brother back. Let's make it count."

The room was silent, filled with a sense of anticipation and hope. Everyone knew how important this moment was, and they were ready to do whatever it took to succeed.

Grandma Tara looked at Matt and said, "My dear Matt, we know that you did your best, and we all appreciate your hard work. In case we don't get the result we're hoping for. I want to thank you for everything you've done. You've given it your all."

She paused, then added, "I don't know where I'm supposed to sit, so just tell us what to do or where to sit, and we'll do it. Tonight is about teamwork and harmony. This is about partnership and unity. I wish you and all of us good luck and hope communication becomes possible. We are listening to you. Please give us your instructions."

Matt smiled warmly at Grandma Tara, appreciating her words of support. He took a deep breath and began, "Thank you, Grandma Tara, and thank you all for being here and for your unwavering support. Tonight, we need to recreate the exact conditions from four years ago. Each of you has a specific role to play, and it's crucial that we follow the plan precisely."

He gestured to the living room, "Those of you who were here four years ago, please take your original positions. Everyone else, find a spot where you can observe without interfering. Helen, you've done a great job with the symbols. Thank you, Atossa. Keep the stones close—they're vital to this process."

He continued, "Grandma Tara, you can sit near the edge of the sign, where your presence will provide the strongest connection, so just try to sit around the sign. No one would be on the sign, so there's no danger of disappearing. Mrs. Vedetta, I need you to stay close to Atossa. Your bond is important. Remember, stay focused and keep your minds clear. This is about energy and intent."

Matt looked around the room, seeing the determination and hope in everyone's eyes. "We are about to attempt something extraordinary. Let's give it everything we've got. Good luck to all of us."

Grandma Tara took his position and signaled everyone to do the same. The room fell silent, charged with anticipation and the hope that tonight would be the night they brought Artemis and her father back. She spoke proudly, preparing everyone to expect anything. Her main goal was to take the pressure off Matt, who had been trying so hard. Matt stood up, acknowledging Grandma Tara and expressing his gratitude for all her support. He looked around at everyone, feeling obliged to show his courtesy, gratitude, and appreciation. They all held glasses of wine as Matt began his speech.

"This is a great night for all of us. We are here because we share a belief and a hope in the same vision—that there is more to this world than we know. We are united by this belief. All of us did a great job today, especially Helen, who did a wonderful job drawing the signs. She remembered everything detailed we did four years ago, with the help of Megan, Ricky, and Allen, who worked together to complete this task. I thank Atossa for valuing her trust and keeping those stones safe for today. Without them, we wouldn't be able to do anything."

At that moment, Grandma Tara raised her hand and opened her fist, revealing another set of beautiful stones and smiled at Matt and said, "I brought my brother's stones." She explained, "I've been keeping them hidden, just in case Atossa couldn't find hers or lost them." With that, everyone burst into laughter. Matt gave a slight bow to Grandma Tara, a gesture of gratitude for her thoughtfulness.

Then he looked at everyone and said, "I thank Azar for helping her sister to believe again. I thank Mrs. Vedetta for allowing us to prepare everything despite her loss. And a special thanks to Grandma Tara, who gave us the most valuable feeling of trust and support."

He paused, letting his words sink in. "Tonight, we stand on the brink of something extraordinary. We have prepared meticulously and worked tirelessly. Now, it's time to put our plan into action. Let's give it everything we've got and bring Artemis, her father, and maybe even Grandma Tara's brother back home again. Thank you again for believing in me and everyone else in this room." With that, Matt raised his glass in a toast and held it toward Grandma Tara, then Dorsa and to everyone else. "To teamwork, to hope, and to the return of our loved ones. Cheers!"

Grandma Tara, wiping away her tears, stood up with everyone else and they all raised their glasses, echoing, "Cheers!" The room was filled with a renewed sense of purpose and determination. They took their positions, ready to follow Matt's instructions and see their efforts through to the end. The atmosphere was electric with anticipation and hope as they prepared for the critical moment.

Matt glanced at everyone as they settled back into their seats, then continued his speech, "There are a lot of questions about tonight, and I'll try to explain what is going on before we start. I want everyone to be aware of their position. The night after we left four years ago, I went home and couldn't sleep. I had to do a lot of research to be prepared for tonight. Four years ago, when we were still teenagers, We did something incredible without even realizing it. We treated it like a game or play, but we had no idea how serious it would turn out to be. That night, we discovered something extraordinary. We had the chance to re-open what I call the Gate of the Universe. Artemis went through the same way her father did. We were so scared and panicked that night. The real truth is, we could have brought her back that same night with a little more thought, but we panicked, just like everyone else. Our reaction to this incredible discovery was fear, and fear is the enemy of science. We needed to reverse the procedure. Tonight is different for all of us. We're prepared now; we know what's happening and what to expect. Let me explain how we did it four years ago."

He took a sip to soothe his throat, then continued, "Last time, we had all the signs drawn on the floor by our artist, Helen, and much of Ricky's knowledge. We asked Artemis to lie down on the sign that Ricky suggested again. We gave the stones to Artemis to hold, which was Ricky's idea, too. We waited and waited, but nothing happened. It didn't happen at midnight, but way after that, and I'll explain that later. It happened when we all gave up and focused only on complaining. Boom… she was gone." He paused for a second, then he continued, "This time, we won't let panic get in our way. We'll stay focused and keep our minds clear. Now, let's go over the plan step by step. First, Helen, you'll finish the final touches on the symbols. Atossa, you'll place the stones around the designated area the way I told you. Mrs. Vedetta! your presence is vital for emotional support and maintaining the connection. Grandma Tara! You'll sit close to the edge of the sign to help anchor the energy. Everyone else, take your positions from four years ago and for everyone else, please sit on the second row to make our circle more stronger."

Matt was in full control as the room fell silent, everyone acutely aware of the gravity of the situation. They nodded in agreement, ready to follow his instructions to the letter. With renewed determination, they took their positions and prepared for the critical moment ahead.

Artemis's mom started to cry, and Grandma Tara held her in her arms, comforting her. Matt glanced at Dorsa, then continued, "Artemis was the main power in the leap year four years ago. How can we do it without her is not a mystery anymore. Her father went through the same way when she was a little child. Let me tell you how. Artemis's father went through the same procedure and vanished, too. Grandma Tara's brother went the same way even though he wasn't a leap year person, but his sister was close to the sign while he was standing on it. That's why he went through. She opened the gate."

He looked at Grandma Tara and smiled, "Yes, you were the power, but don't feel guilty—be proud of such a gift."

Matt paused, looking around the room. "The gate can be opened with the right combination of elements and the right people in the right places. Every person in this room is like a key to a lock, a living password to a secure area. Tonight, we will recreate those conditions. The signs, the stones, the people—all of it matters. This time, we won't let panic get in our way. We'll stay focused and keep our minds clear."

He turned to Grandma Tara. "Your presence is crucial because you were part of the original opening of the gate. Mrs. Vedetta! you provide the emotional connection. Everyone else, your roles are equally important. We'll start the procedure just before midnight. Remember, it's not just about the actions we take but the intention and energy behind them. We need to stay calm and focused no matter what happens. Let's bring them back."

"Remember," Matt said, "this time, we stay calm and focused. No panic. We are ready."

As the clock approached midnight, the room was charged with anticipation. They all held their breath, waiting for the crucial moment when they would attempt to open the gate and bring Artemis and her father back. As midnight approached, one by one, they walked into Artemis's bedroom. Unsure of where to sit, they waited for Matt's guidance. Matt entered last and he remembered how the sign was placed on the floor. According to his knowledge from four years ago, he was taking charge and pointing to Atossa, Dorsa, Azar, and Anahita, instructing them to sit behind the points of the star.

He directed Azar to sit above the sign, representing fire and handed her the red stone. Next, he asked Anahita to sit at the bottom of the sign, representing water and gave her the blue stone. He positioned Afshin, who was Artemis' cousin, on the right side of the sign, representing earth, and Storm on the left, representing air. Each received their special stone to hold.

Now, Matt needed the spirit power. He chose Padideh to hold the spirit stone and asked everyone else to sit around the sign that had faded from four years ago and Helen retraced it back again.

Matt took a deep breath, feeling the weight of the moment. "Remember, stay calm and focused," He constantly reminded them to avoid making any mistakes. "This is our chance to bring them back."

The room was filled with a charged silence, each person holding their stone, each in their designated spot. All the symbols on the walls and floor began to emit a soft, ethereal glow, casting an otherworldly light around the room, creating an atmosphere both eerie and mesmerizing.

"On my count," Matt instructed. "We will channel our energy by holding hands and focus on opening the gate. Trust in the power within you and the bonds we share."

Matt looked at everyone and said, "It is very important to watch each other's back. No matter what happens, do not leave your spot alone. Otherwise, you will break the connection and the gate will be closed."

Standing behind everyone else, Grandpa Avan, along with his grandson Mehran and his granddaughters Zohreh, Anahita, and Oranous, watched the circle intently. His daughters Padideh, Azar, and Parto were also there, each in their designated positions. His sons-in-law, Cenzio, Dino, and Gino, stood by as well, ready to offer their support.

The room was filled with a sense of unity and purpose. Each person understood the significance of their role in this critical moment. Matt took a deep breath and began the final instructions. "Helen, make sure the symbols are perfectly aligned. Atossa, keep the stones close. Everyone else, focus on your task and keep the energy flowing. We are all connected in this, and our combined strength will make this work."

He then addressed the entire group, "Remember, we're here to bring back Artemis and the others. This might be our only chance. Let's make it count."

As the clock struck midnight, Matt gave the signal. Each person channeled their energy and focus into the stones and symbols, their focus unwavering. The room began to vibrate with an intense energy, the air thick with anticipation. Grandma Tara asked Matt if her husband was okay with staying close to her, but Matt was busy positioning everyone in their correct spots, looked at Grandma Tara and answered politely, "Grandma Tara, you and Grandpa Avan are the most important part of this, and I'm counting on you two. However, we need everyone here to support each other. Grandma Tara and Grandpa Avan, please come here and sit on these two cushions." He pointed to two cushions placed under the window. Grandma Tara and Grandpa Avan moved to the designated spots and sat down, their presence lending a sense of calm and strength to the group. "Everyone else, stay focused and remember your roles," Matt continued. "We're about to start. Keep your energy steady and support one another. Hold hands, and whatever happens, don't let go."

Parto spoke loudly, "What are we supposed to do? I know why we are here, but I'm confused about what we should do."

Matt smiled at her and then addressed everyone. "You have to focus on the sign. If you are one of the elements, you must concentrate on your special stone. You need to touch the stone and make it glow. Last time this happened, they all started glowing, which means it's working. The rest of you, focus on the signs. When we have enough energy to open the gate, it will open. If we are lucky and they are waiting for us on the other side, they will jump through the gate and be home in no time."

He continued, "Everyone else, focus on maintaining the energy flow. Stay connected, keep your minds clear, and support the process. Remember, our combined effort is what makes this possible."

Grandma Tara asked with a happy sound, "How do you know if they are there?"

Grandpa Avan echoed her curiosity in a different way, "How do you know they'll figure out that we are opening the gate for them?"

Aunt Padideh, waiting for the right moment, added, "How do they know where to go and wait for us?"

Matt, anticipating these questions, smiled reassuringly. "These are great questions, and I understand your concerns. Here's what we know."

He took a deep breath and continued, "Artemis and her father are intelligent and resourceful. Four years ago, when this happened, they left clues—like the stones in your hands and the faded signs on the floor—showing they went through the same process we're attempting today. Since they disappeared under similar circumstances, there's a strong chance they're together and aware of what's happening."

He looked around, making eye contact with each person to emphasize his points. "When we start the process, the energy and the glowing stones will create a unique signal—something that can't be ignored. This energy will act as a beacon, guiding them to the right place. They will feel the pull and know to head toward the source of the energy. That's my opinion."

He continued, "We're also working with the same setup and the same elements that were in place when they disappeared. The consistency in our approach is crucial. The familiar energy patterns and the specific arrangements will help them recognize our efforts."

Matt paused, letting his words sink in. "We have to trust in our connection with them and in the process we've prepared. Our focus and belief are key. If we stay united and maintain our intent, they will find their way to us."

The room was silent as everyone absorbed Matt's explanation. The determination on their faces showed their readiness to proceed, fueled by the hope of reuniting with Artemis and her father.

Matt had a merry face, realizing that everyone was genuinely interested and eager to learn. He looked at them and continued, "I know you're all curious about how this will work. Let me explain why I have enough confidence to believe in this. I know Artemis very well. In fact, I know her better than anyone else in this room. Artemis is one of the most intelligent people I've ever met. She always pays attention to details, and even when it seems like she isn't listening, she remembers everything. She is capable of redoing everything without anyone's help.

He took a deep breath to steady himself, then continued, "I don't know exactly where she is, which is why I can't provide specific details on how she'll do it. But no matter where she is, I assure you, she will find a way. I have faith in her, and I know she trusts me—and you should too." Matt's voice softened as he reached the end of his speech.

The room was silent for a moment, filled with a sense of hope and determination. Everyone felt reassured by Matt's confidence and his deep understanding of Artemis's capabilities.

With renewed focus, Matt continued, "Alright, let's get back to our positions. Remember, stay calm, stay focused, and keep your energy connected. We're going to make this work together."

Everyone nodded, focusing back on their designated spots, ready to begin the process. The atmosphere was charged with anticipation, each person holding onto the belief that tonight would be the night they brought Artemis and her father back.

Grandma Tara smiled and said, "Artemis is a very lucky girl to have a good friend like you, Matt, who trusts her this much. She is lucky to have friends like all of you." She became quiet, and as she sat back on her cushion, she discreetly dried her eyes with a tissue, not wanting anyone to see her tears.

Everyone focused intently on the signs. The room was filled with a tense silence as they studied both symbols, their significance hanging heavy in the air. Each person was acutely aware of the importance of these markings, knowing they held the key to bringing them back. Their expressions were serious as they waited for the right moment. Different people imagined different gateways, each envisioning the portal that would bring Artemis and her father back. Matt moved around the room, checking everything to ensure it was all in the right place. He glanced at the time. It was just a few minutes to midnight. Stretching his body, he prepared to notify everyone to be ready.

"Alright, everyone," Matt said, his voice steady and calm. "It's almost time. Remember to focus on your stone and maintain your connection. We need to work together as one. When I give the signal, channel all your energy into the sign. Remember, it might take until morning, but we must stay focused and not lose hope, and most important is to be quiet and focus." Matt reminded everyone, his voice steady and resolute. The room was silent, filled with anticipation. Matt took a deep breath and got ready to give the final countdown. "We have a couple of minutes to midnight. I don't know the exact proper time, but I know it is close. My friends, get ready for anything..." Matt announced.

Grandma Tara asked Matt, "When Artemis vanished last time, what time exactly was it?"

Atossa quickly answered, "It was 4:45 in the morning. Why?"

Grandma Tara turned to Dorsa and said, "Isn't that the time she was born?"

Dorsa, surprised, responded, "Yes, that is correct."

Matt felt a sense of relief as one of the biggest puzzles was solved by Grandma Tara. He looked at her and asked, "What time was your brother born?"

Grandma Tara replied, "It was almost five o'clock in the morning."

Matt then turned to Dorsa and asked, "How about your husband, Mrs. Vedetta?"

Dorsa, excited and struggling to speak, managed to answer, "I think it was around six o'clock in the morning, according to his sister. I think between 5:30 and 6:00."

Helen looked at Matt and asked, "What does that mean, Matt?"

Matt stood by the door, looking at Grandma Tara with gratitude in his eyes. "Thank you, Grandma Tara. You've helped solve one of the biggest puzzles," he said, his voice filled with admiration. Then he turned to Helen and continued, "That means they should be here before seven in the morning."

Dorsa looked at Matt, then at her sister and mother with pride in her eyes. Her gaze returned to Matt, filled with satisfaction and a renewed sense of hope. Finally, she gave Matt a big, heartfelt smile.

The room filled with a renewed sense of anticipation and their belief became stronger. Matt's revelation gave everyone a clearer understanding of what to expect. They had a timeline now, a window in which to focus their efforts.

"Let's use this time wisely," Matt suggested.

"We need to maintain our concentration and keep the energy flowing. Stay focused on your stones and on the connection we share. We're close, and we can do this."

The atmosphere was charged with a mix of nervous energy and hope. Each person took a deep breath, preparing for the hours ahead. They knew the significance of what they were attempting, and their belief in Matt and each other fortified their resolve.

***

THE FINAL COUNTDOWN

There was a big fire in the tallest building on Edna Street, one of the most expensive locations in Flimsy World. People were screaming and crying for help. Fire trucks were everywhere, and the police were holding back the crowd.

Firefighters were shaking their heads sadly when Officer Magdam approached them and said loudly, "Are you going in or not? People in the building need your help. They're trapped in there. You need to act as soon as possible, or the result will be a disaster—the building could collapse any minute."

Mehran, the head of the firefighters, turned to the officer, pulled him aside, and said, "This is a very critical situation. The staircase is completely engulfed in flames and has already collapsed. There's no way to enter the building safely. The first floor is gone, and the entire structure could collapse at any moment. If I send my team in there, there's a ninety percent chance we'll lose them."

Officer Magdam looked at Mehran apprehensively. He pulled her aside again and said, "If you want to do anything, you must do it now, or it's too late. You have to contact her because she is our only hope, I'm telling you."

Mehran replied, "We contacted her and left so many messages, but we haven't heard from her yet."

Before she could finish her sentence, there was a cheer from the crowd. Officer Magdam immediately turned to see what was going on. He saw a small person blowing air forcefully into the building. In no time, she brought the people who were trapped inside out to safety. Officer Magdam and Firefighter Mehran looked at each other, relieved. The small person walked through the fire without getting hurt, helping everyone inside the building to escape and reach a safe place.

Artemis said, "Wow!" loudly and turned to Gilbert, who was standing beside her. "It's a big wow, and I don't know what it is about fires that all the superheroes get involved. I remember seeing Spider-Man's movie where he saved a lot of people from a fire. That's exactly the picture in my mind, but this time, I'm the hero. I feel great today."

Gilbert's gaze swept over the faces of the people Artemis had saved, his expression a mixture of awe and quiet admiration then he turned to her. "You're getting better every day," he spoke with a beaming smile, his voice laced with genuine admiration.

He playfully punched her in the stomach, but Artemis didn't feel a thing and was already heading toward Officer Magdam. Gilbert felt a bit offended when he heard laughter behind him, unsure if they were laughing at him or the situation. When he turned to see who was laughing, he saw the usual ridicule from two teenagers who were still chuckling at him.

"What? We always joke like that. Instead of being jerks, go and help people," he told them.

"Yeah, dude, but the problem is that was a big punch from you, and she didn't even feel a thing." They both laughed even louder this time.

Gilbert felt bad and said nothing, leaving the teenagers and going to Artemis. Today had been exhilarating for Artemis, with hours of nonstop rescuing turning it into a day unlike any other for a superhero. She felt as if she were playing a game, but this time with a sense of honor. Fatigue meant nothing to her—being active made her feel truly alive.

Gilbert stood beside Artemis, who was speaking with the firefighters to ensure everyone in the building was saved. As he scanned the faces in the crowd, a sudden jolt of recognition made his heart stop. A familiar face caught his eye, and he needed to confirm if his mind was playing tricks on him. Turning back for a second look, his worst fears were confirmed—there was no mistake. He saw Corrupt walking toward him, and from a distance, Cranky was watching Artemis with a menacing gaze. He whispered, "That doesn't look good! Oh my God, please help me."

Artemis was surrounded by cameras, reporters, and people thanking her and snapping pictures. Besides being a superhero, she had become a star with a devoted fan base. Ever since she arrived, women had become more independent, and wherever she went, a crowd of admirers was sure to follow. Her fans were always present, whether she was on a daring rescue mission or just having dinner at a restaurant. Even the guys started calling her a superhero.

As Gilbert stood still, Corrupt crossed the street and stopped directly in front of him. Corrupt's eyes scanned Artemis from head to toe, taking in every detail for several minutes. Gilbert kept a watchful eye on him and Cranky, who was lingering nearby. He knew these two were not to be trusted—individuals who demanded constant vigilance and scrutiny. Gilbert remembered the letter Corrupt gave him to hand it to Artemis. He didn't dare look away, his instincts telling him that danger was near. It took Corrupt a couple of minutes, but he finally turned to Gilbert and smiled. He pulled out another envelope from his pocket and held it in front of Gilbert.

Corrupt extended his hand, offering a fresh envelope, a sly smirk playing on his lips. "Give this to my sexy babe, or we'll have to deal with her ourselves—and you know Lord Toohi has the power to ensure that happens. This is the second letter—there won't be a third. You're already as good as dead for disobeying Lord Toohi's order by not delivering the first letter. Whatever happens to her now will be entirely your fault. Understood?"

Gilbert's anger ignited, his voice rising as he shouted at Corrupt, "She's not your babe or anybody's babe. Do you hear me?"

Caught off guard by the unexpected reaction, Corrupt froze in momentary shock, instinctively stepping back—his unease deepening as he realized Artemis was far closer than he had anticipated, well within earshot of every word. His confident facade wavered, a flicker of doubt crossing his face as he realized he might have miscalculated the situation.

Gilbert glared at the envelope and asked, "What is this? Another one of your sick games?"

Corrupt's face grew serious as he stepped closer to Gilbert, who instinctively moved backward until he was pressed against the wall. With a swift motion, Corrupt shoved the envelope into Gilbert's pocket, then placed his hand firmly on Gilbert's chest, pinning him against the wall. The pressure was intense, and Gilbert struggled to breathe. Leaning in close, Corrupt spoke in a hushed, menacing tone into Gilbert's ear.

"This is a gift to her from our almighty Lord Toohi," Corrupt hissed, his voice low and threatening.

"This is a great chance for you from him. You shouldn't question his authority because he's Lord Demah's right hand. You must obey instantly. Do you understand?" Corrupt's intense gaze bore into Gilbert, sending a shiver down his spine.

Gilbert, feeling as if he were hypnotized, lost control and immediately said, "Yes. I will carry this message myself to Lord Artemis." The words slipped out of his mouth before he could even think as if compelled by some unseen force.

At this point, Corrupt released Gilbert with a little distance from Gilbert he said loudly, "Give the letter to her." He confidently returned to Cranky, and together they left the location.

Gilbert stood there, nearly panicked and frightened for his life. He knew those two better than anyone else and understood the danger they posed. His heart raced as he considered his next move. He didn't want Artemis to see him so distressed, but the envelope in his pocket felt like a ticking time bomb. Torn between his loyalty to Artemis and the fear of what might happen if he disobeyed it. Gilbert wrestled with the decision to either hand over the envelope or keep it away from her and destroy it. He pulled out his cell phone and dialed a number, speaking tersely, "They handed me another envelope to give her."

He listened intently, then responded, "Okay, I'll take care of it." and shoved the envelope deep into his pocket, hiding it from view.

He knew those two had some sinister plan for Artemis, likely wanting her to do something for them or for their almighty Lord Toohi. Gilbert feared they would try to take Artemis away from him and everyone else, just as they had done with others before. But this time, he was determined not to let it happen. The thought of losing her to their twisted schemes filled him with dread, but it also strengthened his resolve. Gilbert vowed to protect Artemis, no matter the cost. He wouldn't let them succeed.

Taking a deep breath, Gilbert steadied himself, determined to keep his composure. As Artemis approached, concern etched on her face. He quickly forced a calm expression as he prepared to face her. He knew he had to keep this secret for now, at least until he figured out the best way to protect her.

"Gilbert, are you okay? What did they say to you?" Artemis asked, her eyes scanning him for any sign of injury or distress.

Gilbert forced a smile, trying to mask his unease. "I'm fine, really," he replied, his voice steady despite the turmoil inside.

"They just wanted to stir up trouble, as usual. Nothing we can't handle." He avoided her gaze, hoping she wouldn't press further, but he could see the concern lingering in her eyes. Artemis frowned, sensing there was more to the story but choosing not to push him. "Let's get out of here," she said softly. "We need to regroup and figure out our next steps."

Gilbert nodded, grateful for her understanding. As they walked away together, he silently vowed to find a way to protect her from whatever danger Corrupt and Cranky were planning.

"Gilbert! Coming?" Artemis called out.

Startled from his thoughts, Gilbert ran after her. As usual, they flew to a more secluded spot, away from the crowd. This time, they headed to the tallest tower in the city, known as the Sky-lance Tower. Artemis couldn't help but wonder if others from Earth had chosen to build this tower, as it was identical to the CN tower in Toronto.

Once they reached the top, Gilbert's heart pounded—not just from the exertion of the climb but from the dizzying height. Heights had never been his strong suit, and now, standing at the edge of the tower, a surge of vertigo swept over him. He tried to steady himself, forcing a smile as he looked at Artemis, completely at ease, gazed out over the city, proud of herself for conquering her fear of heights. Then she looked at him and said, "You know, back home, I was just like you—terrified of heights, struggling with acrophobia. I even threw up and passed out once. But here, I faced it head-on and overcame my fear. Heights don't scare me anymore."

Artemis lay on her back, gazing up at the sky. The stars here were brighter than those in Toronto, their light twinkling against the deep indigo canvas. Her eyes settled on one of the moons, and as she stared at its soft glow, an unexpected calm washed over her. The moon's gentle radiance seemed to soothe her, and she relished the sensation of the blood rushing to her face as she took in the celestial beauty above. All the chaos and uncertainty faded away in that moment, leaving her with a profound sense of serenity.

Gilbert stood nearby, trying to steady his nerves while keeping a watchful eye on Artemis. He knew he had to tell her about the envelope, but for now, he chose to let her enjoy the peaceful moment. As he observed her, she was clearly drawing strength and tranquility from the moonlit sky, her worries momentarily forgotten. Gilbert couldn't bring himself to shatter that peace just yet. Instead, he took a deep breath and decided to wait a little longer, allowing her to bask in the calm before they faced whatever challenges lay ahead.

Artemis's voice broke the silence. "Isn't it beautiful, Gilbert? Sometimes, moments like these make everything worth it. Right?" She turned to Gilbert and asked, "Are you okay? Is there anything you want to talk about with me?"

Gilbert nodded, though his thoughts were still tangled with the weight of the envelope in his pocket. "Yeah, it's amazing," he replied softly, trying to match her calm demeanor despite the storm brewing inside him. He forced a smile, hoping she wouldn't notice the tension he was struggling to hide. For now, he chose to focus on the serenity of the moment, even if only for a little while longer.

Artemis stared at him for a few seconds, then shifted her gaze back to the sky. They lingered there, basking in the quiet beauty of the night sky. The stars seemed to hold the world at bay, offering them a brief escape from the burdens they carried. Gilbert knew they couldn't stay hidden forever, but for now, this moment of peace was a much-needed respite from the chaos that awaited them. The stillness allowed him to gather his thoughts, and he found comfort in Artemis's presence beside him. For just a little longer, he allowed himself to enjoy the calm before they had to face whatever was coming next.

Without turning to Gilbert, Artemis asked, "Gilbert! Look at the moon. There are lots of lights on it, just like Earth from space. Am I right?"

Gilbert glanced at the moon and nodded. "Ah! I know what you're talking about. This moon shows up every three months and moves very slowly around Zamin."

He smiled, glad for the distraction, even as the weight of the envelope in his pocket reminded him that their peaceful moment would soon come to an end.

"Are people living on it? I can see lights, lots of them," Artemis asked, her curiosity piqued.

"Yes," Gilbert replied, his fear of heights momentarily forgotten as he, too, gazed at the moon. "There are people living on it. I've never been there physically, but they say it's beautiful. It's only for the rich, though—a place of luxury and privilege."

Artemis continued to gaze at the moon, its mysterious allure capturing her imagination. "It must be incredible to live there.

Imagine looking down at Zamin from the moon, seeing the lights of our cities."

The idea fascinated her, the thought of an entire world above their own, filled with life and wonder. For a moment, the troubles of their world seemed distant, replaced by the dreamy possibility of what lay beyond. Gilbert nodded, his mind briefly drifting away from his worries. "Yeah, it would be something. I've always wondered what it's like up there."

The two of them sat in silence for a while, captivated by the distant, glowing moon. For a moment, all their troubles seemed far away, replaced by dreams of distant worlds and new possibilities. "You said on all of them. How many moons actually are there? I already saw two of them," Artemis asked, sitting up and looking at Gilbert curiously.

"There are three of them," Gilbert replied in a cold voice. "One of them moves faster, and that's the one you always see. But this one is different, and you can only see it every three months."

Artemis's eyes widened with curiosity. "Three moons? That's incredible. I can't believe I've never noticed this one before."

Gilbert nodded. "It's not visible often, and when it is, it's usually a big deal. People talk about it for weeks. They say the view from there is breathtaking." Artemis lay back down, her gaze returning to the glowing orb. "I'd love to visit one day," she murmured, her voice filled with longing. "Just imagine what it must be like to look back at Zamin from there."

The thought of standing on that distant moon, looking down at the world they knew, filled her with a sense of wonder. It was a dream that seemed almost within reach yet still far enough away to remain magical. As she lay there, the idea of exploring new horizons offered a brief escape from their challenges and a small spark of hope for what the future might hold. Gilbert remained silent, lost in his thoughts. The peaceful moment allowed him to temporarily push aside the envelope and the ominous message it contained, but he knew that soon. He would have to decide what to do about it and how to protect Artemis from whatever Corrupt and Cranky had planned. For now, though, he let himself be swept away by the beauty of the night and the dreams of distant moons. The serenity of the moment offered a brief refuge, a chance to savor the calm before the storm he knew was coming.

"You said there are three. What about the third one? How long does it take to orbit the planet?" Artemis asked as she got closer to Gilbert, making him uncomfortable.

"The third one is hard to recognize because it was made by scientists and mainly by Lord Demah," Gilbert said, his tone becoming uneasy. "They say they're watching us from there, studying us. It can move fast or slow or even stay in one spot for as long as they want. It moves when they want it to, just like a craft or vehicle," he explained, marveling at its versatility.

Artemis turned to look at him, sensing the shift in his mood. The idea of being watched from above by something controlled and manipulated cast a shadow over the peaceful night. It added an eerie element to the beauty of the moons, a reminder that not everything in their world was as it seemed.

Gilbert's discomfort was evident now, and he silently hoped Artemis wouldn't press further. Discussing the third moon was risky, and he knew it could put them both in a precarious situation. Sensing his unease, Artemis decided to ease up on her inquiries. "That's fascinating, though," she said gently, offering him a reassuring smile. "I never knew your world had such secrets."

Gilbert relaxed a little, grateful for her understanding. "Yeah," he replied, trying to keep his tone light. "There's a lot more to Zamin than meets the eye." He appreciated her letting the subject drop, knowing she was giving him space, even as they both understood there were still many things left unspoken between them. Gilbert nodded, trying to steer the conversation away from dangerous territory. "Yeah, it's definitely interesting. There's so much about our world that we still don't fully understand."

They both fell silent again, looking up at the moons. The calmness of the night and the beauty of the celestial bodies provided a momentary escape from their troubles, even if the weight of Gilbert's hidden knowledge and the envelope in his pocket still lingered in his mind.

Artemis shot a quick glance at him, checking to see if he was okay, before asking, "What's wrong with you?"

Gilbert couldn't bring himself to explain further, fearing he might lose her—especially today when they had inched closer to a looming threat. It was an ominous sign. A comfortable silence settled between them again as they quietly enjoyed their time together. Artemis's excitement was palpable; she was eager to visit the moon and witness life there with her own eyes. Curiosity brimming, she turned to Gilbert and asked, "I'd love to go there and see what life on the moon is like. Do you think I could go there one day?"

Gilbert hesitated, pushing his worries aside. "Maybe," he said, forcing a smile. "With your abilities, anything is possible. But we'd need to learn more about what it takes to get there. It's not exactly an easy trip."

Artemis's eyes sparkled with curiosity. "I'm sure we can find a way. Imagine all the things we could discover up there!"

Gilbert nodded, though his mind was still occupied with the envelope and the potential danger it represented. "Yeah, it would be amazing. We'd need to prepare a lot, though. It's a whole different world up there."

As Artemis dreamed of visiting the moons, Gilbert silently resolved to protect her at all costs—not with physical strength, but by offering her wise guidance. He understood that supporting her journey required more than muscle; it needed careful thought and direction. The mere thought of losing her to whatever schemes Corrupt and Cranky were brewing was unbearable. For now, he allowed her to revel in this moment of wonder and curiosity, but deep down, he knew he had to remain vigilant and find a way to keep her safe.

Inside Gilbert's mind, a storm raged, though he pretended to remain calm. One moment, he managed to keep it together, and the next, he was utterly exhausted by the conversation. He was weary of the topic and, no longer wanting to hear about Artemis's desire to visit the moons, attempted to steer the conversation away for good, his exhaustion evident. He stood up abruptly, his frustration boiling over as he began to rant angrily, "What do you think is so important about going there? HUH? You think it's worth all this?"

His anger consumed him so completely that he lost track of where he was standing. In his fury, he lost his balance, and before he could react, he began to slide dangerously toward the edge of the Sky-lance Tower. In a harrowing instant, he lost his footing and plunged downward, the world blurring around him.

Artemis, who had been sitting with her chin resting in her hand, sighed deeply. "Oh my god. Lately, he's been losing his temper at the drop of a hat. Ah... I really have to do something about this! She straightened up, determination flashing in her eyes. She looked down at the place where he fell calmly and said, "Oh yeah, I need to save him before he hits the ground."

Peering down, Artemis couldn't see anything through the thick clouds below, but Gilbert's high-pitched screams cut through the air with alarming clarity. Without a moment's hesitation, she jumped off the tower, plunging headfirst toward the sound of his voice. She reached him swiftly, effortlessly gliding alongside him as they plunged through the air. He reached out, desperate to grab Artemis's arm, but she teased him, pulling herself just out of his grasp with an almost playful ease.

"Why are you so tense these days?" she asked, her voice calm and teasing. "Couldn't you just answer my questions instead of all this yelling and screaming?"

Gilbert, plummeting in sheer desperation, flailed as he reached for her sleeve or hand, but his fingers found nothing. Each futile attempt fueled his panic, his screams growing louder, reverberating through the open sky. "WHAT IS WRONG WITH YOU? DO YOU WANT TO ARGUE HERE? YOU'RE SICK. HELP ME!" Gilbert shouted, his anger escalating even further as he continued to fall in the air, desperation edging into his voice, and he passed out for seconds and came back.

Artemis descended at the same pace as Gilbert, maintaining her calm demeanor. Finally, she said, "I will save you if you apologize for your behavior."

Gilbert tried to grab her with his nails, making animalistic sounds as he replied, "WHAT KIND OF HUMAN ARE YOU? SAVE ME, AND I WON'T APOLOGIZE."

Artemis smiled and said, "Let's see."

After hearing Gilbert's screams for a few seconds, Artemis added, "I wish you were always like this."

"LIKE WHAT? FALLING AND DYING?" Gilbert said angrily.

"NOOOOO…," Artemis retorted, her voice sharp but steady. "Like now, when you're being stubborn. It's not like when you got that envelope from those guys this afternoon. You were supposed to give it to me, but you didn't. You weren't honest with me. Even if they're bad people, you could have just said NO to them instead of hiding your anger from me and lying." Her gaze bore into him, the wind whipping around them as they fell, her words slicing through the air with unmistakable precision.

By this time, they were close to the ground, and Gilbert was no longer angry but sad. "But you don't understand. You know what? Let me die—I can't bear to see you hurt," he whispered, his voice fading into the wind. Then, as if surrendering to the moment, he fell silent, his body relaxing, drifting downward like a feather caught in the air.

Artemis felt a wave of misery wash over her, unable to comprehend why Gilbert was acting this way. Time was running out as they neared the ground, so she acted quickly. Moving closer to him, she matched her speed with his fall, then slowly grabbed him by the arms, carefully sliding her hands under her shoulders to pull him up. Gilbert remained silent, his expression one of resignation, as if he had truly given up and no longer cared about living.

With a determined focus, Artemis flew toward the mountain where she had first been attacked after her arrival. She ascended to its peak, landing gently on the flattest part, her heart heavy with the weight of the situation.

Gilbert remained silent, taking a deep breath as he pulled himself together. He leaned back, gazing up at the sky, his mind swirling with conflicting emotions. Artemis sat across from him, equally quiet, the tension between them thickening with each passing moment. The silence stretched on, filled with unspoken words and unvoiced fears.

Gilbert loved Artemis deeply and didn't want her to get hurt, but he felt she didn't fully grasp the danger they were in. His thoughts drifted back to the afternoon, puzzling over how she had seen him receive that envelope.

"But how on earth did she see me get that envelope?" he wondered, his brow furrowing as he tried to piece it together.

Gilbert knew he had to break the silence and warn her. Without glancing in her direction, he finally said, "So, you knew about the envelope?"

"Yes," Artemis replied, her eyes drifting from the moon to the sky, her voice calm yet distant.

"Why didn't you tell me?" he asked, his tone flat, concealing the turmoil within.

"Why didn't you?" she shot back, her gaze still fixed on the moon.

"I didn't want you to get involved with them," Gilbert said, his voice wavering as he felt his resolve beginning to crumble.

"You don't know what you're getting into. You don't know them, but I do." The weight of the truth pressed down on him, threatening to break him entirely.

"Who are they? Why don't you leave it to me?" Artemis's voice trembled with a mixture of anger and sadness. She continued, "You were supposed to tell me if there was any message for me, but you doubted me—even though you know me. No one on this planet can hurt me, and you'd better start believing that because you were the one who told me that. You believed in me, and now you doubt my power?"

Her words hung in the air, heavy with the frustration of someone who couldn't understand why the person closest to her would question her abilities. She knew Gilbert was aware of her power, even before she had fully understood it herself, and the fact that he still doubted her stung deeply. Gilbert fell silent, his eyes locked onto Artemis, shining with a deep, unspoken love. Artemis met his gaze, and in that moment, she felt the full weight of her feelings for him. The intensity of their connection filled the silence between them, each understanding more than words could convey.

But then, Gilbert's eyes shifted. He glanced at the moon, then back at her, as if trying to convey something he couldn't put into words. Artemis frowned slightly, unsure of what he was trying to communicate. He did it again—moon, then her—before his gaze darted quickly into the distance as if something out there demanded his attention or held a secret he couldn't share. Artemis's heart raced as she tried to decipher the meaning behind his actions. Was he warning her? Or was it something else entirely? The uncertainty gnawed at her, but she trusted Gilbert enough to know that whatever it was, it was important.

Gilbert said quietly, "Okay." Then he turned to her and asked, "Are you ready for an adventure? Let's go to the other side of Zamin," his voice laced with a hint of excitement.

Artemis, momentarily distracted by her thoughts, sensed there was something he couldn't openly share with her in this place. She turned to look at him, noticing the familiar smile playing on his lips—a smile that always held a promise of something more and full of love. Despite the uncertainty swirling within her, she couldn't help but smile back. In that brief exchange, they both knew what needed to be done. She had the urge to kiss him, but she knew it could be dangerous for him—She might accidentally hurt him and disfigure his face. There was no doubt that she loved him, and he loved her in return. But deep down, both understood that this wasn't a good match, and their love could never be possible. This relationship was impossible.

In an instant, they were gone, vanishing into the unknown, ready to face whatever awaited them on the other side of Zamin. They embarked on the adventure, hoping it would help them forget the feelings they could never act on. They had been flying for hours when Artemis, with a hint of sarcasm in her voice, quipped, "Are you sure you don't just want me to hug you while we're flying, or is there a specific place you have in mind?"

Gilbert chuckled, the tension between them easing slightly. "I might not say no to that," he quipped with a playful grin, "but yes, there is a specific place. We're almost there. We are meeting someone, and if he's not there, we must go back immediately."

Artemis smirked; her teasing met with his usual charm, but her curiosity piqued even more. Whatever lay ahead, she knew it was important and that Gilbert had chosen to bring her along for a reason.

As they reached the edge of the city, Artemis gracefully landed on the nearest tall tree, her eyes wide with awe as she took in the breathtaking view. The city before them was unlike anything she had ever seen—sleek, pristine, and meticulously organized, a stark contrast to Toronto. Even the outskirts exuded an air of cleanliness and order.

"Wow. What's the name of this city?" Artemis asked, turning to Gilbert, her curiosity piqued.

"This is Gilan City," Gilbert replied, his voice tinged with unease.

"And we shouldn't be here. Let's go, and I'll explain everything on the way back. Okay?" The hint of fear in his voice was unmistakable.

But Artemis, feeling an overwhelming sense of power and confidence, wasn't ready to leave just yet. She knew she was untouchable, invincible even, and the allure of the city drew her in. A simple departure without exploring more felt like a missed opportunity, and the desire to see what lay beyond the city's edge tugged at her.

"You brought me here to tell me only the name of this city is Gilan City? What's wrong with you? I want to see more," she said, her eyes gleaming with determination. "Just a quick tour, and then we can go."

"I brought you here to meet a friend of mine, as I mentioned before," Gilbert explained, his tone firm yet pleading. "But since he's not here, we really shouldn't stay. Please, trust me."

Artemis looked at him suspiciously, then struck a playful flying pose, her eyes twinkling with mischief as she asked, "Do you want to come with me or not? Because I'm going either way."

Gilbert, frustration bubbling over, grabbed her hand firmly. "We have to go now," he said, his voice edged with urgency. "This isn't our territory. Please, don't be selfish. Let's go."

Artemis fixed her gaze on him, her expression wavering between determination and confusion. "If you didn't want me to go into this city, then why bring me here in the first place? Why even tell me about this place? And what do you mean it's not our territory? Why can't we wait for this friend of yours?" she demanded, incredulity lacing her voice.

Gilbert hesitated, the tension between them thickening, "I didn't intend for us to get this close. I just wanted to keep you safe, to warn you about the dangers here. We can only enter the city when he allows us," he explained while his voice softening. "But you need to trust me when I say this isn't a place we should be exploring. There are things you don't know, things I'm trying to protect you from."

Artemis searched his eyes, seeing the conflict within him, but still felt the pull of the city. She knew there was more to the story, and part of her wasn't ready to walk away without understanding what that was.

Gilbert said nothing, looking at Artemis, who had clearly made up her mind. He knew no one could change it. "I guess no one can change your mind," he said angrily. "But remember, I told you because I don't want to say, 'I told you so.”

Artemis held Gilbert's hand firmly, and together, they soared above the city, the breathtaking view unfolding beneath them. It was a magnificent sight—an architectural masterpiece. The streets and houses, all made from the same sleek paving material, created a uniform, harmonious appearance. Everything gleamed, reflecting the sunlight, and the cleanliness of the city was astonishing. The people below moved about their day, appearing normal, yet there was something almost surreal about the orderliness and perfection of the place.

"It's beautiful!" Artemis exclaimed with pure joy,

Her voice rang out above the city. "I've never seen such a beautiful place before. Gilbert, you were stupid to keep it away from me. I'm so happy I didn't listen to you."

The city was vast, and as they flew, Artemis couldn't help but notice the delightful aroma that filled the air. It was a scent unlike any she had experienced—fresh, inviting, and free of the pollutants that often marred other cities. The air was crisp and clear, perfect for enjoying the day.

As they continued to explore, Artemis noticed that each business had its name and number prominently displayed on top of their building. The system was strict—without a business number, operations were not allowed, ensuring that every business in the city was legal and above board. This meticulous organization added to the city's charm, making it feel not only beautiful but also well-governed and safe.

But even as she reveled in the city's splendor, a part of her couldn't shake the feeling that something was off—something Gilbert knew and wasn't telling her. The perfection of the place, while mesmerizing, also felt almost too good to be true. Gilbert's voice rang out in panic, breaking through the awe of the moment. "Move back! Move back as soon as possible. I'm not asking you, I'm ordering you. PLEASE DO IT!"

Artemis felt a strange sensation like something light brushing against her, and when she looked back, her eyes widened in surprise. Hundreds of bright blue balls were streaking toward them, glowing with an eerie intensity. While she wasn't worried for herself, knowing her power could protect her, the thought of Gilbert getting hurt sent a jolt of fear through her. Without hesitation, Artemis changed her course, veering out of the city's airspace and speeding toward the nearest hilltop. They landed swiftly, and as soon as her feet touched the ground, she spun around, grabbing Gilbert by the shoulders.

"Are you alright? Did you get hurt? Can you stand up?" she asked urgently, her eyes scanning him for any signs of injury. Gilbert, catching his breath, nodded shakily. "I'm okay," he managed to say, though his voice was still trembling from the close call. "But that was too close. We should never have gone near that place. Those blue balls—they're a defense mechanism. They're designed to protect the city from outsiders."

Artemis looked at him, her concern etched on her face. "I'm sorry, Gilbert. I didn't realize—"

"It's alright," he interrupted, his voice softening. "But we need to be more careful. This place is dangerous, and I don't want anything to happen to you." His eyes locked onto hers, filled with a mix of relief and lingering fear.

Gilbert, furious at Artemis for not following his orders when they were in danger, vented his anger by punching the rocks a few times. Finally, he turned to Artemis and said, "Why don't you listen to me for once? I know where it's safe and where it's not. "They have powerful weapons here that can even hurt you. Those blue balls are meant for Flimsys, but if we stay there too long, we could face dangerous weapons capable of harming you."

Artemis laughed for a few seconds and replied, "Nothing can hurt me here, and you know that. Why are you trying to scare me? Why?"

Gilbert faced Artemis, his eyes filled with urgency. "In Moallem City, you are safe, but not here. Here, they have knowledge of your world and can hurt you."

Before Artemis could fully process his words, more of the blue balls struck her, one hitting her arm with a force that sent a wave of excruciating pain through her body. She cried out, clutching her arm as the numbness spread, and stumbled toward Gilbert, her heart pounding with a mix of pain and fear.

"What were those blue things?" she demanded, her voice trembling. "My arm is numb now. Who are they?"

But before Gilbert could answer, they were surrounded. A line of soldiers closed in on them, their stances rigid and determined. Artemis tried to grab Gilbert, intending to fly them both to safety, but something was wrong. The pain in her arm made it impossible to muster the strength, and in the chaos, they became separated. She watched in horror as Gilbert was trapped inside a cage made of the same blue shocking balls that had hit her, the energy crackling around him.

"Artemis, fly!" Gilbert shouted, his voice filled with desperation. "Please, go and save yourself. Go... go!"

But Artemis couldn't leave him behind. The thought of abandoning Gilbert tore at her, the sense of responsibility for his capture weighing heavily on her conscience. She glanced around, her eyes blazing with fury, and shouted at the soldiers surrounding them,

"Let him go, or I will fight you all! Leave him alone. Open the cage this instant!"

Her voice rang out with authority, but the soldiers didn't budge, their expressions unreadable. The tension in the air thickened as Artemis stood her ground, ready to defend Gilbert with everything she had despite the searing pain and the fear gnawing at her insides. She could feel the power within her surging, pushing against the numbness, as she prepared to do whatever it took to free him. Artemis continued yelling, demanding that the soldiers release Gilbert when she noticed something strange—everyone around her, including Gilbert, had suddenly bowed in her direction.

Confusion swept over her. *Why are they bowing?* she wondered. Determined to show them that she was not intimidated, Artemis straightened her posture, trying to project confidence and authority. But as she looked more closely, she realized they weren't bowing to her—they were bowing to something behind her. A shiver of unease ran down her spine, and she hesitated for a moment before finally deciding to turn around. Slowly, cautiously, she pivoted, bracing herself for whatever might be there. When she had completely turned, Artemis found herself facing a crowd of people standing side by side, their expressions solemn. Most of them shared a delicate, almost translucent quality, similar to Gilbert. But one figure stood out from the rest, exuding an aura of power and authority that was unmistakable. This being was different—solid, imposing, and with a presence that made Artemis's breath catch in her throat. There was something about him that was utterly distinct, something that made it clear he was unlike anyone she had encountered before. Artemis's heart raced as she met the gaze of this figure, sensing that they held the answers to the questions swirling in her mind—and possibly even more than she was prepared to face. Artemis felt a flutter of butterflies in her stomach, trying her best not to panic despite the growing insecurity gnawing at her. This figure before her must be a human, like her—but he wasn't her father. A sudden wave of fear washed over her as he took a step closer, his presence both intimidating and strangely familiar. Determined not to let him see her fear, Artemis stood her ground, her heart pounding.

The only words she could manage were, "Hi. I'm Artemis. Please release my friend this instant, or I will fight for his freedom."

The human continued to approach, and as he drew nearer, Artemis noticed something unexpected—his eyes were so familiar. The kindest she had ever seen, filled with a warmth that immediately disarmed her. There was something familiar about him, something that eased the fear that had gripped her moments before. As he came closer still, without warning, he pulled her into a warm embrace and laughed loudly, a sound that echoed with genuine joy. Artemis was stunned, her eyes darting to Gilbert, who remained bowed, still not daring to look up. *Is this person crazy?* she wondered, her confusion deepening. *Or is this city just... peculiar?* Everything about this encounter felt surreal as if the world had turned upside down, and she was struggling to keep up. Finally, the man released her from the embrace and stood before her, a broad smile on his face.

"Of course, you are Artemis," he said, his voice brimming with excitement."I've heard about you, your sister, and your mother. I've also seen you on TV and in the newspapers, and I couldn't wait to meet you in person."

Artemis blinked, trying to process his words. "You've heard about me and my sister?" she asked, still trying to make sense of the situation.

"Yes," he replied, his tone gentle and reassuring. "You're quite famous in certain circles, you know. But don't worry, I mean you no harm. Your friend will be released, but first, let's talk. There's so much I need to tell you."

Artemis felt her guard lower further, the tension easing as she realized this man wasn't a threat—at least, not in the way she had feared. But the mystery of who he was and why he seemed to know so much about her only deepened, and she couldn't shake the feeling that this meeting was the beginning of something far bigger than she had anticipated.

Artemis faked a smile, her eyes narrowing slightly as she replied, "If you think you can make me work for you, you're wrong."

"I've never thought of that," the man responded calmly, his voice steady and sincere. "But I'm happy to finally see you," he said, a warm smile softening her features.

Without warning, Artemis blurted out, "Are you a human?"

"Of course I am," he replied instantly, his expression unfaltering.

Artemis scrutinized him from head to toe, noting the peculiar mix of solidity and etherealness in his form.

"But you're not as solid as I am and also not like the Flimsy too. What is your name, and how did you come here?" She looked directly into his eyes, searching for any hint of deception.

"I am Uncle Tim or here they call me Lord Leo," he answered, his voice warm and filled with a familiarity that unnerved her.

Artemis frowned, shaking her head slightly. "I've never had an uncle named Tim. I'm sorry. You must have mistaken me for someone else," with that, she turned her back on him and faced Gilbert, her mind racing.

Leo's voice remained gentle as he continued, "I know you don't know me, but I'm your grandmother Tara's older brother. I came here when I was very young, and your grandmother was a little girl. She must've told you about me, and you've forgotten. Or perhaps she told your mother, and she never told you."

Artemis began pacing back and forth, her thoughts swirling in confusion. Finally, she stopped abruptly in front of Leo, her expression one of disbelief. "That's not possible."

"Why not? What is not possible?" Leo asked, a hint of concern creeping into his voice.

"My grandmother is seventy-five years old. But you look only... thirty-five or maybe thirty-nine years old. How is that even possible?"

She stood there with her arms folded, her gaze piercing as she awaited his explanation.

Leo smiled softly as if he had anticipated her reaction. "Time works differently here, Artemis. The years in our world don't align with the years here. When I arrived, I was younger than your age, and time has moved more slowly for me since. That's why I appear younger than I should. It's a side effect of this place, of the world I've lived in for so long. If you get the chance to go back, you'll be 18 years old, not twenty."

Artemis stood there, trying to digest what he was saying, her skepticism still apparent. "So, you're saying you've been here for decades, but you haven't aged like the rest of us?"

"Exactly," Leo replied. "And I understand how difficult this must be to believe. But I assure you, everything I've told you is true. Your grandmother would have told you stories about me, perhaps not in detail, but enough to make you realize I'm not lying."

Artemis remained silent, her mind racing with questions. If what he was saying was true, it meant her entire understanding of time, space, and her own family was about to change dramatically. Leo burst into laughter, the sound echoing through the air for a few seconds. Artemis, still staring at him with an innocent expression, felt a mixture of frustration and curiosity. He finally composed himself and looked directly at her.

"I understand you're concerned," Leo said, a smile still lingering on his lips. "But tell me this; since you came here, what has been normal? Is there anything normal to you? What is normal? Are you normal here? What does normal mean in this world?"

Artemis found herself at a loss for words. Everything about this place had been strange, defying all her expectations and experiences. She realized she had no answer for him.

Still searching for clarity, she pressed on, her voice firmer this time. "How do you know I'm your sister's granddaughter? Huh!"

Leo's expression softened, and he met her gaze with a calm, knowing look. "Because your father told me so many things about you and Atossa."

Artemis felt a wave of dizziness wash over her, and she could no longer stand. She stumbled, and before she knew it, Uncle Leo caught her, steadying her before she hit the ground. At that moment, a warmth spread through her, the most beautiful feeling she had experienced since entering this strange world—perhaps even the most comforting sensation she could remember.

She looked up at Uncle Leo in disbelief, his breath catching as he softly said, "Help me, Artemis. I can't hold you anymore."

Gathering her strength, Artemis steadied herself, gripping Uncle Leo's hands tightly. The reality of the situation was overwhelming, and her voice trembled as she asked, "Uncle Leo, you're a human too, and yet you struggled to hold me."

Uncle Leo smiled gently, the warmth in his eyes tinged with a hint of sadness. "Not entirely human anymore," he replied, his voice quiet but steady. "I'm not as strong as I should be, and it's all because of this damned place."

Artemis's heart sank at his words. The thought of him being less than fully human, of this world, sapping his strength, filled her with a deep sense of unease. "What do you mean?" she asked, her voice barely above a whisper.

"This place," Leo continued, his gaze drifting to the distant horizon, "it changes you. Time doesn't move the same way here, and the rules of our world don't apply. Over the years, I've lost some of the strength I once had—both physical and... spiritual, you could say. This world can be beautiful, but it comes with a price."

Artemis kept staring at him, trying to reconcile the gentle, kind man before her with the idea that he had somehow been altered, diminished by this place. She struggled to understand how someone so familiar could feel so different as if the environment had subtly reshaped who he was. She squeezed his hands tighter, not wanting to let go, feeling a surge of protectiveness and determination rise within her.

"We'll figure this out, Uncle Leo," she said, her voice stronger now, filled with resolve. "Whatever this place has done to you, we'll find a way to fix it. You're not alone anymore."

Leo looked at her with a mixture of pride and sorrow, his smile returning, though it was tinged with a bittersweet emotion. "Thank you, Artemis," he whispered. "I've waited a long time to hear those words."

Uncle Leo looked at Gilbert with a knowing smile. "Hi, Gilbert. Still the same old petty boy, huh? Did you tell her about this significant world of yours?"

Gilbert avoided Uncle Leo's gaze, a flicker of discomfort crossing his face. When he finally spoke, he directed his words to Artemis. "I didn't know Lord Leo was your uncle!"

Uncle Leo chuckled, shaking his head. "That wasn't my question," he said lightly before turning his attention back to Artemis.

"Dear Artemis," Leo began, his tone gentle but serious, "This world appears beautiful when you first step into it, but after a while, things begin to feel monotonous. The days and nights here stretch out much longer than on Earth, with the planet's rotation being slower and, in many ways, peculiar. As a result, the aging process here is significantly slower, making time seem to drag on endlessly. For instance, I should be seven years older than my dear sister Tara, whom I miss dearly, but while she is now a grandmother, I still appear as a young man. This also explains your ability to fly—something I know you've pondered a lot."

Artemis listened intently, her mind racing to keep up with everything Uncle Leo was revealing. She watched as he paced back and forth, processing his words. The reality of this world, with its slow passage of time and strange effects on the body, began to sink in.

Uncle Leo stopped pacing and looked directly at her. "Do you know why I got tired of holding you? It's because I'm not as powerful as I once was. This place slowly affects every inch of your body. Now you understand why we call this world the Flimsy World. If you stay here too long, it will affect you as well. Look at me. I'm not as solid as you are anymore. You're stronger than me, can't you see it?"

Artemis absorbed his words, the gravity of the situation pressing down on her. This world, so alluring and strange, was also dangerous—a place that could slowly erode her strength, just as it had done to Uncle Leo. But even as she tried to process this, one burning question refused to be silenced.

"Uncle Leo!" she called out, her voice loud and insistent, cutting through the weight of everything he had just said. "Is my father here with you, too? Is he alive? Is he here? Where is he now? Can I see him?"

Uncle Leo's expression turned somber as he gently held Artemis's hands. "Yes, he is in this world too, but no, he is not here with me now. I'm sorry, my dear Artemis. I didn't want to make you sad, but he is with them," he said, pointing toward the sky, then Gilbert.

Artemis's heart skipped a beat, and she tightened her grip on Uncle Leo's hands. "He is with whom? Can I see him?" she asked, her voice tinged with desperation.

Turning sharply to Gilbert, her eyes filled with anger and hurt, she demanded, "What does it mean when Uncle Leo says 'with you'? You bastard, you lied to me again! You knew where my father is, and you didn't tell me?"

Gilbert flinched at her words, his face pale as he tried to find the right response. "Artemis, it's not what you think—"

"Then tell me the truth and tell me what it is!" she cut him off, her voice trembling with a mixture of fury and desperation. "Where is he? What have you been hiding from me?"

Gilbert's eyes dropped, unable to meet her gaze. "I didn't lie to you, Artemis. I was trying to protect you. Your father... he was involved with the people who control everything in this world, the ones who oversee it all. That's why I didn't want you to come here—it's dangerous. They're dangerous. We had to help him escape from them, and now he's in a safe place. I had to ensure you stayed with us, not with them."

Artemis felt a cold shiver crawl down her spine as Gilbert's words sank in. The realization that her father was entangled with powerful, possibly malevolent forces sent a surge of fear and anger crashing through her. But beneath the turmoil, a fierce determination blazed—she would find him, no matter the cost.

"Why didn't you tell me?" she whispered, tears streaming down her cheeks, her voice trembling with deep hurt. "You should have told me, Gilbert."

Gilbert finally looked up, his eyes heavy with regret. "I'm sorry, Artemis. I thought I could protect you by keeping you away from all of this. You deserve to know the truth, and I'll help you find him. We'll reunite you with your father. I promise."

She looked at him doubtfully, unsure of what to make of him. "So... why did you bring me here if you didn't want me to see this area?"

Leo looked at Gilbert and said, "You didn't explain to her, did you?"

Gilbert, desperate not to lose Artemis, felt a mix of anger and disappointment. "I didn't lie to you," he insisted, his voice tense. "Uncle Leo asked me to bring you here because he wanted to see you, and if he wasn't here, we were supposed to leave immediately for security purposes."

Artemis faced Uncle Leo and asked again, "Why do you want to see me now after these years? Now, you tell me, can I see my father?"

"No," Uncle Leo replied.

"Why can't I?" Artemis asked again.

"Because they took him months ago, and he's not on this planet anymore." Uncle Leo leaned back against the wall, his gaze steady as he looked at Artemis. Then, with a slow, deliberate gesture, he pointed to the moon, now a small black dot in the distant sky.

"He is there, and without the proper equipment, you cannot go. That moon has only a one-way trip; there is no coming back," Uncle Leo said, his face telling a sad story as Artemis studied his expression.

Artemis cried quietly, tears streaming down her cheeks like rain. Silence enveloped them, and no one dared to speak.

After half an hour, through her tears and hiccups, she asked, "Is he alive?"

"Yes, he is," Uncle Leo answered.

"How do you know?" she asked.

Uncle Leo looked at Artemis, then pointed at Gilbert. "Because Gilbert is our undercover spy and he has friends there, and your father is there with them. I can't explain more here—I don't know if there are spies among my soldiers. I'll tell you when we're in a secure area."

Another fifteen minutes passed, and Artemis remained in her grief, crying hopelessly. Eventually, she stopped, refusing to feel sorry for herself. She stood up, brushed off her clothes, and felt more determined than ever.

"I've never had a father in my life, and I'm not going to give up on him," she said to Uncle Leo.

Uncle Leo hugged her and said, "My dear Artemis, there's nothing we can do. It's impossible to save him. You have no idea what you're getting involved in. Just save yourself and find a way to go back home."

Artemis pulled herself away from Uncle Leo angrily and said, "I've made up my mind. We are not on Earth, and I'm not that hopeless little girl anymore. I'm on Zamin, and I am mighty Artemis. I'll do whatever is necessary to save my father, and I'm not leaving this place without him. Do you understand?"

Uncle Leo looked at Artemis, gently reached for her hand, and said, "Let's not be rational right now. Let's go and have something to eat. Maybe I'll change your mind, or perhaps you'll change mine. Who knows?"

They both flew swiftly toward Gilan, with the rest following on foot. The city was even more breathtaking from the ground than it had been from above. Everything looked brand new, impeccably clean, and gleaming. The walls and ground were crafted from the same seamless paving material, blending together so perfectly that it was impossible to distinguish from above. The roofs of the houses were lush and green, adorned with branches and trees that seemed to grow naturally from them. The streets were open, free from visible traffic, but shaded by a canopy of branches and leaves. Cars moved silently beneath this cover, hidden from view from above. The level of organization and harmony in the city was astonishing.

The structure of the houses was unique as well. Each had multiple entrances on the sides and on the roof, along with one hidden door. Amazingly, all the hidden doors were connected to each other, allowing residents to move unseen throughout the city in case of any danger.

By this time, they had reached Uncle Leo's home. They entered the house, and when he closed the door, he opened it again from a different direction, revealing a hidden passage. Uncle Leo and Artemis stepped inside, and he closed the door behind them. It was pitch black, making it difficult to see anything. Uncle Leo then opened another door, revealing a brightly lit city unlike anything Artemis had ever seen.

The city was incredibly clean and green, with lights that made the area appear as if it were daytime. They walked for a long time, and Uncle Leo waved to almost everyone they passed. They eventually reached a place known as the secure area and entered. It was a long hallway with numerous doors on both sides. Artemis was speechless, admiring the beauty and intricacy of the place.

She turned to Uncle Leo and asked, "Why do you call it a secure area?"

Uncle Leo smiled at Artemis and said, "That's a good question. It's because here, they can't keep track of our conversations. It is secure."

Artemis looked at him in surprise and asked, "Who keeps track of your conversations, and why and how?"

"That's an even better question. I'm glad you're asking because I was going to explain it to you anyway. Wherever you are on this planet, they can track your movements and conversations and especially you are under their surveillance 24/7 because they are afraid of you. You are never truly safe. How do they keep track of everyone? Did you see the moons?"

Artemis, focused on him, said, "Yes, I saw them, and they're beautiful."

Uncle Leo laughed and said, "Of course they are beautiful, and that's how they keep track of us. They need more people like us, I mean humans on those moons, Artemis... so you must be very careful."

Meanwhile, he opened one of the doors. As soon as they stepped inside, Artemis spotted Gilbert. Surprised, she blurted out, "What are you doing here? Uncle Leo! I thought the way we came was the only way in—and that's how this place stays protected."

Uncle Leo put his hand on Gilbert's shoulder and said, "My dear Artemis, he is the one helping us save your father. He is one of the few people I can trust. When someone comes through the gate, all the humans living here can feel it, and your father senses your arrival. For your protection, we chose the most trusted person on Zamin. Gilbert was waiting for you there, though he had no idea he was waiting for a girl. In fact, no one knew a girl was coming."

"You mean... up there was nothing but play? When they tried to bully me, you could do something, but instead, you preferred to watch me and my reaction to them...? Were they part of this game, too?" Artemis asked.

"Yes and no," Uncle Leo replied, his tone measured. "They were truly dangerous people, but Gilbert was keeping an eye on you. If you were ever in real trouble, he would've stepped in," Uncle Leo confirmed.

Artemis felt a wave of emptiness and asked, "But why did you do that?"

Uncle Leo smiled and replied, "Because we needed to know if you would stand up for your friends or save yourself. We needed to know if you care enough for them." Uncle Leo continued, "You passed the test. But we all knew they were watching you the entire time. Every move you made, every conversation you had—it was all under their surveillance."

Artemis froze, stunned by Uncle Leo's words. But she mustered all her strength to ask, "Why didn't you show up earlier?"

Uncle Leo's gaze remained fixed on her as he replied, "Because we received a message through our contacts within their organization. They warned us that if we made any contact with you, they would use the gun they managed to smuggle from Earth to take you out." His voice was steady, but the weight of his words hung heavily in the air.

"But it's time for you to escape from here tonight and find your father," Uncle Leo said, his eyes shifting to Gilbert as he finished speaking.

"What do you mean by that?" Artemis asked, her confusion growing as she tried to piece together these political maneuvers.

"I mean, we have to put our plan into action to help your dad, and you two must escape to follow through with it," Uncle Leo said, noticing the sparks of determination in Artemis's eyes.

"So, what about the things you said about not being able to save my father? About not being able to go to the moon, that it's a one-way trip and all those other things? Were they just lies?" Artemis asked, struggling to know what to believe.

Uncle Leo sighed, "Those weren't lies, Artemis. The moon is indeed dangerous, and it is a one-way trip for most. But with the right plan and the right people, we can defy the odds. We needed to test your resolve and loyalty first." Confidently, he continued, "Yes, my dear Artemis. I had to make sure you had the courage and determination to save your father. Otherwise, I couldn't involve you in something so serious because they force all human work for them and I don't want this to happen to you," Uncle Leo explained. He looked at Artemis, then at Gilbert, and shrugged his eyebrows.

Artemis felt guilty for the way she had treated Gilbert despite his generous support. Her attempts at compensation had been inadequate. She was ashamed to look at him. She didn't know how to restart the conversation, but Gilbert stood up and walked over to her. "Artemis, I know you feel bad and think you mistrusted me. If I were you, I would have done the same thing. You did well, and I'm happy you're doing the right thing. But right now, we have a bigger problem to tackle. Let's put that behind us and focus on our plan. We don't have much time left—it's almost morning."

"Uncle Leo, I have one more question for you. Why didn't you go to save him? To that moon, I mean?" Artemis asked, her curiosity piqued.

"Because if I go, everything we've built here will collapse, and there would be no one to protect it," Uncle Leo replied. "If I leave, they gain everything, and no one can stand in their way—they could win. When you go, I'll be here to support and help you because I was the only one who could escape from the moon."

"Okay! I'm ready for another adventure, Uncle Leo. I'm all yours," Artemis said proudly.

Uncle Leo turned to Gilbert, pointing at an envelope he held in his hand. "Is this the envelope you were talking about? Let's see what's inside. Open it up."

Gilbert turned to Artemis and said, "This is for you, and they asked me to give it to you. That's why we're here, to open it in front of Lord Leo. May I?"

Artemis nodded. Just as Gilbert was about to open it, Uncle Leo held his hand. He took the envelope and looked through it, then called Artemis over.

"Artemis! Look through and tell me what you see," Uncle Leo asked.

Artemis took the envelope, held it up to the light, and focused on it. As she concentrated, she could see more clearly. She could even read the contents without opening it. Additionally, she noticed a pin or something similar inside. She turned to Uncle Leo and explained everything she saw in the envelope.

"Uncle Leo, I can read the letter without opening it, and there's also a pin or something inside," she said.

Uncle Leo nodded at Artemis, signaling for her to read it out loud, "Dear Artemis, I know you well, and I know that you're searching for your father. He's with me, and he wants you to join him here. I've included a little gift to make your transportation easier. So long, and I'll see you then. Lord Kaila," she read aloud, her voice tinged with both curiosity and apprehension as she absorbed the message.

After finishing, Artemis asked Uncle Leo, "Why don't we open it?"

"That is the whole point," Uncle Leo replied. "I worked with them, and I know If you open it here, you'll activate the pin, and they'll know you opened it here. They won't trust you anymore. You need to open it in Moallem City, the place where you and Gilbert are living now."

"Uncle Leo, what is going to happen when I open it? It'll be activated, then what?" Artemis asked.

"Look into the pin again and tell me what you see," Uncle Leo instructed. "Make sure you're not burning it out."

Artemis looked inside the envelope again and found the pin. She focused on it but didn't understand anything. "Uncle Leo, I don't understand anything. What should I be looking for?" she whined.

Uncle Leo was very patient with her. He stopped her and said, "Artemis, when you open it, the pin will be activated automatically. But focus on the pin before and after activation, and you'll see. You can deactivate it again. I mean, when it is activated, you will be able to go to the mother ship, and as soon as you're there, it will deactivate. For the return, you need it again to return on the Zamin, and you have to re-activate it again. That's why it's a one-way trip and that is why they control everything and as soon as you're back on the ground, you must deactivate it yourself, or they can pull you up there again. "Nobody can do that except us. Of course, if I hadn't told you, you wouldn't have known.

He paused for a moment, then placed a firm hand on Artemis's shoulder and said, "Remember, once you activate it, a glossy shield will envelop your body within seconds. Make sure Gilbert is close to you—otherwise, you'll end up going there alone."

"What happens when I'm up there? Am I the only human there?" Artemis asked.

"No, there are many humans there, and all of them are men," Uncle Leo replied, his voice somber. "But remember, you are the strongest of them all. You're new, still brimming with power, while the others have been here for ages and have grown weak. They're all trapped, unable to escape. You're the only one who can reopen the portal."

"They're trapped and have no way back. They might think you don't realize that, and they'll try to scare you into submission. But one thing is certain—they can't touch you or force you to do anything." Leo took a deep breath and added, "Remember, in this world, you are like a god. If you see muscles or big guys, don't be intimidated—they're weak. No matter how small or slim you are, you're the most powerful human on this planet, and their muscles are jelly."

He waited for the information to sink in, then continued, "I want them to see you and realize they can't control you. Let them feel the fear."

"But how can I recognize them, especially Kaila? I don't know what he looks like, and he's not the only human there," Artemis said, looking irritated.

"Artemis, Gilbert will be with you and keep him by your side and don't let them separate you. You'll recognize Kaila no matter how he looks. Trust your instincts—he'll recognize you too. I'm watching over you and will guide you there," Uncle Leo reassured her.

Uncle Leo handed Artemis a pair of earrings and said, "Wear these so we can stay in touch. But be careful—don't let anyone touch you or the earrings. It's a one-way connection, and I'll know where you are at all times. I can also hear your conversations."

Artemis took the earrings, admiring their beauty. They were a pair of diamond earrings, very cute. She put them on and liked them a lot. Uncle Leo looked at her, held her head in his hands, kissed her forehead, and said, "You have to be very careful. Don't trust anyone. I'll be in touch with you at all times. Don't be hard on Gilbert because he's your only friend up there and keep him on your side at all times. I just want them to see that you're not afraid of them, that you walk in with confidence."

"What about my dad?" Artemis asked, concerned.

"According to our latest report, your dad is up there, but he's not one of them or one of us. "I'm hoping that seeing you will help him make the right choice. Otherwise, if I hear any news about him, I'll inform Gilbert, and he'll notify you," Uncle Leo replied.

"We don't have much time left, so you have to hurry. Good luck," Uncle Leo said before leaving the room, closing the door behind him. As soon as the door clicked shut, the room began to shift. The floor beneath them started to rise, the ceiling sliding aside, transforming the floor they stood on into the ceiling. Without a moment to lose, Gilbert sprinted toward the woods with Artemis close on his heels. They were almost there, the urgency of the situation driving them forward.

Artemis faced Gilbert and asked, "What does it mean we don't have much time left?"

"It means that at a specific time, there is a chance that the gate will be open again. That time is coming soon, and you must be there to ensure it happens. Without you, it won't," answered Gilbert.

"What gate?" asked Artemis.

"The gate you came through to get here! It only opens every two years or so, and if you're not there in time, you'll be stuck here for the next couple of years," Gilbert explained briefly.

Artemis looked shocked and exclaimed, "There was a gate? I didn't see a gate. Are you sure there was a gate?"

Gilbert ignored her and continued, "The gate only opens on leap years. The time moves slower here for humans, so it's already been four years in your world. That means there's a chance you can go back."

That's great! I can't believe it—I'm so happy," she exclaimed, turning to Gilbert to share her excitement.

Gilbert watched her without any emotion on his face, sitting quietly and looking at her. Artemis wasn't sure how to start the conversation but knew she needed to say something to lift his spirits.

"Hey, look! Why don't you come with me when the gate opens?" she suggested.

Gilbert looked at her in disbelief and smiled. He said, "Don't you know I can't live in your world because of the heavy gravity? I'm too weak to survive there, and I'll die. But you can live here and always be the superhero in my world."

Artemis smiled and said nothing. She missed her family, friends, food, and Toronto, and Earth—everything. But she also didn't want to hurt his feelings. They finally reached their location. She took out the envelope, took a deep breath, and looked at Gilbert. "Well, this is it. I'm going to open it. I don't know what's going to happen after, but I know I want to do whatever it takes to see my father and bring him back to my mother so we can be together again."

Gilbert had a faint smile on his lips and nodded. She opened the envelope, pulled out the letter, and tucked it into her pocket. She then grabbed the pin with her two fingers, holding it up to see it clearly. She could see clearly inside of the pin, and as uncle Leo said, she knew how to activate or deactivate the pin, then she turned to Gilbert she said, "This is it, Gilbert. I thank you for everything in advance just in case anything happened to me. I want you to know how I am honored to have you on my side."

Unsure how to attach it to her shirt, she hesitated, thinking it might simply stick. Holding it against her collar, she tried to keep it steady. Then, as she inspected the pin again, three needle-like prongs suddenly emerged from its base. Startled, she glanced at Gilbert before pressing the pin onto her shirt. The prongs pierced through the fabric and tightened, locking the pin securely in place.

Suddenly, a glassy shield began extending from the pin like the way uncle Leo explained, wrapping itself around her body. She watched in astonishment as the transparent barrier formed, slowly encapsulating her entirely, leaving her both awestruck and uncertain of what was happening. She looked at Gilbert, who still had no emotion on his face, and said, "Look, Gilbert! It went through my shirt, which means it's from my world, right?"

Before she could finish her sentence, everything around her started spinning and became blurry. "I feel dizzy. I don't feel good, Gilbert. Help me!" she cried, and then everything went black. She felt nothing more. Gilbert's first impression was how Artemis started floating and being lifted from the ground. She was unconscious, her eyes wide open in shock. Not wanting to leave her like that, He rushed through the narrowing gap of the shield and embraced her as tightly as possible, holding on as if he could protect her from everything. Slowly, they both were lifted and pulled up to an unknown destination. More than fifteen minutes passed, and they were still ascending. Gilbert tried to look down to see how far they had gone, but the distance was too great. Fear gripped him, but there was nothing he could do. Looking up, the only thing he could see was a small black dot. He held Artemis close like she was a sacred being. He felt like she could hear him but couldn't respond, so he thought he might comfort her while they were ascending.

He whispered in her ear, "Artemis, I won't let you go, and in fact, I'm stuck with you forever. I promise I'll never let anything happen to you. You can count on me. Maybe I'm not as strong as other men on your planet, or even here... but that doesn't matter. I'm a thousand times more man than anybody else. When I look into your eyes, I get tongue-tied and can't express my feelings, but I love you!"

He was so engrossed in talking to Artemis and looking into her eyes that he didn't realize how close they were to the black moon. Now, he understood why it was called the black moon because it was simply black, or was it? It looked like a flat-flying saucer. From underneath, they were slowly entering the black moon. Gilbert was very scared; it was his first time seeing the black moon up close, and he didn't know what kind of reaction he might face for being there.

THE GATEWAY TO THE UNKNOWN

As they entered the ship—what they called the black moon—they were safely inside, but uncertainty loomed.

It didn't make sense to Gilbert why they called it the Black Moon. As they approached, its color shifted, revealing a clear, almost transparent surface. The other side was visible through it, with a glass-like ring encircling the moon, resembling a giant window. Perhaps the name was meant to deceive, creating an illusion that changed once inside, transforming into something entirely different. All the technology was inside. To Gilbert, it wasn't a moon at all. It was a ship. They both stood up, and Artemis seemed to still be half asleep. Gilbert couldn't hold on to her because he didn't want to be stuck underneath her, and it didn't look good.

There was a person standing nearby, waiting for her. He looked at Gilbert with anger and surprise, then helped her lie down on the stretcher that was prepared for her. Gilbert thought it was the pin that made her unconscious. One of the staff brought them a pinkish drink. When the second staff member took Artemis's drink and tried to give it to her, Gilbert quickly grabbed the glass from the tray and went to her himself. Calling her name a few times, he asked her to relax and try to sit up. Slowly, Artemis regained consciousness, and after a few minutes, she was able to sit down. To ensure it was safe, Gilbert took a cautious sip from Artemis's drink. Once satisfied, he handed it back to her, his expression calm and reassuring.

"Artemis, drink it; it will help you regain your energy," Gilbert said.

Artemis drank it quickly, like an addict needing a fix. The drink was remarkable, and Gilbert could feel its effects after taking a sip. Artemis squinted at Gilbert in surprise before looking around, trying to take in her surroundings. Everything looked different, and she had no clue where she was.

"Where are we, Gilbert?" Artemis asked.

"We are in the black moon," replied Gilbert.

"How did we get here? Why are you here? You're not supposed to be here. What happened?" Artemis asked, surprised.

Gilbert listened to her, fear creeping in. What if she had forgotten their plan? What if she unintentionally exposed everything? She didn't seem to remember anything, and Gilbert was scared, unsure of how to remind her without raising suspicion.

He leaned closer to her, hugged her head and whispered in her ears, "Artemis, remember our mission. We're here to find your father. Stay calm and follow my lead. Trust me. If you remember, we were on the ground, and after you opened the envelope, you used the pin and put it on your shirt. You felt dizzy and were about to fall when I caught you. After that, you started to lift off the ground and I held you in my arms, and we both flew up here together. I think your absent-mindedness is because of that little pin. That's where the problem lies," said Gilbert.

Artemis tried to process what Gilbert was saying. She touched the pin on her shirt, removed it and placed it in her pocket while the memory started to come back to her. "Okay, I think I understand now," she said, regaining her composure. "We need to stay focused and find my father."

Slowly, Artemis regained her full memory and immediately set to investigate. A guide opened the doors, allowing her to step into a hallway alive with activity. She quickly observed the differences— most of the people appeared human, solid and tangible, unlike the transparent Flimsies she had encountered before. She tried to peer through them again but found it impossible.

Turning to Gilbert, she shrugged, catching a flicker of unease in his eyes. Surrounded by so many men, she felt a wave of vulnerability wash over her, a stark contrast to her usual strength.

"What do you think we're doing here? Why did they bring us here?" Artemis asked Gilbert, her voice tinged with uncertainty.

"I don't have a definite answer," Gilbert replied, "but I think they need you for something, or maybe they just want to see you up close. Or for their request, you're the only one who can accomplish it—no one else has your abilities."

The guide continued opening doors for them, but after they entered the last door, he closed it and left. Artemis tried to open the door, but it no longer functioned. As she stood there, she stared out the window, captivated by the mesmerizing and breathtaking view of the planet, marveling at its beauty from afar.

"What kind of thing?" Artemis asked.

Before Gilbert could respond, the door swung open, revealing a short, heavyset man in his late thirties. The sight of him immediately set Artemis on edge; his demeanor and appearance radiated an unsettling air of mistrust. He looked like someone who belonged on a wanted poster.

But what truly caught Artemis's attention was the door itself. Earlier, it had led to a long hallway, but now it opened into a room brimming with computers and blinking monitors, resembling a high-tech control center. The abrupt and inexplicable shift sent a fresh wave of unease coursing through her, heightening the sense that something wasn't right. Artemis glanced at Gilbert in surprise, only to find him seated on the floor, his posture almost reverent, as though he were praying. He faced the man in the doorway with an intensity that unsettled her, amplifying the already surreal atmosphere of the moment.

He stepped into the room, his gaze briefly sweeping over both of them before settling on Gilbert. "You can go; we don't need you here," he said curtly.

Artemis and Gilbert exchanged a quick glance. Then, with resolute defiance, Artemis stepped forward, positioning herself between the man and Gilbert. "I'm sorry, but he's with me," she said firmly. "If he goes, I go."

The short, chubby man gave Artemis a scrutinizing look before breaking the silence. "I apologize for not introducing myself," he said with an air of practiced politeness. "I am Lord Kaila. You have my assurance that you will be safe while you are here."

Artemis was about to laugh when Gilbert quickly stood in front of her to shield her reaction. He looked directly at her and said, "My Lord lady Artemis, if you no longer need my services, you can dismiss me."

There was a tone of fear in Gilbert's voice, and the look in his eyes unsettled her. Taking a step closer to Kaila, Artemis said firmly, "I want him to stay with me, and that's not a request."

Kaila looked momentarily startled but quickly masked it with a smile. "That's fine," he said, his gaze flickering between Artemis and Gilbert. "He can stay."

After a brief pause, Kaila turned back to Artemis. "Now," he asked, "how about a tour of the Black Moon? What do you think? Would you like to see it?"

Artemis looked around the room they were in. It was quite large and impeccably white, with one side of the room featuring a curved wall made entirely of windows or dark glass, giving the room a fascinating ambiance. The entire universe stretched out before her, capturing her gaze and making her realize the grandeur of the galaxy ahead. It was the most beautiful view she had ever seen. It took her a moment to absorb how deeply this view was affecting her emotionally. She recognized the magic of this moment, something beyond her wildest dreams, a scene she never thought she'd witness in her lifetime.

She looked at Kaila, who was smiling at her. This was a moment she would count as one of the best opportunities she had ever had in her life. she couldn't have even dreamed of being in a spaceship, witnessing the vastness of space firsthand.

She stepped toward the window and softly whispered, "This is my thrilling chance from this world."

She glanced toward the opposite side of the room and noticed a curved, double-sided door resembling an elevator. Turning to Kaila, she said, "I'm ready to explore, but first, I have a question. I opened this door before you came in, and it led to a hallway. But when you opened it, it became a control room. How is that possible?"

Kaila smiled and opened the door again, revealing a different room. He looked at Artemis and said, "On the black moon, every room is an elevator, and it works like a puzzle cube. Only the control center sees everything," Kaila said, his eyes narrowing as the realization dawned. You will never open a door twice to the same room, but this is our way of optimizing space. Now, shall we begin the tour?"

Kaila stepped aside for Artemis to walk toward the elevator, and As soon as they approached, the doors opened automatically, though she had tried earlier before Kaila entered the room, and it hadn't worked. It was as if the doors recognized people. There were no visible buttons or sensors, adding to the mystery of the place.

Artemis looked at Kaila, curiosity piqued. "How does it work?"

With a sly smile, Kaila replied, "It's part of our advanced security system. We have personnel monitoring and controlling these doors to ensure everything runs smoothly and securely."

Artemis nodded and suggested, "Why don't you use automatic doors or sensors for all the doors and elevators? Wouldn't that be easier?"

Kaila replied, "It would be easier, but it's not secure, and it's not our way. This system is for our protection."

Artemis looked puzzled, staring at him as if he were foolish, and asked, "Protection from whom? The innocent Flimsies? Or the other humans you've enslaved under your system? Who could even come this far to enter your command center?"

Kaila gave a faint smile and gestured toward the elevator, signaling Artemis to step inside.

Artemis shrugged her shoulders, her curiosity piqued. Suddenly, the elevator made a soft clicking sound, and the doors slid open effortlessly. She couldn't help but grin at the door, trying to conceal her awe at this magnificent place—or better yet, spaceship. The sophistication of the technology around her was both thrilling and humbling. She felt like she was stepping into a world of endless possibilities, and her heart raced with excitement.

Kaila was walking behind Artemis, while Gilbert followed closely behind him, keeping a watchful eye to ensure Kaila didn't try anything against her. They entered a long, white hallway that curved at the end. The entire left side of the hallway was a dark glass wall, offering a clear view of the space. It was both beautiful and intimidating. From there, the Zamin planet was clearly visible, looking stunningly pretty. Artemis was captivated by the view. She tried to focus on a specific part of the planet. She stopped, chose a focal point, and squinted at her target. As she concentrated, the area of the glass she was looking through began to wobble slightly. Gilbert continued walking, unaware of her actions.

Kaila didn't realize what she was doing at first, but when he saw her, he ran towards her and screamed loudly, "NO! ARTEMIS, STOP!"

He reached Artemis, waving a hand in front of her eyes, obstructing her view. She stepped back, startled, yet remained rooted to the spot. "Why?" she asked, looking at Kaila in surprise.

Kaila straightened up and adjusted his clothes before explaining, "Artemis, you must never do that again. These materials are from the Flimsy world, and your actions could have compromised the integrity of the glass, potentially leading to a catastrophic breach. While the damage appears to be minor at the moment, we need to ensure everything remains secure."

Artemis looked at the glass, now bent and dented, and turned to Kaila. "Why don't you use a better material with higher quality?" she asked.

Kaila laughed and replied, "These are the best materials on this planet. Nothing can penetrate them."

Gilbert giggled and whispered, "Nothing?"

Artemis glanced at Gilbert for confirmation and said, "It doesn't seem like the best option so far."

Kaila walked alongside Artemis, with Gilbert trailing behind until they reached the end of the hallway, which led to another door resembling an elevator. As soon as they approached, the doors opened, and they all entered.

Inside was a magnificent room beyond description. Once the doors shut behind them, the walls, made of clear glass, revealed the other side. It looked like a control center, a programming room, or perhaps something else entirely.

Each side of the room was different, and Artemis looked at Kaila and asked, "What are these rooms? Why can you see them so clearly? Isn't it unwise to let anyone have access to these areas?"

Kaila responded, "I admire the way you think, but no one has ever had the chance to get near the black moon, let alone inside it. Plus, it allows me to monitor everything, even when I'm in the elevator. Besides that, those inside these rooms can't see me or beyond the room itself for security reasons."

She grinned slightly and said, "Then again, why do you need a security system if, as you just said, nobody has ever had the chance to get close to the Black Moon?" Kaila felt uneasy but kept walking in silence. Then, turning to Artemis, he said, "Danger doesn't always come from the outside."

As they ascended, Artemis eagerly took in the view of the surrounding rooms. Her eyes briefly met Gilbert's, who regarded her with a detached expression.

Standing beside Kaila, she asked without turning her head, "So...what is your primary task here? What is the purpose of this black moon?"

Kaila glanced at her, acknowledging her question but choosing not to respond immediately. As the elevator doors slid open, he stepped out. Artemis followed, peeking through the door before stepping into what appeared to be an office. The sight took her breath away—the entire planet was visible through a massive window.

Gilbert, equally mesmerized, quietly moved to a chair in the corner of the office and sat down as if he were familiar with the procedure. He remained silent, observing everything intently.

Artemis gazed at the planet for a moment, lost in its beauty, before turning back to Kaila. "You still haven't answered my question," she said, her tone insistent yet curious.

Kaila settled into his chair and began checking his computer. He didn't seem uncomfortable or upset by her question; rather, he appeared somewhat fatigued by the necessity of answering such inquiries. It was clear this was part of his routine—a requisite part of his role to manage supers and maintain order on the planet.

Finally, he spoke, "You got straight to the point, didn't you? I understood you the first time, Artemis. The black moon is primarily a research facility."

"What kind of research?" asked Artemis.

"We are researching people's behavior," Kaila replied.

"The kind of research you're doing right now?" Artemis asked, her voice carrying a note of confidence. However, Kaila remained remarkably calm, his gaze fixed steadily on her. His intense scrutiny made Artemis a bit uncomfortable, realizing he was studying her behavior. This only served to heighten her irritation.

"Yes, and this is a form of study as well. Am I right?" asked Kaila.

Artemis faced him directly and demanded, "Let's get straight to the point. Why am I here? What do you want from me?"

"This is the Flimsy world, and we are studying it. We have brought balance to their society and their world. Our responsibility is to ensure they adhere to the laws; otherwise, they must face consequences," Kaila explained. He paused for a few seconds to gauge Artemis's reaction, then continued, "You are not the only human here. There are over a hundred of us, and we must support each other to make this world better for everyone."

Artemis felt a strong urge to laugh, especially at the absurd notion of the "balance" they had supposedly brought to these people. She restrained herself, but her quiet anger seeped through as she spoke, "You mean taking away their freedom? Or lowering the dignity of women? Or stripping them of their beliefs and replacing them with your own, putting yourself in the place of their god? Or maybe it's that you're happy, and that's all that matters to you?"

She stood still, her expression hardening as she continued, "You've brought them nothing but ignorance and darkness. I've heard from many of them how happy they were before humans arrived." Her voice trembled with emotion, the weight of her anger and pain palpable.

Kaila turned to Gilbert and asked, "Do you think your world was better before we came here?"

Artemis, glaring at Kaila in anger, snapped, "Don't drag him into our conversation to hide your darkness."

Then she continued, "Do you think I will work with you? If you think that's going to happen, think again. How did you manage to make my father follow your lies?" she suddenly blurted out.

"What do you mean by your father?" Kaila asked, his calm demeanor faltering slightly.

"I mean simply my father, whose name is Arsham Vedetta!" she replied.

Kaila looked genuinely surprised. "He's not working with us; he's with Leo!" he said.

For a moment, Artemis glanced at Gilbert, who was listening quietly. She turned back to Kaila and explained, "My father was with Leo before you captured him, and you know it very well. Where is he? What have you done to him?"

Kaila sighed and replied, "I haven't done anything to him. As a matter of fact, he came to us and offered his help. The black moon is one of his creations. He is one of the most renowned scientists here. Actually, it was he who sent you that letter because he wants to see you. Initially, he wasn't sure if he wanted to, but after observing your time here and watching every move you made, he decided to send you an invitation."

Artemis stared at Kaila, processing the information. "So, my father is here, working with you?"

"Yes," Kaila confirmed. "He has been instrumental in many of our advancements. He truly wants to see you, Artemis. This is his way of reconnecting."

He had an expressionless demeanor, making it impossible to tell if he was happy or angry. Artemis found it difficult to discern whether he was lying or telling the truth. She glanced at Gilbert again, hoping to gauge his reaction, but he remained as still as a statue. Turning to the glass window, she hoped to catch Kaila's reflection, but the glass was non-reflective. With a sigh, she gave up and looked directly at Kaila.

"Why should I believe you?" she asked, her voice steady but filled with skepticism. "How do I know you're not manipulating me the same way you've manipulated others?"

"A minute ago, you said my father is with Leo, and now you say the black moon is my father's creation, and he's one of the most famous scientists here? How many lies have I heard from you in just one minute?" she demanded, trying to calm herself. Taking a deep breath, she continued, "Well! I'm here and tell him that I'm ready to see him."

Kaila continued to look at Artemis as he said, "Well, when it's time, he will see you, but first, I must give you a tour of the black moon. It's my duty."

"Duty? Are you a god here, or do you have to follow orders? Duty to whom?" she asked, her discomfort growing as she tried to make sense of the situation.

He stepped aside, indicating the way forward. Her eyes glanced at Gilbert, who was quietly listening. Gilbert stood up and followed Artemis. They all entered the elevator, which began moving upward again. Silence filled the space; no one wanted to talk. The elevator stopped, and a few seconds later, the doors opened wide. Kaila walked out and stopped in front, waiting for Artemis to follow. Gilbert patiently waited for Artemis to go out first.

Artemis gazed outside in wonder, her eyes widening at the sight of a large room with an expansive glass window stretching from floor to ceiling. The view was breathtaking, and she couldn't tear her eyes away. Her attention shifted from the window to Kaila, who was welcoming her and introducing her to the people in the room. Each person was seated behind a computer, and they all stood up as Artemis arrived. Kaila introduced each person one by one, and they stepped forward to shake hands with Artemis, their excitement palpable. As they greeted her, their eyes eventually shifted to Gilbert, their expressions filled with surprise.

"This is Ratna, head of security. Hoog, the assistant security officer, and finally, Rakh Haluom, our security technician," Kaila introduced as he sat down in his chair.

Artemis shook hands with each of them before taking her seat as well. Gilbert quietly sat on a seat behind her. Hoog was the first to break the silence.

"You are amazing, Artemis. I've seen all of your actions. I particularly enjoyed when you got upset with someone and, instead of hurting him, you blew him away, and he ran off. That was impressive and, honestly, a bit amusing," said Hoog, staring at Artemis with a mix of admiration and curiosity.

Artemis suddenly felt confused, unsure of their behavior. Initially, she thought they were happy to see her, but now it seemed different. They didn't look very pleased. She glanced at Hoog, who was still staring at her, and suddenly stood up, causing her chair to topple sideways onto the floor.

At that moment, the door opened, and as soon as the new arrival entered, everyone stood up. Gilbert quickly righted her chair and stood up like everyone else. Kaila stepped forward and began introducing the newcomer to Artemis.

"Artemis, this is Lord Demah, the leader of all our operations. He is the god of this planet, holding everyone's life in his hands. We all bow to him as a token of our appreciation for the excellent job he has done here," Kaila announced, bowing deeply, followed by Ratna, Hoog, and Rakh.

One by one, they looked at Artemis, waiting for her to bow as well. Artemis glanced at Gilbert, who was bowing too.

Demah looked like an athlete, his muscular build and heartless demeanor giving him a menacing presence. Though not particularly tall, he exuded an air of intimidation. His nose resembled an eagle's beak, with a pronounced curve that only added to his severe appearance. However, to Artemis, he seemed more ugly than frightening. He was large and broad, with a thick beard, and he was surrounded by a group of foolishly loyal followers.

What caught Artemis's attention the most, though, was the nagging sense of familiarity. She was certain she had seen Demah before, though she couldn't quite place where or when.

Then it hit Artemis—she recognized Demah from the pictures on the walls of the streets in Zamin. But the man before her was starkly different from his depictions. In the images, he appeared handsome, with kind and trustworthy eyes, a figure that seemed almost heroic. In reality, however, he was nothing like those idealized illustrations. Perhaps the people had drawn him as they wished he was, a symbol of something greater. Yet, beyond this discrepancy, another memory nagged at her. She was certain she had seen him before, not just in Zamin but on Earth as well. The connection eluded her, leaving her with an unsettling sense of familiarity that she couldn't quite place.

Artemis stood tall, refusing to bow. She locked eyes with Demah and said, "Impressive. You must be very proud of yourself. You've almost got everything under control. But you're not a god, and you never will be. You can kill people for wanting their freedom, but their lives aren't yours to take. They're victims, murdered by you, just like any killer takes a life. What's the difference? At least a murderer admits what they've done. But you? You hide behind the idea of divine will, convincing yourself you're a god. You should be ashamed, but instead, you stand proud." She held his gaze and continued, "I will never bow to a criminal. I bow only to my God. I mean real God—only Jesus is my Lord."

Kaila said, "He has everything under control, Artemis. Don't forget that."

Artemis sneered, looking at him without fear. "I know him very well. His reputation is well-known on this planet, and you don't have to point it out. I judge people's reputations by their acts of war or forgiveness, hate or love, and so on. I've heard great things about you, Mr. Demah, but great things aren't always good. They can be devilish. You don't have everything under control. You are a dictator who has gathered a bunch of idiots around you and you call it control."

She refreshed her breath and looked at people around her, then continued, "I know you because I've lived among these people, and I've felt their pain—the pain that came from you. Yes, I know you very well. Everyone knows you're an opinionated, selfish, and inhuman person, and of course, you don't need to be human here. Well, there you go. You've got your wish because you're not a human. Maybe these people on this black moon bow to you because they think they're nothing without you, or maybe they gain something from being close to you, thinking only of themselves. But I won't. I am Artemis, daughter of Arsham and Dorsa. They taught me well, and they taught me to never, ever bow in front of another human because I believe in myself and in the good people I know. Good people respect each other."

The anger on her face was palpable. She shifted her fiery gaze from Kaila to Demah, her voice sharp and unwavering: "And I don't believe my father helped you at all. Maybe this black moon is his creation, but you stole it from him. He would never work for you because he believes in freedom and equality."

Artemis, tired of the political maneuvering, went straight to the point. "I will not adapt or juggle things to work through this, and I certainly will not help you in making these innocent people suffer. You and these idiots mean nothing to you, but people in this world mean everything to me. I am here for my father first, and I want answers now. I want to know where my father is, and then I will be on my way home."

Artemis's impassioned speech disrupted Demah's comfort. His good mood vanished. Kaila stepped closer to him and, with an even tone, said, "I told you, sir, she wouldn't listen. She's just like her father."

As soon as she heard her father's name, a confident smile spread across her face. She now had no doubt that her father was as stubborn as she was. Looking directly at Demah, she asked again, "Where is my father?" she demanded, her voice trembling with fury. She glanced between Kaila and Demah, her eyes blazing. "Of course, I am like my father. If he were here, I would bow to him—not to a bunch of brainless, selfish people."

Demah glanced at Artemis dismissively and ignored her as he made his way out. Just before leaving the room, he said, "Kaila, this is your responsibility. She's under your supervision and your problem to solve. Deal with it as soon as possible." With a sigh, he left the room.

Kaila's natural resting expression was one of confusion, and his movements were sullen and lumbering. He walked to the window, and Artemis couldn't see his reflection, leaving her uncertain about the extent of his anger.

He turned to Artemis and said, "You think we are harming these people? What do you think about our operations? I want to know. Who are your friends here? I want to know."

Artemis felt trapped. Desperately searching for a way out, she realized it was too late to escape. She needed to come up with something quickly. Standing up, she looked directly into Kaila's eyes and said, "I'm not here to talk about your operations or judge you now or even talk about my friends. I'm here to find my father, and until then, I don't have to answer any questions. I need to see him first."

With that, she sat back down and gazed out the window, determined to stay focused on her mission.

Kaila bit his lips and left the room. Artemis turned to Gilbert, who appeared frightened, yet his eyes shone with immense pride as he looked at her. She asked, "What's going on? Why are you upset? I won't let anything happen to you. I promise you that."

Gilbert looked dejected and wretched. His voice was filled with despair as he said, "Oh, Artemis... you can't fight them. They are like gods and can do anything. The lives of my people are at stake, and no one can help them now."

Gilbert subtly moved his eyes to the right, pointing to the corner of the wall. Artemis realized they were being monitored and that Gilbert was warning her.

"Hey! I'm one of your gods, too and strongest, remember? I'm not going to let this happen," she said, sighing. "Let's go and explore this place—or better yet, this spaceship."

She moved toward the door, the door opened smoothly and they both went through. She saw another door and stood in front of it, but it didn't open. Searching for a handle or doorknob yielded no results. Frustrated, she yelled loudly in the room, "OPEN THIS DOOR OR I'LL BRING IT DOWN!"

There was still no response to her request. Frustrated, Artemis kicked the door with a resounding boom, causing it to crack. Despite the damage, it was still difficult to open. She looked at the broken, dented part, placed her fingers there, and, with several strong pulls, managed to remove the door. She looked at Gilbert and smiled, but he still appeared scared.

"Let's go, Gilbert. We need to search the ship and find my father," Artemis exclaimed.

Artemis started toward the elevator, knowing it was the key to accessing every room. She made a turn but stopped when she heard Gilbert's voice coming from the opposite direction.

Artemis smiled and said, "What are you doing, Gilbert? We have to go this way to get to the elevator."

Gilbert looked at Artemis and pointed to the end of the hallway. "This way... do you remember? We came from this direction, and the elevator is at the end of this hallway."

Artemis immediately recognized the correct path and followed Gilbert. They reached the elevator and waited for the door to open, but it remained closed. Frustrated, Artemis screamed again, "Open the door, or I'll smash this one too! Remember, I used just a little punch on the other door. If I hit this one with full power, half your ship will break down. OPEN THE DAMN DOOR!"

The door swiftly opened, and they both stepped inside. Once inside, she confidently asked, "Command Room, please..."

The elevator started descending with clattering, whirling, and clanking noises. Artemis looked at Gilbert, who appeared worried. "Hold on to something," she said. "Something tells me this isn't going to be our ride." They both struggled to find something to grip, but the elevator's interior was lined with mirrors, offering no handholds. There were no keys or buttons either, leaving Artemis to think quickly.

Gilbert quickly pointed at her pocket and requested, "Active that devise, hurry?"

Suddenly, a voice came through the speakers. She couldn't tell if it was Kaila or Demah. "I'm sorry, Artemis, but if you're not with us, then you're against us. I can't allow you to change anything here in my world."

"IN YOUR WORLD?" she shouted, standing up with a groan.

The elevator filled with the sounds of clattering from above and below, followed by a distinct clink. Artemis heard murmuring and grumbling from Gilbert. She looked at him in anger and said, "What?"

He started nervously, stammering a bit, looking like he had been through this before. "It doesn't sound good. Hold on to something. I think this time I'm dead..."

Artemis let out a muffled laugh, her voice echoing in the elevator. "I am a mighty one, remember?" she said, trying to reassure him and herself.

There was a loud clink, and before Artemis could finish her sentence, the elevator floor began to open like a can of beans. They had no choice but to plummet down into the air. This time, Artemis felt genuinely scared and a bit dizzy. She suddenly remembered what uncle Leo said about the pin and fast, she grabbed the pin, focused, and reactivated it. The shield opened again, but there wasn't enough time to cover both of them. In an instant, they fell, watching as the ship—the Black Moon—grew smaller and smaller above them.

Looking around, she saw Gilbert unconscious, falling uncontrollably. She quickly flew toward him, grabbing him by his t-shirt. They were descending rapidly, but there was still no sign of the ground. As they got closer, Artemis managed to slow their fall, taking control and making their descent more gentle. Finally, they landed on the outskirts of the city. She landed and found a bench, gently laid Gilbert down on it, and sat beside him, catching her breath as time seemed to stretch endlessly, with hours slipping away like grains of sand falling to the ground.

Gilbert opened his eyes for a moment and asked, "What happened?"

"I think the pin only opened halfway," she replied, closing her eyes as the feeling slipped away, leaving her in numbness.

The sun's light woke her up, and she instantly sat up. Looking around to see if Gilbert was awake, she was surprised to find he wasn't there. Scanning the area, she saw him approaching from a distance. A smile spread across her face, and she leaned back comfortably.

Gilbert sat beside her, carrying several bags. He opened one, retrieved a small sandwich, and handed the remaining four bags to Artemis.

Artemis glanced at him, her brow furrowed in confusion. "What are these bags?" she asked.

Taking small bites from his sandwich, Gilbert replied, "These are your breakfast."

Artemis felt a rush of pleasant surprise and gratitude, her hunger so intense she could have eaten anything.

"When did you wake up?" she asked, taking a bite of the sandwich and watching him expectantly.

"I always wake up early," he replied with a warm smile before resuming his meal.

After finishing their breakfast, they set off walking. Gilbert, uncertain about what lay ahead, kept stealing glances at Artemis. Though her steps were steady, her gaze betrayed her wandering thoughts; her mind was clearly elsewhere.

Turning to her with a hint of hesitation, he asked, "Artemis, what's next? Should we go undercover?"

"Undercover...?" She burst into laughter, the sound catching him off guard. His discomfort was evident as he looked away, assuming she was mocking him. Noticing his reaction, Artemis quickly stifled her laughter and composed herself.

Clearing her throat, she said softly, "I'm not laughing at you; I'm laughing at the idea. Your innocent suggestion made me smile, but hiding isn't an option. We need to prepare for a fight. I will find my father, and we'll go back home together. I promise you that."

"What do you have in mind?" he asked, his voice laced with curiosity and concern.

"I know exactly what to do and where to go this time. We're heading to Gilan City—we need to see my Uncle Leo," she declared confidently.

As she turned toward Gilbert, he stood there holding two helmets with matching bike goggles, a playful smile lighting up his face. A wide grin spread across hers as she took one and slid it on. "This is perfect for flying," she said, glancing at him with a spark of excitement.

With a quick nod to signal she was ready, Artemis pressed her feet against the ground and began to ascend, her movements steady and deliberate. Gilbert clung tightly, his grip firm as they soared into the sky together.

THE DAWN OF COLLABORATION

The flight was smooth, as Artemis deliberately kept it steady to ensure Gilbert's comfort. With their new goggles and helmets, the journey was seamless, offering a perfect view of the world below. Artemis glanced at him occasionally, her heart swelling with joy at the sight of his calm, loyal presence beside her.

His peaceful expression, paired with the way he marveled at the scenery, showed he was enjoying the flight—especially now that the goggles allowed him to see everything more clearly. The moment filled her with pride and happiness, a quiet satisfaction in her ability to achieve such extraordinary feats. From saving lives to sharing these simple yet meaningful experiences with her friend, Artemis felt the weight of her purpose transform into something beautiful.

As they approached the gates of Gilan City, Artemis was pleasantly surprised to see Uncle Leo waiting for them. A wide smile spread across her face as she landed gracefully in front of him.

Gently lowering Gilbert to the ground, she wasted no time running to Uncle Leo, throwing her arms around him in a heartfelt embrace. Uncle Leo held her tightly, his strong arms offering comfort and reassurance, letting her linger as long as she needed.

She looked at him in surprise and asked, "How did you know we were coming?"

Uncle Leo smiled, gently touched her earring, and said, "I told you, I can hear everything." They both laughed, but the lighthearted moment was short-lived. Suddenly, Artemis's laughter dissolved into tears.

"Uncle Leo," she choked, her voice trembling, "they sent us back to the city again, and they wouldn't let me see him. Gilbert says he isn't on the black moon, and I don't know how to find him. I could go back to the black moon and smash it to pieces, but all I want is to find him and bring him home."

Uncle Leo held her tightly, his embrace steady and reassuring. "Artemis, I understand your frustration and pain," he said gently. "We will find your father, but we need a plan. Acting impulsively could put him—and us—in even greater danger."

He paused, his voice firm yet comforting, "We've learned that he escaped from the black moon, but we have no idea where he is now. Let's think this through together, step by step, and figure out the best way to find him and bring him home safely."

Uncle Leo stood patiently, offering silent comfort as he absorbed her words. His calm demeanor showed no sign of judgment, only understanding. He knew how deeply it hurt her to be separated from her family, especially when her father was her only beacon of hope in this unfamiliar world.

"My dear Artemis, please listen to me carefully," Uncle Leo said, his voice soft but resolute. "I promise you, I won't let you or your father down. That's my vow to you. I anticipated their attempts to deceive you, and I understand what you've been through."

Artemis met his gaze, her eyes a blend of hope and determination. Sensing her readiness to act, Uncle Leo continued, "We need to be strategic. They're counting on rash decisions, but we will outsmart them. I've devised a plan that could help us locate your father without exposing you to unnecessary danger. Trust me, Artemis. Together, we will find him and bring him home."

"If you knew, then why didn't you tell me? You could've been more honest with me," Artemis asked, wiping away her tears.

Uncle Leo sighed, his expression soft but firm. "I didn't tell you because you had already made up your mind. I didn't want to stand in your way or stop you. I knew you'd be safe, but I also knew you needed to have your own experience. Besides," he added with a faint smile, "I wanted them to see you—to realize they can't compete with you. To scare them a little."

He paused briefly, letting his words settle before continuing. "And look at what you've done. You faced them, and you're not afraid of them anymore. You did exactly what you were meant to do, and it was incredible. It made me so proud. But if I'd told you that I wanted them to see you and be intimidated, you wouldn't have approached the situation in the same way. Am I right?"

He looked deeply into her eyes, ensuring she understood the weight of his words before continuing. "Artemis, sometimes the only way to truly learn and grow is through experience. I didn't want to undermine your determination. Now that you've faced them, you're not afraid of them anymore, are you?"

He gave her a reassuring nod, his tone shifting to one of quiet confidence. "Now we can move forward together. We need to be smart about what comes next. I have a plan, but I need you to trust me on this."

Leo leaned forward slightly, his gaze steady as he emphasized his point. "We can make our plan now. You've seen them, you've had contact with them, and you understand them. You're not afraid of them anymore, are you?"

Artemis met his eyes with unwavering resolve. "Yes. I'm ready, and I'm listening," she replied firmly.

"Our contact told me that your father is on Mahtob, the second moon," Leo explained calmly.

Before he could continue, Artemis cut him off, her voice rising with anger. "Uncle Leo! Why didn't you tell me this before? You knew where he is?" she demanded, her frustration evident.

Uncle Leo sighed deeply, his expression a mix of understanding and patience. "I understand your frustration, Artemis," he began. "I didn't tell you earlier because the situation was too volatile, and I wasn't certain of his exact location. I needed to confirm where he was and figure out the safest way to reach him without putting either of you in danger."

He paused briefly, his gaze steady. "We have people on the moons, and I only received confirmation a short while ago—while you were on the Black Moon. He contacted me as soon as he reached Mahtob." Leo's eyes held hers firmly. "Can I continue without interruption?" he asked pointedly, waiting until she gave a reluctant nod before proceeding.

Now that we have more information and you've had your experiences, we can form a plan to get him back safely."

"Your father opposes them, as far as I know," Uncle Leo began, his voice tinged with both confusion and concern, "but I can't understand why he started working for them. We used to work together, both of us despising their policies and rules—especially the plans they had for this planet."

He gestured around him, his frustration evident. "These people were once peaceful. Of course, they had their own struggles, but nothing compared to what they endure now. Look at what's happened to the women here, how everyone has been turned into slaves. And the Flimsies—they revere them as if they're a religion. The worst part? The Flimsies willingly offer themselves as slaves, seeing it as an honor."

Uncle Leo shook his head, his expression dark. "How can you help people free themselves when they reject the very concept of freedom?"

Uncle Leo paused, his eyes locking onto Artemis's, ensuring she grasped the weight of the situation. "We need to approach this carefully. Your father's involvement is likely a strategic move. We have to uncover his plan and support him. This isn't just about rescuing him—it's about dismantling the system of oppression from within. Are you ready for that challenge?"

Before Artemis could respond, Gilbert's voice broke through the tension, his question cutting straight to the heart of his concerns. "Are women on your planet free? Can they even speak in public?" His tone was sharp, his words laden with curiosity and frustration, revealing the question had been gnawing at him for some time.

"Do you see me, Gilbert? I'm a woman too, and we are as free as men in most parts of our planet," Artemis replied firmly.

"But… you're gods and live differently," Gilbert said, his confusion evident.

Artemis sighed, her expression softening. "Our status as 'gods' here doesn't reflect the reality of our world," she explained. "We're not so different from you, Gilbert, except in how others choose to perceive us."

Leo nodded, adding, "On our planet, men and women generally have equal rights and freedoms."

Artemis quickly interrupted, her voice firm but passionate. "Uncle Leo! Men and women aren't as equal as they should be—but it's far better than it is here. The situation here is different, far more complex, because of the deeply entrenched systems of control and oppression."

She turned to Gilbert, her resolve unwavering. "What we need to focus on now is finding my father and supporting those who want to break this system. It won't be easy, but it's the right thing to do."

"You listen to me, Gilbert," Leo said firmly, his voice steady but kind. "There are no gods here. There is only one true God—the creator of all galaxies, including yours and mine. God is not a figure or a face; God is a powerful energy that connects everything."

He paused, making sure Gilbert was following. "You can talk to God anywhere, anytime. There's no specific prayer required—you just speak from your heart about anything, and always remember to thank God for everything you have. There's no need to point to the sky or any direction because God is everywhere, including within you and me."

Leo's tone softened as he continued, "We are all part of God, and when we die, we return to that divine energy. We're here in this world to gain experience, to grow, and to learn. That's the real purpose of our existence."

"No man, Flimsy, or any other being is a god," Uncle Leo continued, his voice steady but impassioned. "We are people, just like you and your kind—only from a different galaxy or perhaps another realm. Don't be fooled by these so-called religions. On my planet, people fight over their religions, each one trying to prove theirs is the real one. They don't realize that religion is often just a tool—a distraction used to cover up the real agendas of those in power. And God only knows what they're truly hiding."

He paused for a moment, his tone softening. "The only thing that matters is being kind to one another, helping each other and being kind to others. That's God's will—pure and simple. No killing, no torture, no slavery. Just kindness and compassion," True kindness is what really matters in this world, more than any ideology or belief system."Uncle Leo said firmly.

Artemis stepped forward, her voice firm and resonant. "Because of those religions, there have been countless wars. Billions have been killed, tortured, and displaced. Kaila and Demah are nothing but frauds following the fallen angels. They're exploiting you and your people for their own selfish gain, robbing you of your freedom. And that's not fair to anyone."

She took a deep breath, her eyes locking with Gilbert's. "If religion is so perfect, why don't they let us choose it willingly? Why is it forced upon us? The truth is freedom and kindness are the only paths to true harmony. I hope you can see that now, Gilbert. Together, we can rise above their lies and fight for what's right."

"You are truly Arsham's daughter. I'm very proud of both of you. You said it all," said Uncle Leo.

Gilbert was still staring at Artemis, her words not fully sinking in. It was as if he was caught in a daze, unable to process what she had just said."What do you mean, Artemis? Are you saying we should change our religion?" asked Gilbert.

"I'm only saying be yourself and believe in you. Did you have any religion or law before mankind appeared in your world?" asked Artemis.

"Yes, we did have our own rules," answered Gilbert.

"What were they?" asked Artemis.

"Our law simply stated that you can't lie, and you are free to do whatever you want as long as it doesn't hurt someone's feelings or life. It didn't differentiate between men and women; it applied to everyone," replied Gilbert.

"So, it means you can believe in anything, even a stone, and I wouldn't say anything unless you tried to throw the stone at me. Am I right?" She paused for a couple of seconds before continuing, "Can you tell me why you changed that? Was it because it was too honest or too simple?" asked Artemis.

"Our ancestors were forced to change their beliefs and adopt the new religion," Gilbert said gravely. "If they refused, they faced crippling taxes—so high that it consumed their entire income—or worse, they were killed by the so-called soldiers of God.

I've always known that Mallcie is hiding the truth from our people. They've fed us lies, claiming our ancestors willingly embraced their faith. They tell us it was God's decree that we had to follow these so-called divine rules because our own laws were not from God. But that's not the truth—it's manipulation, pure and simple."

"I know our laws never killed an innocent person," Gilbert said, his voice heavy with emotion. "But this religion has. Ever since we adopted the Mallcie religion, there have been wars—countless wars. And our women? They're not happy. They're treated as less than people as if they don't matter. To silence them, they're fed lies, told they hold a 'special place' in front of God. But what good is that when their voices are ignored, their rights are stripped away? I had a sister," he continued, his voice faltering slightly, "one of the brightest, most brilliant minds on our planet. She committed suicide because she knew she would never be allowed to continue her studies. They took that from her. They took everything she dreamed of, and for what? To uphold a system that crushes anyone who dares to question it."

His eyes grew distant, the pain of his sister's loss etched on his face. "This is what they do—break people, break spirits—and call it the will of God. But it's not. It never was. I'm helping you to help my people because of my sister. I don't believe in Mallcie anymore. I know it is a fraud designed to make my people serve them unquestioningly. I am with you, and I am ready to do anything to make my people free again," Gilbert said, his voice trembling with emotion.

"Do you have a specific prayer, Gilbert?" Leo asked, his tone curious yet gentle.

"Yes, we do. We have to pray every day before breakfast and dinner and again before midnight. Why?" asked Gilbert.

"How do you do it?" Artemis inquired.

"We must point to God in the sky and toward the Black Moon when we pray," Gilbert explained earnestly. "We can even make requests to God, and sometimes, He grants our wishes. It's surprising how often our desires come true—especially for those who pray regularly and with devotion."

Leo sighed before asking, "The black moon, you said? You were there—did you see any god accepting humans?"

Gilbert glanced at him and replied, "Of course I did. Lord Kaila and Lord Demah were there."

Uncle Leo shook his head firmly. "We just talked about God, Gilbert. Those are not God, and the Black Moon is nothing but a fraud. You know they're listening to people from there, manipulating them. Don't let yourself be fooled by their lies."

Artemis gazed into Gilbert's eyes, recognizing his unwavering determination to fight for what was right. She could feel the strength of his resolve and his deep commitment to making a difference.

Gilbert nodded, his resolve strengthening. "I'm ready to fight for my people's freedom. I won't let my sister's sacrifice be in vain."

Leo placed a reassuring hand on Gilbert's shoulder. "We'll do this together. We'll free your people and bring true peace to your world."

Artemis spoke softly, her tone thoughtful yet concerned. "Gilbert, when we were up there, I noticed many command rooms, and I have some knowledge of computers. I think they're using your prayers to gather energy. The fact that you have to point at the Black Moon when you pray makes it seem like you're channeling your energy directly to them. That's the only explanation that makes sense to me," she said, her voice tinged with a mix of realization and unease.

She paused briefly, letting her words sink in before continuing. "Did you know that without your prayers, the Black Moon wouldn't even function? It seems to be powered by the energy of your people. They've built systems to siphon that energy, and the more people pray, the more power they gather—and they use it against you. That's why they want you and your people to pray. That's why they attack other civilizations, forcing them to become Mallcie. They need more energy to sustain their control, and they don't care how much you suffer in the process," her voice carried a mix of urgency and sadness, the weight of her realization clear in every word.

Gilbert's eyes widened as the weight of Artemis's words settled on him. "So, our prayers… they're not for us at all? They're exploiting our faith, our energy?" he asked, his voice filled with disbelief.

He paused, his expression darkening as realization dawned. "That's how they know who's praying and who's not. They use it to monitor us. And those who refuse… they punish, sometimes even execute them, all under the guise of serving God," His voice trembled with a mix of anger and betrayal, the truth cutting deeply.

Artemis nodded. "Exactly. By stopping these forced prayers, you weaken their power. We need to spread the truth and help our people realize they hold the power within themselves. Together, we can dismantle their control. That's why it's crucial to know your enemy, to understand both their weaknesses and strengths."

At that moment, Leo walked to his chair and sat down with his head lowered. Artemis watched him, her eyes filled with shock and pain. Gilbert leaned back against the wall, his face contorted in anguish. He looked at Leo and said, "We need to make people aware of this and tell them to stop their prayers. This way, we can stop them and crash their system."

Leo turned to Gilbert and said, "Look, Gilbert… It's your job to talk to your people and let them know that their prayers are empowering their enemies. They must stop praying to them and start to talk to the real god if they want to regain their freedom and dignity. Go back to your original pray."

Gilbert nodded, understanding the gravity of his task. "I'll do it. I'll spread the word and make sure everyone understands the truth. We need to unite and fight back. I have a lot of connections."

Artemis placed a reassuring hand on Gilbert's shoulder. "We're with you, Gilbert. Together, we'll free your people and bring down the black moon's control."

Leo looked up, determination in his eyes. "We have a plan now. Let's put it into action and give your people the freedom they deserve."

Gilbert nodded with happiness and said, "I will do that. I have many connections and friends with influence." He kept repeating

Leo turned to Artemis and said, "You have to go to the second moon, Mahtob, and convince your father to come back to us."

Artemis's eyes glowed with determination. "I will. When can I go?"

"You can't just go there," Leo explained, his tone cautious. "Mahtob is nothing like the Black Moon; it's outside the atmosphere. You'll need proper spacesuits, an oxygen tank, and a power engine capable of crossing the ozone layer—"

Artemis interrupted him, her determination cutting through his explanation. "Uncle Leo, I don't care how hard it is. Tell me what I need, and I'll figure it out. Also, how can we come back?" Artemis asked, her concern evident. "My father doesn't have special spacesuits or an oxygen tank."

"Don't worry about that," Leo reassured her. "On Mahtob, there are plenty of spacesuits. People come and go all the time. You'll find what you need there to return safely."

Artemis couldn't wait another minute and stood up, ready to go. Uncle Leo smiled at her, pointed to the seat, and asked her to sit down. "I know you are anxious to see your father and bring him back, but we must be very careful with our plan. We can't afford any mistakes. Don't rush it; be patient."

Artemis reluctantly sat back down. She looked at Uncle Leo, who was drinking water, and asked, "Uncle Leo, what do you want to do? What is your plan?"

He looked at her and said, "I have to reach the people's minds and hearts and explain the truth about their so-called gods. If Gilbert tries to do this, it won't work, and his life will be at risk. This message needs to come from another 'god' for the Flimsies to accept it."

"But they have special guns from the gods that will kill you!" said Gilbert, his voice filled with concern.

Artemis felt a surge of fear and looked at Uncle Leo. "Uncle Leo, I don't want to lose you. I want us to go back to our world together."

Uncle Leo placed a reassuring hand on her shoulder. "I understand, Artemis. We must be careful and strategic. We need to find a way to undermine their control without putting ourselves at unnecessary risk. We will do this together, and we will return home safely. But for now, patience and careful planning are our best allies."

He took a deep breath before continuing, "In reality, nobody is waiting for me. This is where I belong. I'm just helping you out here, and I don't want you to end up like me. Remember, you didn't even know I existed." Leo's voice was tinged with sadness as he spoke, the weight of his words hanging heavily in the air.

"How do you know that? Maybe there's a reason my grandma never mentioned you. But I know you have a big family waiting for you on the other side. Do you know how many people hurt my mother, accusing her of being involved in my father's disappearance? Just imagine what it was like in my grandmother's time. I bet they laughed at her and called her names when she told the truth. Maybe they even threatened her into silence—that's why she never spoke. Maybe my mother knew about you but didn't want us to be sad. There could be a thousand reasons I had no idea you existed."

Artemis's eyes glistened with tears as a few drops rolled down her cheeks, and she wiped them away.

Uncle Leo looked at her with a mixture of gratitude and sorrow. "Artemis, your words mean a lot to me. Perhaps you're right. Maybe I do have a family waiting for me. But for now, our focus must be on freeing your father and the people here. We have to do this together."

Artemis nodded, her determination renewed. "We will, Uncle Leo. We'll free them, and we'll find a way back home. Together."

Leo's face brightened as he looked at Gilbert and said, "I want you to go with Artemis. She is powerful, but she still needs your help. Don't leave her alone and do whatever is necessary to save her."

"I will. Don't worry about her. I will take good care of her," Gilbert replied, smiling at Artemis.

"Where do you want to start?" Artemis asked Uncle Leo.

"I have to take control of the main TV station. It's the only way I can speak to the people without interference," Leo said, glancing at his watch, then continued, "It's nine o'clock in the morning. You two have twelve hours to reach the second moon, and I need to prepare the people to stop their prayers and rise against the chaos that's consumed this world by six o'clock and beyond. By nine tonight, you must be there—it'll take time to find your father. But remember, you have less than three days for the entire mission to find him and convince him to return. Gilbert is with you, and he has plenty of connections there. We all need to be in position,

Artemis stared at Leo, her voice trembling with a mix of surprise and urgency. "Uncle Leo! What do you mean we only have three days?"

Leo, shuffling through papers, didn't look up as he replied calmly, "The gate will open only when you're there. And if you're not on time, we'll have to wait until the next leap year."

Artemis's expression shifted to one of disappointment and frustration. "Uncle Leo! Why didn't you tell me this before? Why am I only hearing it now? How many other surprises are there that I need to know about?" Artemis demanded, her frustration clear in her voice.

Leo smiled at her, his calm demeanor unwavering. "Don't waste your time," he said gently. "And remember, I'm counting on both of you."

Artemis and Gilbert exchanged a nod, fully grasping the urgency of the plan. In unison, they declared, "We'll make it." Then, with steely resolve, Artemis added, "Let's get moving."

As they prepared to leave, Leo gave them one last piece of advice, "Stay focused and stay safe. Trust each other, and you'll succeed. Remember That Friday is the night the portal will open, but only if both you and your father are there. If you don't make it, then you'll have to wait two more years in this world, which is four years in ours," Leo explained.

Artemis suddenly turned pale and sat back down in the chair. She was so shocked that her heart started beating rapidly, causing her to feel extremely hot. Gilbert could sense the heat emanating from her and stopped in his tracks, unable to get closer.

"You mean in three days is a leap year, and we have a chance to go back?" she asked, breathing heavily. "How do you know where the portal is?"

"The portal is in the same place where you entered this world. Yours is very close to here. Mine is in my room here; I built my room there, but it never opened. Maybe because nobody ever tried to open it. But for you, and the way you explained about your friends, it's different. They might help you go back, and they might be waiting for you. When the portal opens, any of us can cross it," Leo explained.

"Uncle Leo! You mean the gate only opens from our world?" Artemis's gaze locked on Leo, her eyes wide with urgency and disbelief.

Leo walked toward her, placing a steady hand on her shoulder. "If we had those stones here, there might have been a chance to open the gate from this side as well. But for now, we don't have them, and we'll have to rely on the other side to make progress."

Artemis took a deep breath, trying to calm herself. "Alright, we have no time to lose. Gilbert and I will head to Mahtob moon immediately. We must find my father and be back here by Friday before midnight."

Leo nodded. "Remember, stay focused and stay safe. Trust each other, and you'll succeed."

Artemis stood up, her determination renewed. "Let's go, Gilbert. We have a mission to complete."

With a final nod from Leo, Artemis and Gilbert headed out, ready to face the challenges ahead and reunite with her father in time to make it back home.

"How will I know where to go?" Artemis asked again.

"After you come back here, we will take you there. It's not far from here," Leo reassured her.

"I wish I could go too," Gilbert asked, looking between Artemis and Leo.

"I'm sorry, Gilbert, as I explained to you before, it's too dangerous for you. The gravity on Earth is too strong, and I don't know if you'd survive it. The force could crush you. It's a huge risk, as I've told you many times before," Leo explained gently.

Gilbert, standing just a little taller than Artemis, watched as she teased him with a playful, childlike tone. "Gilbert! Be happy because if you were on Earth, you'd be shorter. It's only the lighter gravity here that's making you taller than me."

Gilbert nodded quietly, though the disappointment was evident in his eyes. He ignored Artemis and faced Leo, "I understand. You've told me so many times, but I still hoped there might be a way for me to go with you. For now, I'll do everything I can to help."

Gilbert smiled back, his resolve strengthening. "You can count on me like always."

Artemis turned to Leo. "Alright, we're ready. Let's get to Mahtob moon and find my father."

Leo nodded, giving Artemis a final look of encouragement. "Stay focused, and remember the plan. We'll see you both back here in three days before midnight."

Artemis looked at Gilbert, feeling the warmth of his love but unsure of what to say. He was willing to risk everything just to be with her. Meeting his gaze, she softly said, "I don't want you to put yourself in danger. I promise I'll come back and visit you after I return to Earth." She took a deep breath and added, "Look, Gilbert, even if we could create a place with less gravity, it would still be like staying in one spot, like a jail. You wouldn't be able to leave that place—ever. I don't think you want that."

Gilbert stepped closer, taking her hands in his. "I can't live without you anymore. I'd rather die or stay in that jail if it means I get to see you every day. It's my choice. Just think about it."

Artemis opened her mouth to respond when Leo came back and called to both of them, "That's enough. We are short on time. We have to hurry. Walk with me."

Leo opened the door, and Artemis and Gilbert followed him silently down the hallway, their footsteps echoing in the quiet. He opened another door, and they stepped into the room. Turning to his assistant, he called, "Gira, are the spacesuits ready?"

"Yes, Leo. They are ready for an adventure," Gira replied.

Leo nodded and turned to Artemis and Gilbert. "Get suited up. We have a mission to accomplish, and time is of the essence."

Artemis, feeling the weight of the situation, approached the line of spacesuits hanging nearby. She touched one, running her hand over it with a sense of hopelessness. "There are so many," she muttered, her voice tinged with uncertainty. "I hope there's one that fits me. This is a lot for a teenager to handle, but... this might be my last mission." She paused, her expression softening with emotion. "I just hope I see my father before I die."

Leo sensed her despair. To a teenager, this mission must feel like a trip to Mars. He pressed the button again, and the spacesuits moved back to their original place. Confused, Artemis asked, "Why did you do that?"

Leo grabbed a drink, sat on a chair, and took a deep breath before turning to Artemis. "Look, Artemis, these are people living in hell because of us."Demah and his people deceived us, using us to open the portal for their gain, only to bring in equipment that turned these innocent lives into misery. It's our responsibility to make things right before we leave."

"The problem is that you only wish to see your father before you die? Is that your idea of rescuing? I can help you get back to Earth, but I can't promise anything else. With your current hope, I don't think we will succeed. We are wasting our time."

Artemis felt a surge of determination. "You're right, Uncle Leo. I need to stay focused and believe in our mission. I want to see my father, but more importantly, I want to save him and free these people from their suffering. Let's get these spacesuits on and get moving. We don't have any time to waste."

Leo nodded approvingly. "That's the spirit, Artemis. Let's get suited up and make this mission a success."

Artemis felt miserable and ashamed of herself. She stood frozen in her spot, staring at the floor, when she felt Gilbert's hand on her shoulder. He hugged her and looked into her eyes, saying, "Artemis, it's okay if you don't want to do it. I don't want anything to happen to you. Please, when the port opens, just go home safely to your family."

Artemis looked at Gilbert for a few seconds, then turned to Uncle Leo and asked, "Uncle Leo, why do they need us? The same way they came here, they can go back. Why don't they do it?"

Leo, anticipating the question, smiled and said, "Artemis, coming here is easier than going back. To return, we need a triangle of power from the same family. Plus, the gate has to be opened from the other side, and from the Flimsies, it can't open unless we have those stones and you are the most important part of it. That's why they need you. You're special—a leap year child, your father and grandmother are leap year too and that's why you are able to keep the gate open longer than anyone else or maybe for as long as you please, and you can open it from both sides. You can even bring non-leap year people here. All the equipment you see in this world is from that time when you were little when they discovered your power. They've been trying to turn this place into some sort of luxury vacation spot. That's why they tricked you into the spaceship and tried to impress you. It's also why I had to make sure you were strong enough to resist.

A long time ago, many people came here the same way."They used your father to bring you into that room, keeping the gate open for as long as they needed. But when they tried to bring you here without your parents' permission—because your father wasn't willing to involve you—Demah grabbed you and attempted to jump through the gate. That's when your father intervened, blocking him. Demah fell into the gate, dragging your father with him, and both disappeared. You were terrified, and when you're not happy, the gate doesn't work. Your father fell into their trap, and everything came to a halt. They used to come a couple of times to open the gate under the name of the ceremony and they were able to bring more equipment here, but after that, your mother refused to let them return to your home and continue their so-called ceremony. By then, Demah wouldn't allow your father to come back. But once you showed up, everything changed—they were excited again. They can't force you to open the gate because it won't work that way, so they tried to impress you with their ship."

Artemis looked at uncle Leo and asked, "You mean my father used me as equipment for their adventure?"

"No... No… No. Sweet-heart, They tricked your father and your father didn't know that you are the main power of the gate. When he found out it was the time, he didn't want to involve you," Leo explained

Artemis absorbed his words and was shocked, her resolve strengthening. "So, they need us to return. That means we have the upper hand. We can use this to our advantage."

Leo nodded, his expression resolute. "Exactly. They underestimate you, but that's their mistake. We can turn this situation around. Let's get suited up and ready to go. Remember, you have the power to change everything. And be careful not to step into any traps. That's why Gilbert is with you—he's smart, he knows everyone here, and he'll make sure you stay free. They might try to capture you, to chain you up for their advantage. But we won't let them."

Gilbert squeezed Artemis's hand reassuringly. "We're in this together. Let's do this."

With renewed determination, Artemis and Gilbert donned their spacesuits, preparing for the journey to the Mahtob moon. They knew they understood the risks but were ready to face them head-on, driven by their shared goal of freeing Artemis's father and bringing justice to the oppressed people.

Artemis and Gilbert quickly put on the spacesuits with the help of Gira and her assistant, feeling the weight and protection they provided. Artemis looked at Gilbert, her determination renewed. "Let's do this, my friend."

Gilbert nodded, his resolve matching hers. "Together."

Leo gave them a final nod of encouragement. "Stay focused, follow the plan, and trust each other. We'll see you both back here, along with Arsham, before midnight. Got it?"

This time, Artemis and Gilbert together said, "Got it, we're ready.

With that, they were ready to embark on their mission to Mahtob moon, determined to find Artemis's father and bring him back safely. Gira had a happy expression on her face as she looked at Artemis and Gilbert with pride. She pressed a button, and a door opened with a crashing sound, followed by a beeping noise.

Artemis asked, "What is that sound?"

Gira, without looking at her, answered, "It's quirky because these systems are old. This beeping sound happens all the time." They all burst into laughter.

Uncle Leo looked at Artemis and said, "He tricked you into coming here, and now they have to pay for it—with the only hope they have left."

Artemis looked at Uncle Leo in surprise when she asked, "What do you mean by tricking me? Who tricked me? Matt?"

Uncle Leo ran his fingers through his hair, pushing it back before looking at Artemis and saying, "No, Matt is your friend. He was only curious to know what would happen if you all followed the book. But your other friend, Ricky, is the one who brought up this subject."

Artemis recalled Ricky's suggestions and how he influenced Matt. "Yes, I remember him. Bastard… but how did he know about these?"

"I'll tell you, but how did you two become friends anyway?" asked Uncle Leo.

"He wasn't my friend," Artemis said, a flash of memory hitting her. "Last year, in the middle of the school year, his father moved to Toronto from Montreal. At first, he was Allan's friend, and slowly, he joined our team," she paused, the pieces of the puzzle starting to fall into place.

"His father is here, and his uncle prepared his registration at your school," replied Uncle Leo.

"What do you mean his father is here? Who is his father?" Artemis asked, her worry growing.

"Demah is his father, and his brother, who is Demah's twin brother, knew about the Flimsies. They've been planning this for a long time," Uncle Leo explained. "Every time they asked your mother to hold a ceremony for your father's disappearance, she always rejected them, and that's why they couldn't get to you. So they came up with a new plan—having Ricky become your friend."

Artemis felt a surge of anger and betrayal. "So Ricky and his family were part of this all along. They used us to get what they wanted. Now I know why Demah looked so familiar to me—I saw Ricky's father, I mean uncle, one day at school in front of the principal office and he kept asking me questions and he told me he knew my father," her voice trembled with the realization, the pieces finally falling into place.

Uncle Leo nodded. "Yes, they used Ricky to manipulate you and your friends. But now that you know the truth, we can turn the tables on them. Let's get ready to head to Mahtob moon and rescue your father. We'll need to be careful and strategic."

"Uncle Leo, How do you know about all this, anyway?" Artemis asked, her curiosity piqued. "After my father came here, there was no connection between the two worlds. So how do you know what's been happening?"

"They predicted everything from the beginning," Leo explained. "It was part of their plan, even when Ricky was just a little boy. I worked with them for a while at first and they needed me because I knew everything here, and I overheard their conversations. That's why they shared everything with me. They set all of this in motion a long time ago."

Uncle Leo sighed and continued, "Because I know them and I helped them a lot. We used to work together back then. They studied your family and learned about you. At first, I didn't know who you were, but when they talked about your family, I realized that Arsham is your father and your mother is my niece. That's when I got closer to your father, and we started talking about you and everyone else. We knew they had a plan, but we didn't know what it was. We knew they were planning to bring you here and keep you against your will for their own gain, but we didn't know how to stop them."

He looked at Artemis, his expression a mix of regret and determination. "I tried to protect you and your family as best as I could, but they were always one step ahead. Now that we know the full extent of their plans, we have a chance to fight back. We can stop them and rescue your father."

"Demah was my father's friend? At least he said the truth for once," Artemis wondered aloud.

"Yes, your father knew him very well. He told me everything about him," Leo replied, glancing at Gilbert.

"What kind of person was he?" Gilbert demanded.

"Arsham said they used to be co-workers. There were many rumors about Demah, and your father didn't believe them at first," Leo began, trying to keep his explanation concise. But before he could continue, Artemis interrupted.

"What kind of rumors?" she pressed.

Leo sighed and continued, "Your father didn't believe these rumors until they came here. There were rumors that Demah was a child molester and had been in jail for that, including rape. Your father didn't believe it because Demah seemed very well-behaved. He acted like a gentleman, and your dad had a lot of respect for him." He walked back and forth, then continued, "Demah was the one who discovered the stones and asked your father to work with him. After they arrived here, they helped people for years, just like you do now. During that time, there were reports of missing children and women. Your father wasn't suspicious of Demah, and they both tried to find the kidnappers. Over the years, they gathered many people and formed an organization. With your father's help, more humans kept coming here, but the gate wasn't stable and kept closing after a few seconds. Anyhow, your father wasn't allowed to get close to the gate and he always had to stay with a couple of guards."

Artemis interrupted again, unable to contain herself. "Are you saying my father is part of the problem? After all he's done, how can he ever return home?"

"Don't rush to judgment before you hear the entire story," Uncle Leo admonished gently.

"Anyway, they used to bring so much equipment here along with technicians, computer programmers, engineers, and so on. They built a lot here and I didn't go back because I thought that I was forgotten. But their problem was to open the gate from the other side. That was a challenge. It must always be from earth. Until one night, you stepped in and fell in the gate and started laughing. Amazingly, the gate stayed open and that's how they discovered your true power. From that moment on, they start planing to have you for their gain. The amazing part is when they want to open the gate, you must've been awake with positive energy, which means be happy to make it work. When Demah tried to grab you and your father blocked him, they both fell into the gate. You started to cry, and the gate immediately closed. It seems that when you're scared, cry, or fall asleep, the gate stops working—likely why it shuts so quickly. According to your account, Demah's brother used a different method to gain access to your house, and unfortunately, he succeeded. Demah was unaware of Arsham's connection to my family, and we deliberately kept it that way."

"How did you find out Demah was the kidnapper?" Gilbert asked.

"I discovered the truth by accident," Uncle Leo began. "One day, I wandered into a restricted area and saw children, young girls, and women, some in dire condition, others dead. The exploitation between humans and the Flimsy caused irreversible harm, often leading to the death of the Flimsy. When I confronted Demah, I realized he wanted my silence—he wanted me to be part of their operation. We fought viciously, and I barely escaped. I tried to help those who were held captive, but by the time I returned, they had vanished without a trace. It took me years to contact your father, only to find out he had already escaped. Recently, I managed to reach him again, and we've been communicating via radio ever since," Uncle Leo finished his sentence and looked at Artemis.

"How did this religion become so prominent in Flimsies?" Artemis asked.

"They would be killed or beheaded," Uncle Leo replied grimly. "They created this doctrine and called it Mallcie, after Demah's father. Initially, no one wanted to be part of it because Flimsies had good rules and were very happy. However, Demah and Kaila began coercing the Flimsies, ruthlessly killing anyone who refused to join them. They were powerful, forcing the people into submission. Afterward, they compelled the Flimsies to speak English, imposing severe punishments on anyone who dared to use their native language. After a few decades, they forgot their own language. Flimsies were peaceful and did not believe in war or fighting. As time went on, they pushed it even further. They demanded that people donate their young girls to Lord Demah, instilling fear by claiming it was a sacrifice to protect their world from collapsing and to keep their planet and universe safe. They fabricated countless stories, making the people very superstitious. The Flimsies became victims of Demah's twisted mind and forced women to stop challenging and become easier to capture and own."

Uncle Leo paused, unable to continue as Artemis, relentless in her questioning, pressed for more answers.

"Uncle Leo! Did my dad ever tell you about Demah's life on Earth?" Artemis asked curiously.

"Yes, of course he did. We talked about it a lot. Demah is originally from Oklahoma City but moved to Montreal when he was very young. He struggled to find a suitable job, facing constant rejection. During this time, he met his wife, who was much older than him but very wealthy. She helped him start a business, and without her assistance, he couldn't have succeeded. They married a year later, and she gave birth to two children, a girl named Vicky and a boy named Ricky. His wife controlled everything, and Demah had no say in their lives. He feared leaving her because, without her, he felt he was nothing. Demah was your father's boss and was the one who introduced the idea to him, getting him involved. According to your father, their meeting was accidental, happening in a coffee shop where they talked for an hour. Demah offered him a job with twice the salary of his current position, knowing your father had unique abilities and had been targeting him ever since. Later on, your father found out that the meeting wasn't accidental and Demah planed it. He would speak to your father almost daily. Demah despised his wife, coveting only her money and wealth. He cheated on her frequently, but she loved him deeply and repeatedly forgave him. However, he was, and still is, a maniac with a sick mind," Leo took a deep breath and looked at Artemis and continued, "Here, this place is a paradise for him. He makes his own laws and does whatever he wants, and no one is to stop him. That's why we must help these people and save them from the real evil."

"Uncle Leo! I am proud to be part of this mission. We have to stop this abominable regime from being such a horrible government. We must help these people retaliate and rebuild their society. As you always said, 'Let's light up the darkness'."

Uncle Leo's face brightened, and he immediately went toward Artemis, hugging her. "Artemis, you are my star. I knew I could depend on you."

Artemis smiled and replied, "No, Uncle Leo, you are the star. You rocked my world to its core and made me the person I am today."

Gilbert looked confused and disappointed. He would do anything for his people, but he didn't want to put Artemis in danger.

"Whoa, I highly doubt that because you just saw your uncle a few days ago! Isn't it funny?" Gilbert murmured.

Gilbert gulped and looked at Artemis quietly. Uncle Leo called out Gira and Sean to help Artemis and Gilbert put on their spacesuits. It took almost an hour to get the suits on. Artemis had no problem walking around and even running, but Gilbert had a different reaction. He couldn't move a muscle. Uncle Leo tried to explain how to move in the suit, but it wasn't working.

"He can't move at all but don't worry about that because he just needs to be connected to you. He doesn't have to do anything else. You just have to drag him with you," Uncle Leo said, turning to Artemis.

Gilbert sighed, and Artemis held his hand, saying, "Don't worry about anything. I will help you all the way to our destination. We are exploring space."

She clicked her tongue and smiled at him. She repeated, whispering to herself, "We are going to space! Oh god…"

Uncle Leo explained the routine and how to navigate through the atmosphere. "We built this ship—small but incredibly powerful. This is the new model, and you two are the first to ride it. I'm telling you, it's ninety percent better than the old one. It's easy to operate, and you can travel back and forth with ease. It has space for five people." He meticulously guided them through the ship's features and controls.

"Why should I take Gilbert with me? I can do it myself without putting him in danger," Artemis groaned.

"You need Gilbert on that planet because he knows how to infiltrate their camp where your father is. He knows every corner of that moon, every inch of it. He also knows the people and how to contact them. Without him, they might attack you on sight, and they could have Earth weapons—you could get hurt," Uncle Leo explained.

Artemis glared at Gilbert, her voice edged with anger, "You told me you've never been there. What the hell—never mind."

Gilbert glanced at her, "I told you I've never been there physically in person."

"Anyhow, Mahtob Moon consists of different tribes that have no respect or tolerance for foreigners. Without their help, you would be lost. They don't like alien intervention. To them, we are the aliens who disrupted their way of life, and that is true. Because of this, they hate humans," Uncle Leo explained, making it clear to Artemis the challenges they would face with the people living on that moon.

"Why do we need this ship to go to the moon when I'm capable of flying easily?" Artemis asked.

"You need a powerful engine to get through the ozone layer, and even if you're strong enough, you still need protection when entering space. Once you're in space, you'll still need the engine. Space is space, whether it's Earth or another planet—you can't just enter without a specialized suit and oxygen. You have to be extremely careful and head directly for the moon," Uncle Leo explained once more.

"What if we faced a problem?" Artemis asked hesitantly.

"We won't leave you alone up there. We'll be watching and guiding you. We'll let you know when the time is right," Leo replied reassuringly.

Leo looked at both of them and handed them each a transmission device. "These are transmitters, and you have to place them in your ear."

Artemis's hands trembled as Leo gently held them, looking into her eyes. "I know you're scared of going into space, and I understand how you feel, but there's no other way if you want to save your father and bring him back." Artemis nodded.

Leo called Gira, taking Artemis by the hand while Gira assisted Gilbert. Together, they walked out of the building and into an open area almost barren of trees. Before them stood a rocket that looked like a giant toy, yet imposing in size. Inside, there were five seats.

Artemis and Gilbert climbed in, preparing themselves for the journey ahead.

"Artemis, be very careful. Since Demah established his base on the second moon, there has been a fanatical fight between civilians and Demah's troops. There are many different cults living there with diverse lifestyles. They will do anything to harm Demah. They can't physically harm you, but they can mislead you and divert your plans to serve their purposes. They worship themselves and possess some weapons of Earth origin, which can hurt humans. Watch out for yourself and Gilbert. He is your guide while you are there. As soon as you find your father, tell him about the gate and move back immediately."

Artemis looked at Leo and asked, "Uncle Leo, why can't I just talk to him on the transmission device and ask him to come here?"

Leo smiled and replied, "Because he needs you to bring him back."

"What do you mean by that?" she asked, surprised.

"Do you remember the time I couldn't hold you? That's the reason," Leo explained.

"But operating the ship doesn't require power—it's just pressing buttons, right?" she wondered.

"You're right," Uncle Leo said kindly, "his body is frail due to the effects of this planet, but once you're in space, you'll understand what I mean."

Artemis glanced at him, puzzled, but nodded, absorbing the weight of Leo's words. She tightened her grip on Gilbert's hand, feeling the weight of the mission ahead. They prepared to embark on their journey, ready to face the unknown challenges on the second moon. Artemis listened carefully to all the information Leo was sharing. He described the moon, its inhabitants, Demah, and his followers. Despite feeling a tinge of fear, she knew she could do it.

Leo looked at them and said, "I know you're wondering why you need this. It will help your speed, especially when you're heading to the moon. I've never used either of them, actually. I've never even left the planet, but I can tell you this one is incredibly safe."

Artemis shot him an angry glance and shouted, "You've never left the planet before, so how do you know it's safe?"

In no time, Leo closed the cockpit hatch and signaled for them to proceed while Artemis stared at him with a look of sheer terror. They soared into the sky as fast as a cutting-edge rocket, with Leo watching proudly. He kept his eyes on them until the ship became a tiny dot, vanishing from sight.

THE LAST STAND OF UNITY

Leo rushed to the control room, his attention fixed on the monitors. He checked their heart rates, oxygen levels, and other vital signs, meticulously tracking Artemis and Gilbert's condition as they ventured further into space. He selected Aden, one of the top system operators, to monitor Artemis and Gilbert's journey. Speaking into the microphone, he introduced Aden and explained his role before handing it over to him. Aden immediately began a conversation with them. Leo's plan was to have the people of the Flimsy world take over their land, planet, and society.

Leo, accompanied by Gira, Sean, numerous followers, and twenty humans, crammed into the army truck and sped toward Channel Six, the Flimsies' favorite TV station. Only three remained behind, ready to assist Artemis and guide her safely to the moon if needed.

It took them half an hour to reach the station. Upon arrival, Leo and the team swiftly secured the building, sealing all entrances from the inside. Seven humans stood guard outside in front of every entrance, protecting the station and those within. The TV station's perimeter was isolated and fortified. Regular programming was interrupted and replaced by an urgent message broadcast across all channels.

Leo turned to his computer engineer and asked, "Is the system ready to broadcast on all channels? Were you able to take over all the channels?"

She nodded confidently. "Yes, Leo, it's ready."

Leo turned to Gira and said excitedly, "You have no idea how long I've been waiting for this moment, and thankfully, Artemis made it possible for us."

Gira nodded in agreement, her face glowing with happiness as she exclaimed excitedly, "We're going to take our planet back!"

The screen flashed with a series of urgent notices,

- "We will be right back in one hour."

- "Approximately in one hour, Lord Leo has a message for Flimsies."

- "Don't miss this important message from Lord Leo."

As soon as people saw Lord Leo's name—their beloved and favored leader—flashing on the screens, they rushed to the station, gathering in ever-growing numbers. The crowd became a sea of anticipation. They assembled in support of Lord Leo. Suddenly, signs began to appear in their hands, displaying messages such as, "WELCOME BACK, LORD LEO!"

Another prominent sign was Lord Leo's favored flag, which featured a turquoise background with the image of a Sheebr at its center.

They chanted, their voices rising in unison. Over and over, they repeated their slogan, "Lord Leo is the best—Send evil to its nest!"

They quickly turned into protesters, chanting their slogans fervently. It was evident they were eager for someone they could trust to stand up against Demah and his soldiers. Many had been waiting for this moment, and Leo was counting on their support. The number of demonstrators swelled rapidly. In less than half an hour, the streets surrounding the TV station were jam-packed with people, swelling from thousands to hundreds of thousands, approaching close to a million. There were trucks, buses and cars coming from different cities to join them. The entire city echoed with their unified cry, "Welcome back, Lord Leo."

"Lord Leo is the best—Send evil to its nest!"

They chanted in unison, "GO HOME DEMAH... GO HOME DEMAH."

Others said loudly and repeatedly, "DEMAH! DEMAH! GO BACK HOME!"

Other groups were yelling, "GUN, GUN! HUMAN GUN! GUN, GUN! HUMAN GUN."

A person leaped onto the stairs, pointing toward the black moon and shouting, "WE HAVE HUMAN WEAPONS, AND WE ARE NOT AFRAID TO USE THEM AGAINST DEMAH AND HIS FOLLOWERS. WE WILL STAND WITH LORD LEO UNTIL THE END AND OUR FREEDOM!"

They now had the courage to voice their pain and desires. They wanted their own leader, free from the oppression they had endured. They demanded freedom for both men and women, no longer asking, but They demanded Demah leave their world, vowing to stand and fight to the last person if necessary and they declared they would no longer tolerate oppression. Leo wasn't surprised to see all these Flimsies gathered because he understood their pain and needs. He knew they would fight, even if it meant many would die. They didn't want to live like this any longer. Finally, at six o'clock, Gira, the host, announced an important message from Lord Leo. There were a few big TV screens outside of the TV station. As soon as they heard that Lord Leo was about to speak, they all began urging each other to be quiet. "Shh Sh… Lord Leo is about to speak. Quiet… QUIET!"

The crowd erupted in cheers every few seconds, chanting, "LORD LEO, YOU'RE THE BEST!"

Gira waved at everyone and continued, "At this moment, I respectfully ask all of you to keep quiet while Lord Leo explains the situation to us. Thank you."

She paused for a moment and then announced, "Ladies and gentlemen,... here is Lord Leo."

The crowd cheered excitedly and happily, then fell silent, anticipation thick in the air, as Lord Leo stepped forward in front of the cameras to address them. The crowd cheered and screamed happily again for Lord Leo. He waved back at them with a smile and began his speech, "Hello, lovely Flimsies. Today is a special day for all of us. Today is the day we must decide between freedom and slavery. I have lived here for almost half a century. I have studied your culture, people, religion, weather, and nature. I am familiar with the laws before Mallcie took over your world and after. But I have always wondered how free people like the Flimsies could say yes to the nonsensical laws that were imposed upon you, dragging your world down under the guise of religion. You were forced to accept it, becoming victims, and that was painful enough for me to witness. Whether you did this to yourselves or it was done to you by force, it was a grave injustice.

"I remember that your culture amazed me and made me want to be part of it when I first arrived in your world. Men and women were in politics; they were doctors, engineers, and teachers, among other professions equally. This world was the color of happiness. When I came here, I was a child and I learned everything from you and your world. I felt safe and honored. Happiness was the first rule of your world.

"What happened to you? Instead of attending school and university, you are always praying. In the middle of the street or wherever you are, you can't hesitate to stop and pray to the so-called God, who is a regular human.

"But you don't need to be a scientist to understand the differences between that time and now. The vibrant, progressive society you once had has been overshadowed by fear and oppression. Instead of advancing and thriving, you have been forced into submission under the guise of religion. This change has not only stifled your growth but has also taken away the essence of what made your culture so extraordinary.

"Before Mallcie, you had universities. You never wasted your time and were always eager to learn more. But now you have to pray six or seven times a day to the black moon—why? If you want to talk to God, you can do it anywhere, and there's no special way required to speak with Him."

"You had a safe and happy life without this false god, yet you had everything else, including your freedom. They claim you have a god to protect you, but from what? I really don't understand. You have a god but no money to survive. You have Mallcie, but half of your population—your women—are forced to stay away from society, living miserable lives. They must muzzle their voices and have no right to speak up.

"You have this god, yet you must sacrifice your children to stay safe? Before Mallcie, you didn't need to sacrifice anything to be safe—you already were. I can't understand how you can bear it. The freedom and happiness you once had have been stripped away, replaced by fear and subjugation. It's time to reclaim your lives, your society, and your world from this oppressive regime.

"I'm going to explain Demah's life on Earth now. Demah was divorced when he was on Earth, and his wife took everything from him. She was wealthy, and he had nothing—she took everything, including their children. It happened because he wasn't a good husband or father. The court made that decision, but he never accepted it. Unable to confront or fight his wife, he's taking his revenge on her through the women in your world. Do you know why she gave up on him? He was constantly cheating on her. Demah has a sick mind, and he needs to be stopped. On Earth, he's just an average person, nothing special or important.

"Now, he's using his pain and bitterness to oppress and control you. But you don't have to endure his cruelty any longer. It's time to reclaim your freedom and restore the dignity of your society. The strength and resilience you need are within you, and together, we can put an end to his reign of terror."

The Flimsies screamed, "Yes, Lord Leo!" every time he spoke, their voices echoing in fervent agreement.

"You women, stand up for your rights and say no to dictatorship and bondage if you want to live with happiness. Stand up, remove your muzzles, and declare proudly that you are a woman and you will stay a woman."

Women on the streets screamed with joy, and one by one, they removed their muzzles, celebrating the reclaiming of the freedom they once had but had been denied.

There is another plan for you as well. They are planning to export young Flimsies to our world. No Flimsy can live on Earth due to the strong gravity. You will suffer unbearable pain and perish within hours of arrival.

According to new documents we have received, Demah is planning to start a big business on Earth. I know he has made many promises to you, but they are all lies. He wants to take you to Earth and sell you as pets to other humans. You'll be slaves for the rest of your lives if you survive.

Demah is exploiting you on your own planet and plans to profit from selling you on Earth. It's time to take a stand against his cruel intentions. Reclaim your freedom, your dignity, and your future. Together, we can stop Demah and his vile schemes."

The crowd was cheering for Leo and saying, "We will stand by you, Lord Leo."

"Do you know what your prayers are doing for them and you? Every six or seven times a day, when you are praying and focusing, they have a system that harnesses your prayers as energy. Do you know where they use that energy? It's used against you. You are unknowingly helping them to abuse you. Each time you pray in their way, it's as if you're saying, 'Yes, I authorize you to abuse and torture me however you want, and I'm giving you the power to do so'. By allowing them to use your energy, you are contributing to their power and preventing yourselves from having a wonderful life.

"They are planning to bring more equipment from Earth. Do you know what that equipment will do to you? It will further their control and oppression over you. These machines are designed to enhance their ability to monitor, manipulate, and subjugate you even more. It's crucial to understand that your prayers are being weaponized against you, turning your faith into a tool of your own suppression. Finally, You will become a puppet. I'm not against God; I believe in God too, but the real one—not an ordinary human. If you want to talk to the real God, you don't need to point anywhere. Just speak to God directly.

"It's time to break free from this vicious cycle. Stand up for your rights, refuse to be exploited, and reclaim your lives. Together, we can dismantle their systems of control and restore the freedom and happiness you deserve.

"We must unite against them. You must defend your world. We can use their own laws against them. Your prayers provide them with the energy they need to stand against you, but without that energy, they will collapse. Remove your muzzles, come out, and claim your own freedom. This world belongs to you.

"Your freedom is not something they will offer you; you have to fight to take it back. Yes, freedom is not easy to obtain, but it is worth fighting for. The only time I will fight is for freedom. Nothing is more sacred than freedom.

"Stand together, refuse to be oppressed, and reclaim the life and society you deserve. Let us break the chains of tyranny and build a future where every Flimsy can live with dignity, peace, and happiness. This is your world and must stay that way, and it's time to take it back. If not today, tomorrow will be too late."

Every time Flimsy yelled, "YES, LORD LEO. WE WILL. WE ARE WITH YOU, LORD LEO."

"I am asking you to come to the streets and sit there. Don't pray, just be present. If they attack you, then you attack back, but otherwise, do nothing because they can use your energy for their equipment. Soon, the portal between our two worlds will be opened. Let's throw them through the portal and return them to their origins. We know what to do with them once they are back where they belong.

"Artemis is on her quest to help you and her father. Let's support her in her mission. She is the only one who can open the portal from this side. Let's help her to help us. Together, we can achieve our freedom and end this tyranny. Your presence and courage today will make a difference. Stand strong and united, and you will reclaim your world."

After Leo's speech, music played as the crowd cheered enthusiastically for him. The roads quickly became even busier. Leo yelled at Gira, "Any updates so far?"

Sean opened the door and cheerfully exclaimed, "Leo! Channel Mallcie has been destroyed. Flimsies attacked the station, and Mallcie Station is no more... Yahoo! Bravo, my friends…"

Gira hung up and turned to Leo, saying, "Leo! Seven stations, including Lesson of Kaila, have been destroyed. People are rising up; our revolution will succeed, and we will be free soon."

From the other room, Gira called out, "Leo! You have to see this. Hurry up."

Leo ran to the other room and joined Gira, who was looking out the window with a cheerful expression. As soon as Leo stood beside her, she grabbed his arm, hugged him, and said, "Look, Leo! Look at the women! They are removing their muzzles and joining the protesters. They are singing their revolutionary slogans loudly." She sighed.

Sean joined them and said, "Mission accomplished, Leo."

Leo looked up at the sky and said, "Not yet."

Sean looked at Leo and said, "Leo! They say there were humans alongside the Flimsy when they attacked the other stations. I believe they were in hiding as well, too afraid to show themselves."

Leo nodded to confirm.

Suddenly, a horrendous crash echoed from a remote area, and everyone's attention turned that way. The noise was loud and clattering, followed by the sound of something falling to pieces. Leo ran outside and saw a large satellite crushed on the ground. The crowd noticed Leo and cheered, exclaiming, "Lord Leo! We will stand for as long as possible."

Leo waved with a big smile and went back into the building. He pointed at Gira and said, "I'm going on air again. Prepare everything."

Gira started the countdown, and when she reached one, she pointed at Leo to begin.

"Dear Flimsies! A few minutes ago, one of Demah's satellites crashed to the ground and fell to pieces. This is good news because it means you're no longer praying to it, and it answered you back. They cannot watch you anymore. Congratulations to all of you. Good job."

There was a big cheer outside the building, followed by revolutionary slogans once again. Everyone was looking at Leo, who seemed to be waiting for something else to happen. He went to the window and looked up at the sky.

Gira approached him to offer comfort and said, "Don't worry, Leo... she is a strong and smart girl."

"I'm not worried about her," Leo explained. "I'm waiting for the moment of truth. It should happen any moment now. If it's not tonight, it should be tomorrow."

Before he finished his sentence, there was another big scream outside. They all ran out to see what was happening and were surprised to find everyone looking up at the sky. Leo turned to say something to Gira and noticed her astonished expression. His curiosity followed her gaze. It was the most beautiful sight he had ever seen. The black moon glowed ominously, bathed in flashing red lights that pulsed in unison, clearly visible against the night sky. The sound of alarms echoed with unsettling clarity while the red lights flickered rapidly, casting an eerie glow.

Leo asked Gira to bring the speaker, and as soon as he had it, he began his speech, "My friends, you are my allies, and I am very proud of you all."

One of the Flimsies asked on behalf of everyone else, "Lord Leo, what is happening?"

Leo smiled and continued his speech, "That is the second biggest step of tonight. That is the black moon, and it is falling apart. They don't have any more energy to light up, and the red lights are the emergency power, which will be out in a few more hours or maybe days. They are done and as good as dead. You didn't supply their energy tonight. They were already running low on energy, and I was expecting this to happen within a couple of days. Do you know what that means?"

There were so many conflicting thoughts when Leo waved at them and said, "It means many of you have already stopped your prayers and feeding them."

There were cheers everywhere as people danced and sang, celebrating their exhilarating freedom. The city was alive with joy, celebrating their independence day and returning to their roots. However, the joy was short-lived when everyone noticed that Lord Leo had no reaction. He stood still, looking up at the sky, a solemn expression on his face.

Some of the Flimsies approached Leo and asked, "Lord Leo! Are you happy that we've gained our freedom?"

Leo, still gazing at the sky, slowly turned his eyes to them for a couple of seconds before looking back up and saying, "I am happy, but it's not done yet."

"It isn't? My Lord, why not?" asked the Flimsy again.

Leo continued to stare at the sky as Sean and Gira, standing beside him, covered their mouths and looked scared. Without looking at anyone, Leo answered, "That's because the war has only just begun.".

The Flimsy followed Leo's gaze and said, "God help us. Thank God that Lord Leo is here."

From the sky, a few small lights were descending, and Leo knew exactly what they were. It was Demah and Kaila coming down to take their revenge on him. Leo had anticipated this from the beginning and was prepared. He turned to the Flimsies, waving his hands to signal them to calm down and be quiet.

Then he held the speaker and said, "Please listen up! We don't have much time left. They're going to be here any minute. I want everybody to leave the streets and go home. This is not your war anymore, and you will only put your life on the line. They are coming for me and only me. There is nothing you can do because, as you know, they are indestructible. Please go home and follow the safety instructions in the flyer that Gira is handing out. Follow the instructions step by step. Go... Go... Go."

"Lord Leo! Do you think we are cowards? We can help you. Let us do so," one of the Flimsies said.

Leo looked at him with pride and smiled, then he got closer and said, "My dear friend... I know you are not timid. I think all of you are incredibly brave, and it has been my honor to live among you. But the situation is different right now. You can't win this fight because it's like trying to extinguish the most dangerous fire caused by an atomic bomb with a glass of water. If you think that's possible, then you're welcome to stay."

All the Flimsies looked at each other in horror, then turned to Leo and said, "Good luck, Lord Leo. We will pray for you to win."

Before he could respond, there was a loud crash that shook the ground, followed by a powerful wave of air rushing toward them.

"Ka-boom... m... m"

Leo looked towards the sound, seeing a large cloud of dust spreading. He turned to Sean and said, "He's coming. This is the moment we've been waiting for. Tell everyone to get ready because I believe he's coming with Kaila, his executioner and torturer." Sean ran inside, and within moments, every human gathered on the porch while all the Flimsies who worked for Leo rushed inside, anxiously awaiting the enemy. The ground trembled, the shaking intensifying with each passing second as if the approaching forces were deliberately stomping to instill terror in the hearts of the Flimsies. The vibrations reverberated through the air, a menacing reminder of the impending confrontation. Leo's eyes were fixed on the dust cloud, straining to see through the thick haze as the ominous figures grew more distinct. The air crackled with tension, and the sense of impending doom hung heavy over them all.

He walked into the street and stood in the middle, facing the oncoming threat. With a deep breath, he straightened his posture and lifted his head high. This was the moment he had been preparing ever since his arrival. As the dust settled, the figures before him became unmistakably clear. Demah led the charge, with Kaila at his side, their presence exuding menace. But what struck Leo to his core was the sight of numerous Flimsies among them, more than he had ever anticipated. The realization that his own people were aiding their oppressors, turning against their brethren, cut him deeply. The betrayal was palpable, a tragic twist that added weight to the confrontation. Leo's heart ached as he stood firm, ready to face the formidable force, knowing that the battle ahead was not just against his enemies but against the painful reality of his people's division. Leo stood tall, surrounded by the others at his side, waiting in tense anticipation.

In no time, they were all standing together in front of Leo, who stood resolutely with his followers lined up behind him. Demah's grin was a twisted mask of victory, his eyes gleaming with malevolence. Both he and Kaila held wickedly sharp daggers, their blades glinting ominously in the dim light.

Demah slowly looked Leo up and down, his voice a venomous blend of ridicule and rage. "Hello, Leo, my old friend! Is this your army?" he sneered. "These pitiful few who dare to stand against us?" The disdain in his tone was palpable, each word dripping with contempt as he taunted Leo and his loyal followers.

At that critical moment, Flimsies from every direction surged forward, rallying around Leo and Demah and their followers, then transforming his modest line into an imposing and formidable army.

The sheer number of resolute faces caused Demah's Flimsies to falter, instinctively stepping back in hesitation. The air was electric with the sudden shift in power dynamics.

Before Leo could utter a word, Gira, Sean, and the loyal Flimsies who had accompanied Leo to the station stepped forward, raising their weapons in unison and taking their places at his side. Their defiant stance was a powerful testament to their unwavering loyalty and courage, amplifying the resolve of Leo's growing ranks.

Kaila, seething with bloodlust and barely able to contain his fury, glanced at Demah, whose expression was a volatile mix of rage and frustration. The sudden swell of support for Leo had rattled Demah, his mask of control slipping as the reality of the situation set in.

The scene was charged with anticipation, each side poised for the inevitable clash. Leo's calm determination stood in stark contrast to Demah's crumbling composure. The once triumphant grin on Demah's face was now replaced with a scowl of uncertainty.

With unwavering confidence, Leo addressed his adversaries, his voice echoing with the strength of his convictions. "This is not just my army," he declared, his eyes blazing with defiance. "This is a united force driven by a shared desire for freedom and justice. We stand together, not out of fear, but out of the unbreakable bond of our shared cause. I invite the Flimsies who came with Demah to join their people—stand with them, not against them. Fight for your freedom, not for Demah. This is your last chance to choose a side while the choice is still yours to make."

One of the Flimsies raised his hand and said, "Don't worry, Lord Leo. Punishing these Flimsies would be our honor."

The powerful declaration resonated through the crowd, further solidifying the unity and determination of Leo's followers and a lot of Flimsies left Demah and joined others. The tension in the air was palpable, the impending battle promising to be not just a clash of forces but a decisive moment that would determine the fate of their struggle.

Kaila, itching for the fight, could barely restrain himself. He looked to Demah, who, though visibly enraged, was struggling to maintain control. The tide had turned, and the true battle was about to begin, with Leo and his newfound army ready to face whatever came their way.

Demah laughed derisively and said, "That's all you've got? After all these years fighting for these worthless people?" At that moment, the remaining Flimsies who had still stood by Demah shifted sides, moving over to join their own people. Meanwhile, the camera-man filmed and broadcast-ed the footage live, as Gira had ordered, allowing everyone to witness the events. The headlines across all media platforms were dominated by the news of the battle between the gods.

His voice dripped with contempt, but before he could finish his sentence, the sound of footsteps began to echo throughout the city. More Flimsies emerged from every corner, joining Leo's side until it seemed the entire population had risen to support him. The scene was powerful; all the Flimsies, united and resolute, stood behind Leo, their faces etched with determination and anger at Demah's words. One of Flimsys held his fist, pointing at Demah and screamed, "Demah Demah, go back home!"

Suddenly, all Flimsys followed him and repeated after him, "GO HOME DEMAH... GO HOME DEMAH. GO HOME DEMAH... GO HOME DEMAH."

Another Flimsy stepped further and said, "WE HAVE HUMAN WEAPONS."

Another Flimsy continued, "AND WE ARE NOT AFRAID TO USE THEM AGAINST DEMAH AND HIS FOLLOWERS."

WE WILL STAND UNTIL THE END!" There were huge cheers from all over, and it was followed by, "GUN, GUN, HUMAN GUN. GUN GUN, HUMAN GUN. GUN, GUN, HUMAN GUN. GUN, GUN, HUMAN GUN."

Another reporter captured the moment on camera, broadcasting the scene live across all privet media outlets and TV channels. Excitement filled the reporter's voice as he urged, "Come out and join Lord Leo while you still can! Tomorrow will be too late. Stand with us—don't abandon Lord Leo! This is a fight between Evil and God. Which side are you in?"

As the newly arrived Flimsies passed by Demah and his followers, they cast fierce, reproachful looks at those who had aligned themselves with the enemy. The visual narrative was compelling, showing the stark division and the overwhelming support for Leo.

One of the Flimsy standing behind Demah pointed at the others and said, "Fear Lord Demah. Tomorrow, you will answer for today."

Fear was palpable among the Flimsys as Sean glanced at Leo, then boldly stepped forward to face them and said, "He's right—you'll be held accountable tomorrow and executed by Demah. But listen, in this fight. There's a chance you might die because you're fighting for your freedom, your family and your loved one. However, if Demah wins today, you'll be dead for certain tomorrow. If you win today, tomorrow belongs to you. So, are you seeking a death sentence or a chance to live? Choose your death." He cast a cold, unwavering look at Demah, grinned, and returned to Leo's side.

Suddenly, it felt as though the entire city's heart and soul stood united behind Leo. The economy, the spirit, and the hope of the people all converged in his favor. The tide had turned decisively, and the stage was set for a confrontation that would determine their future. Demah's initial confidence faltered as he realized the magnitude of the opposition.

Leo, with a powerful presence, addressed the crowd, his voice unwavering. "This is more than a battle; it is a declaration of our unity and strength. We stand together, undivided and determined, ready to reclaim our freedom and our future."

The energy in the air was palpable, each side bracing for the impending clash. Leo's supporters were fueled by a newfound sense of purpose, ready to face whatever came their way with unwavering resolve. The moment was charged with the promise of change, the dawn of a new era driven by the unyielding spirit of the Flimsies united behind Leo.

Leo looked at Demah and said, "I question your so-called intelligence. When your power began to fade, you should have paid attention to who stands with me—and where that leaves you now."

At this point, Kaila, trembling with rage and barely able to contain himself, turned to Demah and said, "Let me kill him! He is against you, and no one should be left alive if they do not stand with you. Let me finish him!"

The tension in the air was almost unbearable as Kaila's bloodlust threatened to explode. Leo's words had struck a nerve, and the unwavering support of the Flimsies only served to heighten the stakes. The imminent confrontation was more than a clash of wills; it was a battle for the very soul of their world.

A couple of Flimsies behind Demah grew visibly frightened as they watched the overwhelming crowd rallying behind Leo. The mass of people flooded every road, encircling the entire city. A giant screen beside the TV station displayed the streets, all packed with Flimsies, poised and ready for Leo's command to charge and Demah glanced at it. The sheer size of the demonstration was staggering, a clear sign that the tide was turning against Demah and his forces, but they remained in their positions.

The weight of his words hung heavily in the air, pressing on the hearts and minds of those standing on the wrong side. The power of Leo's resolve and the solidarity of his supporters created a palpable sense of urgency. Each second ticked by, a countdown to a decisive moment that would shape their future.

Kaila's eyes burned with fury, and his muscles tensed, ready to strike. Demah's grip on control seemed tenuous, the certainty of his power crumbling under the pressure of the burgeoning resistance.

"Choose wisely," Leo urged to who ever Flimsy still left behind Demah, his voice steady and commanding. "Your freedom, your future, depends on it."

The Flimsies hesitated, torn between fear and the desire for liberation, their eyes darting between Demah's sneering face and the hopeful, resolute expressions of their fellow Flimsies behind Leo. The moment of decision was upon them.

In no time, all the Flimsies who had been standing behind Demah joined their fellow Flimsies, leaving Demah and Kaila. The only Flimsys who stayed by Demah were Ratna, Nieso, and Khalli, isolated and exposed. Ratna, Nieso, and Khalli were notorious for their unspeakable tortures inflicted on the Flimsies. Leo knew he had to confront Demah and Kaila while the enraged Flimsies would deal with the traitors.

The Flimsies were quickly organized into two groups. One surged towards Ratna, Niesoh, and Khalli with righteous fury. These three traitors, despite their formidable skills, found themselves facing thousands of Flimsies, driven by anger and the desire for justice. Ratna, a despised spy, had betrayed countless Flimsies to Lord Demah. Niesoh, a deceitful murderer, had never hesitated to kill in the name of Demah and Mallcie, wielding his dagger against anyone who defied him. Khalli was infamous for executing innocent Flimsies who refused to obey Malice's tyrannical laws.

Despite their combat prowess, Ratna, Nieso, and Khalli were no match for the overwhelming numbers and determination of the Flimsies. Men and women fought side by side, their unity and strength overpowering the traitors. The sight of Ratna, Nieso, and Khalli being overwhelmed brought a palpable sense of satisfaction and justice to the Flimsies. Their defeat was swift and merciless, the Flimsies' eyes gleaming with the relief of long-awaited retribution.

Ambulances were on standby, ready to care for the injured. Flimsies wounded and bleeding from the battle were swiftly taken away for treatment by Leo's order.

As the traitors fell, the Flimsies shifted their focus to the central confrontation. Demah and Kaila stood before Leo, who had a group of humans gathered behind him. Leo met their gaze with a confident, defiant smile, unshaken by the tension. The Flimsies, now united and empowered, formed a protective circle around Leo, Demah, and Kaila. Their solidarity was a powerful symbol of their newfound strength, a living testament to their resolve to stand together and reclaim their future.

Kaila spat and said, "Go home, Flimsies. There's nothing here for you. You've already crossed the line, and we'll deal with that later. For now, just go home." He grabbed one of the Flimsy by the neck, holding her in front of Leo when a shot rang out and Kaila's arm started bleeding. At that moment, all the Flimsys traced the origin of the bullet and saw one of their own atop a house, pointing directly at Demah and Kaila.

In unison, they erupted into a thunderous cheer, "Hooray! Hooray!"

They exchanged cheerful glances before turning to Leo. With a confident shrug, he said, "I came prepared. I came to win. And as you can see, they're not indestructible."

Kaila glanced at his wound, losing his grip as Flimsy escaped. Glaring at Leo with anger, he shouted, "This is your justice? Pathetic and weak!"

Everyone burst into laughter as Gira shouted, "You think grabbing that helpless Flimsy woman made you a hero? Made you powerful?" The laughter grew even louder, echoing through the air. Demah glared at the Flimsys, his eyes burning with fury.

Gira glanced around, seeing the fear in the eyes of her fellow Flimsies. She stepped forward, her voice cutting through the murmurs, strong and unwavering. "You think you're right, Kaila. Maybe Flimsies seem insignificant to you, easy to destroy. But you've forgotten one thing, when we are united, no one can touch us. Remember the old lesson we all learned—one slim branch can be snapped easily, but when bundled together, it becomes unbreakable." She turned to the Flimsies around her and continued, "Kaila, they know it's now or never."They know they must stand together, for your threats are no empty words. When you vow punishment, it means either torturing them to their death or executing them in cold, unspoken silence."

Her words struck a chord. The crowd began to stand taller, their shoulders straightening as fear gave way to determination. The metaphor of unity resonated deeply, rekindling the Flimsies' collective spirit. One of the Flimsies stepped forward and spoke out loud, voice strong and clear, "We are not alone anymore. Together, we are stronger than we ever imagined. Today, we reclaim what is ours!"

"Listen, my friends!" one of the Flimsies shouted, voice full of conviction. "These so-called Lords are threatening us, but only because they fear our unity! Just imagine what they'll do to us if we go home, how they'll use us as an example to scare our people. They don't care for us! We must stay strong and remove them from our world forever!"

A woman boldly stepped forward, her voice loud and clear. First, she removed her muzzle and hurled it at Demah, then locked eyes with him, her gaze unwavering and fearless. "We are not animals, as you said, and we will not follow your stupid rules! Those muzzles might look good on you, but we will follow the laws that came before you!" She then raised her fist in the air and shouted the slogan with defiance.

"Down with Demah, Down with Demah, and his so-called religion and his followers! Victory to our Lord LEOOOOOOOO…!"

The crowd echoed her words with growing fervor, the momentum of the revolution swelling with every shout. Seeing how deeply her words had affected the crowd, the Flimsy leader raised his voice even louder, repeating to her with all his strength, "Down with

Demah and his so-called religion and his followers! Victory to our Lord LEOOOOOOOO…!"

The crowd erupted in unison, repeating his chant with fierce determination. Their voices thundered through the streets as they stood guarded and ready to fight, prepared to reclaim and defend their world.

Leo, sensing the shift, stepped forward to stand beside Gira. "We stand united," he declared, his voice strong and clear. "Together, we are unbreakable. Now! It is us who are indestructible. This is our moment, our fight, and we will not back down."

The Flimsies erupted in cheers, their voices rising in a powerful chorus that echoed through the streets, a defiant proclamation of their newfound courage. The sound reverberated, challenging the authority of Demah and Kaila. The once frightened crowd now stood as a formidable force, their unity and determination palpable.

Demah's sneer faltered, his confidence shaken. Kaila, seething with anger, barely restrained his impulse to attack. The tension was thick, the air charged with the anticipation of the impending clash.

"Let's see if your unity can save you," Demah snarled, his voice trembling with barely contained rage. But just as he finished speaking, several more humans who had once served under Demah stepped forward and crossed the line between him and Leo, moving toward Leo with smiles on their faces. They approached and stood behind Leo and Gira, facing Demah with a newfound determination.

One of them, who was called Ron, stepped forward and spoke up, "Demah! We are tired, and we want to go home cause we miss our family and friends. That's enough of torturing these innocent people. Leave their world! They clearly don't follow or respect you anymore. Enough is enough. You can't tell us we are stuck here anymore. The gate will be open soon and we are going home."

The Flimsies shouted in unison, their voices rising in a powerful chorus, "Hooray… Hooray!"

Then, Ron turned to Leo and continued, "Leo! We're ready to go home, as you said. We know Artemis is the key to open the gate, and we'll help you drag them through it and save these people once and for all."

With that reaction from another human, the Flimsies formed a solid line behind Leo and Gira, ready to defend their hard-won freedom. The final showdown loomed, with Leo and his allies standing resolute, ready to face whatever came their way. The unity and courage of the Flimsies had brought them to this pivotal moment, and they were prepared to witness the culmination of their struggle for freedom and justice.

Kaila looked at the crowd, then at Gira. He sensed the threat but remained silent, casting a glance at Demah and then behind them, which was almost empty. Gira's face, taut with anger and determination, shouted, "My friends! Let's finish this."

The crowd surged forward, with humans at the front row shielding the Flimsies, tightening the circle more and more with every step. Demah and Kaila were surrounded in a circle by all humans. Kaila, undeterred, swung his dagger wildly, injuring a few as blood began to flow. Yet, they stood their ground, refusing to break the circle or give up. Everyone in the circle pressed on, refusing to give up. They encircled Kaila, tightening their grip until he could barely move. The relentless pressure from the combined forces of the former followers eventually immobilized him completely. Just then, Ron stepped forward, got close to Kaila, and with a swift punch to the face, knocked him unconscious then Gira tide him up.

Ron straightened and turned to Leo, saying with satisfaction, "I knew I could do that. He was here long before me and was already weaker."

Seeing that Kaila was subdued, Gira clapped to capture everyone's attention, then turned to Leo with a calm yet resolute expression. "As you requested, Demah is yours. Go ahead and end this war."

Leo glanced at Gira, nodding his thanks with a slight tilt of his head. Standing tall at 185 cm, his powerful build and strong muscles radiated an air of unshakable strength. Stepped forward, his gaze fixed on Demah. In contrast, Demah, in stark contrast, stood shorter at 160 cm, weighing around 250 pounds. His large, protruding belly made every movement a struggle, underscoring his lack of agility. The crowd parted to let him through, their eyes filled with a mixture of hope and determination. Demah, now alone and vulnerable, looked around desperately, then at Kaila, who was bleeding from his nose and wounded arm and unconscious on the ground, realizing the gravity of his situation.

They both ran towards each other. Demah wielded a long, razor-sharp dagger. As soon as it touched Leo's hand, it inflicted deep cuts, and blood began to flow. Leo glanced at the dagger and smiled. Demah, sensing victory, grinned and said, "Isn't it beautiful? It was custom-made, especially for people like us."

Leo laughed, looking at the Flimsies, who watched with bated breath. "Did you hear that?" he called out. "He said 'people' like us."

The Flimsies murmured among themselves, their anger and resolve only growing stronger at Demah's arrogance. Leo, ignoring the pain, advanced once more. He added, "Even if I lose here, the Flimsies won't disappear—they're fighting for their call and their freedom. You see, Demah," said Leo, his voice steady and filled with defiance. "I'm not like you. You may have a weapon, but we have something far more powerful, unity and the will to fight for our freedom."

Demah's smile faltered as Leo's words resonated with the crowd. The Flimsies cheered, their collective strength echoing through the streets. Leo used the distraction to his advantage, dodging another wild swing from Demah and countering with a swift, precise strike that disarmed him. Demah stumbled, his confidence visibly shaken. Leo pressed on, not giving him a moment to recover.

"Your reign ends today, Demah. No more fear, no more oppression."

Demah, red with fury, lunged at Leo, aiming to punch him. But Leo was ready, swiftly defending himself and throwing a powerful punch that sent Demah crashing to the ground. "I came here long before you, but I stayed younger and more powerful because I spent a long time on the Mahtob moon. The gravity there is stronger, and it helped rejuvenate my muscles."

With a final, decisive move, Leo knocked Demah to the ground. The crowd erupted in jubilant cheers, their voices a thunderous wave of triumph. Gira, Sean, Ron and the others rushed forward, their faces lit with hope and relief. Leo stood over Demah, his expression a mix of exhaustion and victory.

"It's over, Demah. Your time is done."

Demah, seething with anger, glared at Leo and snapped, "You teamed up with them and forgot who you are?"

Leo laughed, shaking his head. "Do you hear yourself? This isn't your world. They're not your slaves, and you are certainly not a god. But no, I haven't forgotten who I am. That's exactly why I'm with them. I'm a human who believes in freedom and justice. Actually, it's you who has forgotten who you are. "You think you're a god, but you're nothing more than a child molester, a rapist, a criminal, and a selfish man who has no respect for anyone." Still chuckling, Leo turned away, leaving Demah to be handcuffed by the other humans, ready to be sent back where he belonged.

The Flimsies closed in, their unity and determination a testament to their newfound freedom. Together, they had overcome their oppressors and reclaimed their future. Leo's victory was not just a personal triumph but a powerful symbol of the Flimsies' unbreakable spirit and their fight for justice and liberty.

Demah opened his eyes again, humiliated and seething with rage. He tore the rope apart and pulled out a shorter dagger-like weapon. and lunged at Leo once more. Each time, Leo effortlessly deflected him. With a furious roar, Demah charged, wildly claiming his dagger again and waving it, and aimed straight for Leo's chest. The blade struck true, and the crowd erupted in screams of horror and anger.

Demah stood over Leo, triumph written all over his face. "Is that your power and strength?" he sneered, relishing what he thought was his victory.

Leo, gripping the dagger embedded in his chest, slowly stood up. With a defiant glare, he pulled the blade free, revealing it had shattered into two pieces. Holding the broken dagger in front of Demah, he threw the pieces to the ground and said, "Yes, exactly! Your dagger may be forged from some rare material, but my T-shirt is woven from the spirit of Earth itself and belongs to Artemis." With a swift motion, Leo pulled up his shirt, revealing underneath it a tight, worn T-shirt belonging to Artemis, stretched snugly over his broad frame.

Demah's eyes widened in disbelief. Leo continued, his voice strong and unwavering, "Strength isn't just about weapons. It's about resilience, unity and the indomitable spirit of these people."

Leo turned to Gira and said, "I told you to tie him up with these ropes. "The one you used isn't from Earth—it was made here, designed specifically for Flimsys, who might choose to stay with Demah." He gestured to the Flimsies standing behind him, their faces filled with determination and resolve. Leo stepped forward, his presence commanding and resolute. "Your reign of terror ends today. These people are no longer afraid of you; they see now that you're nothing but a fraud."

The crowd, inspired by Leo's defiance and courage, erupted in cheers. The Flimsies surged forward, closing in around Demah, their unity and resolve unbreakable. Demah, realizing the tide had completely turned against him, stumbled back in fear.

"This is for every life you've ruined, for every injustice you've inflicted," Leo declared, his voice ringing out like a battle cry. "Your power is broken, just like your dagger."

With one final, powerful push, the Flimsies overwhelmed Demah, their collective strength bringing him to his knees. Leo stood tall, a beacon of hope and victory, as the Flimsies celebrated their newfound freedom. The era of fear and oppression had ended, replaced by a future of unity and liberty. The roar of their victory echoed through the streets, a testament to their unwavering spirit and the triumph of justice over tyranny.

Before Ron and Gira tide him up again, Demah attacked Leo by punching him in the face and stomach. Leo pushed him back, then grabbed Demah by his collar and, with a surge of righteous fury, began to punch him relentlessly in the face and stomach until Demah finally passed out. Make them ready, we are going to get ready for our departure.

The crowd, still buzzing with the energy of their victory, moved into action. Gira and Ron stepped forward, helping Leo lift the unconscious Demah. The unity and determination in their movements were a powerful reminder of the strength they had found together. As they carried Demah and Kaila away, The Flimsys took Ratna, Hoog, and Rakh away to face their punishment later on. The Flimsies began to chant, their voices rising in a powerful chorus that echoed through the streets. The chant was not just a celebration of their victory but a declaration of their newfound freedom and solidarity.

Leo, walking at the front, felt a profound sense of accomplishment and relief. They had faced incredible odds and emerged victorious. The oppressive regime that had ruled over them with fear and cruelty was finally overthrown. The journey ahead would still be challenging, but for the first time, they faced it with hope and unity.

When they reached the holding place, Leo and his companions secured Demah and his remaining followers. As they waited for Artemis, the sense of anticipation and liberation was palpable. Leo looked around at the faces of the Flimsies, each one reflecting the same determination and hope. Gira approached Leo, her eyes filled with pride. "We did it," she said softly.

Leo nodded, his expression serious yet relieved. "Yes, we did. And now, we begin to build a better future."

As they stood together, the first rays of dawn began to break on the horizon, symbolizing a new beginning for the Flimsies and their world. The era of fear was over, and the era of hope had just begun.

Leo handed a rope to Gira and said, "This rope is from Earth, too. Don't ask me how I got it. Tie up Demah and Kaila tightly and make him ready for departure."

He smiled as he spoke, his confidence unwavering. Gira took the rope, nodding as she moved to secure Demah and Kaila. Meanwhile, Ron approached Leo, concern evident in his eyes. "Leo, your chest is bleeding." Leo glanced down at his chest, noticing the blood soaking through his shirt. "I know," he replied calmly. "The dagger was made of material partly from Earth, so it hurts a little because the bleeding is from a little scratch. But my shirt is completely from Earth, so I was well protected. Thanks to Artemis for pushing me to wear it."

Ron nodded, still worried but reassured by Leo's composure. As Gira finished tying Demah and Kaila, the Flimsies gathered around, their faces a mixture of relief and determination. The immediate danger had passed, but the work was far from over. Leo looked at the gathered crowd and addressed them, his voice strong and steady.

"Today, we took a stand. Today, we showed that we are not afraid and that we are united. Our journey is far from over, but together, we will build a future free from tyranny."

Leo turned to the Flimsies, his voice strong, commanding and authoritative. "Once we've crossed over, we'll handle Demah and Kaila. As for his Flimsy followers, you will deal with them according to your own laws. If possible, forgive them and offer them another chance. But make sure everyone understands the price of betrayal."

One of the Flimsys approached Leo and asked, "Lord Leo, who do you recommend to become our first president and leader of Rouhar?"

Without hesitation, Leo replied, "Gilbert. He's educated compassionate, and has dedicated his life to helping others while supporting me in aiding all of you. Without him, this journey would have been far more difficult. He's the best choice. Gira, too, would make an excellent candidate as prime minister."

The Flimsies nodded in agreement, their faces resolute as they prepared to restore justice to their land. The air was charged with a sense of finality—both vengeance and liberation on the horizon. The Flimsies cheered, their voices rising in a unified cry of triumph and hope. Gira stepped back, having secured Demah, and stood beside Leo. "We're ready," she said. Leo nodded, glancing at the horizon where the first light of dawn was breaking.

"Let's move," he said. "Artemis will be here soon, and we need to be ready."

As they moved Demah and his followers to the designated holding area, the sense of unity and purpose was palpable. The Flimsies, once oppressed and fearful, now stood together, strong and resolute. They had faced incredible odds and emerged victorious. The era of fear was over, and a new era of hope and freedom was beginning.

Leo, Gira, Ron, and the others walked at the front, leading the way with determination. The journey ahead would be challenging, but for the first time, they faced it with hope, unity, and the promise of a better future. The dawn of a new day was upon them, and together, they were ready to embrace it.

RECLAIMING HER LOST

Artemis and her companion, Gilbert, journeyed toward Mahtob, the second moon of Zamin. Everything was unfolding seamlessly, just as they had planned. A rush of exhilaration swept over Artemis, her thoughts racing, "This is amazing, like a dream come true."

She knew that such an opportunity to witness the vastness of space was a once-in-a-lifetime experience, something she would treasure in her memory forever. Every kilometer, Aden's voice would come through the comms, announcing their progress, and Artemis and Gilbert could hear the updates. The silence of space was profound, amplifying the sense of adventure. Despite the underlying fear of venturing into the unknown, it felt good to be part of something so bold and daring. Artemis occasionally glanced at Gilbert, ensuring he was okay. The sense of camaraderie between them was reassuring. The mission's significance weighed heavily on their minds, but the sight of the stars and the vast expanse of space filled them with awe and determination.

"How are you holding up, Gilbert?" Artemis asked, her voice calm but filled with excitement. Gilbert smiled, a mix of nerves and enthusiasm in his expression.

"I'm good, Artemis. This is incredible. Just thinking about what we're doing and the impact it will have... it's beyond words," Artemis nodded, sharing his sentiment. "It's history in the making. Let's make sure we do everything right."

As they approached Mahtob, the moon loomed larger in their view, its surface illuminated by the distant sun. The sense of anticipation grew stronger. They both knew that their mission was crucial, and they were ready to face whatever challenges lay ahead. The silence of space, combined with Aden's steady updates, created a rhythm that was both soothing and exhilarating. Artemis felt a deep sense of connection to the mission, to Gilbert, and to the Flimsies they were helping. This journey was more than just a mission; it was a testament to their courage and unity.

As they neared their destination, Artemis took a deep breath, feeling a mix of nerves and excitement. "Almost there, Gilbert. Let's make this count," Gilbert nodded, his eyes reflecting the same determination.

"Let's do this without fear. Space may be daunting, but when you have a goal to achieve, you must set aside your fears, Artemis. For Leo, for the Flimsies, and for our future," with those words, they pressed on, resolute in their journey toward Mahtob. The challenges ahead were daunting, the mission far from over, but united in purpose, they were ready to face whatever lay in their path and see it through to the very end.

They reached the critical distance to the ozone layer, and Aden's voice crackled through the comms, announcing their distance to the ozone lay. Artemis felt a mix of readiness and fear at the same time. Beyond the ozone lay the vast unknown of space, and though she didn't know what awaited them, she knew she had to make it work for herself and her father to return home.

This time, Leo's voice crackled through the comms again, filled with urgency and encouragement. "Now, you're getting closer— make sure the engine is at maximum power... Artemis, this is it. Good luck. If we lose contact, don't worry—we're all waiting for you here. Your mission is to find your father. I'm heading to Moallem City to end this war, but Mark and Aden will be here to assist you, ready to support you every step of the way. They're incredible with technical issues, so if you run into trouble, he's got your back. Good luck, and see you soon." He sighed deeply, then put down the microphone, the gravity of the moment clear in his voice. Aden rested her hand on Leo's shoulder and said, "Don't worry, she's smart and she'll come back. She'll succeed. I have a good feeling."

Leo sighed, his worry momentarily easing at Aden's reassuring words. "I hope you're right, Aden. This mission is everything. If Artemis finds her father and makes it back, it will change everything for us."

Aden nodded, his confidence unwavering. "She has the strength and determination of her father. And she has our support. We've done everything we can to prepare her. Now, we just have to trust in her abilities and wait."

Leo turned to look at Aden, drawing strength from his calm demeanor. "You're right. We have to believe in her. She's proven herself time and again." As they watched the sky, the silence of the base was filled with the collective hope and anxiety of everyone waiting. The Flimsies around them continued their tasks, but their thoughts were with Artemis and Gilbert, forging a path in the vast unknown of space.

Aden gave Leo's shoulder a reassuring squeeze. "She'll come back, Leo. And when she does, it will mark the beginning of a new era for all of us." Leo nodded, a small but determined smile forming on his lips.

"Yes, Aden. The weight of their mission was shared among them, each hoping and believing in the success of Artemis and Gilbert."

Artemis took a deep breath, her hands steady on the controls. "Here we go, Gilbert," she said, her voice filled with both resolve and a hint of fear. "This is it."

Gilbert nodded, his expression serious but supportive. "We've got this, Artemis. Let's make it count."

The spacecraft surged forward, breaching the ozone layer and entering the vast, silent expanse of space. The stars stretched out endlessly before them, a breathtaking and intimidating sight.

"Leo, we're through," Artemis said into the comms, hoping for a response. But there was only silence. She glanced at Gilbert, who met her gaze with calm assurance.

"It's okay, Artemis," he said. "We knew this might happen. Let's focus on the mission."

Artemis nodded, her resolve hardening. "Right. Let's find my father."

The spacecraft glided smoothly through the void, guided by the coordinates programmed into its navigation system. Every kilometer felt surreal, the beauty and isolation of space pressing in on them. Artemis marveled at the sight, even as her thoughts remained fixed on the task ahead.

"Look," Gilbert said, pointing to a distant object. "There it is. Mahtob."

Mahtob, the second moon of Zamin, loomed larger with each passing second, its surface illuminated by the distant sun. Artemis felt a surge of hope and determination. "We're almost there," she said, her voice resolute.

Gilbert smiled at Artemis and reminded her, "Not yet. We still have seven more hours. It looks close, but it's still far off."

After a couple of minutes, Gilbert looked over at her and asked, "You look tired. If you want, you can rest for a while." Artemis nodded and closed her eyes. As they neared Mahtob, Artemis prepared for the next phase of their mission. The uncertainty of what lay ahead was daunting, but the urgency of finding her father fueled her.

"Hold on, Dad," she whispered to herself. "We're coming."

With Gilbert by her side and Leo's encouraging words echoing in her mind, Artemis felt ready to face whatever challenges awaited them. Together, they would find her father and complete their mission, no matter the obstacles. The vast expanse of space might be filled with unknowns, but their determination was unwavering, and their goal was clear. After hours of napping, Artemis opened her eyes and stared through the window.

"It's so amazing, Gilbert. It's so peaceful. I love it," Artemis said, her voice filled with awe. Gilbert nodded, his eyes still fixed on her.

Gilbert smiled a hint of pride in his eyes. "Yes, I still remember our mission. I studied the maps and coordinates thoroughly."

Artemis felt a surge of confidence. "Alright, let's head towards it. We've come this far; there's no turning back now."

With Gilbert's guidance, Artemis adjusted their course towards Mahtob. The silence of space enveloped them, a stark contrast to the noisy ascent. The peacefulness was almost surreal, making the vastness of their journey feel both daunting and exhilarating. As they approached Mahtob, the moon's surface became more detailed, its craters and ridges casting intricate shadows. The sense of adventure and purpose-filled Artemis with a renewed sense of determination.

"Gilbert, we're getting closer," Artemis said with a sense of excitement. "Let's find a suitable landing spot and start our mission." Her anticipation was palpable as they were prepared to enter the planet's atmosphere. The thought of finally beginning their task and getting closer to her father filled her with determination and hope.

Gilbert nodded, his focus sharp. "I'll keep an eye on the coordinates. We need to land safely and then we can begin the search for your father."

Artemis guided the spacecraft toward the Mahtob surface, excitement and anticipation building with every passing moment. This was more than just a mission; it was a journey of hope and discovery. Hours passed, and as they broke through the planet's ozone layer, preparing to land, Artemis took a deep breath.

Artemis was so excited when she said, "We're almost there. Let's make this count."

Gilbert looked at her, his expression resolute. "We will."

With that, they descended toward Mahtob, cautious and mindful of the residents, wondering how they would interact with them and gain their trust. Their resolve was unwavering, their spirits high. Artemis floated motionless, her laughter echoing through the silence of the spacecraft. She seemed entranced, almost intoxicated by the weightlessness and the surreal beauty of space. For the first time,

Gilbert was floating as well. Excitedly, he looked at Artemis and exclaimed, "Look! Now I know how you feel—it's amazing. I'm floating, too!" But as the novelty wore off, his excitement gave way to growing anxiety. Unable to contain himself any longer, he finally abandoned his patient waiting.

"Artemis! What are you doing? Aren't we supposed to go now?" he asked, his voice tinged with frustration.

Artemis continued to laugh, her eyes wide with wonder. She seemed lost in the moment, wanting to stay suspended in this dreamlike state forever. To Gilbert, it looked like she was drunk on the experience, and his concern deepened. If she didn't snap out of it, they could be in serious trouble.

"Artemis! Where are you? What are you doing?" Gilbert started yelling, his fear spilling over.

"You are wasting time. Are you out of your mind? Remember, we don't have much time left. If you want to stay here, fine, but I don't want to see you regret this for the rest of your life. Please pull yourself together and take action. Think of your father! WAKE UP!"

His urgent tone and hearing about her father finally broke through to her. Artemis blinked, the spell of weightlessness slowly dissipating. She realized how much time had slipped away and how critical their mission was. "I'm sorry, Gilbert," she said, her voice shaking slightly as she regained her focus. "I got carried away. You're right. We need to move."

Gilbert sighed in relief, his expression softening. "It's okay, Artemis. Let's just stay on track."

Artemis took a deep breath, grounding herself. "Alright, let's get back to the controls and head towards Mahtob."

They both adjusted their positions, shifting back to the control panels. With renewed determination, Artemis guided the spacecraft toward the moon's surface, following its coordinates precisely, the urgency of their mission clear in her mind. As they approached Mahtob, the details of its terrain became clearer, and Artemis's focus sharpened. She carefully navigated the descent, aligning their landing with the predetermined coordinates. "We're almost there," she said, her voice steady and confident.

Gilbert nodded, his eyes fixed on the approaching surface. "Just a little more. We're doing great."

She tried to make conversation to ease the tense in them and she remembered a joke and she thought it would be fun if she tells Gilbert.

"Gilbert! We are like two little flies inside a blonde's head," Artemis said, trying to lighten the mood.

"What? Why?" Gilbert asked, clearly confused.

"Because they call them space invaders, just like us. Like a fly buzzing inside a blonde's head! They call that fly... a space invader! Ah!" She finished with a chuckle, hoping to bring a smile to his face. Gilbert's lips twitched into a reluctant smile, the tension easing slightly as he caught her playful spirit. But Gilbert didn't laugh or respond. He remained very quiet, his eyes fixed on Artemis, filled with a mixture of concern and determination.

Artemis, realizing her joke had fallen flat, glanced at Gilbert, sensing the tension between them still there. She thought a moment and then remembered another joke that always made her laugh. Hoping to ease the mood, she smiled and said, "Hey, do you want to hear another joke?"

Gilbert gave her a hesitant look but nodded. "What's the joke?" Then, with a sigh, he relented and said, "Sure."

She grinned, "So, why did the astronaut break up with his girlfriend?"

He raised an eyebrow, unsure. "Why?"

"Because he needed space!" Artemis chuckled, hoping Gilbert would too.

A small smile finally crept onto his face, and the tension eased ever so slightly. "That was... okay," he said, shaking his head, but the laughter in his eyes showed he appreciated the effort.

Artemis sighed and said, "This is our ultimate trip into space, and I know all this is tedious and repellent changes in your life." She said this because she noticed Gilbert's intense focus on her. Gilbert finally spoke, his voice soft but steady.

"It's not the changes that bother me, Artemis. It's the uncertainty. But seeing you determined and trying to stay positive helps. We've come this far, and I trust we'll make it through."

Artemis smiled, grateful for his words, "You're right, Gilbert. We just need to keep going. One step at a time."

"Gilbert!" Artemis called out, her voice carrying a mix of curiosity and distraction as she looked away at the horizon. "Are you afraid of space?"

Gilbert sighed, his exhaustion evident as he rubbed his temples. "It's probably too late to ask this, but are you mocking me again?" he asked, his voice laced with tired frustration.

Artemis quickly turned back to him, realizing the weight of her words. "No, I wasn't mocking you," she said softly. "I just… I'm nervous, too. I wanted to talk about something, anything, to keep us both from thinking too much."

"You do think I'm afraid of space, don't you?" Gilbert groaned, his frustration evident.

"That's absurd. As I said, I'm not mocking you! I'm just trying to ease the tension before we get to Mahtob moon," Artemis replied, her voice defensive.

Artemis's throat tightened, her words caught in the swell of emotion. She drew a deep breath, steadying herself, and sought a way to steer the conversation elsewhere.

"You're not afraid! But let me tell you something. I want to be honest with you. You have every right to be scared of space, and I am afraid, too. I just wanted to have a conversation with you to kill the time. That's all."

Gilbert looked at her, his expression softening as he saw the sincerity in her eyes. "I'm sorry, Artemis. I guess the stress is getting to me. I know you're just trying to help."

Artemis nodded, relieved. "It's okay. We're both under a lot of pressure. But we're in this together, and we'll get through it together. I'll make sure you are safe, too. I'll care for you just as deeply as you care for me."

Gilbert sputtered, his face contorted with anger. "Maybe you're the one afraid of space, but not me. Just because you think I'm delicate or breakable—like you could blow me up with a glance or burn me with your eyes or lift me with your pinky toe." He paused as if suddenly aware of his own vulnerability, then finished his sentence, "You assume I must be scared?"

Gilbert sighed, then continued, "I must be sensitive and scared. Maybe I am just a sidekick to you, but I'm also affectionate. I'm tired of your preaching about being strong like humans. Maybe I'm not humanoid and I'm just a Flimsy, but my instincts tell me that the Mahtob moon is freaky, with lots of different cults, tribes, and thugs there. That's why I'm freaked out. I don't know if your father is there and if he is, how he could survive them. But I know they're supplied with those Earth guns. We need to be certain of our landing spot."

Gilbert's outburst took Artemis aback. She could see the genuine fear and frustration in his eyes. She took a deep breath, trying to compose herself. "Gilbert, I'm sorry. I didn't mean to make you feel like that. I know you're just as capable as anyone, and I respect you for that. It's just... I'm scared, too. We're in this together, and I need you to know that I trust you. I made it this far just because of you."

Gilbert's expression softened slightly, though the tension remained. "It's not about being capable, Artemis. It's about understanding the risks. Mahtob is dangerous, and we need to be prepared for whatever we might face there. I'm worried about your father, too, but we need to stay focused and not let fear control us.

I've already contacted our allies, and they're waiting for us. But I'm not sure exactly when we'll land—they're there too."

Artemis nodded, feeling the weight of his words. "You're right, Gilbert. We need to be cautious and smart about this. Let's approach Mahtob with a clear head and work together to find my father."

Gilbert sighed, the anger ebbing away. "Okay. Let's just stay alert and be ready for anything. We'll find him, Artemis. I believe that."

They both took a moment to gather their thoughts, the silence of space pressing in around them. Artemis adjusted their course towards the Mahtob moon, the vast landscape coming into clearer view. As they prepared for landing, Artemis glanced at Gilbert, her determination mirrored in his eyes. "Let's do this, Gilbert. Together."

Gilbert nodded, his resolve firm. "Together."

With that, they descended towards the surface of Mahtob. Their mission was daunting, but their unity and determination would see them through. Artemis remained silent, her mind swirling with doubt and fear. The thought that something terrible might have happened to her father weighed heavily on her heart. Tears began to flow, soaking her face. Gilbert, seeing her distress, felt a pang of regret. He hadn't meant to break her spirit, but he also didn't want her hopes to be crushed.

Realizing he had gone too far, Gilbert tried to mend the situation. "Artemis," he said gently. "I didn't mean to hurt you. I'm just worried about you. I didn't find you by coincidence; I chose to be here with you because I believe in you. I'll do anything to support you, not with my muscle, but with my experience on this planet. I just want you to be careful and prepared for whatever we might face," Gilbert said softly, his tone earnest as he reached for Artemis's hand.

Artemis wiped her tears, looking at Gilbert with a mixture of gratitude and sadness. "I know, Gilbert. I appreciate your honesty and concern. It's just hard... thinking about what might have happened to him."

Gilbert nodded, understanding the depth of her pain. "I understand. But we have to stay strong and focused. We're here now, and we have a mission. We'll find your father I promise that."

Artemis took a deep breath, trying to steady herself. "You're right. We need to stay strong. For my father and for ourselves."

They shared a moment of silence, both drawing strength from each other's presence. The mission ahead was filled with uncertainty, but their bond and determination gave them the courage to press on.

"Thank you, Gilbert," Artemis said softly. "For being here with me. For everything."

Gilbert smiled, his earlier frustration giving way to a warm sense of camaraderie. "We're a team, Artemis."

As they approached Mahtob, the moon's surface became more detailed and foreboding. Artemis guided the spacecraft carefully, her mind now clear and determined.

"Let's land and start our search," she said, her voice steady.

Gilbert nodded. "We're ready. Let's find him."

Artemis immediately took control, expertly maneuvering the spacecraft as they glided above the city. Gilbert pointed to an area to their right and said, "It's better if we land over there."

The area he indicated seemed abandoned, with buildings and walls that appeared untouched yet neglected. The entire section of the city looked like it had been deliberately left to decay. Artemis turned to Gilbert, surprise evident in her eyes.

"Why here, Gilbert...? There is nothing here."

"I know. It's Because... here is the safest place on this moon, and I have lots of friends here who can help us in our journey," replied Gilbert while his eyes were searching the area.

"But you said you've never been on this moon?" Artemis asked, her voice filled with surprise.

"I did," Gilbert replied, nodding. "This is my first time here, but I was here by VR means so many times and I can see it for real. I know them from before, through... connections. Sometimes, you don't have to visit a place to understand the people living there."

"What's VR? Is this VR something like sky-glasses, but where you can see another world, too? I mean, an imaginary world?" she asked.

"It stands for virtual reality. You can go anywhere you want, but it's not real. I mean, you're there but not physically, and everything you see is real, but you can't use it and only you can watch it. Your father created it here. He said he first saw it on Earth, but it was too expensive, something not everyone could have," Gilbert explained, his eyes lighting up with excitement.

"My friend Matt has one, and it's amazing, but the way you describe it sounds different. It's like a telephone, but not like those apps. It's like you're face-to-face with the other person. Am I right?"

Gilbert nodded and said, "Exactly!"

After sitting there for a while, they finally decided to step out and explore their surroundings. Artemis smiled at Gilbert, acknowledging his concerns as they looked around the place where they had landed. Up close, the area appeared viciously torn apart without regard for civilians. Despite the desolation, Artemis began moving toward a shadow behind a wall. Gilbert grabbed her hand, trying to find the right way to convey the seriousness of the situation.

"What are you doing? I just told you about the danger of this location," Gilbert said angrily.

The shadow moved into the light, revealing a young girl holding a gun. Her fatigued face suddenly changed, and she smiled cheerfully. She moved forward, dropping her weapon and whistling loudly. Approaching with a courteous manner, she pointed at Artemis a few times and said, "You are Artemis, the daughter of Arsham." She stood tall in front of Artemis, like a soldier saluting her leader, and said, "Proudly, I introduce myself—I am Nina, and it's an honor to finally see you and speak with you in person."

Artemis felt a surge of emotion upon her welcoming action and hearing her father's name. She couldn't wait another second and asked, "Do you know my father?"

"Do I know your father? Do I know your father? Are you kidding me?" the girl repeated, astonishment in her voice.

Artemis was shocked and paused in her spot, confused by the girl's tone. She couldn't tell if the girl was happy to see her or if she was angry.

"I mean, do you know my father?" she hesitated, repeating her question doubtfully.

"Of course, I know him. As a matter of fact, everybody knows him around here. But the real question is, do you know where he is now?" the girl answered, her voice teasing as if she wanted to play a game.

Artemis realized how silly her question had sounded. She quickly corrected herself, "Let me rephrase that. Do you know my father personally?"

"Of course I do," the girl answered with pride.

"Is he here and does he know that I'm here?" Artemis asked, her voice trembling with a mix of excitement and fear.

"Why don't you ask him yourself?" the girl replied, pointing somewhere behind Artemis.

Artemis's knees felt weak, nearly buckling beneath her. A flutter, like butterflies, danced in her stomach. Her heart raced as she turned to look at Gilbert, who was smiling warmly and subtly pointing with his eyes. She knew then that her father was standing behind her. Slowly, she turned around. Standing before her was a handsome man in his early thirties. In an instant, she recognized him exactly as he had been when she was just a little girl. Tears welled up in her eyes as she struggled to comprehend the moment she had dreamed of for so long.

He opened his arms to her and said, "Artemis... my lovely Artemis... God knows how much I've missed you and how long I've waited for this moment."

As soon as she heard his voice and her name, Artemis ran toward him, tears streaming down her face. "Dad! Dad! Where were you? I missed you so much. I love you." She jumped into his arms and hugged him tightly, determined never to let go. Gilbert, standing nearby, wiped away his tears repeatedly, not wanting anyone to see him cry. When he glanced around, he noticed everyone else doing the same, overwhelmed by the emotional reunion.

Arsham held Artemis in his arms, shocked at how much his little girl had grown up. He was crying, too, as he kissed her forehead. "I was here all the time, keeping track of you. Uncle Leo has told me how beautiful you've become."

"Why didn't you come to me or send me a message?" Artemis asked, sobbing.

"Demah has a weapon that can kill humans, and he brought it here from Earth. He sent me a message saying that if I got close to you or tried to contact you, he'd kill you. I had no choice but to work for him, under his control, because I couldn't risk anything happening to you."

"How come you're free now?" Artemis asked, her voice trembling.

"Uncle Leo told me the day you and Gilbert went to see him. He assured me you were safe at his place. That's how I found the chance to escape and make it here," Arsham explained, pulling her closer. Artemis buried her face in his shoulder, overcome with a mix of relief and joy.

"I'm so glad you're safe, Dad. I was so worried." Arsham kissed her forehead again. "And I'm glad you're safe, Artemis. We're together now, and nothing will separate us again."

Artemis looked at her father and asked, "Why didn't you come to Zamin instead of here?"

Arsham smiled, gently brushing her bangs aside as he explained, "Demah placed a tracking chip on all his employees, and I didn't have the equipment to remove it. But here, they do. If I had gone to Zamin with that chip, he could have tracked me or found Leo's location. That's why I came here and asked Gilbert not to tell you where I was—I wanted it to be a surprise."

Gilbert stepped forward, his eyes still wet with emotion, but his face set with determination. "We need to get you both to safety. There's still danger ahead. We brought the spacecraft to take you back to Zamin."

Arsham nodded. "We will. But for now, let's cherish this moment."

The group, filled with renewed hope and strength, began to prepare for the next steps in their journey, "They were prepared to confront any challenges that awaited them."

Arsham, still holding Artemis tightly, continued, "How's your mother? I'm so sorry to put her through all of this. I wasn't there for any of you, especially for you and Atossa. I'm sure your mother is frustrated by now. She probably thinks we're dead, and I didn't know how to get back. Every time I went to the place where I came into this world, I couldn't open it again. Nothing happened. But Demah had a chance to open it, and I think two times, and that's how he was able to bring those guns, and I couldn't even get close to the gate because he would've stopped me from entering and I didn't want put any of you in danger."

Artemis, still overwhelmed with emotion, replied, "Mom has been holding on, but it's been so hard for her. She tried to stay strong for us, but she misses you deeply. We all do. As you mentioned, Demah came to our house twice, asking Mom to hold a ceremony— they said they might be able to bring you back. After the second time, Mom said no and didn't let them come anymore and She suspected they were involved in something illegal."

Arsham nodded, tears welling in his eyes again. "I think he used you to open the gate, which is why he's so desperate to have you on his side. But I never stopped thinking about all of you. Every day, I tried to find a way back, even when it seemed impossible. Knowing you're here now gives me hope that we might find a way to return together."

Artemis stopped him, a sudden realization dawning on her. "Dad! After tomorrow night is the night that the portal will open again. We all can go back home. If we miss it, there's a chance it might never open again." Arsham's eyes widened with hope and urgency. "In two days? Are you sure?"

Artemis nodded vigorously. "Yes, Uncle Leo told us about it. We have to be there on time. We can't miss this chance."

Gilbert, sensing the urgency of the situation, stepped forward. "Then we need to move quickly. We can't afford any delays. Let's gather our things and head to the portal site immediately."

Arsham looked at her, pulling her into another hug as he explained, "Artemis, I don't have the strength to board the ship again. If something goes wrong, I can't fix it. That's another reason why I'm here—I can't move like I used to. This place... it's draining us, melting our muscles, turning us into something frail, like a Flimsy. "Leo and I, along with all the humans, are in constant pain because this place slowly drains our power and inflicts pain until we become like the Flimsies. But the Flimsies aren't affected because their bodies are built differently; this environment feels as normal to them as Earth does to us."

Artemis's tears flowed freely as she looked into his eyes. "That's why Uncle Leo sent me—to find you and bring you back. He didn't want me to know how much weaker you've become. But I'm here now, and I won't let you go, not again. If you don't go with me, then I'm staying too. But we have to take this risk—even if it's just a slim chance, we have to seize it and go back."

Arsham smiled weakly and said, "If it means that much to you, then I'll take the chance. But I have to warn you, I'm very weak and fragile."

He paused, his voice trembling, looked into Artemis's eyes and asked, "How can you be so sure about that? And the gate opens in two days? Why now?" He paused for a few seconds, then continued, "I mean, I know you're the main key here, but we don't have the resources, and someone must operate everything from the other side. How can you open the gate from this side when no one is preparing on the other side?"

"Because I have a friend who's been through this with me," Artemis replied, her voice tinged with excitement. "He won't stop— he's not the type to quit. He's a brilliant little scientist, and he promised that if anything went wrong, he wouldn't give up until he fixed it. But if we're not there, even he might lose hope eventually, and we'll be stuck here forever."

Arsham's eyes widened with a mix of hope and urgency. "Then we must not waste any more time. We need to get to that portal as soon as possible."

Arsham embraced Artemis once more, his voice filled with a mix of relief and determination. "We're going home, Artemis. We're going to be a family again."

Artemis, feeling a surge of hope, replied, "Yes, Dad. We're going home. I can't wait to see Mom, Atossa and my friends again and tell them about this world."

The group quickly gathered their belongings and prepared for the journey to the portal site. With renewed purpose, they set off, determined to seize this rare opportunity and return to their loved ones. The path ahead was uncertain, but their shared goal gave them the strength to push forward, united in their mission to reunite their family.

Arsham looked at Artemis, then Flimsy's around him. "But we can't just leave these people here with Demah and his twisted religion.

We have to make sure they are safe. We need to take everyone with us, no matter the cost," Arsham said, his voice filled with sadness and resolve.

"Dad...? But there is no time left, and Mom really needs us," Artemis replied, her voice tinged with urgency.

"Uncle Leo said he'll take care of it. He has the same idea, and I think he has a good plan." Arsham looked into Artemis's eyes, seeing the determination and hope there. He took a deep breath, his resolve wavering but recognizing the importance of their mission to reunite with their family.

"Alright, Artemis," he said softly. "If Leo has a plan, and we can trust him to take care of things here, then we must go. Our family needs us, and we need to be together."

They held a grand celebration, and the Flimsies prepared a lavish, delicious feast. As darkness fell, they danced, ate, and drank, savoring every moment. Arsham turned to Artemis and Gilbert and said, "We start early tomorrow morning, and by afternoon, we'll be on the planet."

They didn't have any light since the black moon had fallen and broken apart. In no time, all the Flimsies brought numerous candles along with wine to celebrate this great moment. A young girl approached Arsham and Artemis with a tray and a glass of milk, offering it to Artemis. She looked at her father and asked, "Dad? What is this?"

"My dear Artemis... You are not an adult yet, and that's why I can't allow you to drink wine. But I promise you, I will share your first glass of wine with you," Arsham said with a broad smile.

Artemis grabbed a glass of wine and said, "Dad, I'm technically an adult now. If I were on Earth today, I would be twenty years old."

Arsham gently took the glass of wine from Artemis and said, "My dear Artemis, you are not yet an adult in the Flimsy world, which means it's probably not good for you yet."

Artemis took the glass of wine again and said, "I am a grown woman, and I know I am twenty years old in Earth time. Moreover, in the Flimsy world, I am eighteen and allowed to drink wine. Thank you."

Artemis drank her first glass of wine with her father on an alien planet, a moment that felt like a dream come true. Arsham smiled, looking at Artemis proudly, and said, "At least I kept this promise, and you had your first glass of wine with me." Everyone burst into laughter.

The next day, early morning, they all were awake, they quickly gathered their belongings and prepared for the journey to Zamin and to the portal site. The weight of their decision hung heavily, but the promise of reuniting their family and the hope that Leo would protect those they left behind gave them the strength to push forward. As they set off toward the portal, Artemis couldn't help but feel a mix of excitement and anxiety. The path ahead was fraught with uncertainty, but their shared goal and the support of their friends fueled their determination. They were ready, united in their mission to return home and ensure the safety of their loved ones.

There was a big cheer all over the city, and Arsham stood up and asked, "What is going on there?"

The girl ran toward Arsham and Artemis and said, "Lord Leo defeated Demah. He is in custody along with Kaila and the others."

Arsham looked at his daughter and asked, "How long do we have?"

"We have until tonight at midnight, I guess?" Artemis answered immediately.

Arsham then turned to the Flimsies and said, "You all are heroes to me. Each and every one of you deserve a free country, and this world belongs to you. Men and women alike must support each other in rebuilding your world. This is the beginning of a magnificent and marvelous relationship between all of you from every country and region. I am very proud of you all. It was an honor to be with you, and I am saddened that I cannot share this moment of joy with you here. But know that each of you will remain in my heart forever."

Suddenly, Artemis glanced at the time and said, "Dad... We have to go. We can't lose even a minute more."

"What time is it now?" Arsham asked.

"It is seven forty-five, and we have twelve hours to get there and by seven thirty at night, we will be there, and immediately we must move to the location and Gilbert knows where exactly that place is," Artemis answered.

Arsham held Artemis's hand, taking a deep breath, his face lighting up with happiness and the most beautiful smile. Don't worry too much. We will be there."

Gilbert came running toward them, shouting urgently, "We have to go now… we have to go now! Tonight is the night, and the portal will open."

Arsham turned to Gilbert and said, "You two come with me. We have to wear our spacesuits. Let's go." With a renewed sense of urgency, they moved swiftly, knowing that every minute counted.

Artemis and Gilbert followed Arsham along a path, making their way into the woods. After ten minutes of walking, they finally saw a hut. They rushed inside, finding it full of spacesuits, and quickly began changing. Within one hour and fifteen minutes, they were back in front of the hut, where all the Flimsies were gathered for their final farewell. Some were crying, while others stood in silence, sadness etched on their faces.

Arsham looked at them with pride, struggling to control his emotions. The Flimsies were crying, too, and one by one, they came to hug him and Artemis. Finally, he stood still for his speech.

"It is hard for me to say goodbye to you all because we have shared both pain and joy together. I am deeply honored to have known you, and I hope that if I return home, there will be another chance to come back and visit you. Words cannot express my feelings, but I am always grateful to have known you all. This might be our last conversation, but I will never forget you. Thank you all."

Artemis stepped forward and added, "Remember this freedom and do not let anyone take it away from you. That's important. Thank you for helping me find my father again. I love you all." With these heartfelt words, they prepared to embark on their journey home, carrying with them the memories and gratitude for the friends they had made.

Gilbert remained quiet throughout because he knew he would miss her. He understood that Artemis belonged to her own world, but when you love someone, there is little you can do to change that. He wanted to hold her and beg her to stay, but he knew it wouldn't be fair to play with her emotions. He worried he might make her feel guilty. Though Gilbert's world was now free, he felt the sadness of letting Artemis go.

Artemis faced a huge spacecraft or, better to say, a spaceship. It could carry a lot of people. Arsham turned to Artemis and said, "Look, we can go back with this beautiful, but it belonged to Mahtob moon and it must be returned. That's why one of my friends is taking us there and he will return again.

Artemis sat in front of her dad and kept looking at him. She said, "Dad! You look so handsome, and I'm so happy to have you back in my life."

Arsham smiled then turned to Artemis and said, "Do you know why exactly I'm here?"

Artemis just stared at him and, confused, said, "Yes, you mean there's more to it than what Uncle Leo told me?"

Arsham continued, "The night I disappeared was incredibly hard for me. Like every other time, my friends and I gathered, performed the signs, and did everything as usual. The portal would always open for less than a minute. But that night, when you entered the room and asked me to hug you, the portal stayed open longer, its power holding us all in place. The strangest part was how much longer it stayed open. Demah looked at you, then at me, and asked if he could bring you here, offering me millions of dollars. He believed he could open the gate from this side, too." He paused to relax his breathing, then continued, "I refused, and he got furious. Suddenly, he grabbed you and pulled you through the portal. I managed to grab you back and push you into the hallway, but before the portal could close, he grabbed my leg and dragged me inside. In an instant, the portal shut tight."

Artemis was furious over what had happened to her father. Tears filled her eyes as she immediately hugged him tightly. "Dad! You were trying to save me, and you got stuck here? I'm sorry, Dad."

"I'm not. Why are you sorry? I'm happy I could save you. Share in my happiness," Arsham said gently, trying to soothe Artemis. "Any parent would do the same, and when you're a mother, you'll do this for your children too."

They were about to load the craft when they suddenly found themselves surrounded by soldiers, guns raised, standing shoulder to shoulder. Arsham glanced at the menacing circle, then turned to Artemis and said, "They're Demah's soldiers."

"Why are they surrounding us? Don't they know what happened to their so-called Lord?" Artemis remarked with a hint of sarcasm.

Arsham stepped into the center of the circle, scanning the soldiers to spot their leader. The leader, standing behind the line of soldiers, began to move forward, and the circle parted to let him through. He approached Arsham, stopping directly in front of him, and demanded, "Where are you going? Lord Demah wants you to come back."

Arsham glanced around, then burst into laughter before fixing his gaze on the leader. "I think you're a couple of days behind on the news. Your Lord Demah has been captured, and the true Lord, Leo, is ready to send him back home to cool off and face who he really is."

"That's not the message we've received from the Black Moon. He's waiting for you," the leader replied coolly, his voice laced with confidence.

Arsham glanced at the soldiers, a faint smile on his face, before turning back to the leader. "The Black Moon is on the ground, and we all have a way to reach Zamin. If it's still functioning, we'll go to the Black Moon together. But if it's broken, you can choose to return home or help your own people rebuild your own world instead of serving as a soldier for an alien force that's brought nothing but misery and pain to your people. And tonight, the portal will open, giving every human here the opportunity to go back home and reunite with their loved ones."

Nina returned and announced, "The Black Moon is on the ground and non-functioning. Demah and Kaila are in the custody of Lord Leo." She brought pictures of the black moon on the ground along with the pictures of Demah, Kaila and others in capture, and she showed them to the leader.

The soldiers exchanged uneasy glances before turning to their leader, who stared at Nina with discomfort as she invited him to the command room to view the live feed on the screens. He walked through and entered the command center, his face flushing red as he watched the live news showing the Black Moon on the ground, broken and powerless.

He returned, faced Arsham, and said, "Lord Arsham, I'll see you on Zamin." Without waiting for a response, he turned and walked away.

They landed safely on the ground, and as soon as they removed their spacesuits, Artemis held Gilbert's hand and said, "It was wonderful being with you. I am deeply grateful for the time we've spent together, but I promise you, I will be back."

Gilbert managed a smile, feeling the weight of the farewell and the hope of her return. "Thank you, Artemis. I'll hold onto that promise."

Gilbert remained silent, wanting to watch her, listen to her, and never let her go. It was one of the most painful moments of his life. As soon as she held his hand, he squeezed it gently, and they all ran into the woods toward Uncle Leo's location.

Gilbert was panting, struggling to catch his breath. He turned to Artemis, his voice laced with urgency. "We're too far… I'm afraid we'll be late."

Artemis glanced at her father, then at Gilbert, determination flashing in her eyes. "Wait for me here. I'll be back."

Before anyone could respond, she took off like a streak of light. Within minutes, she returned—this time astride Sheebr. The magnificent creature's presence alone was enough to send Gilbert into a panic. He bolted behind Arsham, his voice rising in alarm. "He's going to eat me!"

Arsham burst into laughter, shaking his head. He turned to Artemis with an amused expression. "You know him?"

Artemis grinned. "Yes. While Gilbert was sleeping, I went to his location, and we played for hours."

Arsham's smile widened. "That's right. I played with him a lot too."

Then, turning to Gilbert, he reassured him. "Don't worry. He's harmless. And with him, we'll be there in no time."

Without hesitation, they all climbed onto Sheebr's back. In less than five minutes, they arrived at Leo's location. Before approaching the Flimsies, who had gathered to bid farewell to their Lord, they released Sheebr back into the wild.

Gilbert's face lit up with exhilaration. "Can you believe it? Sheebr was a legend to us—no one had ever seen him! And not only did I see him, but I got to ride him too!"

With that, they turned and walked toward Uncle Leo.

Uncle Leo was waiting for them with the others. Time was running out, and they had to be there on time. Nothing was certain;

they weren't sure if they would go home tonight, but they still hoped the portal would open. It was almost midnight, and they were still running.

Uncle Leo pointed into the distance, a smile spreading across his face. "There they are," he said, his voice filled with happiness.

Artemis looked at the location but it didn't seem right. Helplessly, she turned to Uncle Leo and said, "But Uncle Leo...! It's..."

Leo looked at her and said, "My darling Artemis...! This is it, but you don't remember when you came here. It was so sudden, and you were attacked by Sheebr a few times. They moved you to different places, and when they couldn't do anything to you, they gave up and left you there. When we were notified of your presence here, we came as soon as possible, but you were gone, and we couldn't find you."

Uncle Leo paused, then continued, "We're certain this is the place, but we don't know the exact spot where you came through. That's why we need to keep searching."

Artemis listened, trying to recall the disorienting events of her arrival. She trusted Leo's words and felt a glimmer of hope amidst the uncertainty. The urgency in their hearts drove them forward, determined to seize this chance to return home.

Artemis felt awkward. After a moment, she said, "Yes, I remember I was soaked and wet, but I didn't know it was Sheebr's saliva. How do you know it was exactly here if I wasn't there?"

Leo looked at her and smiled as he answered, "I know it was here because when we got here, the portal was still open for five more seconds before it suddenly vanished."

"Uncle Leo! Why didn't you go back home? That was your chance," Artemis asked.

"Because they don't remember me anymore, and probably I am forgotten, and I know my loved ones are gone. There was no point in going back," Leo answered.

Artemis hugged him and said, "Uncle Leo! But that's not true. Your sister is still waiting for you, and we are your family. You are my Uncle Leo."

"But you said she has never mentioned me, and you didn't even know that your grandmother had a brother," Leo replied.

Artemis nodded. "That's true, but there must be a reason for that. You can ask her when you get there but don't judge her too harshly. I always saw pain in her eyes, and I didn't know why. Now I know the reason." Artemis tried to convince him.

They reached the location, but nothing was happening. Artemis looked at her father and said, "They might have forgotten about me. I had hoped that Matt would do something, but I guess I was wrong."

Arsham walked toward Leo and stood next to him. They both gazed at the area where the portal should be and asked, "Are you sure this is it?"

Arsham asked in surprise, "Bring whom?"

Leo burst into laughter and pointed to some people approaching them. "Lord of nothingness. Of course, we can't let them stay here, so I decided to bring them with us."

They all turned to see who was coming, and to their astonishment, they saw Demah, Kaila, Ratna, and Hoog, their hands tied up. Artemis giggled, winked at Gilbert, and said, "You see, Gilbert. We're taking them with us to make sure they won't bother you guys ever again."

Gilbert pointed in a direction and said, "Artemis! Look! That's the portal. It's open."

Everyone looked in that direction happily. They all were so happy going back home. "Artemis, go before it collapses," said Uncle Leo urgently.

Artemis looked at Uncle Leo with worry and asked, "Uncle Leo...! You're coming too, right?"

Uncle Leo's face was calm, and he smiled at Artemis. "Not before they come," he said, pointing at Demah and the others who were tied up. Everyone burst into laughter.

Artemis hugged Gilbert for the last time and said, "Thank you for everything. I'll see you later, and that's a promise." She turned to her father and said, "Dad! I'll see you on the other side."

"Of course... I'll see you there," replied Arsham with a big smile.

Artemis walked toward the gate and noticed, strangely, a very handsome man searching for something, wandering about. To her, he was striking—tall, with dirty blond hair. He didn't look like a Flimsy—he was a human, emerging from behind a rock, calling out to Artemis repeatedly. "Artemis… Artemis…" She moved closer to him, and when he finally turned and saw her, A big smile spread across his face, and his eyes, glistening with tears, shone like two silver diamonds. His eyes welled up, shining with emotion.

He froze in place, his voice trembling as he repeated, "Artemis, I found you. I kept my promise. I missed you."

He walked toward Artemis and wrapped his arms around her, holding her tightly as if he'd never let her go.

VOICES OF THE FORGOTTEN

At Artemis's home, everyone was prepared. Her room was crowded with relatives, all anxiously watching the sign in the center of the room and another on the wall, placed there at Matt's request—just in case either one opened. If the one on the wall did, they would simply walk through. They waited for the right moment, each person imagining different gateways. Matt meticulously checked everything, ensuring all was in place. He glanced at the clock—it was just a few minutes to midnight. He stretched, signaling everyone to be ready.

"We have a couple of minutes until midnight. I don't know the exact moment, but I know it is close. My friends, be prepared for anything," he said, his voice filled with both anticipation and determination.

Grandma Tara asked Matt, "My son Matt, what time was it exactly when Artemis vanished?"

Before Matt could respond, Atossa jumped in and answered, "It was four forty-five in the morning. Why?"

Grandma Tara turned to her daughter Dorsa and said, "Isn't that the time she was born?"

Dorsa, surprised, replied, "Yes, that is correct."

Matt felt a wave of relief as one of the biggest puzzles had just been solved by Grandma Tara. He looked at her and asked, "What time was your brother born?" Grandma Tara replied, "It was almost five o'clock in the morning."

Matt then turned to Dorsa and asked the same question about her husband. "How about your husband, Mrs. Vedetta?" Dorsa, feeling a surge of excitement, tried her best to answer.

"I think it was between 5.30 and six o'clock in the morning, according to his parents."

Helen looked at Matt and asked, "What does that mean, Matt?"

Ricky excitedly interrupted, "It means we have a long night ahead of us."

Matt stood by the door, trying to ignore Ricky's enthusiasm, and said, "It means they should be here before seven in the morning."

Ricky interrupted again, "The rest doesn't matter. I'm convinced it's Artemis's birthday that's key to opening the gate from the other side. The others just need to step through."

Matt shot him a skeptical look and asked, "How can you be so sure?"

Ricky shrugged, his shoulders lifting in a nonchalant gesture. Matt, visibly frustrated by the situation, invited everyone to keep quiet during this critical procedure. His voice was serious as he addressed the room, pointing at everyone to stay seated.

"Please listen to me. It is important that you do not move under any circumstances because it might worsen the situation," he said. Turning to Dorsa, he continued, "Mrs. Vedetta, I understand how you're feeling, but if Artemis or your husband shows up, please remain seated. Otherwise, you'll put them in a dangerous position, or the portal may shut down. You and Grandma Tara are very important parts of this process."

Dorsa nodded, tears streaming down her cheeks. To show his support, Matt placed a comforting hand on her shoulder. He reviewed everything once more, then clapped to get everyone's attention.

"Listen up, everyone! From this moment on, everyone in the circle must hold each other's hands and maintain the connection for as long as necessary. Now, please focus."

They were all exhausted, and still, nothing was happening. The time was four forty-five, and hope was diminishing. Dorsa, losing her composure, felt tears streaming down her cheeks once again. She was ready to give up when Matt spoke up, "Mrs. Vedetta, I understand how difficult this is for you, but this is our last chance. We must ensure we don't lose it. I know it's past four forty-five, but let's give it a little more time. We don't know what might be delaying them, but we have done our part."

Matt struggled to find more words of encouragement as Dorsa's tears flowed even harder, though a smile flickered on her face. He feared she might have lost her mind when, suddenly, the sign on the floor began to illuminate. He quickly turned to the other sign, and it was glowing, too.

Matt suddenly recalled the importance of maintaining the chain. He turned to Dorsa, who was both laughing and crying, and gently said, "Please, don't move. Stay put until it's safe to let go."

Everyone stared at the glowing opening, captivated by the strange light that seemed to make believers out of them all yet showing nothing beyond. Suddenly, with a whoosh, the portal on the wall burst open, revealing a landscape of trees and large rocks on the other side.

Matt's eyes desperately searched for any sign of life. He moved closer to the gate, cautiously touching the frame with the tip of his finger, a gesture that only fueled his eagerness to step closer. He extended his hand through the gate and through his pen on the other side, watching it flow and slowly land, and when nothing happened, he called out, his voice filled with urgency, "Artemis… Artemis… where are you?" Anxiety gripped him as he waited for a response when suddenly, Ricky ran through the gate, screaming, "I'm here… I'm here, Dad!"

Ricky had vanished from sight by the time Matt crossed through the gate to the other side. He turned back, pointing at everyone in the room, instructing them to stay put while he searched for Artemis. "This gate couldn't have opened without Artemis being here… she must be close by," he assured them.

Dorsa, beginning to calm down, called out loudly, "Don't worry, Matt, we won't move until you come back."

Matt searched the area frantically, calling out for Artemis, his eyes scanning every corner, but he found no one and no clues. Desperately, he shouted her name, his voice echoing back across the mountain in every direction. As he retraced his steps from a narrow path between two massive rocks and returned to the front of the gate, he suddenly spotted a teenager standing before him. Her hands covered her mouth, tears streaming down her cheeks. Matt blinked, unable to speak, overwhelmed by the moment. Tears filled his eyes as he stretched out his arms and rushed toward her, hugging her tightly and covering her face with kisses. "I knew you were somewhere. I knew I could get you back. Artemis… I missed you so much, and you didn't age at all. I love you, Artemis…" he whispered repeatedly.

Artemis looked at Matt with excitement, her voice trembling with emotion as she said, "I love you too. You're a young man now and so handsome. I missed you even more."

Both stood stunned by Artemis's response—she had never told Matt she loved him before. He looked at Artemis, his voice filled with surprise. "So, you love me? You just said that."

Artemis smiled softly and replied, "Like I've told you before, I want to be involved with someone older than me."

Arsham, passing by, turned to Artemis with a smile and said, "Well, Artemis, now you're two years younger. I guess that solves the problem." He then turned to Matt and asked, "You must be the young scientist Artemis told us about. You're Matt, right?"

Matt looked at Arsham and replied, "Yes, I am. And you?"

Arsham extended his hand for a handshake and said, "I'm Arsham, Artemis's father."

Matt felt dizzy with excitement, his knees nearly buckling beneath him. With trembling enthusiasm, he shook Arsham's hand and said, "It's a pleasure to meet you, sir."

As they were talking, Matt suddenly heard a faint cry and looked past Artemis. Behind her stood Ricky, blood dripping from his nose. Matt's gaze shifted to Artemis, who was saying with a hardened expression, "Let's take this bastard back. Everything we've been through—it's because of him and his father. We've faced so many problems because of them. I'll explain later."

Matt immediately responded, "Okay," and, without hesitation, grabbed Ricky's arm, pulling him along as they moved together.

Matt looked back, unable to believe what he was witnessing. A group of people was following behind Artemis, and four of them were bound with ropes. Artemis gripped Matt's hand even tighter and said, "Matt, my father was here too, as you predicted. We're all coming home. And it's all thanks to you."

Artemis glanced back, pointing at her father, then turned to find Matt. That's when she noticed Gilbert, standing pale and sad, watching her and Matt. She walked over to him and gently embraced him. Gilbert hugged her back, his face filled with quiet contentment, reluctant to let her go.

"I'll be back, I promise," she said softly, "because I know a good friend of mine is waiting for me." She smiled warmly at him. Gilbert nodded, unable to find the words, then turned to Matt and whispered, "Please take good care of her."

Matt stood there, momentarily lost for words, until Artemis said, "Matt! This is Gilbert—he's the one who saved me and helped me." Matt softly shook hands with Gilbert and nodded.

Suddenly, Matt's voice rang out loudly, "Wow… what is he? Are they human or alien?" He was pointing at Gilbert and the others who were following their Lord to say goodbye to Lord Leo, Lord Artemis and Lord Arsham.

Artemis smiled and replied, "They're our friends, and I'll explain everything later, I promise."

Matt explained the chain they had rigged to keep the gate open, then cautioned Artemis, "We need to wait until everyone's through before we start celebrating. Save the hugs for later."

Artemis appeared at the gate and crossed through. Leo looked at Gilbert and said, "She'll be back, and this is the beginning of a good friendship. Once she comes, she'll be here with you again." Gilbert looked at Lord Leo, trusting him implicitly as he had never lied to him before. Leo's words brought him some comfort, and he gazed at the portal, hoping to see Artemis again.

Dorsa, tears streaming down her face, held tightly to the hands that anchored the chain. Leo winked at Arsham and said, "Go. They are waiting for you."

Arsham took a step forward and said, "Promise me you are coming too."

Leo smiled reassuringly. "Don't worry. I'm coming."

Then Arsham came through, and Dorsa nearly fainted with relief. Artemis quickly moved behind her, wrapping her in a hug, showering her with kisses, and whispering how much she loved and missed her, giving Dorsa the strength to stay on her feet. As the others entered, tears filled their eyes, overwhelmed by the moment.

But Artemis's gaze remained fixed on the gate, worry gnawing at her as she feared it might snap shut at any moment. Uncle Leo was still out there, and the thought of him choosing to stay behind terrified her. Desperate, she rushed to the gate and began calling out for him. Artemis screamed, "It's not done. Still, one person is left."

"Uncle Leo... Uncle Leo... you promised!" Artemis cried out, her voice breaking as tears streamed down her face.

Just then, Leo appeared at the gate then pulled Demah and the others, throwing them one by one into the portal. Finally, he took a last look around him before stepping into the portal himself. She looked at Grandma Tara and then suddenly exclaimed, "Uncle Leo! Welcome back." Leo turned to the gate and waved at all the Flimsys on the other side of the gate who were saying goodbye to them.

Matt looked at Artemis and asked, "What's wrong with them? Why do they look like a jelly?"

Artemis smiled and said, "I'll explain everything later."

Leo looked at Artemis and said, "I kept my promise. I'm here. But it was so hard to say goodbye to the friends I've had since childhood—they helped me so much."

Leo was looking for his sister and looked to Artemis then at the group in the room and looked to find his sister. With a glance and a gesture, Artemis pointed toward Grandma Tara. Leo wasn't sure which one was his sister and he wasn't expecting his sister to be this old, but he recognized her and walked over to her, his voice soft as he said, "Hi, my little sister. I'm Tim. It's been a long time." He gently held Grandma Tara's hand and kissed it with reverence as if she were a queen.

Grandma Tara looked between Artemis and Leo, her expression confused and visibly shaking. "What's going on, Artemis? What is this?"

Artemis smiled warmly and replied, "Grandma, in that world, people don't age as much. He's your brother, Uncle Leo or better I say, Uncle Tim—Mom's uncle."

Grandma Tara burst into tears, cradling his face in her hands. She kissed him back and whispered, "I missed you too."

He continued to embrace his sister as Grandma Tara, her voice trembling with emotion, said, "I can't believe it. You don't know how difficult it was when you vanished. I've missed you all my life, and I'm so happy I have the chance to see you one more time. You look great! How have you stayed so young?"

Leo then took a handmade craft from his pocket and handed it to Artemis, saying, "Artemis, Gilbert sent you this and asked me to tell you that he made it himself. He wants you to remember him."

Artemis took it and marveled at its beauty. It was a carved likeness of her face, intricately crafted on a piece of wood. Matt held it and said, "Who is Gilbert? And why is this so wobbly? It's amazing. Is it really wood? It's priceless."

Arsham stepped in to explain, "Gilbert was someone who helped all of us immensely. I sent him to assist Artemis, and he did so in the best way possible. He was amazing."

Allan hugged Artemis too and said, "Artemis! This year, you're going to have your birthday with your dad and your uncle as well. By the way, do you remember your last birthday? What was your birthday wish anyway?"

Artemis replied with a playful smile, "I'm not telling you." Then she looked at her father.

She looked at her family and saw her sister, Atossa, hugging their dad and still crying. Atossa looked at Artemis, opened her arms, and they embraced as if they'd never let go of each other. Then she turned to her friends and said, "I love you all, and I missed you so much." She hugged every one of them one by one, then she said, "Excuse me! My family needs me."

She went to her mother and hugged her tightly. Dorsa, unable to get enough of hugging her family, said to Artemis, "My Artemis...! You came back with your father." She burst into tears again, overwhelmed with joy.

At that moment, Matt asked if everyone was accounted for, and Leo looked around before confirming, "Yes." Matt then told everyone to relax. The gate surprisingly remained open when Leo said, "My theory was right! Artemis is the only key to open the gate,"

Matt glanced at everyone and very softly said, "I guess we didn't need the chain after all—just the three of you were enough to keep it open or only Artemis was enough to open the gate."

Everyone burst into laughter, but suddenly, Demah and Kaila stood up just as Leo was untying their hands. Demah motioned for Ricky to go. Their eyes locked onto Arsham, Leo, and Artemis. "It's not over," they said ominously, "let's go, hurry." Without another word, all three of them and their followers immediately ran out of the house.

Artemis, Matt, Megan, Helen, Allan, and Atossa were all surprised. Artemis turned to Matt and said, "Now I remember where I saw Demah. It was at school, and he was coming out of the principal's office. This was all planned by them. You remember that night—Ricky suggested the entire thing and what to do. He knew what was happening and what we needed to do to open the portal."

"But he was his twin brother, Ricky's uncle," said Arsham, then he turned to Leo, bewildered. "Why did you untie them and let them go?"

Leo smiled calmly and replied, "Did you want to call the cops? What would their charge be? How would you even explain to the police what they did? In the end, they'd still go free, and you'd be the one sent to the insane asylum," he continued, "by the way I figured as long as they can't return, everyone is safe. We have to be especially careful around leap years and make sure we're not in the same area or even the same city. Don't worry about them—this world is hell for them, and they are trapped in it."

Arsham hugged Artemis and said, "You must be super careful 'cause you are able to open the gate even without us."

Everyone burst into laughter, and Arsham believed every word. While he was kissing Dorsa, he looked around the house and said, "It's amazing—nothing has changed. It's exactly the way I left it. But we have to make some changes now." Then embraced Atossa and kissed her gently again, then turned to Dorsa, wrapping her in a hug so tight it was as if he'd never let her go. He kissed her tenderly. Dorsa couldn't take her eyes off Arsham, occasionally kissing him. She was amazed at how young he looked, even younger than she did, despite being six years older.

Finally, she couldn't hold back any longer and asked, "You look as handsome as ever. You haven't aged a day. If we go out together, everyone will think I'm your mother. How did you do that? How could you stay young? I'm so impressed."

Artemis looked at her father, and they both laughed. Arsham hugged Dorsa and kissed her on the cheeks and then on the lips. "My love, Dorsa, you are as beautiful as you were when I left. As for how I stayed young, it's a long story, and we will explain it to you. And don't worry about this because I have a good plan to balance our ages. I'm going to send you and your mother on a vacation for a few years until we are the same age again."

Arsham looked at Artemis and winked. They both burst into laughter and hugged Dorsa, who was very interested and, confused, asked, "Where?"

Arsham chuckled, kissing her again before saying, "Don't worry about it. Next time, you, Grandma Tara, along with Grandpa and Atossa, are going there for a long vacation until we all look the same age we're supposed to be IN FLIMSY'S!" Everyone burst into laughter.

Leo, still embracing Grandma Tara, chimed in with a smile. "Sister, you and your lovely husband should go there, too, until we can catch up and close the gap in our ages as well."

Matt called out to Artemis, "According to Flimsy, how old are you?"

Arsham replied, "She is eighteen years old."

Matt took Artemis's hand and said, "I'm older than you now. Will you marry me?" He pulled out a ring box, opening it to reveal the most beautiful ring with a large diamond sparkling inside. Artemis, stunned and speechless, finally replied, "But I'm still twenty years old, and because of the Flimsy world, I aged slower."

Allen, confused, asked Matt, "You bought the ring even though it was only a possibility she might come back?"

Matt ignored him and looked at her and said, "I'll take it, whatever your age. I love you, and I want to spend the rest of my life with you by my side. With you, I'm complete."

He was about to continue when Artemis gently placed her hand over his mouth, stopping him. "I love you too, and my answer is yes," she said softly. With her answer, Matt swept Artemis into his arms, lifting her off the ground. He kissed her just the way he had always dreamed, full of love and joy.

Thank you for joining the journey.
Until the next adventure
Farewell and stay curious.

GLOSSORY

1-*Avicenna-*

Avicenna, also known as Ibn Sina (980–1037 AD), was a Persian polymath who made profound contributions to various fields, including medicine, philosophy, astronomy, and mathematics. His most celebrated work, *The Canon of Medicine*, became a foundational text in both the Islamic world and Europe for centuries. It detailed medical knowledge, practices, and discoveries and remained a standard reference in medicine until the 17th century.

Avicenna's philosophical writings drew heavily on Aristotelian and Neoplatonic traditions, and he sought to reconcile them with Islamic thought. His influence reached far beyond his era, shaping medieval European and Islamic philosophy, particularly in metaphysics and epistemology. Known for his rigorous intellectual curiosity, Avicenna is often considered one of the greatest minds of the Islamic Golden Age.

Avicenna, while often associated with Islamic philosophy, was indeed Persian and lived during a period when Persia was under Islamic rule. The prevailing rule restricted the use of the Persian language in scholarly works, with severe consequences, including potential death, for those who defied it. Although he is frequently labeled as a Muslim philosopher due to the cultural context of his time, Avicenna's beliefs and philosophical inquiries were deeply rooted in Persian heritage and heavily influenced by Greek philosophy, particularly Aristotelian and Neoplatonic traditions. His work often transcended religious dogma, exploring universal questions of metaphysics, ethics, and medicine with remarkable independence.

2-*Artemis or Artemisia*

Who was Artemisia? Artemisia of Caria is a fascinating historical figure, especially as the only female commander in the Persian navy during such significant battles. Her loyalty, strategic acumen, and unique role in the Greco-Persian Wars make her an inspiring character in ancient history.

3-*Arsham*

The name *Arsham* (آرشام) is Persian and carries a strong historical and noble significance. In Old Persian, *Arsham* roughly translates to "strong leader" or "heroic leader." The name combines *Ar* (meaning "hero" or "strong") and *sham* (possibly derived from *kshathra*, meaning "ruler" or "power").

In Achaemenid and ancient Persian history, *Arsham* was also the name of a Persian prince, showing its association with nobility and strength. It's a name that suggests qualities of bravery, authority, and resilience, making it a fitting choice for a character with leadership traits or a strong moral compass.

4-*Azar*

Yes, the name *Azar* has deep significance in Persian culture. In Persian, *Azar* (آذر) means "fire." It's associated with warmth, light, and passion and has historical and cultural importance in ancient Persian traditions, where fire was revered as a sacred element.

Azar also represents the ninth month of the Iranian calendar, which roughly corresponds to November-December in the Gregorian calendar. The name embodies qualities of strength, illumination, and resilience, reflecting the powerful symbolism of fire in Persian culture.

5-*Dorsa*

In Persian, *Dorsa* (درسا) can mean "pearl of the sea" or simply "pearl," symbolizing something precious, rare, and beautiful. It's a name often associated with elegance and grace, carrying a connotation of purity and value, much like a pearl.*Dorsa* is the intended name, with qualities like strength, beauty, and resilience, as pearls are treasured and enduring. It's a lovely choice for a Persian-inspired name!

6-Atossa

Atossa* is a name of Persian origin with historical significance. In ancient Persia, *Atossa* (آتوسا) was the name of a prominent queen—Queen Atossa, the daughter of Cyrus the Great and wife of Darius the Great, two of the most powerful figures in the Achaemenid Empire.

The name *Atossa* is thought to mean "skilled," "well-adorned," or "beautiful body" in Old Persian. Queen Atossa is remembered for her influential role in the royal family, her wisdom, and her status as the mother of Xerxes I. The name carries a sense of nobility, strength, and elegance deeply rooted in Persian history.

7-Padideh

The name *Padideh* (پدیده) is Persian and means "phenomenon" or "wonder." It's a unique and beautiful name that conveys a sense of awe, rarity, and distinction. In Persian, *Padideh* is used to describe something extraordinary, remarkable, or even miraculous, like a natural wonder or an impressive talent.

The name *Padideh* evokes qualities of being one-of-a-kind, standing out, and having a special presence. It's a name that celebrates individuality and the idea of being remarkable or unforgettable.

8-Parto

The name *Parto* (پرتو) is a Persian name that means "ray of light" or "radiance." It evokes images of brightness, illumination, and warmth, symbolizing hope, positivity, and inspiration. *Parto* can also refer to enlightenment or wisdom, as light is often associated with knowledge and clarity in Persian literature and culture.

Parto could suggest that they bring light, guidance, or inspiration to others, symbolizing a hopeful presence or a beacon of knowledge. It's a lovely and meaningful name, celebrating qualities of clarity, kindness, and positivity.

9-*Tara*

The name *Tara* (تارا) has Persian origins and means "star." In Persian, *Tara* symbolizes brightness, guidance, and beauty, drawing parallels with the night sky and the stars' role as navigational aids and sources of wonder.

The name *Tara* is also used in other cultures with various meanings, in Sanskrit, it means "star" or "savior"; in Irish, it's associated with the Hill of Tara, an ancient ceremonial site. In all contexts, *Tara* conveys elegance, light, and a guiding presence, making it a name that suggests inner beauty, wisdom, and the ability to inspire or lead others.

10-Cenzio

The name *Cenzio* is of Italian origin and is derived from *Vincenzo,* which in turn comes from the Latin name *Vincentius,* meaning "conquering" or "victorious." *Cenzio* carries a similar meaning, symbolizing triumph, resilience, and strength. It's a relatively rare name and has a classic Italian charm, often associated with determination and a victorious spirit.

11- *Zamin*

"Zamin," derived from Persian, translates to "earth," "land," or "ground." The term carries rich cultural and linguistic significance, often symbolizing stability, growth, and a connection to the natural world. It is a word deeply rooted in Persian literature, poetry, and philosophical contexts, reflecting humanity's bond with the earth and the environment.

In historical and cultural references, "Zamin" has been used metaphorically to describe concepts such as homeland, heritage, or even the broader notion of the planet itself. Its use extends beyond language, appearing in art, names, and philosophical ideas that emphasize the importance of grounding and belonging.

12- *Parandeh*

The word **"Parandeh"** (پرنده) is Persian and translates to **"bird"** in English. It is derived from the Persian root "par" (پر), which means "feather" or "wing."

13- *Shoosh*

"Shoosh" (شش) is a Persian word that means **lungs,** which are the essential organs responsible for respiration in the human body.

14 - *Ariassp*

The name *Ariassp* likely has roots in ancient Persian or Avestan languages. Breaking it down:

- **"Ari-"**: Derived from the Old Persian or Avestan *Ariya*, meaning "noble," "pure," or "Aryan."

- **"-Asp"**: A common suffix in Persian names, from the Avestan word *Aspa*, meaning "horse." In ancient Persian culture, horses symbolized power, nobility, and status.

Thus, *Ariassp* can be interpreted as a "Noble Horse" or "Pure Horse," reflecting qualities like strength, nobility, and purity. It's a name that would carry significant cultural and symbolic weight in ancient Persian tradition.

ABOUT THE AUTHOR

From the very beginning, she had a deep passion for writing. In 1999 and 2001, she wrote two novels that she hoped would find a place in the world, but unfortunately, the publishers did not accept new authors at the time. Undeterred, she printed the manuscripts, stored them away in the pantry, and eventually moved on, leaving them forgotten. As the years passed and she began to think about revisiting her books and pursuing publication, she faced new challenges, particularly with grammar. Needing professional assistance, her younger son stepped in to support her during this time.

Years later, her elder son introduced her to someone who became an instrumental help in completing her novel. Special thanks to her loving sons. One of the main characters, Matt, is based on her younger son, Ariassp[14]. She chose the name Matt to avoid any confusion with similar character names, ensuring her readers would not be misled. Ariassp is one of the most intelligent people she knows, with a remarkable knowledge of computers. Her first son, Arsham, possesses an incredible personality and a wealth of knowledge. Dorsa, the character based on her daughter, is a gifted artist who has won numerous competitions thanks to her natural talent and artistic abilities. She is extremely proud of all of them.